DOMINION

BENTLEY LITTLE

A SIGNET BOOK

SIGNET
Published by New American Library, a division of
Penguin Group (USA) Inc., 375 Hudson Street,
New York, New York 10014, USA
Penguin Group (Canada), 90 Eglinton Avenue East, Suite 700, Toronto,
Ontario M4P 2Y3, Canada (a division of Pearson Penguin Canada Inc.)
Penguin Books Ltd., 80 Strand, London WC2R 0RL, England
Penguin Ireland, 25 St. Stephen's Green, Dublin 2,
Ireland (a division of Penguin Books Ltd.)
Penguin Group (Australia), 250 Camberwell Road, Camberwell, Victoria 3124,
Australia (a division of Pearson Australia Group Pty. Ltd.)
Penguin Books India Pvt. Ltd., 11 Community Centre, Panchsheel Park,
New Delhi - 110 017, India
Penguin Group (NZ), 67 Apollo Drive, Rosedale, North Shore 0745,
Auckland, New Zealand (a division of Pearson New Zealand Ltd.)
Penguin Books (South Africa) (Pty.) Ltd., 24 Sturdee Avenue,
Rosebank, Johannesburg 2196, South Africa

Penguin Books Ltd., Registered Offices:
80 Strand, London WC2R 0RL, England

First published by Signet, an imprint of New American Library,
a division of Penguin Group (USA) Inc.

First Printing, March 1996
10 9 8

Copyright © Bentley Little, 1996
All rights reserved

 REGISTERED TRADEMARK—MARCA REGISTRADA

Printed in the United States of America

For my wife,
Wai San Li

PROLOGUE

New York City, 1920

Girls!

They were all girls, every last damn one of them. He stood at the top of the stairs, staring down into the dimly lit basement below. The infants crawled through the blood and mud and filthy, rancid water, mewling, crying, screaming. The mothers, chained to the wall, lay limply against the stone, heads lolling, half dead, their nude bodies still smeared with blood and afterbirth, gnawed umbilical cords angling stiffly from between their spread legs.

His eyes darted from one newborn to another, searching hopefully for a penis, but he saw none, only small, hairless cracks.

Mother had been right. He was not a man.

He began to cry. He could not help it. Hot tears of shame forced their way out from under his eyelids, streaming down his cheeks, only adding to his humiliation. An unintentional sob escaped from his mouth, and one of the women looked dazedly up at him. He saw her through the blurred curtain of his tears. He did not know whether she knew what was happening, but he didn't care.

"It's your fault!" he screamed at her, at the others.

One of the women moaned incoherently.

Still crying, he retreated into the kitchen, where he opened the cupboard doors underneath the sink and unwound the hose. He turned on the water full force and carried the hose back across the floor through the basement doorway, dropping the streaming snake end down the stairs.

He would fill up the basement and drown them all.

The water poured from the hose in a steady flow, coursing down the steps before merging with the low, dirty puddle which already existed at the bottom. Three of the women heard the splash-babble of the water and groggily raised their battered heads, expecting their daily hosing off, but when it didn't come, their heads slumped again with a muted rattling of neck and arm irons.

He watched as the water level in the basement slowly rose, his tears stopping, drying, disappearing. He wiped his eyes. It would be two hours, maybe three, before the basement filled up above their heads and drowned them. He would come back later, after it was done, and drain the basement and dispose of the bodies.

He stepped into the kitchen and closed the door, standing uncertainly for a moment before walking down the dark, narrow hallway toward the front of the house. Outside, he could hear the loud rumble of motorcars on the street, the excited screams of children at play. He stood for a few minutes at the front window, staring at the lawn outside, before realizing that the spot in which he was standing was the precise spot in which Mother used to stand while spying on the neighbors.

Blackness rushed over him, and he stepped away from the window, taking slow, deep breaths until he again felt all right. He looked down at his hands. Mother had always said that his hands were too big for his arms, were out of proportion compared to the rest of his body, and he had always tried to keep them hidden in pockets or behind his back. Now, though, they didn't seem that large, and he found himself wondering if they had shrunk. He wished Mother was here so he could show her his hands, ask her.

He wandered disconsolately through the empty house, past the drawing room, down the hallway, up the stairs, and found himself, as always, going to Mother's bedroom.

Mother's bedroom.

He sat on the red silk bedspread and picked up the leg chains attached to the tall wooden posters at the foot of the bed. He had not opened the windows since Mother died, and the room still smelled strongly of the mingled odors of wine and perfume and old sex. He breathed

deeply, inhaling the delicious fragrance, at once sweet
and sour, tangy and musky. He glanced around the room.
The Oriental carpet was still stained with blood from the
last time, dark red now faded to a dusty brown which
blended in with the multihued rococo pattern. On the
dresser in front of the oversize mirror were empty flagons. The soiled undergarments of various ladies and gentlemen were strewn about the room, many of them torn
and tattered, ripped off willing bodies in the heat of passion.

His eyes were drawn to the door next to the closet, the
door to the room where the *unwilling* participants had
been brought.

He stood up and took the long brass key from its hook
above the bed, using the key to unlock the door. This was
the room in which she had worshiped, in which she had
given herself over to her rituals. Precisely what these rituals were he did not know; she had always refused to tell
him. He knew only that they demanded many sacrifices,
that he had been forced to find for her two, three, sometimes four victims each time. Mostly men. Women if necessary. And he knew that the rituals were loud. He'd been
able to hear the cries echoing through the halls of the
house, feel the bodies being flung to the floor, slammed
against the wall. It was good that they lived in such a
large city. Otherwise the sacrifices Mother had required
would have been missed, the noises heard by all. As it
was, the victims' absences had seldom been noticed (he'd
always chosen them well), and the sounds had merely
blended in with the noises of the street.

Mother, however, always said that having to perform
the rituals in this room, instead of in their proper place,
was what had perverted their purpose, was what had led
to his mistaken birth.

He stood in the doorway and slowly scanned the silent
room. Broken bones were still scattered about the floor in
no particular order, as if thrown there in a frenzy. The
bones were clean, all flesh stripped. The walls of the
room were painted with pictures of trees, painstakingly
detailed renderings of forestation for which Mother had

paid a substantial amount to a local artist who had later joined her for two days in the bedroom.

He stepped into the room and breathed deeply. The odor here was stronger due to the fact that the room had no windows, but it was more blood smell than sex smell and was not nearly as pleasant as the scent of the bedroom. He walked forward, kicked a jawbone out of the way. He had brought in the sacrifices, but he had never had to dispose of them. After Mother had finished her rituals, there had never been anything left to dispose, only these cleaned bones and blood and occasional isolated bits of meat.

He had often wanted to join Mother in her rituals, but she had told him bluntly that he could not participate. Only in the last year, after she had reread the prophecies, had she decided that he should be allowed to carry on after her death. Only then had she fully regained her faith. Only then had she told him what he must do.

Now even there he had failed her.

He thought of the infants in the basement. He would give them another hour, then check to make sure they had all drowned.

After that he would try again.

There was nothing more he could do.

He regretted that he'd had to dispose of the mothers as well. It had felt so good when he took them, when he beat them and forced them to submit to his will, when he felt the hot animal passion rising in them as well. Then he had truly felt that he was his mother's son.

But there would be more. He would find them the same way he had found these, and he would take them the same way, make them bear his children.

And if they failed to give him a boy, he would try again.

And again.

An hour later, he returned to the basement. The women had all been drowned—he could see their hair spread outward across the top of the filthy, bloody water like twisted lilies—but the babies were alive and happily swimming.

He stood there, shocked. This could not be!

Furious, he leaped from the top of the stairs and jumped into the cold, dark water, anger coursing through him. He grabbed the head of the nearest infant, pressing her down. There was a sudden sharp pain in his index finger, and he cried out, jerking back, letting the baby up. The thing had bitten him! He shook his hand to clear it of the hurt, then pressed the infant down again, gratified to see small bubbles percolate upward through the water.

He felt a stab of pain in his back and whipped his head around. One of the other infants was digging into his lower back with claw-like fingers. Another baby bit down on the fleshy part of his arm, teeth clenched hard around skin and fat.

The other infants were paddling forward. Laughing excitedly, their little mouths filled with tiny teeth—

newborns didn't have teeth

—they splashed through the water toward him. Frightened now, he let up the first baby, which promptly bit into his stomach. He screamed with pain, then screamed louder as tiny fingers dug into his crotch.

How many babies were there? He could not remember. One of the women had had twins, he thought. His feet touched a box underneath the water, and he pushed off, trying to reach the stairs. A tiny grinning infant head popped up directly before him, and thin hands lashed out at his eyes. He batted the baby away, but she bit into his too-big hands even as she was knocked back.

"Help!" he cried, and his voice sounded high, feminine. *He was not a man.*

"Help!"

But no one heard.

And his children took him down.

PART I

ONE

It was hot as they prepared to leave Mesa, the temperature well into the eighties though the sun had not yet risen. The pale brightening above the Superstitions would soon bloom into a typical August morning, Dion knew, and by noon the lighted display on the side of the Valley National Bank building would be flashing triple digits.

He helped his mom carry the last of the luggage out to the car—the bathroom suitcase, the sack filled with trip snacks, the coffee thermos—then stood next to the passenger door as she locked up the house for the last time and deposited the keys in the mailbox. It felt strange to be leaving, but he was surprised to find that he was not sad at the thought of their imminent departure. He had expected to feel some sense of loss or regret, depression or loneliness, but he felt nothing.

That alone should have made him depressed.

His mom walked purposefully across the brown grass to the sidewalk. She was wearing a thin halter top which barely constrained her large breasts, and shorts much too tight for a woman her age. Not that she looked like a woman her age. Far from it. As more than one friend had admitted over the years, she was the closest thing to a real-life sex symbol any of them were ever likely to meet. He had never known how to respond to that. It would have been one thing if they were talking about a stranger, or someone's cousin or aunt, but when it was your own mother . . .

Sometimes he wished his mom was fat and plain and wore frumpy old lady clothes like everyone else's mother.

His mom unlocked his door and he got into the car, stretching across the seat and pulling up the lock on her side. She smiled at him as she positioned herself in front of the wheel. A thin trickle of sweat was cutting a path through the makeup on the far right side of her face, but she did not wipe it off. "I think we have everything," she said brightly.

He nodded.

"Ready to go?"

"I guess."

"Then let's hit it." She turned on the ignition, put the car into gear, and they pulled away from the curb.

Their furniture was already in Napa, but for them it was going to be a two-day trip. They were not going to drive for eighteen hours straight but were going to stop off in Santa Barbara and then continue on to Napa the next day. That would give them a little more than a week to unpack and get settled before he started school and his mom started work.

They turned onto University and drove past the Circle K, where he and his friends had said their final farewells the night before. He looked away from the convenience store, feeling strangely embarrassed. Saying good-bye last night had been awkward not because of the emotions involved but because of the lack of them. He'd supposed he should hug his friends good-bye, tell them how much they meant to him and how much he would miss them, but he'd felt none of that, and after a few hesitant, misguided attempts on all of their parts to drum up that sort of emotion, they had given up and parted in much the same way they always had, as though they would see each other again tomorrow.

None of them, he realized, had even promised to write.

Now he *was* starting to feel depressed.

They drove down University toward Tempe and the freeway. As he watched the familiar streets pass by, the familiar stores and personal landmarks, he found it hard to believe that they were really going, that they were actually leaving Arizona.

They passed by ASU. He had wanted to see the university one final time, to say good-bye to the walks and bikeways where he had spent so many weekends, but for once they hit all green lights, and the car sped by the campus inappropriately fast, denying him even the opportunity to savor his last look. Then the university was behind them.

He had half hoped that he'd be able to attend ASU, though he knew realistically that his mother could not afford to send him to anything but a community college. Now he knew it would never come to pass.

A few minutes later, they hit the freeway.

A half hour later, they were in the desert and Phoenix was in their rearview mirror.

Ten minutes after that, no buildings at all could be seen silhouetted against the orange globe of the rising sun.

They took turns driving, trading off at the infrequent rest areas they encountered. For the first hour or so they were silent, listening to the radio, each lost in private thoughts, but when static finally overpowered even the rhythm of the music, Dion turned the radio off. The lack of conversation, which had seemed normal and natural up to a few moments ago, suddenly seemed tense and strained, and he cleared his throat as he tried to think of something to say to his mom.

But it was she who spoke first.

"Things are going to be different," she said, glancing over at him. "This is going to be good for both of us. We'll be able to start over." She paused. "Or rather, I'll be able to start over."

He felt his face reddening, and he looked away.

"We have to talk about this. I know it's hard. I know it's difficult. But it's important that we communicate." She tried to smile, almost succeeded. "Besides, I have you trapped in the car and you're going to have to listen."

He smiled halfheartedly back.

"I know I've disappointed you. Too many times. I've disappointed myself too. I haven't always been the type of mother you wanted me to be or I wanted me to be."

"That's not true—" he began.

"It is true, and we both know it." She smiled sadly. "I'll tell you, there's nothing that hurts me more than seeing the disappointment in your eyes when I lose another job. It makes me hate myself, and each time afterward I tell myself that I'm not going to do it again, that things are going to change, but ... well, they don't change. I don't know why. I just can't seem to ... you know." She looked at him. "But they're going to change now. We're going to start a new life in California, and I'm going to be a different person. You'll see. I know I can't just tell you; I have to show you. And I will. It's all over now. All that's behind me. It's in the past. This is a fresh start for both of us, and we're going to make the best of it. Okay?"

Dion nodded.

"Okay?" she said again.

"Okay." He stared out the window, at the sagebrush and saguaro passing by. It sounded good, what she said, and she obviously meant it and believed it herself, but it also sounded slightly familiar and more than a little pat. He found himself wondering if she had taken it from a movie. He hated himself for thinking such a thought, but his mom had given him these sorts of reassurances before, with equal conviction, only to abandon them when she met a guy with a bottle and good buns.

He thought of Cleveland, thought of Albuquerque.

They were silent until they reached a rest area. Dion got out and stretched before walking around to the driver's side. He leaned against the hood of the car. "I don't understand why we're moving to Napa," he said.

His mom, adjusting her halter top, frowned. "What do you mean, you don't understand why? I got a job there, that's why."

"But you could've gotten a job anywhere."

"You have something against Napa?"

"No," he admitted. "It's just ... I don't know."

"Just what?"

"Well, it seems like people usually have a reason for moving." He glanced at her, reddening. "I mean moving to a specific place," he added quickly. "They have family there or they grew up there or they really love the area or their company transfers them or ... something. But we don't really have any reason to be going."

"Dion," she said, "shut up and get in the car."

He grinned at her. "All right," he said. "All right."

* * *

They spent that night in a Motel Six in Santa Barbara, staying in a single room with twin beds.

Dion went to bed early, soon after dinner, and fell asleep instantly. He dreamed of a hallway, a long, dark hallway at the end of which was a red door. He walked slowly forward, certain that the floor under his feet was soft, slimy, and not stable, though he could hear the clicking of his shoe heels on the hard cement. He continued to walk, looking straight ahead, afraid to look to the left or to the right. When he reached the door, he didn't want to open it, but he opened it anyway and saw behind it a stairway leading up.

Down the center of the steps trickled a thin waterfall of blood.

He walked up the stairs, looking down at his feet, following the blood to its source. He reached a landing, turned, continued upward. Now the trickle was thicker, moving faster.

He turned on the next landing and saw seated on the top step a beautiful blond girl of approximately his own age. Her straight hair was tied in a bun at the top of her head, and she was smiling invitingly at him.

She was completely naked.

His eyes moved down her body, over her milky white breasts to her widespread legs. From the hairy, shadowed cleft between her thighs streamed an unending ribbon of blood which cascaded downward from step to step. He walked slowly up to her. She reached out to him, motioning for him to put his head in her lap, and when he again looked at her face, he saw that she had turned into his mom.

They left early the next morning, before dawn, and for breakfast they stopped in the small town of Solvang, some forty miles north of Santa Barbara. A well-known tourist attraction, Solvang was supposed to be a Danish village, but Dutch windmills, Swedish flower boxes, and a varied amalgam of Scandinavian influences could be seen in the architecture of the storybook buildings. They ate at an outdoor café, and Dion had something called a Belgian waffle, a huge, exaggerated waffle square piled high with fresh strawberries and whipped cream. Although he was still troubled by his dream, he felt better today about leaving Arizona, and he looked up at the blue sky, at the green, rolling hills surrounding the community. He knew Napa was still an eight-hour drive away, but he imagined it looking much the same as Solvang—small, cute, beautifully unreal. For the first time he thought he understood why his mom wanted to move to northern California's wine country.

And then they were on the road again, taking with them a white wax sack filled with Danish pastries for the trip. The countryside grew flatter, more farmlike, and though it was initially quite scenic, the sameness of it soon grew monotonous, and Dion, lulled further by the subtle rolling motion of the car, soon fell asleep.

He awoke before lunch and was still awake an hour later as they drove into San Francisco. His mom, obviously excited, grew more talkative as they drew closer to Napa. Her enthusiasm was catching, and Dion found himself anxiously awaiting the moment they pulled up in front of their new home.

His first view of the Napa Valley was disappointing. He had been expecting to find lush green farmland surrounding a small town, a quaint clapboard community with a bandstand in the park and a steepled church overlooking a town square. Instead, the first sight they saw through the white, smoggy air was a crowded Burger King situated next to an abandoned Exxon station. After the build-up, the sight was more than just depressing. He stared out the window. There was no sign of a farm or even a grape arbor, only rather ordinary buildings on typical city streets. He glanced over at his mom. She was still happy, excited, but his own mood of anticipation had been effectively squelched. As they passed through town, he was filled with a growing feeling of dread, a feeling which reminded him for some reason of his dream.

The feeling grew as they drove by shopping centers, through subdivisions, and past tourist traps. The town became more rural, less developed, as they drove north, but it was more than just the physical surroundings which had brought upon him this dread, and he felt as though a great

emotional weight had been placed upon him, a heavy, un-
definable feeling which increased as they headed toward
their new home.

Ten minutes later they were there.

Dion stepped slowly out of the car. The house was
nicer than their house in Mesa. Much nicer. In place of
the small carport and adjoining storage shed they'd had in
Arizona was a beautiful redwood garage. In place of
gravel and cactus was a yard filled with bushes and green
trees. In place of the crackerbox dwelling was a small but
breathtaking wood and glass structure straight out of *Ar-
chitectural Digest*. The house was situated in the flatland
between the hills which surrounded the valley, nominally
part of a subdivision, but the way it was set back from the
road, fronted by shrubbery, gave it a refreshingly rural air.

His mom grinned. "How do you like it? I had someone
at the office pick it out. I figured they'd have an inside
track. What do you think?"

Dion nodded his approval. "It's great."

"We're going to be happy here, aren't we?"

He nodded slowly. "I think we are," he said. And he
was surprised to discover that he believed it.

TWO

April felt good.

They'd been here nearly a week, and it was as if they'd been living here for years. Already Napa felt more like home to her than Mesa ever had.

She stood at the kitchen window, sipping coffee, watching Dion mow the back lawn. He was shirtless and sweating, and she thought that if he wasn't her son, she might try to seduce him. He was turning into a very good-looking young man.

She wondered if he'd grow up to look like his dad.

Not that she remembered what his dad looked like.

Not that she knew who his dad was.

She smiled to herself. Omaha. There'd been a lot of guys back then. Regular lovers as well as one-nighters. And she had never used any form of birth control. She hadn't liked condoms or diaphragms, hadn't liked any sort of barrier to contact, and she hadn't been responsible enough to take birth-control pills on a regular basis. So she'd trusted to luck or fate or whatever, and had just accepted things as they came.

She was glad she'd gotten pregnant, though. She was glad she'd had Dion. She didn't know where she'd be today without him. Dead, she supposed. Overdosed. Or carved up by a Mr. Goodbar.

He turned the mower, started back toward the house, saw her in the window, and waved. She waved back.

On the trip over, Dion had asked why they'd moved to Napa, and she hadn't been able to answer him. Why *had* they come here? As he had pointed out, there was really no compelling reason for them to start over in this place. She had no friends or relatives in the region; her job was one she could have gotten in any mid-sized city or major metropolitan area in the country. She'd told him that it was as good as anywhere else, that it was far enough away that she wouldn't be known, but the truth was that . . .

She'd been Called.

Called. That was how she thought of it. It didn't make any sort of logical sense, but emotionally it felt right. She'd seen an article on the Wine Country in the *Arizona Republic*'s Sunday magazine supplement, and had found herself drawn, pulled to the area. For two weeks the idea of moving had grown within her, making her nervous and anxious, growing from a desire to a necessity in her mind, intruding upon her daily thoughts until she thought she'd go crazy. It was as if something inside her was telling her that she *had* to move to Napa. She'd fought it at first, but she'd finally given in. She had always been one to trust her instincts.

Of course, whether they moved here or someplace else, they still would have had to move. She had no choice in the matter. She had not been laid off from the bank, as she'd told Dion. She'd been fired and threatened with prosecution. Dion probably suspected more than she'd told him and more than he let on, but she doubted that his ideas and suspicions were anywhere near as bad as the truth. The truth was that the boy had been sixteen and that he'd been seriously and permanently injured, and that if the bank manager hadn't been involved as well, she would probably be in jail or on trial at this moment.

What was wrong with her? she wondered. Why did these sorts of things always happen to her? It wasn't as though she didn't try to live a normal life; it was just that this craziness kept intruding. As much as she tried to walk the straight and narrow, there was always someone or something waiting to tip her off balance. She wasn't entirely blameless. Much of it was, in fact, her own fault. But it just seemed like fate wasn't doing her any favors.

All of that was over, though. This time things were going to be different. She was not going to fall back into her old habits, her old patterns. For the first time in her life, she was going to be the type of mother that Dion wanted. The type of mother that he deserved.

She finished one last sip of coffee, dumped the dregs in the sink, then walked into the bedroom to get dressed.

THREE

"First day!"

Dion nodded as he sat down to breakfast. On the table before him was a pitcher of orange juice, two slices of toast with peanut butter, and a choice of two cereals. He looked over at his mom, standing next to the sink and pouring herself a cup of coffee. She was obviously nervous. She only played Harriet Nelson when she was under extreme pressure or extremely worried—ordinarily, they ate breakfast in silence, fending for themselves.

Of course, this was the first day for both of them.

"Are you excited?" his mom asked.

"Not really."

"Be honest."

"More scared than excited." He poured himself a glass of juice.

"You have nothing to be scared about. Everything's going to be fine."

He drank his juice. "You're not nervous?"

"A little," she admitted, sitting down in the chair next to him. He noticed that she was wearing a tight dress which clearly outlined the fact that she was wearing no bra. "But it's only natural to be a little jittery at first. After the first ten minutes, though, it's like you've been there all your life."

For you maybe, Dion thought, but he said nothing. He wished he was a little bit more like his mom in social situations.

He wished she was a little bit more like him.

"Come on," she said. "Hurry up and eat. I'll drop you off at school."

"That's okay. I'll walk."

"You sure?" she asked.

He nodded.

"Embarrassed to have your mommy drop you off, huh?" She smiled. "I understand. But in that case you'd better eat even faster. It's about a fifteen- or twenty-minute walk, I think."

He poured himself a bowl of cereal. "Well, maybe you can drive me part of the way," he said.

She laughed. "Deal."

It was an old redbrick schoolhouse, the kind seldom seen outside of movies. Two stories with indoor hallways, the main building housed both classrooms and administration, stretching parallel to the football field. A tall clock tower topped the adjoining auditorium. The gym, set slightly apart from the other two buildings, was much newer and much uglier, constructed of plain gray cement.

Dion stood across the street from school, waiting for the bell to ring and dreading it at the same time. His mouth was dry, his palms wet, and he wished to God that they had never left Arizona. He was not good at meeting people. He hadn't known that many students at his high school in Mesa, and he had been there since freshman year. Coming to a new school, starting from scratch . . . it was going to be tough.

At least it wasn't the middle of the semester. He was thankful for that. It would have been much worse to walk in on classes already in progress, where all the relationships would have been established and cemented for the year. Now, at least, he would be in on the courses from the beginning. He might be new, but he would be able to start off on somewhat equal footing with his classmates. He would have a chance. There would probably be other new kids here as well, students who'd transferred to the school over the summer, students who, like him, would be looking for someone to meet.

He walked across the street and up the steps into the schoolhouse. Coming to a new school was frightening, but in a way it was also exciting. He knew no one in Napa, so no one would have any preconceived ideas about him. He carried no baggage. He was, as far as the students here were concerned, a blank slate, and he could create of himself anything he wanted. A few well-placed lies, the proper clothes, and he could be a jock or a party animal or . . . anything.

Theoretically.

Dion smiled wryly. He knew himself well enough to know his place in the school hierarchy. He was neither athletic nor spectacularly handsome, neither a class clown nor a bravura talker. He was smart but not in the subjects guaranteed to bring him social acceptability. As much as he might try to alter his personality, his true nature would undoubtedly win out over any self-imposed public image.

He was not going to be Joe Popular here either.

But that was okay. He was used to it.

He stood outside the classroom and looked down at his schedule as if checking to make sure the room number was correct. He knew perfectly well that he was in front of the right room, but this conspicuous display of his newness somehow made him feel more secure, less afraid. Students pushed rudely past him, around him, entering the class. He had half hoped that Napa High would be like those sitcom schools on TV where friendly students would notice his discomfort and immediately try to make him feel at home. No such luck. He was ignored; no one even noticed him.

He walked into class, aware that he was sweating heavily, and glanced quickly around, taking in the lay of the land. The desks in the middle of the room were taken, he saw, but there were a few open spaces in the back row, and the front row was entirely free.

He opted for the back.

He could hide better there.

Seating himself in the middle desk of an empty trio, directly behind a sullen-looking boy in a dirty T-shirt and a heavily made-up Hispanic girl, he looked around the room. He had expected the kids here to be cooler than those in Mesa. After all, this was California. But the students surrounding him all looked faintly anachronistic, the boys' hair a little too long, the girls' appearance a little too casual. Obviously the latest wave of fashion which had crashed over Phoenix had come directly from south-

ern California, its edges lapping only faintly at the northern part of the golden state.

He looked down again at his schedule of classes:
American Government, Algebra II, Classical Mythology,
World Economics, Rock History, and AP English. He was
enrolled in what, for this school, was the standard college
prep lineup. His sole elective, and the only class which
looked like it would be any fun at all, was Rock History.
The others were strict by-the-book academic courses, although in the case of the mythology class he had chosen
the lesser of two evils; the alternative would have been a
foreign language.

At least PE was not a required course at this school.
That was one thing for which he was grateful. He was not
good in sports, and he always felt a little embarrassed un-
dressing in front of other guys.

An average-looking kid with blond mid-length hair
dropped his books on the next desk over and sat down.
His eyes flicked dismissively over Dion, who smiled
bravely, determined to at least try to meet new people this
first day.

"Hi," he said.

The kid looked at him, snorted. "What's your name?
Dick?"

Dion thought for only a second before deciding to take
the plunge. "That's what your mama called me last
night."

The kid stared at him for a moment, then laughed, and
suddenly it *was* like one of those sitcom schools.

He had made his first friend in Napa.

As simple as that.

"What's your real name?" the kid asked.

"Dion," he said.

"I'm Kevin." He gestured magnanimously around the
room. "And this is hell."

It wasn't as bad as all that. The subject was boring, but
the teacher seemed nice, and since it was the first day he
let everyone out early so they would have time to find
their next class. "Where you off to now?" Kevin asked in
the hallway.

"Algebra II."

"Whoa."

"What do you have?"

"English. Then Classical Mythology, then PE, then Rock History, then Economics."

"Looks like we have two more classes together," Dion said. "Mythology and Rock History."

Kevin frowned. "Together? What do you think we are? Butt buddies?"

"I didn't mean—" Dion began, flustered.

"I thought I saw some pixie dust on your shoulder." Kevin backed up, shaking his head. "I'm out of here." And he headed down the hall, disappearing into the crowd which began streaming out of the line of doorways as the bell rang.

Dion stood there stupidly. Apparently he had crossed over some behavioral line peculiar to the subculture of this school, said the wrong word in the wrong way, and had offended his new friend. He worried about it all through math. But when he took an empty seat near the window of his Mythology class an hour later, Kevin sat down next to him as if nothing had happened.

Obviously Kevin's abrupt departure was a perfectly ordinary way of saying good-bye around here.

He would have to remember that.

Dion scanned the room, scoping out his fellow students. Kevin followed his gaze and commented on each individual who came under his scrutiny, revealing tidbits of gossip, information, personality quirks, but he shut up quickly when the teacher entered the room. Mr. Holbrook, a tall, thin man with an angular, bird-like face, put his briefcase down on the desk and strode directly to the blackboard, where he began writing his name in clear block letters.

He was followed through the door by the stairway girl from Dion's dream.

Dion blinked, held his breath. The resemblance was truly remarkable. The girl was wearing fashionable fall school clothes, and her hair was curled and hanging free rather than straight and tied up, but the similarity between the two was nothing less than amazing. His eyes followed the girl as she sat down in an empty seat in the second row. She was gorgeous, almost unbelievably gorgeous, and she had about her a reserved, almost shy quality that made her seem even more attractive and which immediately distinguished her from her dream double.

He wanted to ask Kevin who she was, but it was clear from the silence of the classroom and the unyielding rigidity of the writing teacher's back that talk would not be tolerated during this period.

He settled in for a long hour, content merely to look. After a short introduction, Mr. Holbrook called roll, and Dion discovered that her name was Penelope. Penelope Daneam. It was a nice name, a conservative, old-fashioned name, and he found that he liked that.

Like everyone else, Penelope looked around as each name was called, connecting names with faces in her mind, and Dion grew increasingly nervous as the alphabetical roll call drew closer to S.

"Semele," the teacher called. "Dion?"

"Here," Dion said. He stared down at his desk, too timid to look up at her, too embarrassed to meet her eyes. When Mr. Holbrook called the next name and Dion finally did look up, her attention was elsewhere, on the new student.

Smooth move, he thought.

As the period dragged on, he found himself tuning out the monotonic drone of the teacher to focus on the back of Penelope's head.

Maybe tomorrow he would contrive to sit closer to her.

The hour was as long as he'd expected, but finally the bell rang. Dion moved slowly from his seat, watching through jostling bodies as Penelope rose and picked up her books. The pants she was wearing were not tight, but she had been sitting in such a way that when she stood up they unintentionally rode up the crack of her buttocks.

Kevin noticed the object of his attention and shook his head. "Rapidly approaching the Isle of Lesbos, bud."

Dion looked at him, surprised. "What?"

"She likes 'em fileted."

"Fileted?"

"You know, de-boned. No dick."

"You're lying."

Kevin shrugged. "I call 'em the way I see 'em."

"She's not a lesbian."

Kevin casually grabbed the sleeve of a student pushing past them toward the door, a heavyset guy carrying only a Pee Chee folder. "Hank?" he said. "Penelope Daneam."

The big guy grinned. "Cat lapper."

Kevin let go of Hank's sleeve, turning back toward Dion. "See?"

Lesbian. He wasn't sure he believed it, but he didn't disbelieve it either. He watched her exit the room and disappear into the crowded hall. A lesbian. He had to admit that the idea was rather exciting. He knew he probably didn't have a chance in hell with a girl that beautiful, particularly with his lame opposite-sex conversational skills, but at least he'd been provided with additional fuel for his fantasies, provided with not only the image of her naked but with the image of her in bed with another girl, doing exotic, forbidden, only partially imaginable things.

"Stuff a sock down your pants," Hank suggested as he stepped past them. "Works every time. When she sees that bulging bohannon, she'll be yours."

"Yeah," Kevin added. "Of course, when you whip down your pants and she sees the Vienna wiener you really have, she'll dump you faster'n you can say 'tough titty kitty.' "

Dion laughed. *Fileted. Cat lapper. Bohannon.* He liked the creative obscenities, the idiosyncratic descriptions used by the students here. In Mesa, guys were either "fags" or "dicks," girls "bitches," and the primary adjective used to describe everything else was "shit." The weather was either hot as shit or cold as shit, a person was dumb as shit or smart as shit, a job was hard as shit or easy as shit. In Mesa, shit possessed a number of contrary properties.

But the language here seemed to be more colorful, more interesting, more intelligent.

As did the people.

He might like living in California.

"Come on," Kevin said. "Let's get something to eat."

Dion nodded. "All right," he said. "Lead on."

FOUR

The bus dropped her off at the foot of the drive, and Penelope shifted her books to her left hand, taking out her key, opening the black box, and punching the security combination with her right. The winery gates swung slowly and automatically open. The warm afternoon air was permeated with the rich scent of the harvest, a heady, organic fragrance that overhung the grounds like grape perfume, thick and redolent, undisturbed by any breeze. She breathed deeply as she walked up the winding asphalt road toward the house. She loved the smell of the harvest more than anything, more than the deeper, stronger scent of the pressing, much more than the tart odor of the fermenting processes to come. She had heard it said that olfactory memory was the strongest, that olfactory associations carried the most emotional weight, and she believed it. To her the fresh natural fragrance of the newly picked grapes always conjured up feelings she connected with childhood, joyous, happy emotions not linked to any specific event, and it was at this time that she was most grateful that her mothers owned the winery.

She walked slowly. Ahead, she could see sunlight glinting off the glass and metal of the cars in the parking lot. In the vineyard to her right, several groups of day laborers were cutting bunches of grapes from the vine, gathering the first pick of this year's crop. In the next few weeks, she knew, the ranks of workers would swell until, in early October, the vineyard aisles would be full of crowded, stooped laborers.

One of the women working closest to the drive stopped picking for a moment to look up at her, and Penelope smiled, waving. The woman returned to her work without so much as a nod. Penelope hurried forward, embarrassed. Most of the laborers, she knew, were illegal aliens, many of them unable to speak English, their work overseen by exploitative day-contracted foremen whose only talent was that they could translate orders and requests. It was against the law to hire illegals, of course, but then Mother Margeaux had never been one to be deterred by such trifles as legality. She remembered once asking Mother Margeaux how much the laborers were paid per day. Her mother had replied curtly, "Enough."

She doubted that. And she assumed that that was why many of the day workers seemed to dislike her so. She had never personally done anything to engender any ill will among the grape pickers, but no doubt they viewed her as a follower in her mothers' footsteps.

The salaried employees, on the other hand, the winery workers, always treated her as though she were royalty, taking her much too seriously, behaving very deferentially toward her.

No one treated her like a normal person.

A gull swooped low over her head, a branch of half-dried grapes in its mouth, and she followed its progress as it flew over the cars, over the buildings, toward the hills beyond, nesting finally in an anonymous tree in the heart of the woods.

The woods.

She felt a chill wash over her as she looked at the line of trees demarcating the rear boundary of their land, and she glanced quickly away, quickening her step toward the house.

She had always been allowed to go anywhere she wanted on their property, to roam the grounds, wander the vineyards, but ever since she'd been a small child she had been expressly forbidden to enter the woods. She had been told and retold, warned and rewarned, that the woods were dangerous, home to wild animals such as cougars and wolves, although she had never heard of a single animal attack occurring anywhere near the area. Up by Clear Lake a few years back, a hungry mountain lion had attacked and maimed a three-year-old girl, and near Lake Berryessa there had been isolated incidents of bears frightening away campers. But though she often saw weekend hikers trekking up one of several paths which led through the trees into the woods, she had never read or heard of a single attack on a human being in that area.

Her mothers had obviously instituted the rule because of her father.

Such a stern and seemingly arbitrary prohibition should have caused her to sneak into the woods at the first opportunity, and she knew that most of her friends would have done exactly that. But there was something about the woods which awakened within her a feeling of instinctive dread, a feeling that would have been there even if her mothers had said nothing at all to her about the area. Each time she looked through the barbed-wire fence at the back of the property toward the line of trees across the meadow, she felt the hairs tingle on the back of her neck, felt goosebumps rise on her arms.

The goosebumps were there now, and she pushed the thought out of her mind, running up the last stretch of drive, taking the porch steps two at a time, hurrying between the tall Doric columns which fronted the house. Pulling open the heavy double doors, she walked through the high-ceilinged foyer and past the stairway into the kitchen. "I'm home!" she announced. She dropped her books on the chopping block and opened the refrigerator, taking out a can of V8.

Mother Felice, looking tired and wan, the dark circles around her eyes more prominent than usual, emerged from the pantry, wiping her hands on her apron. "How was it?" she asked. "How was your first day?"

Penelope smiled. "It was fine, Mother."

"Just fine? Not wonderfully spectacularly amazingly stupendous?"

"What did you expect? It was only the first day."

"How are your teachers?"

"I don't know yet. It's hard to tell until the end of the first week." She looked out the window of the kitchen toward the twin buildings of the winery. "Where's everyone else?"

Mother Felice shrugged. "Pressing time. You know. It's a busy day."

Penelope nodded, grateful that her other mothers had not been there to greet her. She had told her mothers she was a senior this year, almost an adult, had asked them not to make a big deal over school for once, and apparently they had gotten her hint.

"Did you make any new friends yet?" her mother asked, washing her hands in the sink.

"I saw Vella and Lianne and Jennifer."

"I said any *new* friends."

Penelope reddened. She finished her V8 and tossed the empty can into the garbage sack next to the stove. "I know what you're hinting about, and, no, I have not met any guys yet. I will probably not have a date this week, okay? God, it's only the first day. What do you expect?"

"I don't mean to—"

Penelope sighed. "I know," she said. "But don't worry. Prom is eight months away."

"It's not that, it's—"

"It's what?"

Her mother tried to laugh lightly, but the effect seemed hollow and artificial. "Never mind. We'll talk about it some other time."

"Okay." She looked again out the window, was glad to see no sign of other mothers. "If you need me," she said, "I'll be in the Garden."

"Don't you have any homework?"

"Mother, it's the first day. How many times do I have to tell you? No one ever has homework the first day. Or even the first week."

"We did."

"Times have changed." Penelope grabbed an apple from the fruit bowl on the counter and picked up her books. She was about to head upstairs to drop the books off in her bedroom when she was stopped by her mother's voice. "Aren't you even going to stop by and see your other mothers?"

Penelope turned around. She licked her lips. "I'd rather do it later," she admitted.

"It's your first day of school. They'll be interested in what happened." She put a hand on Penelope's shoulder. "They care. We all care."

"Yeah," Penelope said.

Her mother punched her playfully on the shoulder. "Knock that off." She smiled at her daughter. "Come on."

Mother Margeaux, dressed entirely in black as usual, was seated behind the massive desk in her office, talking on the phone, berating the person on the other end of the line. She nodded curtly at Penelope, at Mother Felice, then continued unabated with her diatribe. "What I expect," she said in a hard, even voice, "is that you correctly perform the function for which you were contracted. If that is too difficult, our company will find a more effective and efficient means of delivering our product. Do I make myself clear?"

Mother Felice sat down in the dark leather couch against the wall and motioned for Penelope to do the same. Penelope shook her head and remained standing.

Mother Margeaux hung up the phone, coolly and carefully replacing the receiver in its cradle, then glanced up at Penelope, smiling tightly. Light was reflected in her deep brown eyes and in the smoothness of her slick black hair. "I trust your first day of school was satisfactory?"

Penelope nodded, not meeting her mother's eyes. "Yes, ma'am."

"Are you satisfied with your classes? With your teachers?"

"I guess . . ."

"If not, I can arrange to have you transferred. This is your senior year, and it's important that you maintain your grade-point average."

"My classes are fine."

"That's good." Mother Margeaux nodded. "That's good."

Penelope said nothing. The three of them sat silently for a moment.

"Is there anything else you wish to tell me?" Mother Margeaux asked.

Penelope shook her head. "No, ma'am."

"I'd better get back to work, then. Thank you for coming in, Penelope."

She was dismissed. The conversation was over. Mother Felice stood up. "I guess we'll see your other mothers."

"You'll do well this year," Mother Margeaux said to her daughter. "You'll make us proud."

Penelope nodded, following Mother Felice out of the office. She did not notice that she was sweating until they stepped into the hall.

Although Mother Sheila was out somewhere in the fields, overseeing the collection of representative samples of today's harvest, her other mothers were in the testing area of the main building, supervising the analysis of grapes which had been picked this morning. A team of analysts sat at a long counter in front of the window, testing the balance of the must in order to make a preliminary determination of this year's product potential while her mothers looked on.

"Penelope's home!" Mother Felice announced, closing the white door behind her.

Mother Margaret was quietly conferring with two of the analysts. They both looked up at the announcement, smiled absently, nodded, waved, and continued talking. Mother Janine, however, immediately stopped what she was doing and hurried over, her spiked heels sounding loudly on the tile. Penelope felt herself tense up. Mother Janine reached her, threw her arms around her, and hugged tightly. The hug was a little too long, a little too unmotherly, and Penelope anxiously held her breath. As always, she tried telling herself that Mother Janine really loved her and cared about her, but what she told herself and what she felt were two different things. There was something disturbing about her youngest mother, something she could not quite put her finger on, and as soon as Mother Janine let go, Penelope stepped back and away.

"I missed you," her mother said in that cloying little-girl voice she used when talking to Penelope. "I always hate it when summer ends and you have to leave us and go back to school."

Penelope nodded, said nothing. The truth was that for the past two weeks she had not seen Mother Janine except at breakfast and dinner. She didn't know how her mother could miss her.

"Did you meet anyone yet? Any cute guys?"

Penelope frowned. "It's only the first day."

Mother Janine laughed, a strange sound that segued from the high falsetto of a child's giggle to the low chuckle of a deep-throated woman. "Never too early to start."

"Yeah." Penelope nodded and turned toward Mother Felice. "Well, we'd better go, let them get back to work."

"Okay," her mother agreed.

"We'll talk at dinner," Mother Janine said. "I want you to tell me all about your day, everything that happened." She gave Penelope's shoulder a small squeeze.

"See?" Mother Felice said as they walked across the small lawn to the house. "That wasn't so bad."

Penelope grimaced and said nothing.

Her mother laughed.

The two of them parted at the kitchen. "*Now* I'm going to the Garden," Penelope said. She grabbed her books from the kitchen table and went upstairs to her bedroom. Her feet were silent on the heavy carpet as she walked down the long hallway. She glanced into the open doorways as she passed and noted as always how the tastes and personalities of her mothers were reflected in their bedrooms. Mother Margeaux's sleeping quarters were simultaneously imperial and practical, the warring values represented by a huge bed with an intricately carved oak headboard and a large, simple desk topped with neatly stacked piles of paperwork. The off-white walls were decorated with framed original prototypes of Daneam labels. Next door, Mother Sheila's room was the most mundane, filled with bland contemporary furnishings that looked as though they could have come straight out of a catalog photograph, and a single framed print on the wall that always reminded Penelope of hotel art. Mother Margaret's room decor was the boldest and probably most interesting, with its ultra-modern bed, non-dresser, and startling juxtaposition of Old World folk art and original paintings by young Native American artists, but it was in Mother Felice's bedroom that she was most comfortable. Cluttered with lace and flowers, antiques and needlework, a shiny brass bed in its center, the room was crowded and at the same time light, airy. It was a friendly room, and it suited her favorite mother perfectly.

Mother Janine's bedroom had no furniture at all, only a bare mattress centered on the red tile floor. The undecorated walls were painted a deep, unreflective black.

She had never liked going into Mother Janine's room.

She reached her own bedroom and threw her books on the bed. Grabbing her journal and pen from the dresser, she went back downstairs, walking through the library and opening the sliding glass door to the Garden. Or what her mothers called the Garden. To her it had always been much more than a garden. To her it was a sanctuary, a refuge, a place where she could come to relax and to think and to be alone. Her mothers seemed to recognize her feelings and to appreciate her kinship with the location. The Garden had originally been the place where in the summer they read or sunbathed or just lounged around, but over the years their involvement with the area had become less, their visits more infrequent. It was as though they had tacitly agreed that the Garden was her domain and not theirs, and gradually they relinquished their control to her. For this she was grateful.

She glanced around the walled yard. In the center of the quadrangle was a fountain, an exact replication of a Hellenic fountain discovered in the ruined courtyard of an old villa by Mother Margaret on one of her trips to Greece. Spreading outward from the fountain like spokes in a wheel were Mother Sheila's medicinal herbs and rare flowering shrubs, the even rows of greenery subdivided by the purposeful placement of various Old World archaeological artifacts and folk sculpture purchased by her mothers over the years. There were several benches within the Garden, but Penelope had always preferred sitting on the edge of the fountain, listening firsthand to the burble of the water, feeling the spray of light mist against the skin of her hands and face.

Although she hadn't said anything to Mother Felice and probably wouldn't, the question of her mothers' sexual preference had come up again today at school. Last year she had nearly been suspended after fighting with Susan Holman, who had called the product produced by their vineyards "Lezzie Label Wine." She and Susan had no classes together this year, but in the hall after lunch she had heard Susan loudly say something about "the Dyke Factory" while her tough blue-jeaned cronies laughed hysterically. She had ignored the remark, continuing on to class as though she hadn't heard. But she had heard. And it hurt.

It always hurt.

What made her feel worse was that she wondered herself sometimes if any of her mothers were lesbians. That had been the rumor around town for years, and it was not beyond the realm of possibility. Each of her mothers went out periodically on dates, but for all she knew that could have been a cover-up, merely an attempt to maintain respectability for the sake of the business. There were no serious men in any of their lives, and there never had been, at least not in her lifetime.

Besides, her mothers were . . . well, weird. She hated to admit it, but they not only seemed peculiar to outsiders. They often seemed strange even to her.

Particularly Mother Janine.

Of course, if that was the case, if they *were* lesbians, one of them had to be bisexual. Or had to at least have done it once with a man.

Unless she had been adopted.

No, she was not adopted. Of that she was certain.

She sat down, dipping her fingers into the cool water of the fountain pool. She called them all "mother," but she knew that, really, she had only one female parent. She had a pretty good idea of who her biological mother was too. It was something all of them denied when she put it to them, confronted them with it. They all handed her the same line, saying that traditional one-on-one relationships, such as those usually associated with parents and siblings, were ultimately limiting and were not to be established or recognized within this household. They told her she must always treat each mother equally. But she noticed that they did not all treat her equally. Some were kinder to her than others, some were more open and honest with her than others, and so she was closer to some than others.

She felt closest to Mother Felice, and it was Mother Felice whom she believed to be her true mother, her biological mother. The reasons were vague, more feelings than thoughts, but they were consistent and always had been. It was Mother Felice who throughout the years had seemed most concerned with both her physical welfare and her emotional well-being. Like today. It had been Mother Felice who had stayed in the house to wait for her. The apron and the pantry routine hadn't fooled her at all. Her mother was here instead of at the winery because she wanted to know how her first day in school had gone.

That made her feel good.

Sometimes she wished that Mother Felice was her only mother.

She looked down into the water, seeing in the shimmering a distorted reflection of her face. She was pretty, she knew, and she liked looking at herself, though she was by no means obsessive about it. She had never been one to spend excessive amounts of time on makeup or hair care, but if she passed a mirror she invariably looked into it. She found it reassuring to see her own reflection, to know what she looked like, although it always embarrassed her if someone caught her at it.

Sometimes she wondered if she herself was homosexual. It was not inconceivable. Growing up in an all-female environment, it might even be expected. She had always had a hard time talking to boys and had never really made that leap of socialization that most of her peers had made during the awkward years of junior high. At night, in bed, when she masturbated, she liked both the way her fingers felt on her vagina and the way her vagina felt against her fingertips. She enjoyed the pliant softness, the warm wetness, even the subtle pressure of the vaginal walls against her middle finger when she occasionally slipped it into the opening. She could not see herself ever touching another girl's body—the very thought was revolting—but wasn't the joy she felt when fingering herself enough to make her a lesbian?

She wasn't sure.

Maybe the fact that she had trouble imagining herself

in a romantic situation with anyone, boy or girl, meant
that she was asexual.

She splashed her reflection, dissolving her face in a
fluid ripple.

Why was it all so complicated?

There was a knock behind her, and she turned around
to see Mother Felice at the window, waving. She waved
back, then looked down, opened her journal, clicked her
pen. "Today," she wrote, "was the first day of my senior
year ..."

FIVE

As one, the four grandfather clocks lined along the wall next to the door chimed six, and Vic Williams stood up, shut off the cassette player, and moved from behind the counter to lock the door. It had been a long day, a boring day, and not a very profitable one. Tourist season had pretty well run its course, and only five people had come into the shop since he'd opened this morning, all of them browsers, not buyers. It was a taste of things to come, he knew. School had started, vacations had ended, and from now until mid-October business would be pretty much hit-and-miss.

Time was when the antique market was bullish all year, when he didn't have to depend on outside trade, when even local women wanted stained glass windows to decorate their living rooms and conservative middle-aged men bought Victrolas for their wives' anniversaries. But antiques were out these days. People bought Nagels and Neimans now, mall art for their walls, and anniversary presents consisted of televisions or VCRs.

Vic pulled the shade on the window. He was hungry and wanted to grab a bite to eat, but there were still three cartons of Depression glass he'd purchased at an estate sale a few weeks back which needed to be catalogued. He could have, and should have, done that earlier today, during the long slow stretch between lunch and closing, but he hated going through purchases during business hours. Somehow, the ritual of examining, appraising, and pricing items seemed more suited to evening than morning or afternoon.

He'd pick up a burger on the way home.

Vic retreated behind the counter once again and walked

through the beaded doorway into the back room. The three cartons were on the floor, and he hefted the largest onto the long metal table which ran the length of the side wall. He took a razor blade out of the desk drawer and cut two cross slits through the layered masking tape which sealed shut the top of the box. Dropping the blade on the table, he pulled up the cardboard flaps and, one by one, began unwrapping the individually stacked plates. The pieces were good. Rose glass from the mid-thirties. He held each up to the light, checking for flaws and chips and scratches before setting it carefully down on the tabletop.

After unwrapping, examining, and setting down the last plate, he looked into the box. At the bottom, lying as if thrown there by accident or afterthought, was an old waterstained paperback. *In Watermelon Sugar.*

In Watermelon Sugar.

Richard Brautigan.

Whoa, did that bring back memories. He picked up the book, flipped the pages. Half of them were stuck together, glued by the hardening of some spilled beverage. The photo of Brautigan on the front was almost completely obscured by a brown stain, although the woman next to him stared out of the picture undamaged. It saddened Vic to see the book in such shape. It had been originally purchased, no doubt, by a member of what had then been called "the counterculture," someone young and enthusiastic, hungry for new ideas. Now that person was probably balding and overweight, dully establishment, interested only in interest rates and IRAs, the book and its fallen idol author now not even a memory.

Vic dropped the book in the wastepaper basket and sighed heavily.

He had come to Napa as a college student in the late sixties, and though he now wore his hair short and dressed respectably in the fashions of today, he still aligned himself with the sentiments of that era, still considered himself a part of that generation. Of course, those days were long gone, even here in northern California, where small conclaves of ex-hippies still lived in converted Victorian houses amidst the faded relics of psychedelia. People these days were harsher, harder, more willingly insensitive. The pace of life was faster now; there was less time to talk with friends, less time to be kind to strangers, less time to stop and smell the roses.

It made him feel depressed.

A lot of things made him feel depressed lately.

Last night he had watched a television program on the Vietnam War which, straight-faced, had portrayed the army as an upright organization of highly moral men bravely doing their patriotic duty despite the protests of an obnoxious and misguided crowd of drug-crazed college students. He had turned the program off before it ended. If there was one thing that really drove him crazy, that made him absolutely furious, it was the revisionist history now fostered by the media which characterized the sixties as an anarchic aberration, a decade in which the traditional values of America had been trashed by rioting long-haired, dope-smoking freaks. Jesus, couldn't people even remember what it had been like? What the hell had happened to the nation's short-term memory? Of course there had been a harsh element—a protest against the amoral complacency of the establishment and the immorality of the war—but there had also been a kindness, a gentleness of spirit which had gotten lost in the translation, which was never captured by movies or television shows or news retrospectives. It had been a time of turmoil, yes, but the people of that time had been open and giving and trusting and honest, filled with an optimistic generosity which in today's pragmatic light seemed quaintly naive. He shook his head. Even the hip today, their counterculture counterparts, seemed much more materialistic and opportunistic, less real, much phonier, pretenders to the throne, pseudo-beatniks dressed in black turtleneck costumes of the past, capturing only the surface details of a much more serious movement.

The times they had a-changed.

Vic lifted the box off the table, put it on the floor, and was about to crush its sides when he heard a noise from the front room, the sound of someone bumping into a piece of furniture.

He frowned. What could that be? There was no one in the store.

The bump came again.

He stood up and walked out to the counter. The front door, he saw immediately, was still closed and locked, the window shade pulled down. Could someone have been shopping in one of the rear aisles and not heard or noticed that the shop had closed?

He heard footsteps from behind a row of armoires to the left.

"Hey!" he called. "Who's there?"

There was no answer, but the footsteps retreated down the aisle away from the counter. The thought occurred to him that someone had been deliberately hiding in one of the trunks or armoires while he closed up, waiting until he left in order to rob the place. Common sense told him to call the police, but instead he walked around the front of the counter.

"Who's there?" he called again.

From the other end of the store, the dark furniture aisle farthest away from the windows, came the sound of a woman singing. Vic stopped. The sound sent a chill through him. There was nothing threatening in either the voice or the song, a folkish tune sung in another language, but the incongruity of the circumstances lent the situation a decidedly surrealistic tinge.

"We're closed," he said, instantly aware of how ineffectual his announcement sounded.

The woman continued to sing.

Heart pounding, he proceeded slowly down the aisle toward the source of the sound. *I should be carrying a baseball bat,* he thought, *some type of weapon.*

Then he was around the corner and it was too late.

The woman was of approximately his own age and was dressed in a long, sheer gown which recalled the earth dresses of the past. She was obviously drunk or stoned and was humming to herself as she swayed back and forth in the center of the aisle, eyes closed. Next to her on the floor was a stick about half the size of a broom handle, tipped with what looked like a small pine cone.

Vic stood silently for a moment, watching the woman

instead of announcing his presence. She was beautiful.
Her hair was long and black and hung in naturally uncombed splendor over her shoulders and down her back.
Even in the dim light he could see the smoothness of her
perfect complexion, the classic line of her well-formed
nose, the sensuous fullness of her lips. Through the
transluscent gown he could see a dark thatch between her
shifting legs, the outline of nipples where the light material caught at her breasts.

What was she doing here? he wondered. How had she
gotten in?

He was about to clear his throat, let the woman know
that he was here, when her eyes suddenly snapped open.
The effect was so startling and unexpected that he nearly
jumped. Her eyes fastened on his. There was hunger in
her expression, and a wildness which seemed totally at
odds with the makeup of her face. Although she had
seemed spaced out a moment before, there was in her features none of the vagueness associated with being high.
Her gaze was sharp and focused, crystal clear.

"I don't know what you're doing here," Vic said. "But
you'll have to leave." His voice sounded more authoritar-
ian than he'd intended, than he'd wanted.

The woman closed her eyes again, began humming, began singing.

"You have to leave," Vic repeated.

Smiling, swaying, almost dancing, the woman moved
forward until she was directly before him. One arm
snaked around his waist, the other lightly cupping his
crotch, as she tilted her face upward to kiss him. He did
not draw her to him, but he did not push her away. Unsure
of how to react, he allowed her to control the moment, silently acquiescing as she kissed him, her soft tongue sliding gently between his lips. He felt himself growing. It
had been a while since he'd been to bed with anyone, and
to his body even this casual contact felt good. She gave
his crotch a small squeeze.

Pulling away, still humming, she dropped to her knees
and began unbuckling his belt.

This isn't happening, he thought.

She's crazy, he thought.

AIDS, he thought.

But he remained in place. He wanted to back away, to put a stop to this—it was too strange, it was happening too fast—but he stayed rooted, his body refusing to listen to the arguments of his mind.

She pulled down his pants, pulled down his underwear. He was hard and quivering, and slowly, expertly, she began massaging him, stroking him. He found himself putting his hands on the top of her head. Her hair felt smooth, soft, wonderful. He closed his eyes.

The rhythm changed. What had been gentle became aggressive, then just plain rough. He opened his eyes, looked down. The woman was smiling up at him, and there was something in the expression on her face that chilled him.

She grabbed his balls tightly and with one quick pull yanked them out by the roots.

Vic screamed, a primal, instinctive expression of agony, as his erection disintegrated in a wash of warm blood. The woman, still on her knees before him, lifted her hands to catch the spurting blood, smearing it on her face and in her hair, laughing with drunken, ecstatic glee. He staggered backward and would have fallen had it not been for the armoire behind him. And then she was wielding her pine-cone stick, shoving it deep into his stomach, thrusting upward. New agonies flared within him as the serrated, irregular end of the spear pushed in farther, piercing skin, rending muscle, ripping veins. She pulled the stick out and dropped it, trying to shove a hand into the hole she'd made. Her gown was covered with a Pollock canvas of red, and still she was tearing at him, her mouth open to catch the spray, greedy fingers bathing in the hot liquid.

He kicked out at her with what strength and coordination was left to him, all the time screaming, but she absorbed the blows happily, laughing, her head whipping back and forth in a frenzied motion as she clawed into his abdomen, grabbing viscera, squeezing. He slumped to the floor, his vision clouding, coherence slipping fast.

The last thing he noticed was that she had ripped off her gown and was naked.

SIX

After Mythology, Dion followed Kevin out of the building to the cafeteria. He felt pretty good. He had been here less than a week, but already he had settled in to the familiar rhythm of school, making the adjustment with unusual ease. The teachers, the classes, seemed not much different than those in Mesa, certainly no harder, and most of the students he met seemed all right, although he hadn't really spoken in depth to any of them except Kevin.

He was still not sure of Kevin's status in the school social structure. His friend clearly did not belong to any of the identifiable cliques, but neither was he a true loner or outcast. He seemed to fall through the categorical cracks. Kevin knew almost everyone, was on good terms with most of the people he knew, yet he chose to spend his lunches with Dion. The two of them were still not completely at ease with each other, were still in fact defining their roles within the friendship, but a friendship it was, and for that Dion was grateful. Kevin talked tough, but between the frequent obscenities there lurked evidence of a mind, a sharp one, and Dion suspected that Kevin had latched onto him because he sensed a soul with similar interests. Indeed, their taste in everything from music to movies to schoolteachers seemed remarkably in sync, and Dion thought that perhaps that was one reason why he and Kevin seemed to get on so well.

He was surprised to find that his interest in Penelope Daneam had not abated. He had half thought that his first-day attraction to her was the result of her resemblance to the girl in his dream, but as he heard her talk in class, as he eavesdropped on her conversations with the friend seated next to her, as she grew into a person of her own, distinct from his mental image, he found that his interest had increased. She too seemed intelligent, far more aware of events and ideas than the girls he'd known in Arizona, and that impressed him. What's more, she appeared to be approachable. She was gorgeous, of course, no doubt about that, but she did not seem as far out of his league as he had initially thought. She was not in the least stand-offish or stuck up. There was an easiness to her manner, an unaffectedness obvious even within the confinements of the classroom. She seemed like a real person, not a phony.

She also did not seem like a lesbian.

The problem was that he didn't know how to go about meeting her. In class, he imagined what he would do if she accidentally dropped her books and he picked them up, their eyes meeting, but he knew that sort of thing happened only in film or fiction and wasn't a feasible possibility. He could, and did, however, move his seat closer to hers each day, changing and exchanging desks. In this class the teacher did not insist on a seating chart, allowing students to sit wherever they pleased, and this was an opportunity he was determined to take advantage of. He was not sure what he would say to her when he finally reached the adjoining desk, not sure of how he would initiate a conversation, but he would deal with that problem when he came to it.

That would be Friday, according to his calculations.

Luckily, Kevin continued to move forward through the seating ranks with him. It was always easier to bring a third party into an existing conversation than to start a conversation cold with someone you'd never talked to before.

Kevin bought a Coke and a burrito at the cafeteria, and Dion purchased a hot dog and milk. The two of them battled their way against the stream of traffic, and sat on a low wall next to the vending machines, watching the passersby.

Kevin took a bite of his burrito. He shook his head. "Do you realize," he said, "that every one of those girls has a pussy? Every one of them." Dion followed his gaze, saw a well-endowed girl wearing a tight T-shirt and form-fitting jeans. "Between each of those legs is a hungry hole, ready for dick." He grinned. "It's a wonderful world."

Dion nodded. Yesterday, Kevin had called women's bodies a "life-support system for the vagina." Kevin's macho comments were funny, but Dion wasn't sure if they were simply public posturing or reflections of his real attitude, and it was something that bothered him, that made him slightly uncomfortable.

The two of them watched the girls pass by. Dion's eyes were caught by the sight of Penelope, carrying a brown sack lunch, buying a carton of orange juice from one of the machines. Kevin saw who he was staring at and laughed. "I knew it. The siren's song of Lesbos."

Dion reddened, but was determined to appear nonchalant. "So tell me something about her."

"Tell you what?"

"Anything."

"Well, she's a lesbian. But I told you that, right?" He pretended to think. "Let me see. She lives with a bunch of other lesbians at the Daneam Sisters Winery. They're all related somehow, her aunts or something. You can't buy the wine in stores. It's strictly a mail-order business. Sold to other lesbians, I believe."

"Be serious."

"I am. At least about the winery. The references to sexual preferences are my own editorializing."

Dion felt his chances slipping away. "So she's rich?"

Kevin nodded. "Nice work if you can get it."

The two of them watched Penelope take her juice carton out of the drawer and disappear into the crowd. "Don't worry," Kevin said. "There are plenty of other beavers in the valley."

Dion forced himself to smile. "Yeah."

Kevin offered Dion a ride home with one of his friends after school, but Dion declined and said he'd rather walk. Kevin and his friend took off in a squeal of burnt Mustang tires that left twin skid marks on the lighter black of the faded asphalt.

Dion walked down the tree-lined street. He usually avoided most forms of exercise—he was by no means a jock and he truly hated PE—but he'd always enjoyed walking. It offered him a chance to move about in the open air, to think without concentrating. He glanced around at the quiet residential neighborhood as he walked. He liked their house, liked the school, liked the people he'd met, and Napa itself seemed to be a pleasant enough town, but there was still something about living here that made him slightly uncomfortable, a lingering residue from that initial reaction. It wasn't anything as obvious or specific as a street that seemed sinister or a building that gave him the creeps. No, the feeling he got was more subtle, more generalized, and seemed to apply to the entire Napa Valley. There was a heaviness here, an indefinable sense of unease which he had never experienced in Mesa. It was not something that he felt would affect his day-to-day living, but it was persistent, a hum of white noise underlying everything. He could live with it, though. He could ignore it most of the time.

Most of the time.

He stopped walking. He was supposed to turn right at this corner, but in front of him the street continued onward, heading straight toward a grassy section of hill.

The hill.

He stood, staring. The view before him seemed somehow familiar and somehow unpleasant, and he felt cold suddenly, chilled.

He forced himself to look away and hurriedly turned down the cross street toward home. It was probably psychological, he reasoned. A reaction to the pulling up and transplanting of his roots. Yeah. That was it. That had to be it. He would no doubt get over it soon, once he'd fully adjusted to his new surroundings.

He hurried forward, not looking to his left, not looking toward the hill.

His mom was not home when he arrived, but Dion was not worried. She wasn't scheduled to get off work today until five. Besides, he'd been keeping a close eye on her, and was surprised to see that she actually seemed to like her job and to get along well with her coworkers. As she described each day's events over dinner the past two nights, the behavior of the other loan officers in the bank, the customers, he'd listened carefully, trying to read between the lines, to ascertain the truth behind the facts. But her attitude of professional objectivity seemed real, not feigned, and he quickly decided that she wasn't attracted to anyone in the bank. That was a good sign. At her last two jobs, in Mesa and Chandler, she'd been inviting people over for what she called "a little get-together" even before the first week was out.

Maybe she really had turned over a new leaf.

He walked into the kitchen, took out a bag of Doritos, poured some salsa into a bowl. He walked into the living room, picked up the remote control, turned on MTV, but was quickly bored by the sameness of the music and the videos. He flipped around the cable channels, but there was nothing on, and he turned the set off. After he finished eating, he would put on the stereo, listen to music, and do his math homework. He had to have twenty algebra problems solved by tomorrow. His mom would be home soon after that.

Dion finished his snack, finished his math, read the front page and entertainment sections of today's paper, and glanced through a two-week-old *Time* they'd brought from Arizona.

When his mom hadn't come home by six and still hadn't called, he found himself worrying. He turned off the stereo and turned on the TV, settling into the couch to watch the national news. It was strangely comforting to watch the news, though the majority of the stories concerned murders, disasters, and other tragic events. It was a stupid attitude, he knew, an ignorant, uneducated attitude, but he found it reassuring to see the incidents of the day categorized, dissected, and discussed on national television. It made him feel that no matter how chaotic the world seemed, someone was on top of things and doing something about them, though he knew, intellectually, that was probably not the case.

The first commercial break passed, and then the second and the third, and then it was six-thirty. He stood up and looked out the window. Already the sky was getting dark, the orange color of dusk dimming into the bluish purple of evening. She couldn't be starting again, could she? Not so soon after her last job. Not after promising him she'd change.

He almost hoped that she'd been in an accident instead. *No.*

He pushed that thought from his mind.

Dion sat down again to watch the local news. He tried to remain optimistic, to tell himself that she'd merely stayed after work and forgotten to call, but he didn't believe any such thing.

He just hoped that she had enough sense not to bring the guy home.

He was in the kitchen and was about to make himself dinner—macaroni and cheese or one of the frozen dinners in the freezer—when he heard the familiar sound of the Pinto's brakes in the driveway. He wanted to go out front, to peek through the living room window, to see what was going on, but he remained in the kitchen, rooted in place. His muscles were tense, his palms sweaty.

He heard the front door open. "I'm home!"

He stepped through the doorway into the living room, and felt relief flood through him as he saw that his mother was alone.

"Sorry I'm late," she said, dropping her briefcase in the entryway.

She was not drunk, but she had obviously been drinking. Her voice was louder than usual, happier and more vivacious, and her movements were loose, expansive. "I met the greatest people!" she said.

The worry returned. "Mom . . ."

"No, I'm serious. I think even you'd like them."

"Who are they?"

"Well, I met them at happy hour—"

Dion took a deep breath. "Happy hour? Mom, you said—"

"Don't worry. A couple of people from work decided to go there after they got off, and they asked me if I wanted to go. But when we were there we met these people who—"

"Male or female?"

She stared at him, understanding dawning in her expression.

Dion shifted his weight nervously from one foot to the other. "You said you were going to change," he reminded her gently.

Her mood shifted. "I have," she said angrily. "And don't give me that accusing look. People at work asked me to go. What was I supposed to do, say no?"

"Yes."

"And ruin my chances for advancement?" She pushed past him into the kitchen. "Sit down," she ordered. "I'm making dinner."

"That's okay—" Dion began.

"I'm making dinner!"

He knew it was useless to argue. He watched her take out a pot from beneath the sink, slam it down on the counter. Sighing, he walked out to the living room. He watched TV as outside the night darkened and inside the kitchen his mother swore loudly to herself, banging spoon against pan as she made their meal.

SEVEN

On Friday, Mr. Holbrook greeted them with a pop quiz. Immediately after the bell rang, announcing the start of class, the Mythology teacher told the class to put all books under the desks and to take out pencils and paper.

"Number from one through twenty-five," he said, "leaving two lines between each number." He stood up from his chair and walked over to the blackboard, turning his back on the class and picking up a stubby piece of white chalk. "You are to copy down each question and write the answer on the line immediately beneath it."

"Fucker," Kevin whispered, holding up a middle finger.

Dion stifled a laugh.

The teacher began writing on the board. "You may begin."

There was a rustle of papers, a sighing of seats as the students settled in to do their work. Dion was already trying to figure out what grades he would have to get on the paper and the regularly scheduled tests to balance out the F he'd get today. He rubbed his pencil sideways on the desktop to sharpen it. At least Holbrook could have warned them ahead of time, told them he would be popping quizzes on them throughout the semester. The teacher had given them an outline of the course, had told them which pages in which book were supposed to have been read by which date, but he had said nothing about quizzes. At least he could have had the decency and courtesy to explain to them how his class was run, how grades were determined.

Of course, looking back on it now, Dion recalled that the teacher had said several times, "I expect you to keep up with your reading." He realized now that that cryptic warning had been a foreshadowing of things to come.

Unfortunately, he had not read a word of the assigned text. He did not study that way. Never had. He had always worked better under pressure, cramming at the last moment, force-feeding his brain with information. He always completed questions and turn-in assignments on time, but the reading he left to the very end.

Now he was going to pay for it.

What made it even worse was that this was the day he had finally completed his sneaky maneuvers, had unobtrusively slid into the empty seat next to Penelope.

Things were not going well.

Dion dutifully copied the questions written by Mr. Holbrook on the board. He did not know the answers to any of them, was only vaguely familiar with some of the terms after hearing them in class, and he simply wrote down on the paper whatever single-word answers came into his head. He turned the paper over, putting down his pencil, to signal that he was finished.

When everyone had completed the test, the teacher faced the class. "All right," he said. "Please exchange papers with the person seated next to you."

The person seated next to him. That meant either Penelope or Kevin. He looked to his left, saw Kevin exchanging his paper with a short boy on the other side of him. Dion looked at Penelope, forced himself to smile, handed her his paper. She handed him hers. He stared down at the writing. Her letters were light, formed with almost calligraphic precision, definitely feminine.

"Question one," the teacher announced. "Zeus."

Dion went down the paper, marking plus signs next to answers which were correct, minus signs next to those which were incorrect, just as the instructor had explained. Penelope had gotten two wrong, for an A-minus. He was right. She was smart.

Of course, that meant nothing now. They exchanged papers and Penelope handed back his quiz. He did not meet her eyes, did not look at his score. He had blown it. She probably thought he was a dim-witted jerk. His chances of getting to know her had probably shrunk from fair to zilch. He glanced miserably at Kevin, then looked down at the paper in his hand.

He blinked.

He'd gotten a perfect score.

He had not missed a single question.

As always, the cafeteria was crowded, and he and Kevin sat on top of one of the round plastic tables in the adjacent eating area outside as they waited for the lines to die down.

"You really know your mythology," Kevin said, running a hand deliberately through his hair. Like Dion, he too had not studied, planning to wait until the week before the test to crack the books, but unlike Dion he had missed nearly a fourth of the questions, putting him in the low-B range if the teacher graded on the curve.

Dion shrugged self-consciously. "Not really," he said. "I guessed. I was just lucky."

"On multiple-choice tests you can guess and be lucky. On short-answer tests you can guess only if you have knowledge to begin with, if you have some names to choose from. I mean, shit, you were the only one to get a perfect score in the whole class."

It was true, but Dion did not know why it was true or how. He was embarrassed, and he said nothing. He found himself glancing down at the tabletop to read the graffiti penciled on the faded plastic. He looked up as a skinny blond kid in a black heavy metal T-shirt walked belligerently up to them, frowning. "What do you think this is? A pussy convention? You're sitting on my table."

Kevin calmly raised his middle finger.

"You think that's cute, Harte?"

"Not quite as cute as your mama's titties, but it'll do for now."

"Get off."

"Fuck you."

"Your ass, Harte." The kid left, scowling, his own middle finger raised aggressively.

Dion said nothing. He had been silent during the verbal exchange, half afraid that the newcomer might try to pick a fight with one of them or, even worse, return with his bigger, tougher friends, but he let none of his feelings show. Kevin seemed to know how to handle this guy, or at least acted as though he did, and Dion trusted that his new friend knew who could be pushed and how far, knew when to speak out and when to shut up.

At least he hoped so.

"Guy's a needledick," Kevin said, as if reading his thoughts. "Don't worry about him. All talk and no show."

Dion nodded as if that was what he had suspected all along.

"Hey," Kevin said. "Check it out." He nodded toward the cafeteria lines. Making their way between the tables toward the open double doors were Penelope and a short black-haired girl with thick glasses. "Here's your opportunity, bud."

Dion jumped off the table. "You come with me."

Kevin snorted. "Hell, no. This is your move. You go over there and talk to her alone. I'll still be here when she shoots you down."

Penelope and her friend were at the back of one of the lines, and Dion knew that if he didn't move now, someone else would take the spot behind her. He quickly zigzagged through the crowd of teeming students.

He was in luck. He got in line behind her just as a group of cheerleaders got in line behind him. It had all happened so fast, he had moved without thinking, and now he didn't know what to do. His hands were sweaty, his stomach churning. He didn't want to tap on Penelope's shoulder to get her attention or to speak to her before she noticed his presence, so he simply readied himself in case she turned around, trying to relax and put on a show of comfortable ease he did not feel.

When she did turn around a moment later and saw him, he pretended to be surprised. He cleared his throat. "Hi," he said. "I didn't recognize you."

She looked surprised too, but she smiled when she saw him. She had a nice smile, he thought. A friendly smile. A real smile.

"Hi," she said.

"My name's Dion. I'm in your Mythology class." He

knew it was stupid the moment he said it, but there was no way to take his sentence back.

She laughed. Her laugh was warm, casual. "I know who you are. I corrected your paper, remember?"

He reddened, unsure of what to say or how to respond, afraid he would say something even dumber.

"I was really impressed by how well you did on the test," she added.

"Yeah, well, thanks."

"No, I mean it. You really know your stuff."

The line moved forward, and Dion realized with something like panic that it was his turn to say something, but he could think of nothing to say. There were at least six people between Penelope and the food. This was his one and only chance; he'd better think of something good, or they'd wait the rest of the time in silence and it would be all over. He glanced toward Kevin, who gave him a thumbs-up sign.

What the hell was he supposed to say?

It was Penelope's friend who saved him.

"I don't remember seeing you here before," she said. "Are you new?"

He relaxed. Now he was home free. "Yeah," he said. "I'm from Arizona. My mom and I just moved here a little over a week ago."

"It must be tough to come to a new school," Penelope said.

He looked at her. Was he imagining it, or was there more than just casual interest in her expression, in her tone of voice? She had spoken almost wistfully, as if she understood how he felt, as if she had been there herself.

As if she cared.

No, he was just reading nuances which were not there.

"Yes," he said. "It is tough. I don't know anyone yet."

"You know us," Penelope's friend said, smiling.

Dion smiled back. "That's true."

"And you know that Kevin Harte," Penelope said. There was something in the way she said "that Kevin *Harte*" which implied that she did not like his new friend.

"Well, I just met him," Dion said.

And then they were through the line and at the food,

their opportunity for conversation at an end. Penelope took a covered bowl of salad and a can of V8 from the buffet. Dion grabbed a hamburger, a small cup of fries, and two Cokes, one for him, one for Kevin.

"I'll see you Monday," Penelope said, heading with her friend over to a cash register. She smiled that radiant smile. "It's nice to meet you."

"Yeah," her friend said.

"Yeah," Dion echoed. He wanted to say something else, wanted to invite the both of them to Kevin's table, wanted to ask Penelope if she would like to study with him some time, wanted to ensure that they would talk again, but he did not know how. He paid the two dollars, watched the girls walk away.

It was a start, and he should have felt good, but for some reason he felt disappointed, sort of let down. It made no sense. Things had gone well. It was the first week and they were already talking, but he still felt depressed about the encounter. He made his way through the crowd toward Kevin.

"So," his friend said, grinning, "how'd it go? She dive for your ding-dong?"

"Asked for it by name," Dion said, setting down the tray.

Kevin laughed, almost spitting out the sip of Coke he'd taken. He wiped his mouth with the back of his hand. "Penelope?" he said, laughing.

Dion smiled, chuckled, and then laughed himself. "Yeah," he said. Already he felt better. He picked up his hamburger. "And her friend wants you."

"In her dreams," Kevin said.

Dion laughed. He thought of Penelope. Things *had* gone well, he told himself. Things might work out.

He unwrapped his hamburger and settled down to eat.

EIGHT

Lieutenant David Horton used the landlord's key to open the heavy glass door and stepped inside Something Old. The antique shop was empty, its dead air silent save for the low drone of outside noise. He was followed inside immediately by the two uniforms. "Mr. Williams!" he called out. He waited a beat. "Anybody here?" His voice died flatly in the stillness.

Horton nodded to the policemen behind him. "Check it out," he said.

The two officers spread out, taking both sides of the front desk, entering the back room in tandem. They emerged a moment later, shaking their heads.

"Check the aisles," the lieutenant said. He lit a cigarette, watching his men take parellel paths away from the center of the store.

The antique shop had been closed for a week. No crime there. But it was highly unusual, noted by owners of several of the adjoining businesses. And when rent had come due a few days ago and the landlord received neither a check nor an excuse from the usually punctual antique dealer, he'd suspected something was up. He'd called Williams' house, gotten no answer, called Williams' sister in Salinas, learned that she hadn't heard from him for over a week. Then he'd called the police.

Disappearances were not that unusual in the Wine Country. Northern California's reputation for fostering a laid-back lifestyle, combined with outsiders' perceptions of what life in the valley was like, attracted to the area a lot of flakes and transients, drifters who saw the wine industry only in terms of its alcoholic output, not realizing that mundane work went into producing recreational beverages, that life here was not one long, constant party.

But Victor Williams was not a transient. He was a local businessman with roots in the valley. And Horton had serious doubts that he'd just up and leave on a whim, telling no one, letting his store remain closed. It was out of character, it didn't fit.

Which meant, Horton thought to himself, that Vic Williams was probably dead.

The lieutenant took a drag on his cigarette, sighed, exhaling smoke. There had been a time when he'd hated this job, when the novelty of wearing a badge and wielding a little power had worn off, when the fact that his work consisted of looking up society's asshole day after day had really begun to get to him. He had almost quit then, had almost told the department to Johnny Paycheck it, but he'd realized that he was not qualified to do anything other than police work; he had no other skills and was too old to start over.

Now he just tried not to think about it. He didn't regret lost career opportunities, didn't piss and moan that he'd never finished college, didn't compare himself to other men of his age who were more successful. He simply put in his hours, did his job, and counted the days toward retirement.

And he bought a lottery ticket twice a week.

A man had to have something to hope for.

"Lieutenant! Over here!"

Horton turned around, taking the cigarette out of his mouth. He saw Deets, the youngest uniform, frantically beckoning him from down the end of an aisle. He dropped the cigarette, stubbed it out, and hurried toward the rookie. "What did you—?" *Find,* he was going to say, but there was no reason to ask. The floor in this section of the shop was stained brown with dried blood, forming a huge irregular amoeba pattern against the dusty faded slats of the hardwood finish. Small speckles of blood could be seen on the lower portion of a beveled mirror, though the droplets were smeared and it was clear that someone had tried to wipe them away.

Protruding from underneath a piece of furniture was a small, ragged, fleshy segment of torn muscle.

"Jesus," Horton breathed. He glanced toward Mc-Comber, standing on the other side of Deets. "Call the lab," he ordered. "Get some dusters and photogs over here now."

The younger cop nodded, frightened, and hurried down the aisle toward the front desk.

"Don't touch anything," the lieutenant told Deets.

"Yes, sir."

"And stop that 'sir' crap. This isn't the goddamn marines."

"Okay, sir, uh, Lieutenant."

Horton looked at the rookie, shook his head. He reached into his pocket for another cigarette, pulled out the package, but found that it was empty. He crumpled it up, put it back in his pocket, and looked wistfully up the aisle to where he'd dropped his other cigarette. It was going to be a long afternoon.

NINE

After dinner, Penelope went out to the Garden. The air was warmer than it was inside the air-conditioned house, and more humid, but to her it felt wonderful. She sat on the edge of the fountain, bracing her arms against the rounded concrete, and leaned back, peering upward. The winery was far enough from town that the lights of the business district did not seep into their air space, and the sky above was a deep purple, dotted with patterned clusters of millions of microscopic stars. Her eyes picked out the Big Dipper, the North Star at its corner, and her gaze swept across Orion's belt and the Little Dipper to the dot of pinkish light that was Mars.

She had always been fascinated by the stars, the moon, the planets, the movements of the heavens. It seemed amazing to her that the progress of celestial bodies had been noted and charted so long ago, the patterns of such an immense canvas identified and understood by peoples who had not even known the rudimentary rules of science grasped by today's grade schoolers. She had taken an astronomy course last semester, hoping to learn more about the subject, but had been disappointed to discover that the class dealt more with the mathematics of trajectories than with the background stories of heavenly bodies and their earthbound discoverers.

Which was one of the reasons she had signed up for, and really looked forward to, this Mythology class. Glancing through the book after the first meeting, she had seen that three full chapters were devoted to the constellations, and she had read those chapters immediately.

This was what she'd wanted to learn.

She had also met Dion in the class.

She found herself thinking of him now, just as she'd thought about him at odd times during the week. She didn't know Dion, didn't know anything about him, but there was something about the way he looked, the way he talked, the way he acted, which interested her. He was obviously intelligent, but he also seemed very nice, very down-to-earth, although that was not a quality to which she would have expected to be attracted.

Did he like her? She thought he might. Twice during the week she had caught him staring at her from the next seat over when he thought she wasn't looking, and he had always looked immediately away, acting guilty, as though he had been caught doing something he wasn't supposed to do.

And then today at lunch he had actually spoken to her. Vella, afterward, had said that Dion was obviously interested, but Penelope was not sure she could read that much into the few words that they had spoken together. The suggestion had flattered her, though, and the rest of the day she had found herself tuning out her teachers, going over each sentence they had spoken, looking for clues that backed up Vella's hypothesis.

Penelope looked up into the sky. She smiled. Maybe it was fate. Maybe their signs had coincided, and that's why they had met in this place at this time.

She closed her eyes. Several times today she had tried to imagine what it would be like to go on a date with Dion, but the image just wouldn't come. It was not that she wasn't attracted to him, or at least interested, but she had never before gone on a date, and it was hard to imagine herself carrying on the sort of vacuous conversation favored by high school daters in movies.

Movies.

All of her perceptions of dates had been formed by film, books, or television.

She heard a soft click and opened her eyes, sitting up. Mother Felice opened the sliding glass door and smiled at her. "Maybe we should bring your bed out here."

"And my dresser and TV."

"A refrigerator and microwave?"

They both laughed. Mother Felice crossed the gravel

and sat down on the rim of the fountain next to Penelope. The two of them said nothing for a while, simply enjoying the quiet and each other's company. They often sat this way. It would have driven Mother Margeaux mad to sit for so long without doing something actively productive, and Mother Margaret and Mother Sheila would have had to talk, get up, move around. She would not have wanted to be alone with Mother Janine. But Mother Felice enjoyed the quiet, was thankful for silence after spending all day in the hurricane of the household. She was like her daughter in that way, which only served to reinforce Penelope's theory.

Mother Felice leaned her head back, trying to reduce the tension in her neck, then sat up. She looked casually at her daughter. "Is anything wrong?" she asked.

Penelope frowned, puzzled. "No. Why?"

Her mother smiled. "Well, you seemed kind of distant today at dinner. I just ... well, we sort of thought ... I mean, we were wondering if maybe you'd met someone. You know, a boy."

Was it that obvious? She hadn't thought she'd acted any differently than usual. She looked at her mother. She wanted to tell the truth, and probably would have if her mother hadn't made mention of the rest of the family, but that "we" implied that the subject had been discussed, that Mother Felice had been sent out here deliberately. She had no doubt that Mother Felice had been the one to notice—she was always the most observant in emotional matters—but this obvious collusion, this attempt to invade her privacy, no matter how well intentioned, hardened her against revealing anything. "No," she said.

Mother Felice frowned. She looked confused, as though she hadn't understood the answer. "Haven't you even met someone who looks like he might be interesting?"

Penelope shrugged. "It's too early to tell." She shook her head. "God, Mother, it's only been a week. What do you expect?"

"You're right, you're right." Her mother's voice was understandingly apologetic, her smile sympathetic, but there was still a slight look of mystification on her face.

They were silent again, although the silence this time

was not quite as comfortable. Penelope stared up at the recently risen moon, yellow and disproportionately large above the hills in the east. When she was little, around eight or nine, she had seen the movie *A Connecticut Yankee in King Arthur's Court* with Bing Crosby. It had been light entertainment, a romantic musical comedy, but the thing that had made the biggest impression on her, that had stayed with her for years to come, had been the fact that Bing had been able to save his life by remembering the date of a solar eclipse, passing himself off as a powerful magician, pretending to the medieval men and women intending to burn him at the stake that he was able to make the sun disappear by simply making absurd hand gestures at the appropriate time. It had been a terrifying scene to her, and had been the cause of many a nightmare-filled sleep time. Throughout grammar school she had been obsessed with learning the dates for solar and lunar eclipses, past and present, just in case a similar situation ever happened to her.

There was still some of that fear in her as she looked up at the moon now. Her rational mind told her that it was merely earth's satellite, a dead, inanimate orb reflecting back the refracted light of the sun, but on a deeper, more visceral level she could not help feeling a little intimidated by it, as though, like the moon in a children's book, it was sentient and possessed some sort of magic that could affect her life. The feeling was strange but not unpleasant, and she was grateful that even the cold facts of astronomy had not been able to completely dissolve for her the mystery of the night sky.

Penelope looked over at her mother. "Do you like looking at the moon?" she asked. "Looking at stars?"

Her mother smiled. "Sometimes."

Her father had liked to look at the stars.

Or so her mothers had told her.

She found herself thinking of her father. She did not think of him often, and sometimes she felt guilty about that, but she had not really known him; to her he had been little more than a face in an old photograph. He'd been a handsome man, that she knew. Tall and broad-shouldered, with longish brown hair and a mustache, he looked in his picture as if he could be either a carpenter or a college professor. There was about him that appearance of both intelligence and physicality which suggested that he was equally at home with books and tools, adept at both mental and manual labor; a romantic assumption which was born out by the descriptions of her mothers.

When she was younger, her mothers had talked about her father a lot, answering her myriad questions, invoking his perceived wishes in regard to discipline and learning, endeavoring to make his presence felt through affectionate stories and detailed reminiscences. But as she'd grown older, the talk had ceased, as if her father had been an imaginary entity like Santa Claus or the Easter Bunny, invented to aid a period of her development, as if the spectre of his life had performed its function and outlived its usefulness. By the time she'd hit her teens, the subject of her father seldom, if ever, came up in discussion, and her infrequent questions concerning him were often redirected elsewhere. It was all very confusing to her, and sensing the shift in attitude, she had stopped mentioning him at all. Gradually, the details of her father's life began to blur and fade, blending in with the other secondhand stories of childhood.

The details of his death, however, remained sharp and clear.

Her father had been killed shortly after she'd been born, brutally murdered, torn apart in the wild woods beyond the fence by a stray band of rabid wolves. She knew the story by heart. It had been spring, late April, and her father had gone out for one of the evening strolls he enjoyed so much. Mother Felice and Mother Sheila had been preparing dinner in the kitchen, with Mother Janine watching television in the next room. Mother Margeaux had been in the office with Mother Margaret. All of them, even Mother Margeaux and Mother Margaret, had heard the screams, and all had come running out, only to see the gray-white blur of wolves savagely attacking a human figure on the dirt path which led between the tall trees. The screams had already stopped, but though it was night, they could clearly see in the distance the fall of her father's upraised arm, the sleeve of his yellow shirt torn and streaked black with blood.

Mother Janine had screamed, and Mother Margeaux had rushed into the house for the rifle, ordering Mother Felice to call the police. Mother Margeaux had led the charge across the meadow, firing into the air, and the wolves had fled, scattering and disappearing into the woods.

There had been nothing left of her father's face. His chest had been chewed open, his entrails devoured, and large chunks of his arms had been bitten off. Only his legs, for some reason, had sustained minor injuries.

The six of them had carried his body back to the house themselves, his cooling blood dripping down their arms and over their clothes, and waited for the ambulance to arrive.

The tale had been told to her and retold hundreds of times, and looking back now, Penelope wondered why her mothers had felt compelled to dwell on the end of her father's life, why they had insisted on telling a small child such a horrifying story. For it had been horrifying. And frightening. And her mothers had always gone into gruesome detail in their descriptions of the blood and the body. She had had a series of ultra-vivid recurring nightmares in which her mothers had killed her father. What, she wondered now, had she been meant to learn from all that?

She didn't know.

But she knew that her life would probably be a lot less confusing if her father was still alive.

Mother Felice nudged her elbow, stood up. "Come on," she said. "Let's go inside. It's getting late."

"But it's a Friday," Penelope said. "It's not a school night."

"You still have a lot of chores to do tomorrow. Besides, your other mothers will be wondering where we snuck off to."

"Let them wonder, then."

Her mother laughed. "You want me to tell that to Mother Margeaux?"

"No," Penelope admitted.

"Come on, then."

Reluctantly, Penelope stood. She followed her mother into the house.

TEN

He dreamed of high hills, white outcroppings of rock punctuating the dull green of late summer meadow grass. There were no houses or buildings in sight, no roads, only a thin, slightly worn dirt path which looked as though it had been formed by the continued passage of animal hooves. To the right, the path wound up the nearest hill toward the summit. To the left, it meandered toward a stand of trees in the flat bottom of a gently sloping valley.

He walked barefoot across the ground toward the path, rocky gravel beneath the grass digging deep into his heel and sole but not hurting. The air was hot but not humid, dry and desertlike, the sky above a light pastel, bleached by the sun.

He felt good. His senses were heightened; he could see clearly for miles, he could hear the rickety click of insects moving in the grass, he could smell the heavy, warm, comforting odor of dirt and on top of that the lighter scent of growing weeds and grasses.

He realized that he was very tall.

He reached the path and turned toward the valley and the trees. The warm dirt felt smooth on his feet, and he began to walk faster, suddenly anxious to arrive at his destination. On his tongue he tasted the faint remembrance of grape, and for some reason that spurred his interest in hurrying.

Ahead he saw movement on the path, smelled the fetid odor of an unwashed animal. He reached the spot and stopped. On the path before him was a goat, a she-goat, breasts heavy with milk. He found that he was thirsty, and he lifted the animal until its multiple teats were above his face. He took three in his mouth and began suckling. The warm, sweet milk slid smoothly down his thirsty throat.

When he was finished, he put the goat down, and he noticed for the first time that next to it, just off the edge of the path, was the body of its kid. Or what remained of its kid. The small goat had been killed, gutted, mutilated, and sharp wooden sticks protruded from the bloody wreckage of its torso. Its legs and head had been ripped off and tossed aside. Small segments of skin, tufts of bloody hair, hung from the low, sturdy stalks of grass.

He knew that this meant he was getting close to home, and it made him feel good.

He heard screams from the trees, screams of joy and pain, and, smiling, he began to run toward them.

Dion spent Saturday with his mom, the two of them unpacking the last of their belongings, making adjustments to what was supposed to have been the final rearrangement of the living room. The work was monotonous, but Dion enjoyed doing it. Particularly since his mom seemed to be having a good time. Instead of moaning and complaining, making a big show of how much she hated doing domestic labor the way she usually did, she put on some records—Beatles and Beach Boys, music they could both agree on—and sang along as she dusted and cleaned the items she unpacked. She had been home from work on time both Thursday and Friday, acting like Holly Housewife, cooking dinner, cleaning dishes, watching television, making a visible effort to gain his trust, and she was low-key and conscientious in both her work and her conversation today, clearly trying to show him that things really had changed. He was willing to give her the benefit of the doubt. It was obvious from the effort she was making that she'd meant what she'd said, that she really did want things to be different.

Everything was going to be okay.

On Sunday, the two of them spent the day exploring the Napa Valley. Life had been moving forward at such a hectic pace since they'd arrived, with school and work and unpacking, that they hadn't really had much of a chance to see the area beyond their own small section of the city. Both of them figured it was about time they got to know their new home.

They hit all the tourist spots, following a map of the valley given to his mom by the Auto Club. They drove past Lake Berryessa and Mount St. Helena, went to the Bale Grist Mill, and paid to see Old Faithful and the Petrified Forest, lesser publicized cousins of the identically named natural wonders. The land was not spectcular, but it was beautiful in a quiet, subtle sort of way, the country roads winding between cultivated vineyards, skirting rolling hills and low, wooded mountains.

Although they drove as far as Sonoma to see Jack London's house, they did not stop at any of the wineries. It would have been too awkward right now, too tense. Nothing would have or could have happened, but the mere fact that they were at a winery would have served as a reminder of things past, would have dredged up recent memories neither of them wanted to face. The subject of visiting a winery did not even come up between them.

While his mom drove, however, Dion looked on the map for Daneam Vineyards, hoping to see where Penelope's family business was located. Unfortunately, the winery was not listed. They passed several unnamed vineyards with both large and small complexes attached, any of which could have been the one owned by Penelope's family, but though he carefully scrutinized each gate and signpost, Dion did not see Penelope's last name written anywhere.

They returned home around five, travel-tired and sightseeing-worn, and while his mom took a hot bath, Dion drove to Taco Bell and bought a junk food feast for both of them. They pigged out while watching *60 Minutes* and afterward watched a TV movie together. For the first time in a long while, his mom seemed to him like a mother, not like a sister, not like a peer, not like an adversary, and Dion fell asleep happy. He did not dream.

ELEVEN

In the year and a half that he had worked as night watch-man at Pauling Brothers Winery, Rob Fowler had never had occasion to investigate even a minor disturbance. There had been a few false alarms at first, brought about by his own jitters and inexperience rather than anything substantive, but those had disappeared after he'd learned the layout of the operation. Of course, Pauling was not Beringer's or Mondavi or Sterling or one of those other high-profile wineries. Those, he understood, often had problems with vandals. But Pauling was a small concern, out of the way, off the main drag, and tours were given by invitation only. This meant that ordinarily he had a pretty cushy job. He read his mystery novels, watched his por-table TV, did his crossword puzzles.

Which was why he now felt so woefully unprepared.

Ron walked slowly through the silent, empty building toward the entrance of the fermenting cave, peering anx-iously in all directions, listening for any sound out of the ordinary. The huge room was empty, the only noise his own loudly clacking heels and the amplified drumming of the blood in his head. He was scared, much more scared than he'd thought he'd be when he'd imagined this sce-nario in his head. This was not something he was really trained for, not something he felt comfortable with. He had taken this job because it was supposed to be a cake-walk, not because he had any aptitude for it. As a retired maintenance worker, he drew a pension that was a step above bird crap, and he'd just wanted an easy way to pull in some extra cash. He'd been assured every step of the way that there was nothing to this job, that the gun he'd been issued was little more than a prop, part of the uniform, that he would never have to actually confront anyone.

Why the hell hadn't he got a job at McDonald's with the other senior citizens?

He walked slowly forward. He knew he didn't have to do this. Despite what it said on his job description, despite the gun and the uniform and the ersatz police trappings, he could have simply alerted the cops and waited in place until they arrived. But he still wasn't absolutely sure that this was anything. He had been at his station, in the small office next to Purchasing, reading an old Ross McDonald book, when the black-and-white picture on the screen monitoring the cave suddenly disappeared in a burst of snow. He caught the shift with his peripheral vision and immediately glanced up at the row of monitors above the desk, scanning quickly from one to the other. He had not counted on seeing anything, had assumed there had merely been some type of technical malfunction, but on the screen showing an overview of Distilling Room One he saw the door to the cave, which was supposed to be closed and locked at all times, swing slowly and deliberately shut.

His heart had leaped in his chest.

He'd immediately jumped up, grabbing his key ring and unholstering his weapon, and had hurried across the dimly lit parking lot to the distillery.

Scared as he was, though, he was glad that he had not alerted the police. Calling in a false alarm, making a fool of himself in front of them, probably would have lost him his job quicker than anything else.

Ron continued forward, toward the closed door leading to the cave. His hand on the butt of the pistol was sweaty, slippery, and he quickly switched hands, wiping his palm on the rough material of his pants before switching back.

Something clicked against the other side of the door.

He stopped in mid-step. The room suddenly seemed much darker, the tanks to each side much larger, more threatening. Even with the lights on, pools of shadow still existed, ill-defined patches of night which had seeped past the technology of electricity and phosphorescence into the building. There were a million hiding places here, he realized. An army of vandals, corporate spies, or terrorists could be staying in place, waiting for him to pass by so they could jump him.

The door clicked again, but this time the sound was wet, faintly organic.

Monsters.

It's vandals, he thought, clinging to the idea, trying to take comfort in it. It's corporate thugs, burglars, arsonists, murderers, terrorists, escaped lunatics. His mind ran down the list of possible assailants, possible *human* assailants, in a desperate attempt to keep that other idea at bay.

Monsters.

That was what he really feared, wasn't it? After all these years? Monsters. The decades had passed, he had grown up and grown old, but inside he was still that little boy who was afraid of the garage, who heard noises in the bushes outside his window at night, who saw shadows in the hallway grow and move after his parents turned off the light. The rationality that had come with responsibility and adulthood was merely a mask, a thin covering over the real self he had never really outgrown or left behind.

The door to the fermenting cave was before him, a few steps away. He could clearly see the point at which the concrete foundation of the building met the side of the limestone hill. He wanted to run, to flee back to his office, to the homey comforts of his book and his TV, to pretend he had seen nothing and feign ignorance in the morning when the break-in was discovered, but he forced himself to put out his hand and knock loudly on the closed steel door.

"Who's in there?" he demanded.

There was no answer.

He tried the handle and, as he'd expected, the door was open. He pushed open the door with his left hand and gripped his gun firmly with his right.

He staggered back, gagging.

The floor of the cave was covered with blood, a thick red, viscous goo which looked like congealed Jello and smelled like rancid feces. Blood had splashed onto the sides of the wooden casks, and the odor of the blood mingled with the strong aroma of the fermenting vintage was almost overpowering. He pinched his nostrils together with his fingers so he could breathe, and held the door open with his foot. Flung randomly about the cave, on the floor, on top of the casks, against the limestone walls, were the rent and mutilated carcasses of dozens of small animals: squirrels, cats, rats, opossums. In the refracted light let in by the door, he could see peeled fur skin backed by white-veined flesh, discolored and deflated organs clustered about lifelines of arteries and intestines.

There was a quiet pop, the sound of falling liquid, an alcohol blast of scent. Heart racing, he reached around the side wall, feeling the stone with his fingers, searching in vain for a light switch. He peered into the gloom at the far end of the narrow cave, and cursed himself for not bringing a flashlight. "Who's there?" he called.

There was no answer, but the liquid noise stopped. Now there was another sound.

Chewing.

"Come out now!" he ordered, but his voice was not as strong as it had been.

Monsters.

"Now!"

No answer. Only chewing. A low laugh.

He squinted into the gloom, and, to his horror, his eyes adjusted.

Dwarfish figures were crouched in the shadows against the far wall, low, hairy, misshapen forms clutching long, pointed spears. A tough, cynical part of his mind saw the entire scene in terms of a grocery tabloid headline—Night Watchman Attacked by Trolls—but the more instinctual portion of his brain was making him scream, had let loose the bladder muscle which held back his piss.

Now the shapes were moving, growing, becoming more human, evolving upward through the evolutionary scale until they stood erect. The smells of blood and wine were strong in the air, combined with a familiar underlying muskiness. One of the figures was eating something and threw it in front of him. A partially devoured chipmunk.

Turning, still screaming, trying to run, trying to escape, Ron slipped on the bloody floor. His right foot flew out

from under him, twisting painfully, and the door which
he'd been holding open with his left foot began to close.
In the last few seconds of light, he saw with exaggerated
clarity the wet red cement in front of his face, the segment of muscled animal bone beneath his nose. Desperately in the sudden darkness, he tried to push himself to
his feet, tried to pull himself along the floor, but he was
not quick enough.

Behind him, the creatures were laughing, screaming,
jabbering excitedly.

The first spear entered through his crotch.

TWELVE

From ten to twelve, between the crowded first hour and the noon rush, the bank was virtually dead, the only sounds in the light, air-conditioned lobby the relaxed, easy banter of the tellers, the muffled click of calculator keys, and the low drone of the soft rock Muzak which played incessantly over the bank's ceiling speakers.

April hated this time of day. For most of her coworkers it was the high point of their shift, the time when they could drop the public mask of servile civility, when they could relax and catch up on the bookkeeping or other behind-the-scenes paperwork which kept the bank running smoothly and efficiently. But these two hours always left her feeling bored and restless. Whatever else she was, she was a good loan officer, and she seldom if ever had any extra paperwork or leftover duties to perform. As a result, she usually found herself desperately searching for something to do, some way to look busy. Once she was settled, she knew, things would be different, she would be able to hang a little looser, but for the first few weeks on the job it would not do to look idle in front of her supervisor.

As far as she could tell, her new supervisor was a nice, if rather boring, soul, a family man with framed photos of his overweight wife and two pre-teen daughters set up on his desk. He was dedicated to his job but not fanatic and not overly strict, someone with whom it would be easy to work.

Someone of whom Dion would definitely approve.

It was strange to think that way, to use her son as a behavioral guideline, to mentally consult his taste and beliefs while making simple day-to-day judgments and

decisions, but she respected him, she trusted his opinions.
Somehow, despite her best unintentional efforts to screw
him up, Dion had turned out to be a boy she not only
loved but admired, a person with both feet firmly planted
on the ground, who knew who he was and where he was
going. She was aware of the fact that in many ways their
relationship was the inverse of what it was supposed to
be. She often looked to him for guidance and support, for
strength she did not possess, and though this was something she felt comfortable with, she knew her son did not
feel the same way. He would have been happier with a
more traditional mother, the kind who offered heartwarm-
ing advice while making brownies, the kind who had all
the answers all the time and could not only run her own
life perfectly but could make sure that the lives of her
family ran the same way.

Not the kind of mother she was.

And definitely not the kind she'd had.

All these years later, it was difficult to remember her
childhood without seeing it through the socially conscious
filter provided by endless TV movies. Her real mother,
her biological mother, she could not even remember.
She'd been abandoned at birth, and had been passed from
foster home to foster home, from uncaring foster mother
to uncaring foster mother, suffering the litany of abuses
that continued to provide topics for daytime talk shows.
She finally ran away from the last home at seventeen, and
at nineteen she was a bank teller in Omaha and pregnant
with Dion.

She had not done so badly, all things considered. She
had not gotten trapped in the welfare cycle, had been for-
tunate enough to avoid the minimum-wage circuit, but
she had never really been as independent as she wanted to
be, as she felt she should be. There had always been the
men, paving her way with sheets, assisting her financially
and opportunistically in each of her attempts to better herself, to gain more experience or education.

And there had been mistakes.

Lots of mistakes.

Big mistakes.

Cleveland. Albuquerque.

But all of that was behind her now. She was going to try to start fresh here, to learn from the past. It was not going to be easy. She knew that. She was like a recovering addict—there were temptations everywhere. But she just had to be strong, to focus her sights on the future, and to always, always keep Dion's welfare—financial, educational, and emotional—first and foremost in her mind.

Mr. Aames, her supervisor, walked across the carpeted lobby carrying a stack of folders, which he proceeded to hand to her. "Backlog," he said. "From your predecessor."

"Thank God," she told him, accepting the pile. "I was running out of things to do."

He grinned. "You never have to worry about that around here. Anytime you run out of things to do, you come and see me. I'll find something for you."

She looked up at him, her eyes level with his gold wedding band. Was that a come-on?

Did she want it to be?

She wasn't sure.

She smiled sweetly at him. "Thanks," she said, putting down the folders. "I'll get started right away."

The afternoon was slower than usual, particularly in the loan department, and April found herself finishing all of Mr. Aames' backlog before closing. She was cleaning off the top of her desk, putting papers in their proper drawers, preparing to go home, when she heard a familiar voice.

"Hey there."

She looked up to see one of the new friends she'd met the other night when she'd come home late and she and Dion had had the fight. She couldn't immediately remember the woman's name, but she didn't need to.

"Margaret," the woman said. "Remember? Joan Pulkinghorn's friend?"

"Yeah. Hi." April glanced over at the teller's cage, but Joan was either in the vault or in the back office, not at her station. Her gaze focused again on the woman in front of her. "So what brings you around here? Did you come to see Joan?"

"Actually, I wanted to see you." Margaret sat in the overstuffed chair reserved for loan applicants. "We all had a great time the other evening, and we were just wondering why you hadn't been by. A couple of us usually stop off at the Redwood Terrace after work to unwind a little before going home, and we were kind of hoping that you'd be one of our regulars. I mean, you certainly breathed some new life into the old group the other evening. I asked Joan about you, and she said she'd invited you to come along, but you were busy. I just wanted to make sure we didn't offend you or anything, or scare you away."

"No."

"So where've you been keeping yourself?"

April shrugged awkwardly. "You know. I've been busy with my job, my son, getting settled . . ."

Margaret nodded. "Yeah, I know how that is. When we were just getting our business started, I never saw the light of day. I was up before dawn, not home until after sunset. Work-eat-sleep. That was my life." She smiled. "But now I have time for play. So what about after work today? You're almost off. You want to come along, have a few drinks?"

"I'm not sure."

"Come on. It'll be fun."

April looked down at her desk, concentrated on picking up a paper clip. The offer was tempting, the pull was strong. It was not just the inducement of a good time. There was something else as well, something more subtle; the promise of belonging, the same sympathetic camaraderie she'd felt the other night. She looked up at Margaret, thought of her other new friends, and felt her resolve slipping.

But then she thought of Dion, sitting alone at home, waiting for her, worried about her. What the hell kind of mother was she? How could she even think about leaving him to fend for himself while she was out on the town?

But then, he was old enough to take care of himself.

"Okay," she said.

Margaret smiled. "Great!" She leaned forward conspiratorily. "Do I have some stories to tell you. Remember that construction worker I told you about?"

"The one with the—?"

"Yeah. Well, that wasn't the end of that tale." She raised her eyebrows comically and stood. "I'm going to stop by and talk to Joan. I'll meet you back here in a few minutes, okay?"

"Okay." April watched her new friend walk purposefully across the lobby to the teller window where Joan now stood counting her money. The two talked for a moment, and Joan glanced over, smiling and waving.

April waved back. She looked down at her phone, thought of calling Dion to tell him she'd be a little late, then decided against it.

Five minutes later, the bank closed.

Ten minutes later, the three of them were in Margaret's car, laughing about the construction worker, heading down Main Street toward the Redwood Terrace.

THIRTEEN

The week passed in that quirky time rhythm which always seemed to be generated by school—individual days that crept slowly by yet somehow added up to a quick week overall. Dion had planned out several conversational paths to take with Penelope, but she was absent Monday, and by Tuesday his bravery had fled. They nodded to each other, said hi, but the tentative stab at friendship they had made at lunch on Friday did not seem to have survived the weekend. They were strangers again, awkward and distant with each other, merely classmates. On Thursday, however, Dion caught her looking at him when she thought his attention was directed elsewhere, and that cheered him up immensely.

He and his mother had not spoken since the beginning of the week, the night she hadn't come home until nearly ten. This time she really had been drunk, old-style drunk, staggering, laughing, talking to herself, her speech slurred. She had ignored him that night, ignored his attempts to talk to her, to find out what had happened and why, and he had been ignoring her ever since, trying to punish her with his pointed silence, although it didn't seem to be working. He was more disappointed than anything else, more hurt than angry, but she probably thought he was furious at her. It was a tense situation, and one that wasn't getting any better, and he was dreading the weekend.

Dion saw Kevin in the parking lot after school, standing next to a red Mustang, talking to a long-haired boy he didn't recognize. He'd been planning to walk straight home, but Kevin called out his name, motioned him over, and Dion crossed the asphalt to where the other two boys waited.

Kevin turned toward Dion as he approached. "So what're your plans for tonight? What're you doing? Twanging your tater?"

"Could be. I got this picture of your sister I bought last week."

Kevin laughed. "Well if you're not doing anything, you want to go cruising around with us? Who knows? Maybe we'll get lucky and find us some hitchhikers." He pointed at the license plate frame on the back of the Mustang. Written on the thin metal was the stock phrase "Ass, Gas, or Grass: No One Rides for Free." Underneath this had been attached an addendum: "And I have a full tank and I don't smoke."

Dion laughed.

"Whattaya say?"

"I don't know."

"You're not gonna pussy out on us, are you?"

Dion thought for a moment. The phrase *cruising around* carried connotations of passed bottles and passed joints in dark car backseats, images which made him extremely uncomfortable. On the other hand, he didn't want to alienate the only friend he'd made here so far. He looked at the long-haired kid leaning against the hood of the Mustang, and turned back toward Kevin. "Where're you going to go?"

"We're going to have some fun with Father Ralph."

"Who's Father Ralph?"

"Episcopal priest," Kevin said.

The long-haired kid grinned. "My dad."

Dion shook his head. "I'd like to, but I already have some plans. Maybe next time."

Kevin looked at him. "What plans do you have? Sitting at home with your mom? Come on, it'll be fun."

Dion felt his options narrowing. "What are we going to do?"

"You'll see when we get there," the long-haired kid said.

"Paul always likes to keep it a secret," Kevin explained, "retain the element of surprise. But I guarantee you it'll be great."

"It's not illegal, is it?"

"Fuck it," Paul said. "This guy's a pussy. Let's leave him."

"No." Kevin moved defensively next to Dion. "I go, he goes."

"That's okay—" Dion began.

"No, it's not. You want to sit with your momma and watch the damn TV while we're harassing Father Ralph and looking for bimbos?"

Yes, Dion wanted to answer, but he said, "No."

"Fine." Kevin nodded to Paul. "We'll meet you at eight at Burgertime."

Paul shrugged his shoulders, smiling indulgently. "See you there, then."

Paul got into the Mustang, racing his engine, and Dion and Kevin walked across the parking lot toward Kevin's Toyota. "He's kind of a wang sometimes," Kevin said apologetically, "but overall he's all right. You get used to him."

"You guys hang out together a lot?"

"Not as much as we used to."

"So why does he hate his dad so much?"

"He doesn't hate him. It's just ... well, it's a long story." They reached the car, and Kevin used his key to open the door. "We'll go by your place, tell your mom the plan, then we'll cruise by my house."

"Okay," Dion said. "Sounds good."

"Unless you want to skip telling your mom, give her a little scare, pay her back, let her wait up for you this time."

"I'd like to, but I'd better not."

"It's your call," Kevin said.

The two of them got into the car, and Kevin put his key in the ignition. "Fasten your safety belts."

Before Dion could comply, they were off.

Kevin's room was the type usually seen only in movies. The walls were decorated with what looked like authentic posters of old horror films sandwiched in between an amazing collection of metal signs: stop signs, street names, yield signs, Coke signs. From the ceiling hung a lit display advertising 7-Up. The shelves above the king-size waterbed contained row after row of records. In the corner, next to the free-standing television, was a working traffic signal, flashing green-yellow-red in sequential order, and next to that stood an old life-size cardboard cut-out of Bartles and Jaymes. Dion stood in the doorway, taking it all in. "Wow," he said.

Kevin grinned. "Pretty cool, huh?"

Dion stepped into the room. "Where'd you get all this?"

"Around."

"Did you—?"

"Steal it? No. My uncle did, though. Some of it. He used to work for the transportation department in San Francisco, but they fired his ass. Before he left, he took a few souvenirs." Kevin laughed, pointing toward the stoplight. "I don't know how he got that one."

"This is great!"

"Yeah." Kevin scooped a pile of coins from the top of the dresser into his hand and grabbed a small wad of bills. "Come on, let's hit the road."

"I thought we weren't going to meet him until eight."

"Yeah, but I don't want to hang around here all night. We'll find something to do. Let's go."

They ended up simply driving around aimlessly. Dion asked where Penelope's winery was, and Kevin took him down a narrow road which ran along the edge of the foothills just outside of town. He stopped the car for a moment, pointed at a large white wrought iron gate. "Beaver-chomping territory beyond them there walls."

Dion tried to see something, anything, on the other side of the gate as they passed, but the daylight was gone, no lights were on, and whatever buildings lay within the property blended in with the foliage and the black background hills.

They drove by twice more, but saw nothing either time.

"Give it up," Kevin said. "No one's home. Besides, we'd better move out. Paul's probably waiting."

Burgertime was straight out of *American Graffiti,* a

chrome and tile drive-in complete with uniformed car-hops. Paul was indeed waiting, and three other guys Dion did not recognize were sitting next to him on the hood of the Mustang. Paul grinned as the two of them got out of Kevin's car. "Well, if it isn't the famous butt brothers."

Kevin flipped him off. "Knick knack paddywack, give your mom a boner."

Paul laughed, pushing himself off the car. "Well, we're all here now. You ready to hit the pavement?"

"Yeah," Kevin said.

"All right. We'd better take two vehicles this time." He looked purposefully at Dion. "It's getting crowded."

"We'll follow you," Kevin said, either ignoring or not noticing the slight.

"See you there."

The two cars raced quickly through the Napa streets, slowing to the legal limit only at known speed traps, those intersections where the city's men in blue consis-tently sat in wait to nab unsuspecting motorists. The buildings changed from commercial to residential, the garish glow of signs giving way to the low illumination of lighted living room windows. The houses became spaced farther apart, the roads more winding, as rural ten-drils encroached onto city space. Finally the Mustang pulled to a stop just before a huge oak tree whose massive leafy branches overhung the pavement.

Paul and his friends got out of the car, Paul carrying a brown grocery bag.

Dion and Kevin met them halfway between the two ve-hicles.

"Hope you all wore shitty clothes," Paul said. "This is going to involve some dirty work." He gestured toward a two-story Victorian house on the other side of the oak. "My old man's camped out in the living room in the back of the house, and we're going to have to circle around through the trees and bushes to get to the window."

The rest of them nodded in understanding.

"Let's make this quick." Paul disappeared into the blackness beneath the tree, and the other four followed. The night topography was confusing to Dion, but Paul obviously knew the way, moving swiftly between trees, around seemingly identical bushes, until suddenly the back of the house was before them.

They crouched low between the branches of an oleander. Behind the translucent curtains covering a large double window, backed by the flickering blue glow of a television, they could see the indistinct shadow of a stiff-backed man.

"What exactly are we going to do?" Dion whispered.

"You'll see." Paul grinned. "Come on." He crept forward through the underbrush. The rest of them fell in behind him until they were just below the window. Putting a finger to his lips to shush them, Paul opened the sack. Inside was the object he had spent half of his afternoon working on.

A huge clay penis.

It was hard for Dion not to laugh as Paul placed the gigantic phallus on the windowsill. Grinning, Paul looked from one face to another. "Get ready to roll," he whispered.

Dion's heart was pounding in his chest. He had no idea what Paul was doing, and he was more than a little nervous. Still, he could not help laughing as he looked at the object, silhouetted against the inside light.

"Shut up!" Kevin warned.

Paul suddenly stood up, pounding on the window with both his fists. In the quiet night air, the sound was explosive. "Suck me, Father Ralph!" he yelled at the top of his lungs.

The rest of them scattered, taking refuge in the dark safety of the trees.

Dion ducked behind a bush next to Kevin. He saw the curtains open, saw the priest's expression of shock as he saw the clay cock. A moment later, the front door flew open. "I'll get you punks!" the minister yelled. In his hand was a baseball bat, which he waved threateningly in the air.

"Suck me, Father Ralph!" Paul called from behind a bush.

The rest of them took up the cry:

"Suck me, Father Ralph!"

"Suck me, Father Ralph!"

"Suck me, Father Ralph!"

Dion laughed. "Suck me, Father Ralph!" he cried.

The priest ran toward the nearest bush, toward the sound of Paul's voice.

"Haul ass!" Kevin yelled, and the bushes rattled as all five of them scurried back the way they'd come, heading for the cars.

"I'm calling the cops!" the priest yelled after them.

Dion was still laughing, his heart pounding, blood pumping with adrenaline, as they broke onto the street. "This is great!" he said.

Kevin laughed with him. "Told you."

"Take off!" Paul ordered, rushing to his car. "Follow me!"

"Let's go!" Kevin said.

Dion jumped in the passenger seat. He could not remember when he'd had this much fun. This was the kind of thing that happened in films, not in real life. Certainly not in his life.

The two cars took off in twin squeals of burnt tire.

The lights inside were off when Dion returned home, though his mom's car was parked in the driveway.

Parked in back of it was a red Corvette.

Dion glanced quickly back at Kevin's disappearing taillights, but it was too late to flag him down. He turned back around. It was nothing, he told himself. She had just invited a new friend over for some innocent talk, that was all.

But if that was all, why were all the lights off?

He stepped quietly over the gravel of the front walk, tiptoeing, until he reached the front door. It was locked, but he had a key. He pulled out his wallet, removed the key from its hiding place behind the bills, and opened the door.

He could hear his mom in the bedroom.

She was not alone.

He stood there, unmoving. That was it, then. She was starting again. All that cock and bull she'd given him about turning over a new leaf had been just so much hot air. She hadn't meant a single goddamn word of it.

So where did that leave them now?

How long was it going to be before she screwed things up here and got fired from this job?

He crept carefully across the wooden floor to his bedroom, moving silently, a trick he had perfected long ago. He could smell the pungent odor of whiskey in the still hall air. He wished he was one of those people who just didn't care, who could roll with the flow and accept things the way they were. But he was not one of those people; he could not do that.

He closed the door to his room, took off his clothes, and got into bed. The loud drunken conversation which had greeted him when he'd first come into the house had now degenerated into something else. He could hear the loud squeak of bedsprings through the thin wall, accompanied by short, high, breathless cries. His mother would start her litany soon: "Oh, God, you're good! . . . You're so good! . . . Yes! . . . Yes! . . . Oh, God! . . . You're so big! . . . Oh, God, you're big! . . . Oh, God!" He knew it by heart. It never changed. She never used names, and he'd wondered more than once if that was because she did not know the names of the men she brought home.

He pulled the blanket over his head and plugged his ears, trying to block out the sound, but her cries were getting louder. Did she enjoy this? he wondered. Did she mean any of the crudely flattering things she said, or was it all simply an act? He had never been sure.

He closed his eyes, trying to focus his attention on the earlier events of the night rather than on the show in the next room, but it was impossible to do so.

He hated his mom right now.

It was said that teenagers rebelled against their parents, consciously rejecting their parents' value systems in an effort to forge their own identities. That sounded good in psych class, but he certainly didn't feel as though he was rebelling against anything. He had no doubt, however, that his social awkwardness stemmed from, or was a reaction to, his mother's "overly permissive" lifestyle.

Maybe that was why he'd never had sex.

It was not something which he would ever admit to in public, not something he would share with Kevin, but it was true. He rationalized it to himself, told himself it was better to wait until he had found the right person, but that was just an excuse and he knew it. It sounded good to have such high moral principles, and it did make him feel a little better about himself, as though he was making a conscious decision to do the right thing, but the truth was that he was just like anyone else. He would have jumped at the chance for sex if it had been offered.

Only it had never been offered.

Then again, maybe he wouldn't have jumped at the chance. People always seemed to assume that the children of so-called "liberated" parents had an easier time of it, were more comfortable with their own sexuality, but he knew from experience that this was not the case. If anything, knowing about his mother's love life in such detail tainted the sex act for him, made it seem distasteful and repulsive instead of exciting and desirable. He was also privy to his mother's morning-after comments and could contrast what she moaned in bed and what she said afterward.

And that scared the hell out of him.

"You're so good!" she cried from the other room. "You're so big!"

He plugged his ears more tightly.

He fell asleep still plugging his ears.

Dion awoke in the middle of the night to go to the bathroom and stumbled out of bed into the hall.

Where he ran into his mom's "guest."

He jumped back, startled. "Sorry," the man said sleepily, grabbing Dion's shoulders. "Didn't see you." He was good-looking—weren't they all?—and was tall and muscular, with thick black curly hair and a mustache. He was completely naked.

Dion watched him pad into his mother's bedroom and close the door.

In the morning he was gone, and when Dion woke up and went into the kitchen for breakfast, his mom was already there, reading her paper and drinking coffee. She looked up when he entered, pretending as though nothing was wrong, as though nothing had happened. "What time did you get home last night?" she asked brightly.

"About eleven," he said. He walked over to the counter, took two pieces of bread from the unwrapped loaf, and dropped them into the toaster, pressing the handle down.

"Did you have fun?" she asked.

Did you? he wanted to say, but he simply nodded. He took the butter out of the refrigerator. "I had a hard time sleeping, though," he said pointedly. His mom seemed not to notice the inference behind the words, and he poured himself a glass of orange juice.

She was being nice to him today, all traces of last week's hostility gone, but somehow that made him feel even worse. He thought of what a friend of his back in Mesa always used to say about the girls who treated him like dirt, that all they needed was "a good fucking."

His toast popped up, and he buttered it and sat down across from his mom at the table. She smiled at him. "What do you want to do today?"

"I don't know," he mumbled.

She folded the entertainment section of the paper and picked up the front page. "We'll find something."

He nodded, chewing slowly. He watched her as she read. His gaze focused on a small red stain on the right sleeve of her nightgown.

It looked like blood.

FOURTEEN

Lieutenant Horton looked down at the remains of Ron Fowler.

Remains.

It was an appropriate word. For the tangled mess of red muscle and bone which lay on the stone floor before him was barely recognizable as human. It looked like leftover food, something which had been chewed and rejected by the mouth of some gigantic creature.

He looked away, unable to stomach the sight except in short bursts. A flash went off as the photographer snapped another picture. Horton stepped back, grateful for the battery of fans that were keeping the stench somewhat at bay. He turned toward the coroner. "How long would you estimate he's been dead?"

"Hard to determine without tests, but I'd guestimate two days. Three tops."

Jack Hammond, the detective assigned to assist Horton with the investigation, continued to quiz Jauvert Pauling, the winery owner. "How can you not have discovered this for two or three days?"

"What do you mean 'how?' We just didn't."

"Fowler's car was still in the parking lot."

"What do you want me to say?" The small man's face was getting red. "This is a busy time of year for us. Ron wasn't there when we arrived in the morning, so we assumed he left. When he didn't show up that night, we found our daytime security assistant to take the watch, and when we discovered that he was missing, we called you."

"And no one noticed the body? Not even with all of your cameras and monitors?"

"The monitor to the cave was out; we were in the process of getting someone out here to repair it. And at this time of the season we don't check the cave but once a week. The wine ferments without us."

Horton tuned out the Q & A, looked again at the remains, turned away. He closed his eyes for a second, attempting to push back with willpower the major mother of a headache that was brewing behind his brows and that he knew could only be quelled by a double dose of industrial-strength aspirin.

He was getting too old for this shit.

Footsteps sounded on the concrete floor, and he looked up to see Chief Goodridge, Captain Furnier, and a group of flunkies striding across the concrete floor of the distilling room. The captain nodded at him, as did the chief.

"Capsule review," the captain said, taking the clipboard from his hand.

Horton gave him a shorthand version of the events as currently understood. Both Goodridge and Furnier listened without asking questions, their hardened eyes taking in the bloody scene.

It was the chief who spoke first. "Any theories?"

Horton shrugged. "From the nature of the crime, we're operating on the assumption that it was a cult of some sort, involved in animal and human sacrifice, although as you can see the scene seems more chaotic and unstructured than a ritual would indicate. I'll be checking the computer for the names and practices of our local wierdies when I get back to the station. Hammond'll be interviewing winery workers."

The chief nodded. "I want you to keep this as quiet as possible," he said. "If the media gets a hold of this, they'll blow it all out of proportion—"

"Blow what out of proportion?" Pauling asked, walking over. "What will they blow out of proportion? The fact that satanists snuck into my winery and drank my wine and sacrificed animals in my fermenting room? Or the fact that they killed and tore apart my security guard?"

"It's a story that could easily be sensationalized—" the chief began.

"Because it's a sensational story! Jesus, what do you

want to do? Hush all this up, pretend it didn't happen? It did happen! It happened at my winery! My goddamn shoes are stuck to the goddamn floor with goddamn blood!" He pointed a finger in the chief's face. "I don't give a fuck whether the media knows about this or not. I just want you to catch the bastards."

"You don't care?" the chief said. "What do you think it's going to do to sales of your wine when consumers find out that satanic rituals were performed on your premises?"

"Gentlemen," Horton said, sensing the tension building and stepping between the two men. "There's no reason for us to argue. We're on the same side. We both want to catch whoever did this, and I think we'll have a better chance of that if we cooperate."

The chief looked at him coldly. "I don't need your advice, Lieutenant. I know how to conduct myself in an investigation."

Horton backed off, nodding in acquiescence, swallowing the retort which rose naturally in his throat and which concerned the species of the chief's mother. He was blinded for a second as he accidentally looked into the flash of the photographer, and he quickly glanced down. When the glare cleared, he saw again the security guard's gruesome remains, a shred of tattered shirt glued with blood to bone, fluttering in the fan wind. He turned away.

He was getting too old for this shit.

FIFTEEN

"Ariadne," Mr. Holbrook said professorially, pacing in front of the class, "was the princess of Thebes and—"

"Crete," Dion said.

The teacher stopped talking, stopped walking, looked at him. The eyes of the other students followed those of their instructor. "What?" Mr. Holbrook asked.

"Crete," Dion repeated timidly. "Ariadne was the princess of Crete. You said Thebes." He looked down at his desk, at his hands, embarrassed that he had spoken up, not sure why he had mentioned the misstatement, not sure how he had known that it was incorrect.

The teacher nodded. "You're quite right, Dion. Thank you."

The lecture continued.

Twenty minutes later the bell rang, and though the teacher was writing on the board, still speaking, in the middle of a sentence, books were immediately slammed shut, pencils pocketed, as students stood and rushed toward the door. Mr Holbrook turned around, wiping the chalk dust from his fingers. "Dion," he said. "I'd like to speak to you a moment."

There was a chorus of onimous "oohs" from the departing students. "I'll wait outside," Kevin said, passing by. Dion caught Penelope's eye and was gratified to see that she was looking at him.

The teacher walked to his desk as the class emptied and sat down in the swivel chair behind it. He leaned back in the chair and looked up at Dion, fingers steepled together. "It's obvious," he said, "that you have an extensive knowledge of classical mythology."

Dion shifted uneasily from one foot to another. "Not really," he said.

"Yes, you do. And I just wanted you to know that I can arrange for you to take independent study. Clearly you're just spinning your wheels in this class. This is basically a mythology primer, an overview for beginners. I think you would benefit greatly from accelerated coursework."

"No," Dion said quickly.

"Don't be so hasty. Think about it. I don't know what your future academic plans are, but I can assure you that such a move would look very impressive on your transcripts."

Outside the classroom, the hall was filled with talking, shouting, slamming lockers: the sounds of lunch. Dion glanced anxiously toward the open door, then turned his attention back to the teacher. "Okay," he said. "I'll think about it."

"Discuss it with your parents. I really feel that you'd just be wasting your time in this course."

"I will," Dion said, backing up. He picked up his book and notebook from the top of his desk.

Mr. Holbrook smiled. "I know. It's lunch. Go. Get out of here. But promise me you'll consider this option, okay? We'll talk more about it later."

"Okay," Dion said. "Uh, thanks. Bye." He walked out of the room. In the hall, Kevin, Penelope, and her friend Vella were standing together next to one of the lockers. Dion knew that he was the subject of their conversation, and for some reason the knowledge made him absurdly, unreasonably happy. He walked purposefully toward them, but Penelope, seeing him, waved a quick good-bye to Kevin, and she and her friend disappeared into the stream of people rushing through the building toward the outside lunch area. "What was that about?" he asked Kevin.

"Why? Jealous?"

He hadn't even thought of that.

"Don't worry." Kevin laughed. "She's all yours. I was just talking to her. I don't want to cornhusk her."

Dion grinned. "Oh, you want her friend, huh?"

"For what? I already have a dog." Kevin snorted.

"Come on. We're late and it's getting crowded. Let's grab some grub."

The two of them pushed their way through the crowd toward the cafeteria.

Dion was standing in line next to Kevin, trying to over-hear the sexually explicit conversation of the two jocks in the next line over, when he felt a light feminine tap on his shoulder. A shiver of goosebumps surfed down his arm. He turned around. As he'd hoped, as he'd feared, he found himself face to face with Penelope. This close, he could see the clear smoothness of her skin, the natural redness of her lips. She nodded at him, smiled, but there was a trace of worry in her brow, a subtle hint of concern in her eyes. "What happened with Mr. Holbrook?" she asked. "Are you in trouble?"

Dion studied her face. Did she care? *Was she interested?* His palms were sweaty and he wiped them on his jeans, but his voice betrayed none of his anxious excitement. "He said I should be in an advanced mythology class, but since there was none, he wanted me to take independent study."

The worry turned to alarm. "Are you going to?"

She *was* interested.

"No." He smiled.

A flush of redness spread over her cheeks. "It's just that . . . I mean, I, uh—"

Kevin stuck his head between them. "She likes you, okay? God, just come out and say it. I'm tired of this. I have to listen to you two beat around the bush for an hour and a half, and then I'll have to listen to him analyze it for the next week. She likes you. You like her. You both like each other. Does that about cover it?"

Now both of them were red, embarrassed. They stood awkwardly silent, not looking at each other, neither of them knowing what to say.

"Would you like to sit with us?" Kevin asked, usurping Dion's obvious next line. "Yes, thank you," he answered himself.

Penelope looked doubtfully at Dion, then shifted her gaze toward one of the tables. "I'm supposed to eat with—"

"Bring her along," Kevin said. He motioned for the two of them to move forward in line. "And move up. You're blocking traffic. Jeez, do I have to do everything for you?"

Dion and Penelope looked at Kevin, then at each other, and laughed.

After paying for her lunch, Penelope went to get Vella, who was brown-bagging it, and the girls joined Dion and Kevin at a table near Senior Corner. It was Kevin who initiated the conversation at first, who expertly drew all of them into the discussion, but what began as a four-way dialogue was soon dominated by Dion and Penelope, who addressed most of their words to each other, involving Kevin and Vella only peripherally.

Dion drank his Coke quickly but hardly touched his hamburger as he kept his eyes and attention fastened on Penelope. He had expected the conversation to be stilted and awkward, filled with favorite food–favorite music– favorite movie questions, and there was some of that, but for the most part the conversation flowed naturally, or- ganically, not seeming the least bit forced or false. The two of them did not run out of things to talk about, as he'd feared, but found that each question, each answer, each observation, each reminiscence, opened up entirely new topics and fields for discussion. Neither of them mentioned what Kevin had brought up in line, and for that reason there was an underlying tension in their talk, a tension that maintained a steady rush of intoxicating adrenaline coursing through Dion's veins.

Lunch ended far too soon.

The bell rang, and Kevin stood up, throwing his wrap- pers in the metal trash bin next to the table, waving good- bye, and heading off to his sixth-period class. Vella threw away her trash too and waited a respectable distance away for her friend. Around them the flow of people began streaming toward the classrooms.

Penelope looked at Dion, glanced away. "So what are you doing after school?" she asked, not meeting his eyes.

"Why?"

"Well, I thought maybe we could study together. I mean, I'm having a little trouble in Mythology, especially keeping all those Titans and Olympians straight." She smiled. "Since you're the big expert, I thought you could help me out."

She was not having any trouble, and he knew it, but he decided to play along. "Okay," he said.

"We could meet in the library . . ." She thought for a moment. "Or you could come over to my house. It's not as quiet there, but it's a lot more comfortable."

"Sure," he said. "I'd like that."

"Do you have a car?"

He shook his head, embarrassed. "No."

"That's okay. Neither do I. The bus takes me straight home, though, and you can ride with me. I'm sure I can get one of my—I can get my mother to drive you home."

"Come on!" Vella called from the sidelines. "We'll be late!"

Dion smiled. "You'll be late."

"We'll both be late."

"So where do you want to meet?"

"Outside the library, after school."

"I'll be there," he said.

"I'll see you then."

He waved good-bye and watched her hurry over to Vella. The two girls sprinted across the grassy expanse toward the lockers.

He was still staring at the spot where they'd disappeared into the building when the bell rang.

The conversation on the bus ride was not as relaxed and easy as it had been at lunch. Kevin and Vella weren't there, which put extra pressure on the two of them, and the tension which had been nascent earlier was now full blown and firmly in the forefront, the considerable effort involved in arranging this supposedly casual meeting making it nearly impossible to maintain the illusion that they were classmates simply studying together. Their talk was hesitant, their words infrequent, their discussion consisting of awkwardly worded questions and quick-to-the-point answers. Nevertheless, the natural affinity they shared won out over this more superficial unease, and by the time the bus brakes hissed to a stop in front of the

winery gates, the two of them were, if not talking as
though they were old friends, at least not acting as though
they were terrified of each other.

They stepped off the bus, which pulled slowly away
with a rattle of loose gravel. Penelope used a key to open
a small black box attached to a low pole next to the gate,
and she quickly punched in a series of numbers on the
tiny console. She closed the front of the box, and the giant gates opened with a low whirring noise. She smiled at
him. "Come on."

Dion followed her through the iron gates and up the
winding paved driveway. The single lane was flanked
near the entrance by a line of trees which acted as a natural fence and which disappeared almost immediately,
giving way to a field of staked grape vines, laid out in
parallel rows and spreading over what appeared to be
acres of flat farmland. On the far side of the huge vineyard, he could see Penelope's house and the adjacent
structures of the winery.

He whistled. "Wow," he said.

Penelope giggled.

"I've never seen anything like this," he admitted. He
stared at the tall Ionic columns which made up the peri-
style separating the winery from the parking lot. Beyond
it were three neo-Classic buildings arranged in staggered
order. Concessions had been made to modernity—as they
drew closer he could see metal heating/air-conditioning
units, reflective window glass, clearly marked service
doors—but from afar the complex looked like nothing so
much as an ancient Greek hilltop city. The plantation-
style house, while set slightly apart from the winery and
distinctly American, also contained complementary
echoes of ancient architecture and did not dispel the impression.

Dion thought of the small house he and his mother
rented, realized that he had never even imagined living in
a place this big or this opulent. He looked at Penelope.
The differences between them suddenly seemed enormous.

She looked at him and smiled.

He tried to smile back, tried to think of something to

say that wouldn't make him sound like a fool. He cleared his throat. "I was looking at a tourist map of the wineries the other day, and I didn't see yours listed."

"We don't give tours," she explained. "The winery is not open to the public."

"Really?" Dion was surprised at that. The winery seemed to have been built with tourists specifically in mind. With its pseudo-Greek architecture and distinctive layout, it would seem to be a natural point of interest, much more so than Edinger's or Scalia's or some of the other more pedestrian-looking wineries which did offer guided tours of their facilities. He frowned. "Then why does it look so . . . Why does it look like this?"

Penelope shrugged. "That's how the women of the combine wanted it."

Dion looked again at the complex, and suddenly he didn't like it. The interest and admiration he had felt only seconds before disappeared. A wave of distaste washed over him, an aversion so strong it was almost physical. He glanced quickly away, but not before Penelope saw the expression on his face.

"What's the matter?" she asked.

He waved it away. "Nothing," he said. But he looked again at the winery buildings, and he was afraid. There were goose bumps on his arms, and he was reminded of his equally irrational reaction to the hill last week. He coughed, tried not to let his unease show. "Come on."

Penelope nodded, leading the way. They walked past the rows of vines and lines of pickers, through the parking lot, and down the short path to the house. The fear passed as quickly as it had come, and by the time they had reached the front steps it was just a memory.

"Home sweet home," Penelope said.

Dion looked up at the three-story mansion. "Have you always lived here?"

"All my life."

"You must have a big family."

"No. It's just me and my mother."

"Your dad doesn't—?"

"No."

He shook his head. "Just the two of you in this huge house?"

"Well, it's not just the two of us. My other . . . women in the combine live here too."

Dion nodded, saying nothing.

Penelope stopped at the foot of the porch steps, turned to face him. "I know what the kids say," she said, her voice low, "but I'm not a lesbian."

Dion found himself blushing. "I didn't say you were—"

"And neither are any of the women in the combine." Her voice was strong, her expression serious. For all of her shyness, for all of her earlier hesitancy, she seemed much older than her years, more poised and mature than other girls her age. "Look," she said. "I know how it looks to a bunch of hormone-enraged teenage boys, but the combine is just a business concern. That's it. We all live in the same house, but that's because it's big and it's convenient. Our winery is not some sort of sex club or Playboy mansion or anything. Nothing like that happens here or has ever happened here. I'll admit that the women are all strong feminists, but contrary to what people seem to think these days, there's nothing wrong with that. They're aggressive because they have to be. They're businesswomen. And everything they've done, they've done on their own. No one helped them, no one encouraged them, no one would even hire them when they were originally looking for positions in other wineries. They may have made it in spite of men and not because of men, but that doesn't make them lesbians." She stopped to catch her breath.

Dion smiled softly at her. "I wouldn't care if they were lesbians," he said. "But if I thought you were a lesbian, I wouldn't be here."

Now it was her turn to blush.

Both of them were silent for a moment. Dion's hands were sweaty, and he wiped them surreptitiously on his pants. He had said it. He had taken the plunge. He had spoken aloud what he had been thinking, and now she knew for sure that he was interested. He licked his lips. What would she say? How would she react? How would she respond? The silence dragged on, and he was suddenly certain that he had made a mistake, that he had tipped his hand too early.

Her response was no response. She chose to ignore his remark. "Are you thirsty?" she asked finally. Her voice was gentler than it had been, filled with an emotion he couldn't quite place but which for some reason made him feel good. She motioned him up the porch steps, refusing to look at him. "We have some juice in the refrigerator."

Part of him was disappointed, part of him relieved. If he hadn't been accepted, at least he hadn't been shot down. He was still in the running, and that was good enough for now. He nodded. "Sounds great," he said.

They walked inside.

The interior of the house was less impressive than the outside. Rather than the museum's worth of untouchable antiques he had been expecting, he saw a hodgepodge of furnishings and decorating styles, most of them contemporary, none which fit with the grandiose promise of the exterior. The house was comfortable, though, the rooms warm and inviting. In a family room dominated by a large-screen TV, the day's newspaper was scattered over a low wood and white tile coffee table. On the armrest of the couch was an opened paperback, a Danielle Steele novel. Next to the doorway were two pairs of women's shoes.

Dion felt less intimidated than he had before. Penelope's family might be rich, but they lived the same way as everyone else.

"Kitchen's through here!"

He followed Penelope into the kitchen, where a middle-aged woman wearing faded jeans and a plain white blouse was chopping bell peppers on a freestanding butcher block. The woman turned toward them as they entered. She exchanged a quick glance with Penelope, then beamed at Dion. "Hello," she said.

Dion smiled, nodded. "Hello."

"Dion, this is my mother. Mother, this is my friend Dion."

Penelope's mother looked nothing like her. She was small-boned and dark, whereas her daughter was tall and blond. Her features were plain and nondescript in contrast to Penelope's stunning good looks. She was also older and more careworn than he would have expected. The one thing mother and daughter did seem to have in common was an innate shyness, a natural reserve, although Penelope's mother appeared to be more deferential, less strong-willed.

"Would you two like something to drink?"

"Yes," Penelope said. "Juice?"

"We have grape. Fresh squeezed today."

"That'll be fine."

Mother Felice opened the white refrigerator door and drew out a large glass pitcher filled to the brim with grape juice. She maneuvered carefully over to the counter, holding the pitcher with two hands in order to keep from spilling any on the floor. "Where are you from?" she asked as she put the pitcher down and took two glasses from the cupboard. "I know you're not from around here."

"Arizona," Dion said.

"Really? Whereabouts?"

"Mesa. It's near Phoenix."

"I know where Mesa is. I used to have a friend from Scottsdale, a girl I went to high school with."

Penelope smiled as her mother handed her a glass of juice. Mother Felice had always been able to put people at ease, to make them feel comfortable. Of all of her mothers, she was the kindest, the most solicitous of the feelings of others, and it was she who was always chosen to soothe the waters after Mother Margeaux had bulldozed her way over someone. Penelope was glad to see that Dion seemed to like her mother, and that her mother seemed to like Dion.

The door banged open and Mother Janine stepped loudly into the kitchen, bumping against the frame as she pulled work gloves off her hands. "Who's—" she began. She stopped in mid-sentence, saw Dion, and smiled. "Hello," she said.

"This is Dion," Mother Felice explained. "A friend of Penelope's."

"Dion?" Mother Janine's smile broadened. She reached

out, took his hand, shook it gently. "I am very happy to meet you. Very happy. I'm ... Penelope's aunt, Janine."

"How do you do?" he replied.

Penelope saw her mothers exchanging surreptitious glances, smiling in approval. She reddened, but she did not look away. She was embarrassed but also proud. She had never before invited a boy to see where she lived, and she felt good that the first one she had chosen was Dion, someone of whom her mothers would obviously approve, a boy who was nice, intelligent, good-looking, and respectful.

"Would you like to go on a little tour of the winery?" Mother Janine asked. "I'd love to—"

"We have to study," Penelope said.

"We could study afterward," Dion suggested.

"We have to study," she repeated firmly.

He nodded. "Right," he agreed. "Right." He handed the empty glass to Penelope's mother. "Thanks," he said.

There was silence for a moment. Dion was awkwardly aware that everyone was staring at him: Penelope, her mother, her aunt. He didn't know what to say and was about to make some sort of generic remark when Penelope saved him and suggested that they go out to the Garden.

"Study in a garden?" Dion said.

She laughed. "I'll show you. Come on."

He said good-bye to the two women and followed Penelope out of the kitchen. Though nothing had happened, nothing he noticed, he got the feeling that he had passed some sort of test. He thought of Penelope's mother and her aunt, and he was not sure if he liked that or not.

He followed Penelope through the library as she opened the sliding glass doors and stepped outside.

SIXTEEN

Frank Douglas had been a bartender for a long time, for thirty-three of his fifty-six years, and while he might not have had the academic credentials of a sociologist, he had learned a little about reading people in his time behind the counter. Individuals *and* crowds. He could be pouring drinks, wiping up, engaging in superficial chitchat with the more talkative regulars, but at the same time his senses were always open, his antennae out, working, measuring, gauging, sizing up.

And this crowd was weird.

He poured himself a mineral water and downed half of it in a single swallow. The night crowds had all been weird lately. Or at least weird for this bar. The Pioneer usually attracted a steady, stable clientele of after-work drinkers and evening socializers, a solid blue-collar beer crowd. But in the past few weeks the makeup of the bar had gradually shifted. No, not the makeup. The *personality.* For the people were still the same, and, individually, they seemed no different than they had before. They wore the same clothes, drove the same cars, came and left at the same times. But the configuration of the crowd when these people were together had changed completely, and that had changed the whole tenor of the bar. Gone were the endless public rehashes of the weekend's sporting events, the petty domestic complaints, the boring shop talk. Conversations now were quiet, less public, more intimate, more personal, usually between two people. Usually between a man and a woman.

And these days most of his customers were drinking wine instead of beer.

A lot of wine.

Frank finished his mineral water, washed out the glass.

His gaze wandered to the back wall, where the once empty booths were all full, populated with people who sat very close together in the darkness.

That was the strangest thing of all. Many of these people had known one another for years, had been friends or acquaintances, bar buddies, but had always looked elsewhere for love. Now they suddenly seemed to have discovered each other, and they were behaving like high school students in heat.

It didn't make any sense.

At Josh Aldridge's high sign, he poured the roofer another wine cooler, placing it on a napkin before him.

What made even less sense was the feeling he got that beneath the surface calm there lurked a barely concealed storm. It was a strange feeling, an unfounded feeling, but as much as he tried to discount it rationally, it would not go away. Despite the intimate discussions, despite the quiet nuzzling, despite the lovey-doveyness, he had the impression that it would require only a very slight provocation to stir up this crowd, to bring whatever latent violence lay beneath its thin veneer immediately to the surface.

He had tended bar in a lot of places, a lot of towns. He'd mixed drinks in discos and punk clubs, in cowboy and biker bars. He could sense danger. And though his customers tonight were polite and well behaved, though they seemed to be merely looking for companionship, he could tell that they were looking for something more than that. Something nowhere near as nice.

And it frightened him.

SEVENTEEN

There were buildings on top of the rocky hill, buildings not unlike those that made up the winery. Stately structures with tall Doric columns supporting heavy entablatures decorated with intricately carved friezes. There were three buildings altogether, the largest flanked by two co-equal counterparts. Men were standing in line before the middle building, a long line which wound a considerable way down the side of the barren slope. In their hands were baskets of fruit and samples of recently killed game.

He wanted nothing to do with the men. Though he was hungry, he longed for none of the fruit, coveted none of the game. The sustenance he wanted was located far below the temples, in the valley.

Temples. That's what the buildings were.

He turned away from the line of men and began running down the hill. Fleet of foot he was, possessing a strength and agility that seemed natural but at the same time superhuman. He fairly flew over the rough terrain, feet finding purchase and springing from the ground's inlaid rock.

Then he was at the bottom of the hill, speeding toward the trees. He smelled the sweet frangrance of wine, and the musky odor of women.

He was late. In the meadow, in the valley, the celebration had already started. Vats of wine had been brought here, and two of them were now half empty. Whole and broken cups lay strewn about the grass in scattered disarray. There were nearly a hundred people laughing, screaming, singing. Many of them were naked and most of them were drunk. Couples—men and women, women and women, men and men—were fornicating furiously on the soft grass.

He raced into the center of the meadow. "I am here!" he announced. His voice was loud, booming, echoing over the hills and back.

The people gathered around him. He had been planning to join in the festivities, but he realized that the celebration was in honor of himself. A huge goblet of wine was thrust into his hand, and he swallowed its entirety. The goblet was immediately replaced with another, and that with another, until he had drunk ten such draughts and his thirst was quenched.

He felt good, he felt primed, ready to satisfy his other hunger.

The smell of arousal was all about him, entwined with the fragrance of the wine, the heavy musk of the women, the lighter scent of the men.

He scanned the faces before him. He wanted two today.

His eyes alighted on the robed figures of a woman and her young daughter. He nodded, and both removed their clothes. The woman's breasts were full, milky, her thatch thick. The daughter was hairless and only just ripe. With one easy movement he stepped out of his own garb. The eyes of the two females widened with awe and lust at the sight of his enormous organ.

He took the woman first, bending her over a log and taking her from behind as the other celebrants cheered. She screamed with agony and joy and hot ecstasy, and he became wilder, more feverish in his movements as the wine was poured over them and the woman began to buck. His time was about to come, and he grabbed her head, smashing it against the log with each thrust as his seed shot deep into her body.

She had stopped breathing long before he was through, though the blood continued to pump from her gashed head.

Afterward, the daughter sat on his lap and rode him as he impaled her, tore her apart. His satisfaction came at the precise moment of her death, and he leaped to his feet as he gave a cry and around him the carnage began. Screams of pleasure and screams of pain blended, harmonized, created a music beautiful to his ears. He breathed in the blood and sex and death, looking proudly down at the broken, used, and twisted bodies of the mother and her daughter, bathed in liquid red and white. They were dead, but the life force had not yet fled entirely, and their legs were still twitching in remembrance of ecstasy.

Dion awoke suddenly, his head jerking up from the pillow. The final image was still in his mind, the young girl and her mother covered in blood and semen, twitching. He was disgusted by the image, nauseated, frightened by it. He closed his eyes, breathed deeply, opened his eyes. His room seemed far too dark, its night shadows much more threatening than usual, and he was sweating, drenched with the aftermath of fear.

He also had an erection.

"So did you feed her some sausage?"

Dion slammed shut his locker, ignoring the question.

Kevin grinned. "Come on, man. You can tell me. I'd tell you."

"I wish you wouldn't talk about Penelope like that."

"Whoa, it's love and not just lust!" Kevin reached out to grab a passerby and make some crude remark about the situation, but Dion stopped his hand.

"Hey, I'm serious."

Kevin's smile faded. "I'm sorry. I was just joking."

"No," Dion apologized. "I'm sorry. I didn't mean to be so defensive."

"You must be pretty serious about her, huh?"

Dion shrugged. "I don't know." He shifted the books uncomfortably in his hand.

"You are. I can tell."

"Bell's going to ring," Dion said, changing the subject.

The two of them started walking. "You coming with us Friday?" Kevin asked. "We're going to cruise up to Lake Berryessa, see if we can't scare us some campers."

"Sorry. I hope to have a date that night."

"Hope to? You mean you don't know? You haven't asked yet?"

"No," Dion admitted.

"Don't be such a wimp. Use your balls. You do have balls, right?"

Dion laughed. "Your sister says I do."

"Ask her out, then. I mean, shit, how much more encouragement do you need? You expect her to come out and say she's madly in love with you before you ask her out on a simple date? Be serious. No offense, but if Pussy-Eating Penelope invites you over to her damn winery and introduces you to her mom, that would seem to be a pretty good indication that she likes you. As far as I know, you're the only guy who's ever made it past those gates."

Dion raised his eyebrows. " 'Pussy-Eating Penelope?' "

Kevin held up his hands in an expression of innocence. "I didn't make it up."

The two of them turned toward the east wing.

"So are you going to make your move?" Kevin asked.

"We'll see."

"So that means you'll be coming out with us Friday?"

"Hopefully not."

" 'Hopefully'?"

"Probably."

"Have some guts, dude."

"Okay, I'm not coming with you. I'm going out on a date."

"That's the way it always is," Kevin complained. "A guy finds himself a girl, forgets about his buddies—"

Dion laughed. "I could set you up with her friend Vella."

"I could get a rubber woman with more life."

Around them, the crowd suddenly thinned as students hurried into classes. "I guess that means it's time." Kevin hurried down the hall. "See you in Mythology."

"I'll be there."

Kevin laughed. "I know you will."

Dion and Penelope walked slowly through the vineyard, the late summer sun streaming down on their heads. Penelope talked about grapes as they walked, about hybrids and planting techniques. Dion listened to what she had to say, looked at the examples she showed him. Close up, the vines looked different than he'd thought they would. The plants were not as leafy as he'd expected, and the stalks seemed dry and twisted, strangely grizzled. Even the grapes did not match the image in his mind. The bunches were full and plentiful, outnumbering the leaves on some of the vines, but the grapes themselves were much smaller than ordinary table grapes.

They continued to walk. The picking had stopped for a few days, until some of the remaining grapes had ripened, and they had the field entirely to themselves. They strode side by side as they moved farther away from the drive. The ground here was rough, furrowed, and it was impossible to step in a straight line. More than once the backs of their hands accidentally brushed, and Dion felt tingles of anticipatory excitement pass through him. He wanted desperately to breach the inches between them and hold her hand. It seemed natural, right, and though he thought he sensed a similar desire on her part, he was not experienced enough at these things to know for sure. He might be misreading the signs, and he did not have the courage to act on his instincts. He needed more than a hint, more than a promise; he needed assurance that she felt the same way he did before he attempted to make a move.

They stopped for a moment at the end of a row. Dion leaned his foot against a long, wheeled pipe sprinkler and wiped the sweat from his forehead as he looked around. "What's there?" he asked. "Behind the wall?" He pointed toward the stone fence which ran the length of the field, disappearing in back of the house and winery buildings.

"I don't know," she said quickly.

"You don't know?"

She shook her head.

"Come on, you can tell me." He grinned mischievously. "I won't sell your family secrets."

Penelope did not smile. "I'm forbidden to go back there."

"Forbidden? Why?"

She turned toward him. "Do you want to see how it's done?" she asked. "Do you want to see how we make the wine?"

"Uh, sure," he said, frowning.

"Let's go, then." Without waiting for an answer, she began hiking back down the row the way they'd come, her arms swinging in a carefree manner that was too studied and too perfect to be real.

He looked toward the fence and wondered what it was about the forbidden area behind it that had triggered this reaction. She was obviously afraid of the place and didn't want to talk about it, but her unexpectedly strong response had intensified what had before been only idle curiosity. He would definitely have to ask her about the place sometime when he knew her a little better, when she wasn't so freaked.

She stopped, turned around, motioned him forward. "Come on!"

He hurried down the row toward her, and she began to run. Laughing, they raced over the rough ground all the way to the drive. Dion stopped first. "I give up," he said, breathing heavily. He bent down, putting his hands on his knees. "Whoo!"

"I take it you're not used to exercising?"

"I walk to school and back."

"A whole three blocks!"

"More like six."

Penelope laughed. "Another Arnold Schwartzenegger."

Dion stood, straightened, catching his breath. He smiled at her, acknowledging the joke, but he couldn't help feeling a little hurt by it. She hadn't meant it to be insulting—her tone of voice was light and completely innocent—but he vowed nonetheless to start exercising.

She looked toward him. "Ready?" she asked.

He nodded.

"Let's go, then."

They walked together up the drive and entered the main building through a tinted glass side door. Dion had expected the inside of the winery to be dark and rustic, filled with floor to ceiling oak casks, dimly lit by bare bulbs, the Hollywood conception of a winery. But the long room outside the small glass-walled office into which they'd entered was antiseptically white, with a checkerboard tile floor and a row of gleaming stainless steel tanks along the north wall. He could see a curled hose lying next to one of the tanks, and a drain in the center of the floor.

Penelope nodded to a middle-aged woman sitting at a computer terminal. "I'm just showing my friend around," she explained.

The woman smiled. "Go right ahead."

The two of them walked through the open doorway. "We're kind of taking the backward tour," Penelope said. "Or the sideways tour." She pointed at the row of tanks. "These are used for fermenting. Wineries used to do all of their fermenting in wooden casks, but that's not really an efficient method these days. What we do is allow the wine to ferment here, and then for certain blends we move it into the wooden barrels for final aging."

"Why?" Dion asked.

"Because the wood actually adds flavor to the wine. Redwood will add a slight, barely detectable flavor; oak has a fairly strong effect. So what we do depends on the type and vintage. Whites and roses we ferment and age completely in here. Certain reds we age in the oak barrels."

He shook his head. "It's weird hearing someone my age talk about wines like this. I mean, you're not even old enough to drink, and you act like an expert."

"What do you expect? I grew up here."

"I guess." He looked around the room. "Do you ever help out?"

"Not really. I hang around sometimes, but they never wanted me to actually do any of the work. I never wanted to either."

"Does your mother ever let you try any of the wines? In France, even little kids drink it. They have it with every meal. Do you guys do that?"

"No," Penelope said simply. "I don't drink."

Dion was glad of that.

"Come on, let's go into the pressing room."

Their tennis shoes sounded loud and absurdly squeaky on the silent tile. Penelope led the way down the row of tanks and pushed open the white door at the far end. They passed through another, identical room filled with large, closed metal tanks, where Penelope nodded to two workers, then into the pressing room.

The pressing room was just as modern but not nearly as antiseptic and was the size of a small grocery store. The air here smelled of grape, and there were purple stains on the raised wood-slatted floor. Machines of various shapes and sizes were grouped according to type. Along the opposite wall were what looked like two electrical generators.

"As you can see, we don't all stand barefoot in a big barrel and stomp around to press the grapes. These are different types of presses. The women of the combine bought several kinds in order to experiment with different techniques. They all still work, and we usually end up using most of them at the height of the season, but we usually stick to these." She tapped a long metal cylinder suspended in a sturdy frame. "Air-pressure presses. They squeeze from the inside out instead of the other way around like the rest of these do. For our purposes, it makes a much better must."

"Must?"

"The grape juice that we make into wine."

"Oh."

He followed her around the large room as she opened each press type and explained its workings. After that she led the way into a huge, damp, cavelike room in which hundreds of wooden barrels were stacked almost to the ceiling. *This* was what he'd though a winery would look like.

"This is just where we age the wines. After this the product is bottled and shipped out. I'd show you our bottling apparatus, but it's in another building, and it's closed up right now. The casks you're looking at now are arranged by year. We have wines in this room going back four, five, six years. My . . . aunt Sheila does the testing to determine when the wines are ready."

Dion took a deep breath. The air was rich, smelling of sweet grape and tart fermentation.

He thought of his mom.

What if he and Penelope eventually got married? What

would happen if there was a winery in the family? If his mom had unlimited access to alcohol?

He did not even want to think about it.

"That's the basic tour, the non-technical tour. If you want a more in-depth look at the wine-making process, if you want to follow it from step to step, I'm sure I could get one of my aunts to take us around."

He shook his head. "No, that was good enough." He smiled at her. "You're really an excellent tour guide. Ever think of doing it professionally?"

"Very funny."

They walked out of the room the way they'd come in, but exited the pressing room through a side door which led down a hall. There was only one door in the wall of the hallway. "What's in there?" Dion asked as they passed.

"In there? That's the lab. But we can't go inside. That's Mother Sheila's territory, and she's very protective. Even I've never been in there."

"What's the big secret?"

"Well, that's where they come up with new blends, new wines. That's where the serious brain work is done."

They walked outside, squinting against the sudden brightness of the late afternoon sun. "So where is your wine sold?" Dion asked. "I haven't looked, but Kevin told me your wine's not sold in stores, that you have to mail-order it?"

Her face tightened. "Did he call it 'Lezzie Label Wine'?"

"No," Dion lied.

"Kevin Harte? He didn't mention the word *lesbian* in there somewhere?"

Dion smiled. "Well, yeah, he did."

She shook her head. "We produce what are called 'specialty label' wines. Kevin's right, they are mostly sold by mail order, but that's because most of our customers live out of state. Or out of the country."

"What's a 'specialty label' wine?"

"It's a wine that's sold primarily to collectors or connoisseurs. It's the equivalent of, like, a limited-edition book. A lot of the smaller labels like ours couldn't afford to compete with the big names in the mass market, so we've sort of carved out our own niche. We produce the type of wine that it is just not economically feasible for a big winery to produce. Specialty labels usually specialize in wines made from obscure or exotic breeds or new hybrids of grape. Some use archaic or adventurous pressing, fermenting, or distilling techniques on their product."

"Sounds like you're quoting from a textbook."

She laughed. "Close. Our sales brochure."

"So what do you specialize in?"

"Basically, we make Greek wine, the type of wine they drank in ancient Greece, in Socrates' time and the days of Homer. Wine played an important role in the religious and social life of ancient Greece, but the classic techniques of wine making have been virtually abandoned in favor of the European style of wine making. It's really almost a lost art. The machines you saw in there are all modern, but they're used to duplicate those processes." Penelope smiled shyly. "That's in the brochure too."

"That explains the architecture," Dion said. "And I assume that's why you're taking Mythology."

She looked surprised. "Not really. In fact, it never even occurred to me. But now that you mention it, yeah, I suppose it did influence me."

They walked slowly across the lawn, toward the house. Dion glanced up, saw Penelope's mother and two of her aunts watching them through a window. They smiled and waved when they saw him, and he waved back, but it made him feel a little creepy. He couldn't help thinking that he and Penelope were being spied upon.

"It's getting late," Dion said. "I should be getting back."

"This early?" Penelope sounded disappointed.

"My mom expects me home for dinner."

Did she really? he wondered. From school he had called his mom at work, explaining that he was going over to Penelope's, telling her that he would be home by dinnertime. He had assumed that she would be home before he was, would have dinner waiting, but a nagging voice in the back of his mind kept saying that this would give her free time, that she would use this opportunity to do what she wanted and that she would not be home when he got there.

Stop it, he told himself.

"You always talk about your mother," Penelope said. "Your father doesn't live with you?"

Dion shook his head.

"Are your parents divorced?"

"No." He looked at her, aware she was waiting for more, not sure how much he wanted to reveal. He took a deep breath, took the plunge. "I don't know who my father was," he admitted. He glanced away from her, toward the house, ashamed, embarrassed, though he knew it was something over which he'd had no control.

"But doesn't—"

"My mom doesn't know either."

"Oh."

She was silent then. He wanted to apologize somehow, to say it was not his fault, to tell her not to blame him for the circumstances of his birth, but he said nothing. He tried to read her face, but he could not tell from her expression if she was disappointed, angry, hurt, sympathetic, whether he was tainted in her eyes or it made no difference to her at all. The silence dragged on, and he felt he had to say something.

"My mom's a slut," he said.

He regretted the words instantly. The statement did not really express how he felt, and outside the confines of his brain it sounded much too harsh, much too cruel. He had wanted to disassociate himself from his mother and at the same time show that her values, her lifestyle, were not his own. But he did not like the cold, judgmental tone of his own voice, the thoughtless dismissal implied by his words. And he could tell that Penelope didn't like it either.

"You dare to say that about your mother?" she said, turning on him.

He wanted to take it back, wanted to explain what he meant, but he couldn't. "I don't know," he said ineffectually.

"Don't you have any respect for your parents?"

He was quiet.

"I'm sorry," she said, pulling back. "I didn't mean to jump all over you. I don't really know the circumstances of your life, but I just don't think that you should heap everything on your mother. If you've had a tough time, then she has too. She's probably doing the best she can. It's hard being a single parent, you know? I mean, I don't blame my mothers for . . ." Her voice trailed off.

"For what?"

"My father." She looked away.

Neither of them said anything as they continued walking across the grass. It was Dion who spoke first. "What about your father?"

She did not answer.

"Penelope?" he prodded gently.

"My father," she said, "was torn apart by wolves."

Dion was shocked into silence. He looked at her, turned away, not knowing what to say. He took a deep breath. "I'm sorry," he said quietly.

Penelope nodded slightly, her voice subdued. "I am too." She pulled ahead of him. "Let's just forget about it."

Dion hesitated for a moment, unsure if he should continue with the conversation or let it drop. She'd said she didn't want to talk about it, but he sensed that she did. The subject of his father was a sensitive one for him; he knew how he felt when other people asked about it, and he was sure that she probably felt a thousand times worse. Nevertheless, he hastened forward and caught up with her at the edge of the parking lot. "Do you remember him?" he asked.

Her steps slowed. She stopped walking, turned to face him. "I was a baby when he died. I have pictures of him, and from the way my mothers talk about him, I feel as though I know him. But, no, I don't remember him. My father exists only in my mind." She looked at her watch. "It's almost five-thirty."

"Yeah, I'd better go."

Penelope licked her lips. "Still friends?" she asked.

He nodded. "Still friends."

"You don't hate me?"

"You don't hate me?"

"No," she said. "Of course not."

"I don't hate you either."

Penelope looked toward the house, met his eyes shyly. "My mother said I could drive you home alone this time."

"Good," Dion said.

He meant it. He had nothing against Penelope's mother, but the drive home last time had been extremely uncomfortable. Penelope had been in the backseat, right behind him, but he'd still felt as though he was alone in the car with her mom. Her mother had done most of the talking, asked all of the questions, and most of those questions had been strangely personal. Or just plain strange. There had seemed something vaguely sexual about the way she'd smiled at him, something promising or threatening in the way her eyes had examined him. In a bizarre manner she reminded him of his own mom, and that made him extremely uncomfortable. He had quickly revised his initial impression of her. And he had been grateful when the car had pulled up to the curb in front of his house and he had gotten out.

He'd said nothing to Penelope, of course. And this time when he'd seen her mom again, she'd seemed once more a typical, if slightly mousy, housewife.

But he was glad he wouldn't have to ride in a car with her again.

"I'll get the keys and tell them we're going," Penelope said.

"Okay."

He followed her up the steps and into the house.

Penelope turned out to be a good driver, a safe and cautious driver. She drove with her hands at ten and two on the steering wheel, and she slowed for yellow lights. Dion found himself smiling at her conscientious concentration.

She must have seen him out of the corner of her eye. "What are you grinning at?"

"Nothing."

"Are you making fun of the way I drive?"

"Of course not."

She turned on her blinker to make a left turn. "I don't drive that often, you know."

He laughed. "I never would've guessed."

She left the engine on as she pulled in front of his house and put the car into Park.

"We didn't get much studying done," Dion said, picking up his books from the seat between them.

"No," she admitted.

He looked at her, wanting to touch her, wanting at the very least to shake her hand and say good-bye, but he was afraid to. "Do you want to come in?" he asked.

"Oh, no!" She shook her head, as if shocked by the offer. "I couldn't. I have to be straight back." She looked embarrassedly down at the steering wheel. "Besides, my mothers wouldn't like it."

"Mothers?"

"Huh?"

"Mothers. You said your 'mothers.' "

"Did I?"

"Yes. And you said it before too."

She blushed. "Well, I guess that's how I think of them. I mean, I know it seems weird, but they all take care of me. The women of the combine share business duties, and they also sort of share family duties too. It's ..." She shook her head. "No. That's not exactly true." She sighed. "I might as well be honest with you. I've never told anyone this before, but to tell you the truth, I don't know which one's my mother."

He stared at her incredulously. "You're kidding."

"No. It's true. I mean, I sort of adopted Felice as my mother because I liked her the best, and for school and things I need to have one mother. But to me they're all my mothers, and I don't know which is the real one."

"Have you asked?"

She shrugged. "Indirectly. But it's sort of an awkward subject. It's probably the way most people feel when they try to talk about sex with their parents. It's tough." She looked at him. "I didn't really even care until recently. It probably sounds strange to you, but I was brought up this way. I've never known anything else. So to me it seems natural."

"Natural?"

She smiled. "Almost natural."

"But why? It's just so ... weird."

She shrugged. "My mothers believe that I will turn out to be a healthier and more well-rounded person if I am not subjected to the family pressures that everyone else experiences. If I'm not forced to play a traditional role within our household, I will not be locked into playing a traditional role in society." She smiled sadly. "I guess I'm sort of an experiment."

Dion shook his head.

"A failed experiment."

"I don't think so. I think you turned out very well. And surprisingly normal."

She laughed. "Normal, huh? You know that you're probably the only person who would call me that."

"That's because other people don't know you as well as I do."

She reddened, looked away, and impulsively he reached over and touched the back of her hand resting on the seat. Her gaze jerked immediately up, her eyes locking on his. They stared at each other for a moment. Her skin felt smooth, soft, cool beneath his fingers. She pulled her hand out from under his.

"I'll see you in school tomorrow," she said, putting the car into gear.

"But—"

"I have to go."

"Still have those same old parental restrictions, don't you?"

Penelope laughed.

He got out of the car, closed the door. "Good-bye," he said.

"Good-bye. I'll see you in school."

She waved as she turned around, and he watched the car cruise smoothly down the block until it disappeared with a blink of red taillight around the corner.

EIGHTEEN

April sat in front of the television, waiting for Dion to return. The TV was on, but she was not paying attention. She was thinking about her son, about the way he was growing older, growing up. She saw him in her mind as a child, then thought of him going out with a high school girl, holding the girl's hand, kissing her. It was an uncomfortable thought, and one she did not like. She knew it was normal and natural and that it was long past time that Dion showed some interest in the opposite sex, but she still didn't feel good about it.

She was angry at herself for thinking this way. She had always promised herself that she would not be an overprotective mother. So far it had not been a promise that was hard for her to keep. If anything, she had been underprotective, leaving him too much to his own devices. But then Dion had never needed much supervision. He was not the kind of kid to hang out with the wrong kinds of friends, or party or drink or use drugs.

The things she had done.

Now, though, she worried. It was not that she didn't trust her son. It was more that . . . Well, she hated to admit it, but she was jealous. She knew what Margaret would say if she told her about it. She knew all of them would laugh at her, would tell her it was time to let go, time to stop coddling her son, but she couldn't help wanting him not to change, wanting him to remain forever exactly the way he was now. There was nothing sexual about her jealousy. It was nothing like that. It was just that, for all of his brains, for all of his intelligence and sophistication, for all of the things he'd been exposed to, there was still something essentially naive and innocent about him, something that she alone knew about, that he shared only with her. She didn't want that to change. She didn't want that to disappear.

A commercial came on the television, a commercial for a nationally known brand of wine made here in the Napa Valley. Her eyes focused on the glass of chilled white wine shown sweating on a redwood table before a barbecue.

A glass of wine sounded good right now. It sounded very good. She needed to relax a little, to stop brooding over this situation. What was it Margaret had said about the medicinal value of good wine? She stood up and was about to walk into the kitchen when an unwanted memory of the other night burst upon her. She sat shakily down.

Not all wine was good.

She heard Dion's knock on the front door, heard his machine-gun ringing of the doorbell. She hadn't heard a car pull up, hadn't seen it through the window. She'd been too preoccupied. She stood up again. "Coming!" she called. She opened the door.

Dion rushed in. His color was high, and he was obviously excited. "What's for dinner?" he asked, putting his books down on the seat of the hall tree. "I'm starved."

April smiled. "That sounds suspicious to me. Why are you so hungry? What were you doing?"

He looked at her. "Huh?"

"Come on," she teased. "What's her name?"

He reddened. "Mom . . ."

"Don't 'mom' me. This is exactly the sort of thing we should be talking about. We're supposed to be communicating, remember? We're supposed to be sharing our thoughts and feelings, et cetra, et cetra."

Dion smiled.

"I'm serious." She moved back to the couch, sat down, patted the seat next to her. "Sit down. Let's talk."

"Look, I have to study."

"I thought you wanted to eat."

"I have to study until it's time to eat."

"You're going to talk first. Did you have a good time?"

"Mom . . ."

"If you ever want to leave this house again, you'd better humor me. After all, I'm your mother. I have a right to know. What's her name?"

Dion sat down next to her. "I told you her name last time. Penelope."

"Penelope what? You never told me her last name."

"Daneam. Penelope Daneam."

She frowned. "Daneam? Like Daneam Vineyards?"

"Yeah. You've heard of it?"

She felt a small knot of worry in her stomach. "Is this, uh, serious? Are you two seeing each other, going steady, boyfriend and girlfriend or whatever you call it these days?"

"I don't know," he said.

"What's she like?"

"She's nice."

"Is she good-looking?"

"Yes."

"Pretty, sort of pretty or very pretty?"

"Mom!"

She smiled at him. "Okay, okay. I'm just trying to find out where things stand. Are you going to be going out with her? On a real date?"

"I told you, I don't know. I don't even know if she likes me."

"But you're attracted to her, right?"

He stood up. "I have to study."

"Sit down." She grabbed his belt buckle, pulling him back onto the couch. "You know, you're lucky," she said.

"Why?"

"Because. This is a good time for you, even though you might not realize it. It's frustrating, I know. You can't think, can't concentrate on your homework, you spend half your time wondering what the other person is doing, whether they like you or are thinking about you. But it's exciting. You interpret everything as a sign. You analyze every move they make, everything they say, for clues to how they feel about you." She smiled sadly at him. "Once they're caught, once you have them, you lose that. The magnifying glass is gone. You no longer pay so much attention to the little things they do, you start paying more attention to the text of their words than the subtext." She patted his hand. "I don't mean to say it's not good. It is good. But . . . it's never the same."

Dion stared at her. He had never heard his mom talk that way before, and for the first time he felt as though he partially understood the way she acted. He felt even guiltier for the name he had earlier called her, and he realized that he hadn't told Penelope that he loved his mom. He should have, he thought. He should have told her that.

"I'm hungry too," April said, changing the subject. She stood up, turned on the table lamp to dispel the creeping shadows in the room. "Let's eat."

"What are we having?"

"Tacos."

"All right."

"I'll cook the meat and chop the vegetables. You go to the store and get the tortillas."

He groaned. "I'm tired. I have to study. I don't want to go—"

"Or we have egg sandwiches."

He sighed, conceding defeat. "Give me the keys and some cash."

"I thought you'd see it my way." She grabbed her purse from the table and took out her keys and wallet. She handed him two dollars. "That should be enough."

He walked outside to the car in the driveway.

She watched him get into the car and back up onto the street, feeling worried, apprehensive, and a little bit scared.

Penelope Daneam.

Somehow she wasn't surprised.

And that was the part that scared her.

NINETEEN

Dinner that night was more silent than usual, the occasional conversation more stilted, more reserved, and Penelope could feel a Big Discussion coming on. She sat at her usual place between Mother Felice and Mother Sheila at the long dining room table, trying to eat her spaghetti without slurping, not wanting to disturb the quiet. Her palms were sweaty, her muscles tense, and she waited for that first innocent lead-in question that would broach the topic on everyone's mind.

Dion.

None of her mothers had said anything to her about Dion the first time he'd come over. At least not anything serious or substantial. They'd alluded to him playfully, indirectly, letting her know that they were glad she was finally showing some interest in boys, and she'd found during the succeeding days that she felt a lot less reticent in talking about school, a lot less defensive in regard to her social life. If he had been nothing else, he had served as a validation of her normalcy, tangible proof that, despite her own and her mothers' worst fears, she was not a complete social misfit.

But of course he was something more than that, and she knew that that was what her mothers now wanted to talk to her about.

She looked from Mother Margeaux chewing her food thoughtfully at the head of the table, to Mother Margaret, across from her. She wished her mothers would just come out and say what was on their minds instead of putting so much weight and pressure on everything, turning every minor concern into a major topic of discussion.

But this was their way. Just as the rigidity of the dining

arrangements was their way, although to Penelope, her mothers' insistence of formal dinners every evening had always been something which rang false. Even as a small child, it had always seemed to her that her mothers were feigning civility and sophistication for an audience that was not there, mimicking scenes they had seen in movies or on television. She would never admit it to anyone, but more than once, surrounded by her mothers, eating elaborately prepared meals off expensive imported china, she had been reminded of monkeys dressed in business suits, going through motions they did not understand. It was a harsh assessment and not entirely fair, but the analogy did not seem to her that far off base. There was something wild beneath the calm exterior of her mothers, a sense of something untamed struggling to get out of a package of politeness. Mother Margeaux in particular always seemed so controlled, so unemotional, but Penelope knew from experience that her outward display of rationality was just that: a display. When Mother Margeaux was angry or she drank too much, when she let herself go, the results were truly frightening.

Penelope never wanted to see any of her mothers when they were really drunk.

Finished with her food, she pushed her plate away and swallowed the last of her grape juice. She stood, bowed, and addressed her mothers. "May I be excused? I have a lot of homework tonight."

"You may not," Mother Margeaux said.

Penelope sat back down. In addition to its formality, dinner in their house was also uncomfortably ritualistic, and though she had lived with that every night of her life, it was still something that made her feel slightly uneasy. They dined at precisely seven-thirty every evening, and no matter what any of them were doing, they had to stop at seven, wash up, and change into a green dress. Her mother's dresses were all identical—simply designed full-length gowns—while hers was slightly different, not quiet as expensive. They began each dinner with a song, any song, which they took turns initiating. To leave the table after eating, each of them had to ask the permission of the others; if the decision was not unanimous, the person had to wait. Until she'd been in fifth grade and stayed overnight for the first time at a friends' house, she had thought all people ate this way. She had even begun to panic when she'd discovered that she'd forgotten to bring her green dinner dress to her friend's house. But after embarrassing herself by asking detailed questions of her friend's mother, she'd learned that not everyone ate dinner in such a ritualized manner, that in fact hardly anyone did. The knowledge had made her extremely uncomfortable.

She picked up her empty glass, poured the last few drops of grape juice onto her tongue. She fiddled with her fork.

It was Mother Felice who brought up the subject of Dion.

"So how's your boyfriend?" she asked casually.

"Dion?"

"Of course."

"He's not my boyfriend."

Her mother's next question died in her throat. She looked quickly around the table. There was silence.

"Penelope." Mother Margeaux's voice was quiet, but it was strong.

Penelope looked toward the head of the table. Mother Margeaux dabbed at her lips with a napkin and replaced the napkin in her lap. In the warm low light of the dining room, her lips looked almost as dark as her hair. The whites of her eyes seemed large as she focused her intense gaze on Penelope.

"I thought you and Dion were dating," Mother Margeaux said.

Penelope squirmed in her seat. "Not exactly. Not yet."

"Well, what exactly is your relationship?"

"Why do you want to know?" Penelope felt herself reddening.

Mother Margeaux smiled. "We do not disapprove of Dion. Nor do we disapprove of you going out on dates. We would simply like to know the status of your relationship. After all, we are your mothers."

"I don't know," Penelope admitted. "I don't know what our relationship is."

"Are you planning to go out sometime?"

"I told you, I don't know."

"But you do like him?" Mother Felice asked.

"Yes!" She stood, exasperated, embarrassed. "May I be excused? I really do have a lot of homework."

"Yes, you may be excused." Mother Margeaux looked around the table. There were no objections.

Penelope strode quickly from the room, running upstairs, taking the steps two at a time. She had avoided the Big Discussion she'd been anticipating, but her mothers' quiet probing had been even worse. There seemed something secretive about it, something that made her uneasy. The questions themselves had been innocent enough, but they had been asked in a manner that was anything but innocent, and as Penelope flopped down on her bed, she could not get out of her mind the satisfied way in which Mother Margeaux had smiled.

TWENTY

Lieutenant Horton stood in front of the printer and read the report as it ran out. He held up the long roll of perforated paper and frowned as he read the DUI statistics. Up two hundred percent from last month? Up a hundred and ninety-six percent from the same period last year? That wasn't possible. Someone must have made a mistake. He dropped the paper. The printer continued to noisily click out its dot matrix, one line at a time.

Now he would have to spend an hour double-checking the input.

He was going to have a lot of comp time accumulated by the time this was all over. In addition to working full-time on the murder investigations, he still had to perform his regular duties, which meant that he was putting in twelve-hour days as well as working weekends.

He took a drink of his lukewarm coffee, put the paper cup down on one of the shelves housing the tech manuals, and bent down to peer through the printer's smoked plastic window at the latest lines of the report.

Drunk and disorderly arrests up a hundred and fifteen percent.

Something was definitely wrong.

When he had transferred here from San Francisco over a decade ago, Horton had been surprised by the relatively few alcohol-related arrests made in Napa and the surrounding communities. Incidents of public drunkenness, reckless endangerment, DUI, etc., were surprisingly low, particularly for a region so heavily devoted to the production of alcohol. It was as if people, overly conscious of the area's economic dependence on liquor, made a special effort to behave responsibly when it came to imbibing. It was something that had remained constant during his tenure on the force and which he and everyone else took for granted.

Horton sat down on the low, empty table next to the door and waited for the report to finish printing. He pulled a bottle of Tylenol from his coat pocket, shook out two caplets, and washed them down with the last of the coffee. He didn't have a headache, but he could feel the blood thumping in his temples and his thoughts were heavy, muffled, coming to him as if through a thick fog.

He stared across the room at a faded poster someone had tacked up on the wall years ago: a stylized cancan girl kicking up her leg in a dance. The poster reminded him for some reason of Laura, and he found himself wondering what had happened to her. It was not a thought that occurred to him often these days, but even after all these years it was one tinged with more than a hint of sadness. The alimony payments had stopped when she'd remarried, and though he'd thought at the time that he should still keep in contact with her, still keep tabs on her whereabouts, he had not made the effort. He had moved three times since then. There was no telling how many times she had moved. Periodically, he got the urge to run her name through the computer and find out where she lived now, but he didn't know her current last name, was not even sure if she was still married to the same man.

It was strange to think that two people who had once been so close could now not even know if the other was still alive. There'd been a time when he had honestly believed that he could not live without her, when he had selfishly hoped that they would both live well into their nineties and that he would die first so he would not have to go on alone. He'd been alone for over fifteen years now, and the woman with whom he'd shared his most intimate secrets, his worst fears, was now a stranger, sharing the hopes and dreams of another man he did not even know.

Horton slid off the table, stood. What the hell was he doing thinking about this? Why was he wasting his time on this nostalgia crap? There were enough problems for him to be concentrating on in the here and now. More than enough.

The murders for one.

The murder investigations were not going at all as planned. The police were doing everything they could—interviewing friends, family, and business acquaintances, combing the nearby neighborhoods for possible witnesses, quizzing the appropriate file suspects—but there was no real evidence to go on, and despite the sophistication of their techniques, none seemed to be forthcoming. With the obvious cult angle, he would have thought Fowler's murder would be a little easier to work up a lead on, but both investigations were stalled at the starting point. They were simply going through the motions, following procedure, hoping something new would turn up. If these two killings were connected—and everyone from the chief on down believed they were—the murderer knew his stuff. He was obviously crazy, but he was just as obviously not stupid.

And that was a terrifying combination.

Jack Hammond thought it was something else entirely. He wouldn't say exactly *what* he thought was happening—apparently he belonged to some cult or fringe group that required a vow of secrecy—but he'd hinted around about resurrection and prophecy and all sorts of wacky religious crap. Which was why he'd been taken off the case.

Horton walked into the hallway, glanced up and down the corridor. At the far end he saw the captain still in his office, his silhouette outlined clearly against the lit window that faced the hall. As Horton watched, he saw the older man discreetly pour a shot of whisky into his McDonald's coffee cup. Horton frowned. Captain Furnier drinking on the job? He could not believe what he was seeing. The captain was the most by-the-book officer he had ever met, a man who went into rages if staff meetings were not conducted according to proper procedure. This was definitely not like him.

Hammond. Furnier.

There were a lot of weird things going on.

The captain looked up, out of the window, saw him.

Horton immediately ducked back into the computer room. He stood in front of the printer and began folding the long roll of reports.

A moment later, he heard the captain's heavy footsteps pass in the hallway, but he did not look up and the captain did not stop by.

Officer Dennis McComber pulled out of the Winchell's parking lot, cinnamon roll in hand, a Styrofoam cup of coffee between his legs. He cruised down Main toward the periphery of town, eyes open for drinkers, tokers, partiers, parkers, the usual Friday night offenders. He was glad to be on the street again, happy to be driving. It was routine duty, but it sure beat working with Horton on homicide. It sure as hell beat that. That glamour shit might look good on TV, might impress the women in conversation, but it was a creepy damn business and he didn't like it one bit.

He drove across the Spring Street intersection and slowed down as he passed the park. He was tempted to shine his light in the dark section of the parking lot, underneath the trees, but he was still eating the cinnamon roll and his fingers were sticky. He finished the pastry and drove with his knees while he pulled out a Wet One and cleaned his hand.

He took a sip of coffee. Working homicide was different than he'd thought it would be. A lot different. The academy training had taught him what to do and how to act, but it had not prepared him emotionally for the experience. All the films and reenactments in the world could not adequately simulate the intense pressure and heightened reality of an actual murder scene.

And no dummy or playacting test subject, no matter how good the makeup, could ever fill in for a real corpse.

Particularly not a corpse that had been mutilated.

McComber shivered, turning down the air conditioning though he knew the coldness came from within. He'd had nightmares about Fowler the watchman ever since that day at the winery. Nightmares in which Fowler, bloody and faceless, had stood in the fermenting cave and screamed endlessly with the raw, open hole that had been his mouth. Nightmares in which Fowler had chased him through a tortured, shadowed landscape of living grape-vines to a monstrous vat of black wine. Nightmares in which he had gone to work and everyone in the station had been horribly, bloodily disfigured.

Last night he'd gotten drunk, really drunk, blackout drunk, for the first time since he'd met Julie. She hadn't understood, had been frightened of him, and though part of him had wanted to seek her sympathy, another part had wanted to hit her, hurt her, make her pay for the way he was feeling, and he'd had to force himself not to punch her in the face.

He turned onto Grapevine Road. He took another sip of coffee, but it tasted like shit, and he rolled down the win-dow, dumped out the rest of the cup's contents, and tossed the cup itself onto the floor of the cruiser. He was coming up on one of the valley's busier lovers' lanes, and he slowed down, hoping for some action.

He was rewarded with a red Mazda parked underneath a tree by the side of the road.

McComber slowed, cut his lights, and pulled in back of the vehicle. He grabbed his flashlight, got out of the po-lice car and, putting his right hand on the butt of his pis-tol, walked forward. As his eyes adjusted to the darkness, he saw a teenage boy in the passenger seat of the car, leaning back, his eyes closed, a look of relaxed joy on his face. A moment later, a girl lifted her head from his lap, pushed the hair out of her eyes and back around her neck, and lowered her head once again.

McComber grinned. This was more like it. This was going to be fun.

He put on his most serious expression, strode up to the car, and rapped loudly on the driver's side window, shin-ing the flashlight and peering in.

The chief's daughter sat up and stared back at him dumbly, fingers still grasping the boy's hard, wet penis.

McComber gazed at the pair, shocked. They were both hopelessly drunk. He could see it in their glassy-eyed stares, in the dumb slackness of their mouths. His light reflected off sweaty skin. The fun had gone out of this scare, but he decided to pretend he didn't know who the girl was, and he motioned for the boy to roll down the window.

He waited until the window was down before speaking. He tried not to look at the still stiff organ peeking out from between the folds of hastily pulled up pants. "What are you two doing, exercising in there?" His voice was threatening, official, but though the boy seemed frightened, the chief's daughter was not intimidated.

She picked up a wine bottle from the floor and took a swig, not looking at him. "Fuck you."

Chief's daughter or no chief's daughter, it was time to play hardball. "May I see your driver's license?" McComber said.

The boy licked his lips nervously. "Look, we're sorry. Please don't—"

"Your license," McComber repeated.

The boy dug through his pants and pulled out his wallet. His hands were shaking as he withdrew his driver's license.

"Mr. Holman?" McComber said, reading the name next to the poorly shot photo. "Will you and the young lady please step out of the car?"

"We didn't—"

"Please step out of the car."

He hadn't intended to do anything but scare them, put them through a few sobriety tests, then let them off with a warning, but as he stood there, the wine bottle few over the roof of the Mazda toward his head.

"Fuck off, pig!" the chief's daughter yelled.

The glass shattered on the asphalt.

He knew he was acting out of anger and not reason, that he was making what could be a career decision, but he strode around the car, yanked the staggering girl to her feet, and twisted her arm around her back.

"Police brutality!" she yelled.

"If you do not cooperate, young lady, you will be spending the rest of the night in a jail cell."

"She didn't mean it," the boy said, apologizing for her.

"Fuck you!" The girl was sobbing, but there was no sadness in her tears, only anger and frustration. She glared at McComber defiantly. "It's almost here, and there's not a fucking thing you can do about it!"

"What's almost here?"

"Him!"

"Who?"

Her expression clouded; her gaze seemed to lose some of its intensity. "I don't know." Her voice was confused but still defiant.

"Look, I'll take her home. She's sorry—"

"Shut up," McComber snapped.

It's almost here.

He'd nearly understood that, it had almost meant something to him, and that was why he now held her without moving, why he wanted the two of them to shut up so he could have time to think. Even outside the car, he could smell the wine they had been drinking. It hung heavy in the air, recharged every few seconds by the girl's exhalation of breath, and it made him feel slightly nauseous, gave him a minor headache.

It's almost here.

He felt that too, had felt it ever since he'd seen the watchman's body at the winery, though he never would have thought to express it that way. There was a palpable feeling in the air, a building tension, like the accumulation of energy or the gathering of power or . . . He wasn't sure. But something was coming to a head. Something he did not understand and probably would not believe in if he did. Something the chief's daughter had obviously tapped into.

He suddenly wanted a drink himself.

He looked toward the boy, now buckling his pants. "Mr. Holman?" he said.

The boy looked at him, frightened. "Yes?"

"I could run you in for being a minor and being under the influence, for having an open container of alcohol in your vehicle, for indecent exposure and, if I wanted to get nasty, for statutory rape." He stared at the boy, waited for a response, was glad to see that there was none. "But I'm going to let you off with a warning this time on the condition that you lock your car and walk—I said, *walk*—the little lady home. If I come by later and find that this car had been moved, that will mean that you were also driving under the influence, and I am afraid that is an offense I will not be able to overlook. Do I make myself clear?"

The boy nodded gratefully.

"Fuck you!" the chief's daughter yelled.

"Now get Miss Charm out of here before I haul her in on a drunk and disorderly charge." He let the girl go, and her boyfriend immediately took her arm, pulling her away.

"You can't stop it!" she called. "There's nothing you can do!"

McComber walked slowly back to his car, ignoring her taunts, wondering if he should tell the chief about what had happened or if he should try to keep it quiet. The good mood which had been his upon initially approaching the Mazda had long since fled, and now he no longer felt like cruising the streets at all.

He felt like drinking.

He felt like getting drunk.

It's almost here.

He did not acknowledge the boy's wave as he passed the two teenagers on his way down the road.

TWENTY-ONE

The ground was wet, the sky overcast, the air redolent with the fresh, invigorating odor of recent rain. Above the rooftops, the trees appeared almost black against the gray background, their heavy leaves and branches disturbed only by the cool northerly breeze which blew against his face. Dion felt happy, for no real reason at all. Days like this inevitably put him in a good mood, no matter what had happened the night before. He breathed deeply, smelled fireplace smoke, exhaled, saw steam. In a puddle on the sidewalk he saw a reflection of the sky, silhouettes of trees and rooftops, a charcoal sketch.

Fall had always been his favorite season. While most kids linked the seasons with the school year, waiting anxiously for summer and school's end, dreading fall and the resumption of classes, his perceptions had always been more instinctual, less tied to the workings of the material world. He loved fall, always had. There was something about this time of year which made him feel healthy and alive. Autumn was usually assumed to be nature's dotage, the season before its death, but as he had learned from Penelope, plants such as grapes belied that assumption, bucked the general trend, died when others bloomed, bloomed when others died, and he himself felt a little like that.

A van drove by, its tires hissing on the wet asphalt. He waited a moment, then crossed the street, stepping into and splashing through a shallow puddle. Looking down, he saw muddy black water.

Black water.

He felt cold suddenly, and he shivered, his mood dampened by the remembrance of last night's dream.

It had been a bad one.

In the dream his mom had been staggering through a meadow, drunk and naked, holding in one hand an overflowing skin of wine, in the other a severed penis, blood still dripping from its torn, ragged end. There were other women nearby, also naked, also drunk, but his attention was focused only on his mom. He'd stepped forward, through a pile of rustling leaves. She turned and saw him and let out a great, excited whoop of joy. She dropped the wineskin, dropped the penis, and began dancing, a mad celebratory dance of wild abandon. A goat sprinted by, passing directly in front of her, and she leaped at it, grabbing the animal around the neck and twisting it to the ground. There was an audible snap of bone, and then she was on top of the goat, ripping with fingers, tearing with teeth, ecstatically smearing the blood on herself.

In the space between her legs, he could clearly see the goat's hairy erection.

And then the other women joined his mom, all of them coalescing into one madly carnal, wildly anarchic group of grasping hands and hungry mouths. His mom grabbed the goat's erection, yanking it out and proudly holding it aloft.

And then he was alone in the darkness, floating face up in the waters of a black river, everything, all of his thoughts, all of his feelings, all of his memories, fading, going, gone until he was a blank nothing drifting onward into a bigger nothingness, the black water streaming through his ears, through his nose, through his mouth to fill him up.

He'd awakened cold, shivering, his blanket kicked off the foot of the bed, feeling . . . not frightened exactly, but . . . disturbed. He'd felt depressed as well, filled with a strange sense of loss.

The feelings faded with breakfast, were washed away with his shower, and were forgotten when he saw the gorgeous fall day outside.

But now he was worried. He walked slowly down the sidewalk toward school. There was something about the dreams he'd had lately that didn't sit right with him. They didn't feel like ordinary nightmares, did not seem to come from the same subconscious pool as the dreams he usually had. He was not sure what about them made him feel this way, but whatever it was had him scared.

"Hey, dickmeat!"

Dion looked up to see Kevin hanging out the passenger window of Paul's Mustang.

"Need a ride?"

He shook his head, waved them on. "I need the exercise."

"I thought you got your exercise doing push-ups on Penelope!"

He pointed toward Kevin, then pointed toward his crotch. "Your breakfast, bud!"

Kevin laughed. "Later!"

The Mustang took off, tires squealing on the wet road, splashing water.

Black water, Dion thought, looking at the spray.

He shivered.

Kevin closed his locker. "She called it what? The commune?"

"The combine."

Kevin thought for a moment. "You know," he said, "there used to be a religious cult that ran a winery around Santa Rosa, back, I don't know, a long time ago. Fountaingrove, I think it was called. And it was run by a cult called the Brotherhood of the New Life. If I remember right, they used to use their wine in ceremonies. This sounds a little like that."

"Penelope's family is not a cult."

"It doesn't sound just a little spacey to you?"

Dion twisted his combination lock, pulled on it to make sure it had caught. "A little," he admitted.

"Just keep your eyes open." Kevin grinned. "You've got a rare opportunity here. You're seeing all possible permutations of the female Daneam. You're seeing Penelope's future. In twenty years she's going to look like one of them. Acorns don't fall far from the tree and all that good crap. So you've been given fair warning. If you don't like what you see, back out now. Save yourself some grief and heartache."

Dion tried to smile. "I like what I see," he said.

"I hope so."

Dion tried not to think of Penelope's family as he and Kevin walked to class.

Bacchus, Mr. Holbrook wrote on the board. *Dionysus.* He underlined the words, wiped the chalk dust on his pants, and turned to face the class.

"Bacchus, or Dionysus," the teacher explained, "was probably the most important of the Olympian dieties. More important even than Zeus or Apollo. There are not as many stories about him, but the fact remains that he was, throughout this time, the most popular of the gods, and his followers were by far the most loyal. This can be attributed in large part to the fact that he was the only Olympian god who was both mortal and divine."

A student near the back of the room raised his hand.

"Yes?" the teacher said.

"Which name are we going to be tested on?" the student asked. "Bacchus or Dionysus?"

"We will be referring to him by his proper Greek name in this class: Dionysus. You may be tested on both."

The class was filled with the sound of furious scribbling.

"As I said, Dionysus was both mortal and divine, the son of Zeus and Semele, the princess of Thebes. Zeus was in love with the princess, and after impregnating her while in one of his many guises he swore by the river Styx that he would grant any wish she desired. Zeus' wife, Hera, jealous as always, put the idea into Semele's mind that her wish was to see Zeus in all of his glory as the king of heaven, and this is what the princess asked for. Zeus knew that no mortal could behold him in his true form and live, but he had sworn by the Styx and could not break that oath. So he came to the princess as himself, and Semele died beholding his awesome splendor, but not before Zeus took the child that was about to be born."

Mr. Holbrook turned back to the chalkboard and wrote two more words: *Apollonian. Dionysian.*

"Over the years, over the centuries, Dionysus has usually been misunderstood and misinterpreted. In general, these two words have come to mean 'good' and 'evil.' If something is described as 'Apollonian,' that means it is connected with light and goodness, order and rightness. The word 'Dionysian,' on the other hand, applies to the dark and chaotic, and is often connected with evil. Although Dionysus was by no means a bad or evil god, this mistake is easily understood. As a god who was half human, half divine, Dionysus had a dual nature. This duality was further emphasized by the fact that he was the god of the vine, the god of wine. Wine can make men mellow, and it can make men mean. Likewise, Dionysus could be likable and generous, warm, good and giving. He could also be cruel and brutally savage. Just as the same wine that brings men together in camaraderie can also make them drunk and drive them to commit degrading acts and horrible crimes, Dionysus could bring to his worshipers joy or pain, happiness or suffering. He could be both man's benefactor and his destroyer. Unfortunately, over the years the dark side of Dionysus has tended to overshadow his good side, to the point where today most people's picture of him is highly distorted."

Mr. Holbrook turned back to the board. *Dionysian Rites,* he wrote. *Bacchanal.*

"We will now look at the worship of Dionysus, which was done often through drunken orgies and festivals of debauchery."

Dion felt a pencil in his back. "Now we're getting to the good stuff," Kevin whispered.

Dion laughed.

Vella was absent, Kevin had a dentist's appointment, and for the first time Dion ate lunch alone with Penelope. He was glad Kevin wasn't there, but he felt guilty about it. He liked Kevin, enjoyed his friend's company, but at the same time he found that he preferred being alone with Penelope.

The two of them walked through the cafeteria line— Dion picking up a hamburger and Coke, Penelope a salad and juice—and sat at a table near the low wall which separated the eating area from the softball field.

The conversation was easy, comfortable, free and wide-ranging, shifting from music to school to plans for the future.

"What do you want to do with your life?" Penelope asked. "What do you want to be?"

He smiled. "When I grow up?"

She nodded, smiled back. "When you grow up."

"I don't know," he said. "I used to think I'd like being an archaeologist or paleontologist, dig for fossils and artifacts, travel to exotic locations. I thought it would be exciting."

"Exciting?" She laughed. "You've seen too many Indiana Jones movies."

"Probably," he admitted. "Then I thought I'd like to be a dentist. You know, have a big waiting room with lots of magazines and a saltwater aquarium, work five hours a day in a pleasant environment and rake in big bucks."

"Sounds good."

"I suppose. But I've changed my mind since then."

"What do you want to be now?"

"A teacher, I think."

"Why?"

"I could lie and say it's because I want to help open young minds and expose them to great truths, but actually it's because I'd get summers off. I'm spoiled. I like vacations. I like getting my two-month summer, two-week Christmas vacation, and one-week Easter vacation. I don't think I could survive getting two weeks a year, period." He took a bite of his hamburger. "What about you?"

She shrugged. "The winery. What else?"

"What if you didn't want to work at the winery? What then?"

"But I do."

"What if you didn't? What if you wanted to be a computer programmer? What would your ... your mothers do?"

"I don't know."

"They don't have anyone else to leave the place to, do they? You don't have any brothers or sisters."

"I don't have any other relatives."

He looked at her. "None?"

She stared out across the field, then turned back toward him. She wrinkled her nose mischievously. "What if you could be anything you wanted? Not anything practical or realistic. Your secret fantasy."

"Rock star," he said.

She laughed.

"Thousands of girls screaming for me, groupies galore."

"Hey!"

He smiled, drank his Coke. "You really don't have any other relatives? Just your mothers?"

She reddened. "I don't want to talk about it, okay? Some other time."

"Okay. I understand." Dion finished his hamburger, rolled up the foil wrapper, and tossed it at the nearest trash can. It missed by several feet, and he stood up, picked it off the ground, and dropped it in. He turned around. Through the thin material of Penelope's blouse he could see the outline of her bra. He sat down next to her. "So what are we?" he asked. He tried to make the question sound casual. "Are we friends or are we . . . more than friends?"

She licked her lips, said nothing.

His heart was beating rapidly in his chest, and he suddenly wished he hadn't said anything. "What are we?" he asked again.

"I don't know."

"I don't either." His voice sounded too high.

They were both silent for a moment.

"I want to be more than friends." Penelope said softly.

Neither of them said anything. The surrounding lunch noises faded from background sound into something else, something less. They looked into each other's eyes, neither knowing what to say but neither turning away. The silence was awkward, but it was a pleasant awkwardness, the welcome discomfort of initial intimacy. Dion smiled, embarrassed. "Does this mean that we're, uh, like boyfriend and girlfriend?"

She nodded but looked down at the ground. "If you want to be."

"I want to be," he said.

There was a second's hesitation, an instant of uncertainty, then he took her hand in his. His palms were sweaty. He was embarrassed by their sweatiness, but not embarrassed enough to move them away. He squeezed her hand.

She squeezed back.

He let out the breath he'd been holding. "Well, that wasn't so hard, was it?"

"It wasn't?" She laughed.

He laughed.

And then they were laughing together.

Dion met with Mr. Holbrook after school.

He hadn't discussed the independent study idea with Holbrook since the teacher had originally brought it up, had, in fact, nearly forgotten about it, but he'd received a pink summons notice during his last period, requesting that he meet the mythology instructor after class, and after dumping his books in his locker, he made his way through the rapidly emptying hall to Holbrook's room.

The classroom was empty when he arrived. He waited five minutes, but the teacher still hadn't shown. He would have left then and there, but a message on the blackboard read:

Dion,
    Please wait. I will be back shortly.

There were other words on the blackboard as well, most of them half-erased. Many appeared to be foreign, the characters part of a non-English alphabet, and while Dion didn't know how he knew, he realized that they were entirely unrelated to classwork or school.

That frightened him for some reason.

The door of the room opened, and Holbrook walked in. He was carrying what looked like a folded sheet atop an armload of supplies, and he placed them all on top of his desk. "So, Dion," he said. "How're things going?"

"Well, there haven't been any big changes in my life during my afternoon classes."

Holbrook chuckled, but there was no humor in the

sound. "That's true. We just saw each other this morning, didn't we? In class."

Dion had been leaning against the back counter, and he straightened up. There was something about the teacher's tone of voice that seemed odd, off, unusual.

Threatening.

That was it exactly.

He stared at the instructor, his stomach knotting up. The hostility had been vague, veiled, but it had been there, in the voice, and it was there now in the look the teacher was giving him from across the room. What did Holbrook have against him?

He suddenly realized that the classroom door was closed.

"I . . . got your summons." He held up the pink notice, aware that his voice was quavering, wishing he could stop it.

"Yes," Holbrook said.

"Is this about the independent study thing? I already told you I don't want to do it."

"Why?" the teacher asked. "Afraid of being alone with me?" He grinned.

This was getting too damn weird. Dion started toward the door. "I'm sorry," he said. "I have to go."

"Afraid I'll attack you?"

Dion stopped, turned toward the teacher. The supplies on the desk, he saw now, were rolled-up scrolls of parchment. "Is there a reason you called me here?" he said coldly. He met the teacher's eyes.

Holbrook looked away, moving back a step. "Why do you *think* I asked you here?"

He wished Kevin was with him. If he'd had his friend's moral support, he would have replied, "Because you're a pervert, that's why." But Kevin wasn't here, and he wasn't brave enough to talk back to the teacher.

"I don't know," he said.

The teacher had pulled open the top drawer of his desk. Dion craned his neck, trying to see what Holbrook's hands were fiddling with, caught sight of what looked like a long, shiny knife amidst the pencils and paper clips.

The door to the room opened, and Dion jumped, startled.

"Wait a minute!" Holbrook said.

Dion was not sure if the teacher was talking to him or to the group of men walking into the room, but he quickly pushed his way past the men, through the doorway, into the hall. He was sweating, his heart pounding, and the first thing he noticed was that the school seemed to be empty. There were no faculty or students in sight.

He turned, caught the last of the men looking at him, and quickly sprinted down the hallway toward the exit. There'd been five men altogether, and each of them had been carrying scrolls and white cloth—just like Holbrook. Dion didn't know if he'd been invited to a Klan meeting or what, but there was something about the situation that didn't sit right with him, and he did not stop running until he was outside the building and on the sidewalk headed toward home.

TWENTY-TWO

Pastor Robens looked out over the half-empty church. He tried to smile, though smiling was the last thing he felt like doing at the moment. Three weeks ago, when church attendance had started to drop, he'd attributed it to a flu bug that was going around. Two weeks ago, he'd blamed the playoffs. But last week, as his flock continued to dwindle, as the number of people coming to the already poorly attended fellowship fell to single digits and as the spaces between people in the pews on Sunday became bigger, he'd had to admit that there was something seriously wrong.

He'd spent the last five days trying to nail down the problem, trying to determine what was happening. He'd gone over his notes for the past two months, looking for anything offensive he might have said in one of his sermons, something that might have driven people away, but he had found nothing. He'd even called some of the long-time parishioners who'd quit attending Sunday services and asked them if anything was the matter, if there was some reason why they had stopped coming to worship. To a person, they said everything was fine and promised to show up on Sunday.

None of them were before him now.

And six other churchgoers were missing.

Pastor Robens folded his hands and smiled at the people who had shown up as the organist finished playing. His smile was false, a mask. He did not feel happy today, he did not feel at peace.

He was worried.

The last notes of the hymn faded.

Pastor Robens bowed his head. "Let us pray."

* * *

Polly Thrall gobbled the wafer and enthusiastically gulped the wine. Father Ibarra smiled at her, gave his blessing, and moved to the next person, Bill Bench. He looked over Bill's head at the empty pews, then down at the double row of kneeling men and women. Overall attendance was down, but participation in communion was up.

Way up.

He should have been happy about that. But he wasn't. There was something about the eagerness with which his parishioners drank their small sip of wine which seemed to him sacriligious, almost defiantly so. They were performing the most holy of rituals, enthusiastically going through all of the proper motions, but there seemed something wrong about it, something blasphemous, and he found their enthusiasm both unhealthy and unchristian. They appeared to be more interested in the wine than the ritual, though that did not make any sense to him.

Bill ate the proffered wafer, greedily swallowed the wine.

Father Ibarra smiled, gave his blessing, and moved on.

He didn't like the way things were going.

He didn't like it at all.

TWENTY-THREE

The restaurant was nothing like he'd expected. From its name, and from its stately, rustic, vaguely European exterior, Dion had imagined the Foxfire Inn to be a tastefully elegant eating establishment, a dark dining room filled with Victorian table settings, expensive chandeliers, and dimly heard classical music. Inside it was dark, all right, but the booths were covered with red and rather shabby naugahyde, and the plain walls were decorated with sportsmen's memorabilia: moose heads, antlers, guns. Through the open doorway which led into the smoky bar, he could see neon beer signs and could hear the hyperactive jabbering of a sports announcer from a too-loud TV.

Things were not turning out the way he'd planned.

But Penelope was taking it all in stride. In his mind he had mapped out every moment of the evening, had practiced each intended topic of conversation, and so far nothing was occurring in the way he'd foreseen. The perfect romantic evening he'd envisioned was turning out to be a series of barely avoided misadventures.

But it didn't seem to matter. Penelope had merely laughed when he'd left his wallet at the Shell station and had to turn back for it. She'd politely ignored the fact that when he'd come to the door to say hello to her mothers, his zipper had been down. She'd registered no disappointment when she saw the inferior interior of the "nice" restaurant he'd promised to take her to and for which she had worn her best dress.

The logistics of the evening had turned out to be a nightmare, but Penelope had turned out to be better than he had dared dream.

The food, to be fair, was not bad, and they ate slowly, talking. He told her of his life, she told him of hers. Their rapport was immediate and instinctually trusting, and even though this was only their first date, Dion shared with her thoughts and feelings that he had never shared with anyone else, that he thought he would never share with anyone else. He felt he could tell her anything, and that both scared him and made him feel exhilarated.

Two hours flew by.

After they'd finished eating, the busboy cleared everything but their water glasses, and their waitress returned. "Is there anything else I can get you?" she asked.

Dion looked questioningly at Penelope, but she shook her head. "I guess not," he said.

"I'll be back in a minute with your check."

Dion nodded and smiled, but as he looked at Penelope across the table, he realized that he didn't know how much money to leave for a tip. The dinner had gone surprisingly well, much better than he had expected or had reason to hope, but he had another chance to blow it right here. If he left a tip that was too small, she would think him cheap and miserly. On the other hand, if he left a tip that was too large, she would think him foolish, since she already knew he wasn't rich. But how much was too little in this instance? How much was too much?

"I'll get the tip," Penelope said.

He stared at her. It was as if she had read his mind. But he shook his head anyway. "No," he said.

"You paid for the meal. It's the least I can do." She opened her purse, took out three one dollar bills, and placed them on the table.

Three dollars.

Relaxing now, he picked up the bills and handed them back. "No," he said firmly. "I'll get it."

She smiled. "Macho guy." But she put away the money.

They had paid the bill and were halfway to the door when Dion heard a woman's voice call out, "Young man!" He looked toward the source and saw, off to his left, an elderly woman seated alone at a small table. She was in her late fifties or early sixties and was wearing a tight brightly colored dress inappropriate for both her age and the era. Her dyed blond hair was frozen in an unattractive beehive, and even in the dim light he could see the thick texture of her makeup. She winked at him.

He thought uncomfortably of his mother. It was too easy for him to see her as this old woman, alone and desperate, trying pathetically to recapture days that had long since passed her by.

"Young man!" the woman repeated. Her voice was high, hoarse.

Dion turned to go.

"She's talking to you," Penelope said. "Go see what she wants."

"No. She's talking to someone else."

"Young man!"

"Go see what she wants. Be nice."

Dion walked across the carpeted floor of the darkened room to the old woman's table. She was wearing no bra; he could see her large breasts and the points of her nipples beneath the tight material of her dress. He was disgusted at himself for noticing.

"Sit down," the woman said, gesturing toward the chair next to her.

He shook his head. "We have to go."

This close he could smell the liquor. It hung about her table like strong, cheap perfume, permeating everything, and when she spoke it doubled in intensity. The woman grabbed his arm with bony fingers. He saw liver spots on the wrinkled flesh beneath her bracelet. "See that fish up there?" the woman asked. She pointed to an oversize plastic marlin mounted on the wall behind him. He was aware that people at the tables nearby were looking at him, giggling. His face felt hot.

"See that fish?"

He nodded dumbly.

"The owner of this restaurant caught that fish."

He looked toward Penelope for help, but she was merely looking at him, her face unreadable.

"He caught that fish on the wall."

"Yeah," Dion said.

"The owner caught that fish."

"Well, I have to go now." He tried to pull away.

The woman's grip tightened on his arm. 'That same fish right there. The owner caught that fish."

And suddenly he wanted to smack her, to hit her in the face. The old woman continued to babble drunkenly, inanely, her eyes glued in their fixed position, her mouth open and closing like that of a ventriloquist's dummy, and he wanted to punch her hard, to feel his fist connect with the bone beneath her skin, to hear her cry, to hear her scream as he beat her.

The smell of the alcohol was making him dizzy. He pulled away. "That fish is plastic," he said.

"The owner caught that fish!" The woman sounded as though she was about to cry. Her breasts shifted beneath her tight dress.

"The owner didn't catch that fish. That fish is plastic. And you're drunk." He hurried across the room to Penelope. He heard people at the tables behind him giggling.

"He caught that fish! That same fish there!"

"Come on," Dion said. He took Penelope's hand and pulled her toward the front door.

"Have a nice night," the hostess said as they hurried past her and outside.

The night air was cool and crisp, fresh and clean. The sounds of the restaurant were cut off as the heavy wooden door closed behind them.

"What was that about?" Penelope asked.

Dion shook his head, taking a deep breath. "The old woman was drunk."

"I know, but I mean why did you overreact like that? I thought you were going to hit her."

"Did you?"

"It looked like it."

"It was just . . . I don't know, claustrophobia, I guess. I have a slight headache. I had to get out of there."

She looked concerned. "Are you all right?"

"Yeah, I'm fine." The cool air was already making him feel better. "I don't know what came over me. I just couldn't stay in there." He shook his head, smiled at her. "Let's go. It's a school night, and I need to get you home."

"Are you sure you're okay?"

"I'm fine."

Hand in hand, they walked down the sidewalk to the parking lot, the sound of their heels loud in the quiet. Dion glanced at the news rack as they passed by.

And stopped, holding his breath.

On the front page of the paper was a photo of a man with a mustache.

The man who had spent the night with his mom.

He did not have to read the headline to know that the man had been murdered.

"What is it?" Penelope asked.

He realized that he was squeezing her hand, and he lessened his grip. He licked his lips, which were suddenly dry. "Nothing," he said. He stared at the picture, thought of meeting the man in the hallway at night, thought of seeing his mother in the kitchen the next morning.

Thought of the blood on her sleeve.

He took a quarter from his pocket, dropped it in the machine, and opened the cover to grab a copy of the paper.

"What is it?" Penelope asked, reading the headline. She looked at him. "Do you know that man?"

Dion folded the paper, put it under his arm. He shook his head. "No," he said. "I don't."

He led the way across the parking lot to the car.

His mom was gone when he came home, and there was no note left for him on the refrigerator. All of the lights in the house were off, which meant that she'd left while it was still light outside, probably only a little after he had.

He deliberately placed the paper on the front table—folded, photo up—where she would be sure to see it.

He went to bed.

He was half-asleep when she bustled into his room, drunk and crying, sitting down heavily on the side of his bed. He sat up. Through blurry, half-focused eyes he could see that the digital clock said one-something.

His mom hugged him close, and he could feel beneath her blouse the softness of her body. She smelled sweetly of wine, sourly of breath, and he thought of the old woman at the restaurant. One of her hands massaged his bare back, and he tried to pull away, backing against the headboard.

She let him go, stopped crying, and suddenly turned on him angrily. "What's the matter?" she demanded. "Are you drunk?"

"No!" he said.

"You better not be. If I ever smell alcohol on your breath, you're out of this house. You're old enough to take care of yourself now, and if you don't abide by my rules, you're gone. Do you understand me?"

"Why?" He was getting ready to argue a position in which he did not believe, but he wanted to hurt her.

"Because I say so. Because it's wrong."

"It's not wrong when you go out and get wasted and bring some guy home and fuck his—"

She slapped him hard across the face, a slap as painful as it was loud. He angrily gathered up his covers, scooted to the opposite side of the bed. His cheek was stinging. Unwanted tears formed in his eyes.

She sat there for a moment, inert, blank, then suddenly began crying again. She cried openly, unashamedly. Her face turned red. A torrent of tears rolled down her cheeks. A thread of saliva hung from her mouth, and she did not bother to wipe it away. "Don't make the same mistakes I made." Her words were distorted by her sobs.

He could still feel the pain on the skin of his cheek. "If they're mistakes, why do you keep doing them?"

"I don't know. I wish I could tell you. I wish I had an easy answer. But I don't. I drink. I smoke. I can't help it. I wish I could say it was a sickness or an addiction, but it's not. It's something else. I don't want to be this way, Dion. But I can't help it."

He stared at her from the other side of the bed. There was an urgency to her manner that made him realize that she was not just drunk but that she'd seen his newspaper. It made him think of the man who had been murdered.

It made him think she had been there when he'd died.

* * *

After Dion dropped her off, Penelope went into the kitchen for a drink of water. She could hear her mothers talking in the living room as she passed, and though she didn't want to disturb them, wanted only to sneak up-stairs and into bed, she heard Mother Margeaux call her name. She dutifully walked through the doorway to greet them.

Mother Margeaux was standing near the fireplace. "Hello, Penelope. How was your date?"

She shrugged. "Fine."

Sitting next to Mother Sheila on the couch, she saw a tall blond woman she didn't recognize. The woman wore a short jean skirt and a tight white blouse which accentu-ated the fullness of her large breasts. The woman smiled at her, and Penelope looked away.

"Where did you go?"

"We just went out to dinner."

"Did you have a good time?"

"Yes, ma'am."

Mother Margeaux smiled. "That's good." She looked at her watch. "We're going to be talking a little while longer, but after our guest leaves, we want to talk about your evening."

"I'm tired. It's late—"

"It's not that late. Take your bath and come back down."

"I don't—"

"Penelope." Mother Margeaux's voice indicated that she would tolerate no argument.

"Yes, Mother. I will."

Penelope retreated upstairs. She got her pajamas out of the dresser, and stole a *People* magazine from Mother Felice's room, bringing it with her to read in the bathtub.

A half hour later, she went back downstairs. She walked into the living room. The blond woman was gone, but all five of her mothers sat on the overstuffed couches, facing her in a semicircle. The arrangement was some-what intimidating. None of her mothers were talking, none were smiling. They were all waiting patiently for her to join them. Mother Margeaux was still wearing the business suit she used when meeting potential clients, an ensemble intended to exude an aura of strength and confidence, and its message was coming through to Penelope loud and clear.

She sat quietly down on the loveseat.

"We are going to talk about sex," Mother Margeaux announced.

Penelope blinked dumbly.

"We have never had this discussion before," Mother Margeaux continued, "although perhaps we should have had it long ago."

Penelope's cheeks felt hot. She looked at her shoes, nervously playing footsie with herself. "I know all this," she said.

"Yes, but I don't think you know about birth control."

"I already know." She wished this agony would end.

"Do you know about the pill? Do you know what an IUD is? A diaphragm? A condom?"

"Yes," she said miserably.

"Well, where did you learn all this?"

"I don't know."

"From school?"

"Yeah, I guess. I just . . . I don't know. From reading. Hearing people talk."

"Have you and Dion discussed this? Have you talked about birth control?"

"Mother!"

"You are a senior in high school, as is Dion. I assume you both have the natural urges universally shared by all young men and women your age. This means that you are probably going to have sex. Your other mothers and I simply want to know if you have talked about it."

Penelope looked embarrassedly away, said nothing.

"Have you kissed him yet?"

"It's none of your business."

"It is our business. Have you thought about having sex with him?"

"Look," Penelope said. "It hasn't gone that far. It may never go that far."

"If it does," Mother Margeaux told her, "we do not want you to use any form of birth control."

"What?" Penelope glanced up, shocked. She looked

from one to the other, but though her mothers were smiling at her tolerantly, it was clear that they were totally serious. She felt embarrassed and confused at the same time. Disoriented. She did not know what to say or how to act.

Mother Janine grinned. "Have you thought about his cock?" she asked.

Penelope stared at her. She had never heard any of her mothers use profanity, aside from an occasional "hell" or "damn," and the sound of such a base word in one of her mothers' mouths sounded disgustingly obscene.

"He has a big one. It's nice and long."

"That will be enough," Mother Margeaux said sternly.

Penelope looked around the semicircle. Her mothers were not outraged, as she would have expected. They were calm, unruffled, acting as though this sort of conversation occurred every day.

What was going on here?

"Don't use any contraceptives," Mother Felice said kindly.

Mother Margeaux and Mother Sheila nodded in agreement.

Mother Margeaux smiled. "Invite him over," she said. "We want you to invite him over for dinner tomorrow. We haven't really had a chance to meet him."

She glanced from mother to mother, confused. One moment they were being totally crazy, the next they were behaving like typical concerned parents. She shook her head in disbelief. "Is this some kind of test or what?"

"Test?" Mother Margeaux laughed. "Heavens, no. And we don't mean to put any pressure on you. But, as you know, we have brought you up in an atmosphere of complete honesty and openness, and we just want to state our position at the outset. I'm sure you will agree that acknowledgement of the reality of this situation is preferable to the clandestine deceit and denial practiced by most families. You are now a woman, faced with a woman's choices, and we recognize that fact."

"It's big." Mother Janine grinned. "His cock is big."

"Janine!" Mother Margeaux shot her a withering glance

which wiped the smile from her face. She turned back toward Penelope. "Will you ask him to dinner?"

She nodded, still too stunned to know how to react. "I'll ask him. I don't know if he'll say yes."

"He will."

They were all silent for a moment, looking at one another.

Penelope stood. "Is that all?"

"Yes. You may go to bed."

She left the room and started up the stairs. Halfway up, she heard Mother Janine's off-center giggle. A moment later, they were all laughing hysterically.

Even Mother Felice.

TWENTY-FOUR

The house was dark when Horton arrived home. The bulb in the living room lamp attached to the timer had obviously burned out. He braille-scanned the metal contents of his key ring on the stoop of the unlit porch, feeling for the smooth roundness of the house key. He found it next to the blocky squareness of the key to his long-discarded Thunderbird, and he used it to open the door, automatically flipping on the light switch as he walked inside.

The house smelled old and closed, of dust and dirty clothes, of previous meals. He walked across the dark shag carpet of the living room. Though the light was on, there was still a dimness about the room, a yellowed hint of shadow which stubbornly fended off all attempts at cheerfulness. It looked, he thought, like what it was. The home of a bachelor. Despite the fact that the rooms had been decorated by his ex-wife, that initial woman's touch had not been updated, refreshed or renewed, and an air of lonely maleness hung over the house. Last night's can of Coors sat in a dried ring of condensation on the crowded coffee table next to a pile of newspapers, a stack of half-opened junk mail, and an empty potato chip bag. Yesterday's socks were balled up at the foot of the couch.

The only sound in the house was the muted hum of the electric clock on the cluttered knickknack shelf above the hi-fi, and he quickly turned on the television, grateful for the noise and companionship it offered. His gaze fell upon the framed family photograph atop the TV, and as always his eyes scanned over it without looking.

He walked into the kitchen. Taking a frozen burrito out of the freezer, he slit the plastic wrapping and popped it into the microwave. He grabbed a beer from the fridge.

Sometimes he wished he didn't have to eat or sleep. Sometimes he wished he could work nonstop. He hated his job, but truth be told, he hated his time off even more. At least when he was working his mind was kept busy, he had something to think about besides his own life.

He downed the beer in three quick swallows, but he found that it wasn't enough. He needed something stronger.

The microwave timer rang, and he took out his burrito, dropping it on a plate and pulling off the wrapper. He opened the cupboard above the refrigerator alcove and withdrew a bottle of scotch. He thought of getting out a glass, but decided against it. He didn't need another glass to wash.

He sat down, ate a bite of burrito, drank a swig of scotch.

The burrito and the bottle were finished at almost the same time.

TWENTY-FIVE

In the light of morning, with an all-news station reciting a litany of last night's events on the radio, with the smell of fresh coffee permeating the kitchen, the idea that his mom could have been involved in someone's death seemed not only far-fetched but ludicrous. He stood in the doorway, watching for a moment as his mom, her back to him, stood at the counter, spreading cream cheese on toast. If she had killed that man, he realized, she would have had to have done so between two o'clock, the time he'd met the man in the hall, and six o'clock, the time she'd come down for breakfast. She would have had to have done so without making a noise, and to have disposed of the body just as silently.

He was thankful that his suspicions had faded. If he had still suspected his mom, he would not have known what to do. Would he have turned her in? Told the police anonymously? Confronted her? Done nothing? He did not know.

His mom either heard him or sensed his presence, for she turned around. There were dark hangover circles around her eyes. She tried to smile at him but only partially succeeded. "I'm sorry about last night," she said. She would not meet his eyes.

He nodded silently, equally embarrassed, and busied himself looking through the refrigerator for orange juice.

"I went out with Margaret and Janine and a few other friends after work, and I guess I had more to drink than I thought."

He frowned. Hadn't she seen the newspaper? He glanced over at her. She appeared chastened, ashamed, but not to the extent that he would have expected. He cleared his throat. "That guy was murdered," he said.

She looked at him blankly.

"Your friend. The guy who spent the night."

"What are you talking about?"

"Didn't you even read the paper?" He shook his head at her and strode purposefully out to the living room, but the newspaper was no longer on the table.

"What did you do with the paper?"

"What paper?"

"The newspaper I put there last night!"

"I don't know what you're talking about."

"It didn't just get up and walk away."

"Dion—"

"I left it there for you!"

"Why?"

He was angry at his mom suddenly. "Because that guy you fucked was murdered! I thought you might be at least mildly interested!"

Her expression hardened. She advanced on him, but he backed up behind the couch. She stopped, pointing at him with a furious finger. "Don't you ever speak that way to me again."

"Fine!" Dion said. "I won't speak to you at all!"

"Fine!"

The two of them glared at each other for a moment. Then his mom turned and stalked back into the kitchen.

Bitch, he thought. *Fucking bitch.*

He went down the hall to his bedroom and slammed the door.

Dion wiped his sweaty hands nervously on his pants and pressed the doorbell. From somewhere inside the huge house came the sound of chimes. A moment later, Penelope opened the door. "Hi," she said shyly.

He smiled. "Hi."

The door opened all the way, and he could see, standing behind Penelope, her mothers. The women, all of them, were wearing identical green dresses—tight dresses which accentuated their figures. He could see dark nipples through the sheer fabric, faint triangles of pentimento pubic hair, and he realized that none of the women were wearing underwear. The knowledge embarrassed him.

Penelope too was wearing green. But her dress was looser, less revealing, and made of a different, thicker material.

All of them were barefoot.

He felt awkward. He was wearing blue jeans and a white shirt, with black tennis shoes, and he felt as though he had committed some type of fashion faux pas.

"Come in," Penelope said. "You didn't have any trouble with the gate, did you?"

He shook his head. "No problem."

"That's good." She smiled and gave him a private bear-with-me look, then gestured behind her. "Dion, I'd like you to meet my mothers. All of them this time." She pointed, one by one, at each of the women in line. "This is Mother Margeaux, Mother Felice, Mother Margaret, Mother Sheila, and Mother Janine." She motioned toward Dion. "Mothers, this is Dion."

The women bowed to him in a strange, awkward-looking half curtsy, a movement that seemed familiar to him but that he could not quite place.

"We are very pleased that you accepted our invitation to dinner," Mother Margeaux said. "We have been told so much about you and have been looking forward to formally meeting you." She smiled at him, a wide white toothpaste-commercial smile that he knew was supposed to be welcoming and ingratiating but which instead made him feel slightly uncomfortable.

"Why don't you all go into the other room?" Mother Felice suggested. "You can talk for a while while I get dinner ready."

"We're having lemon soup and chicken with goat cheese," Penelope said. "I hope you like it. I guess I should have asked you first."

"It sounds delicious," he told her, and it did.

Mother Janine grabbed his hand and pulled him away from Penelope, leading him toward the doorway into the next room. He could feel her smooth fingers lightly pressing against his knuckles. "I'm so honored to finally meet you," she said. "I'm so thrilled."

He looked back at Penelope, but she only smiled, shrugged, and followed them.

"Do you have dreams, Dion?"

"Everybody has dreams," he said.

Mother Janine laughed, a low, sultry laugh that somehow put him on edge. "I dreamed last night that I was a flea bathing in your blood—"

"Janine!" Mother Margeaux said sharply.

His hand was let go, and Penelope sidled next to him. "Sit close to me," she whispered. "I'll help you through this."

They walked into the sitting room.

The dining room table was large and regal, the place settings formal. The room smelled of an unfamiliar odor, a scent at once organic and alien. Dion sat near the head of the table, next to Penelope. The pre-dinner conversation had been neither as awkward as he had feared nor as strange as he had expected. Penelope's mothers had asked the usual parental dating questions, subtextually quizzing him on his intentions toward their daughter, and they seemed to be fairly pleased with his responses.

Dinner appeared to be a different story. The moment they had stepped into the dining room, all conversation had stopped, as though they had walked through some sort of soundproof barrier, and the only noise had been the scraping of chair legs and the quiet slap of bare feet on hardwood floor.

Now the only sound was the slurping of soup.

Dion cleared his throat, intending to talk, if only to pay Mother Felice a generic compliment on the food, but the sound was so loud and out of place in the stillness that he immediately gave up the idea of speaking at all.

Across the table, Mother Sheila picked up the carafe from between the twin soup tureens. "Would you like some wine?" she asked Penelope. Her voice was barely above a whisper.

The girl stared at her in surprise. "I'm not supposed to—"

"It's a special occasion. Besides, you're nearly eighteen. You're mature, responsible. I think you're old enough to handle it." She smiled teasingly. "You've lived in a winery all your life. Don't tell me you've never sneaked a taste."

Penelope blushed.

"I don't think she should have any," Mother Felice said, prim-lipped.

Penelope smiled gratefully at her favorite mother.

"She may have some if she wishes," Mother Margeaux said from the head of the table.

Mother Sheila poured Penelope a glass. "Here you go." She looked questioningly at Dion. "Dion?"

He shifted in his seat, feeling extremely uncomfortable. Having seen the destructive effects of alcohol close up, drinking seemed to him neither exciting nor adult. It seemed wrong and somewhat frightening. Still, he did not want to offend Penelope's mothers. His heart was pounding. "Just a little," he said.

Mother Sheila smiled and poured.

Dion took a sip. He had never tasted alcohol before, though he'd had ample opportunity to do so. It was milder than he expected and more pleasant. His mom had often left open bottles around the house, had breathed her drunken breath on him many a time, and after a while the smell alone had been enough to nearly make him gag.

But this was good. He took another sip, a bigger one.

The table had once again lapsed into silence. The other mothers continued to slurp their soup and drink their wine as Mother Felice went out to check on the chicken.

Dion finished his soup and, realizing that he was the first one done, made a concerted effort to sip his wine slowly. He emptied the glass, and Mother Sheila quickly poured him another. He did not touch it. He felt strange, queasy, slightly dizzy, and as he looked around the table at Penelope's smiling mothers, his first thought was that he had been poisoned. They had put a drug in his wine to kill him in order to keep him away from their daughter. But that was stupid, crazy thinking, and he at least had enough sense to realize that the alcohol was affecting his thought processes, impairing his judgment.

Was this what it felt like to be drunk? If so, he didn't like it.

"Have some more," Mother Sheila said, nodding toward the untouched wineglass.

He shook his head. His brain felt heavy, full. "No, that's enough."

"Come on," Mother Janine told him.

He felt a bare foot rub against his leg, caress his calf.

It was getting hard to think. He glanced at Penelope, next to him, and she looked at him and shrugged, not certain of what behavioral clues to offer.

"Don't you like our vintage?" Mother Margeaux asked him.

He picked up his glass and obligingly took a sip. He nodded. "It's very good," he said.

He took another drink. The feeling in his brain changed, and now he found that he did like it. The heaviness, the queasiness was gone, replaced by a subtle sense of exhilaration.

Penelope's mothers smiled at him.

Mother Felice brought in the chicken.

They ate the rest of the meal in silence.

After dinner, Penelope went upstairs, changed into jeans and a T-shirt, and the two of them went out to the Garden alone. The air was crisply cold, but he felt warmed by an inner fire. The alcohol, he assumed.

He wondered if he was going to be able to drive home.

Penelope led the way over to the same stone bench they'd sat upon the last time they'd come here. Leaning against the wall behind it, Dion saw several long sticks tipped with pine cones. He frowned. Like the women's welcoming curtsy, they too seemed familiar, though he could not quite place the reason why.

"Your mothers are nice," he said. His voice sounded different to himself, louder, amplified. He wondered if Penelope noticed any difference.

She nodded. "They are. Mostly. But sometimes they're a little strange."

He chuckled. "I'll give you that one."

They were sitting close on the bench, and Penelope drew closer. Their hands, lying flat on the stone, were almost touching. Dion put his fingers over hers and was surprised at their warmth. He leaned to the left until their shoulders were pressed together. Not knowing what to say, not knowing if he should say anything, he put his arm around her and pulled her to him. He licked his lips to moisten them, then bent down to kiss her.

She was ready, and she moved up to meet him. Lips parted, tongues met, and Dion felt an immediate reaction stirring between his legs. The kissing grew more passionate. Their mouths pressed harder together, their tongues intertwining.

Dion pulled back. "Are your . . . can your, uh, mothers see us here?"

Penelope reached around his neck. "No," she said. "Besides, they trust me."

Dion felt her tongue slide deeply into his mouth, and he tentatively reached around her to cup her right breast in his hand. It was small but firm, and he could feel the raised bump of her nipple. She did not push his hand away but instead leaned into him. He began massaging her, his fingers moving in slow circles, and he felt her body stiffen imperceptibly.

His hand worked its way down to her pants.

This time she tried to push him away. "No!" she said, but the word was muffled in their kiss.

Dion ignored her protestation, slipped the fingertips of his left hand beneath the waistband of her jeans, touched the cool silk of panties.

She pulled away. "No," she said firmly, removing his hand from her waist.

"Okay," he said, withdrawing. His face was hot and he was breathing heavily. "I'm sorry." His words were apologetic, but he was aware that his tone was not. Part of him was embarrassed, embarrassed at what he had tried, more embarrassed that he had been rebuffed. But another, deeper, more frightening part was angry, angry at her rejection, angry at her attitude, angry at her. He wanted to hit her, wanted to hurt her, wanted to feel the warm giving elasticity of her skin as he struck her face, wanted to slap her across the mouth until her blood ran, wanted to throw her down on the hard stone fence and take her

now by force as she screamed in pain and fear and long-
ing.

He realized that his fists were clenched, and he un-
clenched them. He shook his head to clear it.

What was happening to him?

Penelope stood up, straightened her hair and her
T-shirt. "It's getting late," she said.

Dion nodded, and the two of them walked back inside.

All of the mothers walked with them to the door to say
good-bye. Dion thanked them for a wonderful time.

"Why don't you come back next Saturday?" Mother
Janine asked sweetly as he took his keys out of his
pocket.

He looked at Penelope, who looked away. "Okay," he
said. "Thanks. I'd like that."

Penelope closed the door to the bathroom and locked it.
She felt like crying. Life was so unfair! She pulled down
her pants and unrolled a foot or so of toilet paper, which
she doubled and used to take out her maxi-pad. Why the
hell did she have to have her period now? She wrapped
up the pad and dumped it in the garbage.

She remembered the way Dion's hand had felt on her
breast, the way his tongue had felt in her mouth, the way
his erection had felt against her thigh. She had wanted
him then, and when his fingers had slipped inside her
pants she had wanted them to get in all the way, had
wanted to feel his fingers touch her vagina.

Why had her period come now?

She looked down at the soak of red blood through
white tissue paper. Although she hated the fact that she
had to have a period at all, hated the pain and discomfort,
the accompanying pimples and mood swings, the blood
itself didn't bother her. Of the entire ordeal, in fact, it was
only the changing of the pads she enjoyed.

She saw a smear of crimson on the tip of her index finger, and she put it to her nose. The blood smell made her
invigorated, almost excited. She felt like going out and
raping Dion right now.

She sat down on the toilet, feeling a little light-headed.

She shouldn't have touched that wine. It was making her behave strangely, making her think weird thoughts.

She stood, took out a new pad, affixed it to her panties. Before pulling them up, she breathed deeply, inhaling the musky fragrance. She touched her breast, remembering how Dion's hands had felt through the thin T-shirt cotton. For a moment there, when she had made him stop, it had seemed as though he had almost wanted to hit her, to force her to comply to his wishes.

And for a moment, a brief moment, she had wanted him to do just that.

Dion pressed down on the gas pedal as he drove away from the winery. There was a burning in his crotch as he sped down the darkened rural road toward home, a painful aching that demanded to be released. He was hard, extraordinarily so, but there was no pleasure in it. Rather, the feeling was one of extreme discomfort. His penis seemed supremely sensitive, and each turn of the steering wheel caused his erection to chafe against his underwear. It hurt, but at the same time it made him stiffer.

The pressure on his penis increased as he pushed farther down on the gas pedal, hurrying, speeding up, desperately anxious to get home.

He thought of Penelope, thought of the way her panties had felt against his fingers, the cool silk and smooth skin soft to his touch.

His erection throbbed.

He couldn't take it anymore. He swerved off the side of The road, shoved the gear shift into Park, and fairly threw himself out of the car, leaving the engine running. He lurched into the bushes as he frantically unbuckled his belt, ripped open the button fly of his Levi's, and grasped his engorged organ. He held it hard and began pumping, his hand sliding quickly up and down the shaft.

He came almost immediately, a shower of thick, milky white semen falling on dirt and dead leaves.

He kept stroking his penis until it hurt, but he could not come again.

His erection, however, remained as hard as ever.

Oh, God, he thought. There really was something

wrong with him. He needed some kind of help. Medical or psychological or both or . . .

He bent over and threw up into the bushes, his throat and stomach working in sickening tandem, clenching and unclenching until there was nothing left to disgorge.

He wiped his mouth and walked slowly back to the car, buttoning his pants, buckling his belt. He had not cried, had not felt like crying in . . . he didn't know how long. Years, probably. But now he got into the car, locked the doors, made sure the windows were closed, and leaned his head against the steering wheel.

He sobbed like a baby.

TWENTY-SIX

"Miss Daneam?"

Penelope turned around. Her eyes quickly scanned the crowded school hallway looking for the owner of the voice before locking on Mr. Holbrook, standing in the open doorway of the teachers' lounge. He beckoned her over. She gave Vella a quick look of apology, then walked over to where the mythology teacher stood.

"Penelope," he said.

"Yes?"

"Penelope." He stretched the word out, rolled it on his tongue. "A good name. A classical name."

"Yes, I know. Penelope was Odysseus' wife." She looked impatiently back toward Vella.

"You wouldn't happen to know the origin of your last name, would you?"

She shook her head. "I'm afraid my family was never big on geneology."

"Were your ancestors Greek by any chance?"

She shrugged. "Why?"

"Oh, nothing. Just curious. The real reason I called you over is because I was wondering if you were related to the Daneams of Daneam Vineyards?"

She nodded. "It's my family's business."

"I had some of your wine the other night. Remarkable stuff. Very interesting indeed. I was wondering if perhaps you could arrange a tour of the winery for me."

"We don't give tours." She frowned. "And how did you get a bottle of our wine? It's not sold around here."

"A friend of mine, a lady friend, let me try it."

"How did she get it?"

"I believe she bought it at the liquor store."

"Here? In Napa?"

He nodded. "I think so."

"That's strange. I'll have to ask my mother about that."

Mr. Holbrook smiled. "Do you think you could ask about a tour at the same time?"

"I'm sorry. We don't give tours."

"Just thought I'd ask."

Penelope looked at him. "This isn't going to affect my grade, is it?"

He chuckled. "No," he said. "You have the same C-minus you've always had."

"What?"

"Just joking." He laughed. "Don't worry. You and Dion both have easy A's."

"Well, bye, then." She backed away from the door.

"See you in class."

Penelope walked back across the now not so crowded hallway. Weird, she thought. Just plain weird. What was that all about? Did he want to meet one of her mothers? That was the only thing she could think of. Why else would he be acting like that? She tried to imagine Mr. Holbrook with Mother Margeaux or with Mother Janine but could not do so without laughing.

"What is it?" Vella asked, stepping up to her.

"He wanted to take a tour of the winery."

"Why?"

Penelope shook her head. "I don't know. Maybe he wanted to meet my mom."

She and Vella both laughed as they headed toward fourth period.

TWENTY-SEVEN

Mel Scott drove home after work instead of going straight to the hospital. It was stupid, he knew, and completely illogical, but he wanted to change before he went to see Barbara. She would not care what he wore, she would not even know, but dressing up for her made him feel as though everything was back the way it was supposed to be, as though Barbara was still alive.

Not that she was dead. She was comatose, had been so for the past nine months, but she was still alive, and the doctor said there was a slim chance she could come out of it one of these times.

Although the possibility of that occurring grew slighter every day.

She had been hit on a Friday afternoon while walking home from work, a drunk driver ignoring a stop sign and not seeing her as she crossed a corner. He'd plowed into her from behind, and she had bounced over the hood before cracking her head on the asphalt, the blood staining one of the white crosswalk lines so badly that it had to be painted over.

She was lucky she hadn't died.

Ironically, after the trial, after the man had been sentenced to fifteen years without the possibility of parole, Mel had turned to drink himself, and though he made sure he never drove drunk, he had often been intoxicated while visiting his wife in the hospital.

He wondered if she knew that.

Lately, he had switched from whisky to wine, and while this should have been an improvement, should have sharply reduced his intake of alcohol, for some reason he'd also begun drinking more. A lot more. He now found himself drinking wine not only after work and after dinner, but during dinner, for lunch, and, even more recently, for breakfast. He just couldn't seem to get enough of the stuff.

This morning he'd even poured a dash of it into his pancake batter.

He had thought about that all day. Part of his mind rationalized this latest act, told himself that it was no different than the cooking sherry Julia Child seemed to pour over everything, but another part of him warned that this was not ordinary behavior. This was obsessive behavior, addictive behavior.

But he felt no compunction to stop.

Amazingly enough, none of this had affected his performance at work, although even if it had, he was pretty well insulated from possible repercussions. He had less than a year to go until retirement, and the review and dismissal process would take at least that long—if it even got off the ground, which was a long shot for someone with his seniority and his well-publicized problems.

At home, Mel took a shower, combed his hair, and put on his suit. He drove to the hospital, waved to the doctors and nurses in his wife's wing, and went into her room.

Her status was unchanged. As always, he felt a second's flash of disappointment. He'd known she would be unmoving, in exactly the same position on the bed, with exactly the same expression on her face, but part of him always hoped that there would be some response as he opened the door, that she would be sitting up groggily as he entered and ask where she was and what had happened, that she would be waiting for him with open arms.

She was lying prone, however, tubes and sensors in place, machines and oxygen tanks flanking her bed.

He patted his coat pocket. This past week he had taken to bringing a bottle with him to visit Barbara, a flask. He knew it was pathetic, the act of a pitiful, desperate man, but he needed the support. The nurses and doctors had objected when they'd found out, warning him about hospital regulations, but their protestations were perfunctory. They knew how much he cared about Barbara, they could see the toll this was taking on him, and they understood, even if they did not condone.

He was under a lot of pressure.

His hand found the flask and he pulled it out. He made sure no one was in the hallway outside the door and quickly downed the entire contents.

He sat down on his chair next to the bed and closed his eyes for a moment, feeling the wine do its work. When he opened his eyes again, Barbara looked changed. The hospital surroundings and medical paraphernalia now seemed extraneous, fake, and she appeared to him to be merely sleeping.

"Barbara?" he called softly.

She did not answer.

He swallowed back the tears he could feel approaching. She was not merely sleeping. She was in a coma. A deep coma. And she might never come out of it.

"Barbara?" he said again. He touched her cheek, felt warmth there but no life. He looked at the wall, tried to think of what he would have for dinner, tried to think of the assignments he had to complete at work tomorrow, tried to think of anything that would keep the tears at bay.

He wished he'd brought another bottle.

A lone tear escaped from underneath his eyelid and rolled halfway down his craggy cheek before he wiped it away. He sat there, unmoving. A moment later, the mood passed.

Grateful, he held Barbara's hand and, as always, told her of his day. He described to her the minutiae which made up his life and shared with her the thoughts and feelings he would have shared had she been at home with him and cooking dinner. His mind filled in what would have been her responses, and it was almost like having a real conversation.

He stroked her hand as he talked. He continued stroking her hand even after he had run out of things to say.

He thought of all the times that hand had stroked him.

He smiled. They had not done it all that much the last few years. They'd still loved each other, perhaps more than they ever had, but the sex thing seemed to have died down for both of them. They'd done it only infrequently in the past decade, and even then it had not always worked.

But he'd discovered recently how much he missed that part of their relationship. In bed alone, he remembered their early years together, when they had done it almost every night—and when she had continued to please him even when it was her time of the month.

He'd masturbated a lot lately.

He held Barbara's hand and looked at her face. Her slightly parted lips looked wet, full. Inviting.

He closed his eyes. What was he thinking? What the hell was wrong with him? He let go of her hand. It was the wine. He'd had too much of it today. It was starting to get to him.

He opened his eyes, looked again at Barbara's moist lips, and felt a stirring in his groin.

He stood up and, as if underwater, walked across the room and closed the door. He turned back toward the bed. The tubes were in her nostrils, he thought. She would still be able to breathe.

And of course she would want him to be happy.

No. This was crazy.

He stood for a moment next to the bed, staring at her familiar face. He could feel his erection growing. He was hard, painfully so.

He pulled down his pants, crawled on top of her.

He heard the door to the room open behind him. He heard the nurse's gasp. "Mr. Scott!" she yelled.

But his penis was already in her mouth, and he was thrusting.

TWENTY-EIGHT

Penelope was standing alone in the main hallway of the school. Only the school was empty, abandoned, the bare floor covered with the dust of age. It was night, and only a thin sliver of moonlight shone through the boarded windows, but it was enough to show Dion that Penelope was naked. And that she was rubbing herself.

As he watched from the shadows, there came a growing, insistent flapping, like the sound of birds taking off or a helicopter landing. The sound grew, intensified, and from the blackness behind Penelope he saw a shifting shape emerge, descending downward through the color spectrum, growing lighter, grayer, white, a huge fluttering, whirlingly ill-defined creature that he identified to his horror as a monstrous swan. Even in the dark he could see pliant lips on an orange, ungiving bill, calculating human eyes within the tangle of feathers above. As if on cue, Penelope stopped fingering herself and dropped to her hands and knees, waiting on all fours.

Behind her, Dion could see the swan's massive penis.

Penelope arched her back, baring her buttocks for the swan, which mounted her from behind. She screamed once, loudly, a horrible cry of agonized pain, and then the feathers were flying, the swan disintegrating in a rain of white which floated down on Penelope as a baby gruesomely pushed its way out of her exposed forehead, the skin below her hairline ripping, breaking open in a wash of blood that rolled cleanly off the emerging infant.

The baby smiled at him, pulling the remainder of its body from Penelope's head as she fell onto her side. "Father," the baby said in a voice like thunder. "Son."

Dion awoke feeling strange. He sat up. The bottom half

of his body seemed different, unfamiliar, as though it belonged to someone else. He closed his eyes for a moment,
opened them again. He found that he was afraid to move
his legs, afraid they might not work, afraid they might
work in ways to which he was not accustomed.

He turned his head to look out the window. Outside it
was still dark. From this vantage point he could see the
rounded silhouette of the hill, backlit by the moon.

He looked immediately away, frightened.

What the hell was happening to him?

He didn't know, and it was a long time before he fell
back asleep.

TWENTY-NINE

Kevin and Dion walked past the school bus on their way to the parking lot. It had rained earlier in the day and the ground was wet, the sidewalk's ostensible flatness belied by a series of off-center puddles. "You know," Kevin said, "ever since you two got together, you don't do shit with me anymore. Not that I miss having to drag your sorry ass around, but—"

A paper cup filled with ice was thrown from one of the bus windows and landed on the sidewalk to Kevin's right. "Pussy!" a boy's voice called out.

"Don't tell me your problems!" Kevin shot back. He reached down, picked up the smashed cup, and threw it at the side of the bus. It hit with a wet splat.

Dion laughed.

"So what are you plans for tonight?"

Dion shrugged. "I don't have any."

"You're not doing anything with Penelope?"

"I don't know."

"So take a night off. We're going to pay a visit to Father Ralph again. Paul's been grounded for the past week, so this time he's really going to get back at his old man. It should be great."

"I'm not—"

"Come on, don't be a flit."

Dion grinned. "Flit?"

Kevin nodded. "Flit."

"Okay." Dion laughed. "You talked me into it."

They met again at Burgertime. A guy Dion didn't know had brought his van, so all six of them could fit into it. This time there was a bottle in the car, and Paul lit up a joint. Dion frowned. Was it his imagination or did all of them seem a little wilder than usual, a little more on edge? The joint was offered to him, and he shook his head firmly.

"Candy ass," Paul sneered.

Dion ignored him.

As before, they parked a little way up from Father Ralph's house and crept through the bushes and the mud until they reached the backyard. This time all of the lights were out. Only the pulsing blue glow of a television shone from one of the windows.

Paul crept up to the window, peeked in. He crouched immediately back down, giggling. "Check it out!" he whispered. "He's in there boffing some babe!"

The rest of them moved closer and peered into the bedroom.

Dion's stomach dropped. One of Penelope's mothers, Mother Margaret, was on all fours on the floor next to the bed, the preacher kneeling behind her, grasping his hardened organ, positioning himself. Dress and underwear, pants and panties, were strewn across the rug. An empty bottle of wine lay tipped over on the nightstand next to the bed. Penelope's mother cried out, and her large breasts jiggled as the preacher entered her from behind. "Yes!" she moaned. "Yes! Yes!"

Dion turned away, sickened, slumping against the wall of the house.

"Get ready to run," Paul said. He stood, held up the camera he'd brought, and began snapping pictures. Dion could see in his mind the shifting tableaux as the dark was illuminated by a series of quick flashes. He saw the preacher's shock and rage and fear, saw Mother Margaret's confusion as she became aware of the crowd at the window.

"Run!" Paul screamed.

And then Dion was following the rest of them through the brush, crashing through branches, slipping in mud, tripping over roots until they reached the van.

They took off, laughing excitedly.

"Who was that?" someone asked.

Kevin shook his head. "I don't know."

"Nice titties, though." Paul grinned. "No wonder my old man coveted her ass."

Dion closed his eyes as the other boys laughed, and they sped through the night toward the burger stand.

He avoided Penelope the next morning at school, afraid to face her, feeling guilty, almost as though her mother's actions were his fault, as though he was the one who had done something wrong.

He met Kevin next to the lockers before class, but the usual joking insults were nowhere in evidence. His friend's face was grim, his manner subdued. "You heard the news, didn't you?"

Dion shook his head.

"Father Ralph's dead."

Dion stared at his friend, not knowing what to say.

"Heart attack, they think. Paul's really taking it hard."

"What about the woman? Did they—"

"Haven't heard anything about her. I bet she split after it happened."

"Maybe it happened after she left."

"I don't think so. I think she probably brought it on."

Dion closed his locker. "Does—does Penelope know?"

"I have no idea." Kevin frowned. "Why?"

"Nothing," Dion said. "No reason."

Kevin looked at him suspiciously. "No reason?"

"No reason." He swallowed, looked away. "Come on. It's getting late."

Kevin nodded slowly. "Yeah. All right."

The two of them walked together to class.

He talked to Penelope on the phone that night.

She called him, worried, wondering why he had avoided her all day, and he wanted to tell her what he'd seen, what had happened, but instead he lied, told her that Kevin was having some family problems and that he'd felt obligated to be there for his friend, to give him some moral support.

Penelope was silent for a moment. "I thought maybe it was because you'd changed your mind."

"Changed my mind?"

"About us."

Now Dion was silent. His heart was pounding, and his hand holding the receiver was shaking. He swallowed, forced himself to speak. "I haven't," he said.

Penelope, when she spoke, sounded as nervous as he felt. "How do you feel about me?" she asked.

He knew what she wanted him to say, but he wasn't sure if he could say it. Or if he should say it.

He said it anyway: "I love you."

And it was true. He didn't know if he'd felt that way before, if he'd felt it all along, but he felt it now, and his pulse raced as he heard her say softly, "I love you too."

A painful erection was pressing against his jeans. He was in his bedroom, with the door closed, and he unbuttoned his pants with his left hand, releasing his hardened penis. He touched himself gently, and he pretended that she was the one who was touching him.

Neither of them had spoken yet, and Dion was aware that the silence was becoming awkward. "Do you—" he began.

"Are we—" Penelope said at the same time.

They laughed. "You go first," Dion said.

"Are we going to see each other this weekend?"

"Yes," Dion said. He was stroking himself, and he closed his eyes as he pressed the receiver to his ear, wondering if Penelope *would* be stroking him this weekend.

"They're having a fair tomorrow and Sunday," she suggested. "I read about it in the paper."

"That sounds good."

"I can drive if you want."

"No, I can drive," Dion said. He suddenly thought of Penelope's mother, naked on her hands and knees in front of Father Ralph.

And he came. Semen shot all over his jeans, all over the bedspread. He released his softening organ and looked at the mess, disgusted. "I have to go," he said quickly. "I'll see you tomorrow. Okay?"

"Okay. What time are you going to come by?"

"Is ten o'clock okay?"

"That's fine."

"Ten o'clock, then."

"Okay." There was a pause. "I love you."

"I love you too."

"Good night," Penelope said.

"Good"—he had been about to say "bye," but somehow "night" seemed nicer, more intimate, more appropriate—"night."

He hung up the phone, looked around for Kleenexes or a towel or a napkin, something to clean up the bedspread. He grimaced as he wiped his sticky left hand on the cuff of his pants. What the hell was the matter with him?

He didn't know, but he thought again of Penelope's mother, on her hands and knees, and for some reason he remembered the wine he'd had at Penelope's house, how it had tasted, and his penis began to stiffen.

Before he knew what he was doing, before he could think about it, he had pulled his pants down around his ankles and was once again furiously stroking himself.

He climaxed almost immediately.

THIRTY

"Fifteen cents is your change. Thanks." Nick Nicholson dropped the coins into the young woman's open palm and watched admiringly as she walked out of his store to the red Corvette in the parking lot. Her ass swayed gently back and forth beneath the material of her tight skirt. She looked up at him and smiled before unlocking the car door and getting in. He glanced quickly away, caught but not wanting to admit it.

What was in those Daneam wines? He'd received a shipment on Tuesday and had just sold the last bottle of burgundy to the Corvette woman. And he wasn't the only one who couldn't keep them in stock. Jim over at O-Kay Liquor had sold out almost immediately, as had Phil at Liquor Shack.

The amazing thing was that he had never before seen a Daneam label. He'd been aware of the winery, of course, but as far as he'd known, Daneam sold only by mail order and only to specialty collectors. Now, all of a sudden, the company had been supplying its vintages to area stores, offering everything in its catalog.

Just as spontaneously, people had been buying. Not just collectors, not just connoisseurs, but regular people. There'd been no advance publicity, no hype of any sort, but there was now a sudden demand for Daneam wines among seemingly all segments of the general public.

He didn't understand it.

He'd talked to several of his friends who were buyers for some of the area's better restaurants, and they too had started carrying Daneam wines. Two of them had even elevated the vineyard's products to "house wine" status.

All within the past week.

It was crazy.

A bearded, burly man wearing ripped jeans and a Chi-cago Cubs T-shirt walked into the store, jingling the bells over the door. He strode directly up to the counter. "You have any Daneam wines?" he asked.

Nick shook his head. "Sorry, just sold the last one."

The man slammed his fist down on the counter. "Shit!"

"You might try Liquor Barn over on Lincoln."

"I just came from there, asshole." He glanced around the store. "You sure you don't have some hidden in the back?"

"No. Sorry."

"Bullshit! I'm going to check myself."

"No, you're not." Nick reached under the counter until his fingers touched the handgun hidden there. "You're go-ing to leave. Right now."

"Who says so?"

"I say so." Nick looked hard into the man's eyes, trying to stare him down, hoping he wouldn't have to pull out the gun and threaten the man with it.

"Fuck," the man said, shaking his head. He knocked over a small display of Chapstick products and pushed open the front door, causing the bells to ring crazily as he stormed out of the store.

Nick relaxed, able to breathe again, but he did not take his hand away from the handgun until he saw the man cross the street and disappear from view. He stood there for a moment, uncertain, then walked around the edge of the counter, locked the front door, and flipped the sign in the window from Open to Closed. The store wasn't scheduled to close for another half hour, but he didn't feel like remaining open any longer. There wasn't any point to it.

He was all out of Daneam wines.

And he had the feeling that the customers who came in tonight weren't going to be asking for anything else.

THIRTY-ONE

Dion awoke, rubbing his eyes, stretching. The blanket on top of him seemed heavy, and he kicked it off, sitting up. Outside the sun was out, light streaming through the window in pillars roughly the shape of the wood-bordered panes, but the atmosphere felt dark, oppressive. He had never been claustrophobic, but that was how he felt now. Everything seemed close, confining, as though both his room and the world outside were pressing in on him. Even his underwear felt unnaturally restrictive, the cotton much too tight against his skin. He peeled off his T-shirt, peeled off his shorts, but the feeling persisted.

He stood up. His body felt small. It was a strange thing to think, but it was the only way to describe the sensation. He had certainly not shrunk during the night, but his body seemed somehow compacted, as though his being was too large for its physical form.

No, it was not as if his body had shrunk. It was as if, inside, he had grown.

But that made no sense. Why would he even think of something like that?

He'd had dreams. All night. A lot of them. And though he could remember only fragmented images, he was filled with the certainty that the dreams had been all of a piece, that they had been not only related but interconnected, like individual episodes of a serial.

That frightened him for some reason.

Just as frightening were the images that had remained with him: the head of Penelope's Mother Margaret, grinning, impaled on his enormous erection as he paraded before a huge, orgiastic audience in an outdoor amphitheater; a line of ants on the dirt suddenly growing, changing, metamorphosing into men who bowed before him and promised their undying fealty; dead women swimming in a black lake, their faces blank and lifeless but their legs kicking, their arms paddling; Mr. Holbrook, shirtless, pushing a boulder up the side of an incline in a dark cavern; three beautiful nude women standing on top of a high cliff, singing, as men on the flat ground below the cliff ran crazily forward, smashing their heads into the rock.

He wasn't sure why the dreams had frightened him so, but they had, disturbing him in a way that seemed almost more real than real life. What was most disturbing, though, was that there was an element of anticipation in the fear. Despite the fact that he was awake and the dreams were over, the unpleasant feelings lingered, and they were not fading residual reactions to something that he had experienced but growing expectant feelings of dread for something that had not yet happened.

He walked into the bathroom, looked at himself in the mirror.

Perhaps he was psychic.

That was a scary thought.

He took a quick shower, and once again had the sensation that his body no longer fit him.

He pushed that craziness out of his mind.

He hadn't told his mom that he was going out with Penelope today, and after he showered, shaved, dressed, and walked out to the kitchen to grab something to eat, she asked him if he'd mow the lawn this morning. He told her then that he was planning to go out, and to his surprise she paused a moment before giving her approval. He'd expected her to be understanding, accommodating, completely supportive. She'd seemed excited for him until now, happy that he was finally dating, and even this slight hesitation put him on the defensive. His mom hadn't attacked Penelope, but anything less than total backing smacked of criticism, and he felt immediately resentful. Hell, his mom hadn't even met Penelope. What was she doing passing judgment?

Maybe she should meet Penelope.

Maybe.

He'd think about that later.

He ate a quick breakfast of toast and cocoa and borrowed ten dollars from his mom, promising to pay her back.

"Pay me back?" she said. "How?"

"When I get a job."

"Are you planning to get a job?"

He grinned. "No. But when I do, you'll be the first person I'll reimburse."

She tossed the car keys at him. "Get out of here."

He was lucky. The car's tank was full, so he didn't have to waste any money buying gas. He hadn't thought of that before. If he had, he would've borrowed twenty dollars.

He backed out of the driveway and pulled onto the street. He glanced east toward the hill as he drove, and though the sight of the hill had unnerved him in the past, there seemed something familiar and comforting about it now, and he could not remember what had so disturbed him about the hill before.

Although it was only quarter to ten when he pulled up in front of the winery gates, Penelope was already waiting for him, sitting on a bench next to the driveway entrance. He was glad that she was alone, that he would not have to go up to the house and see her mothers. He didn't feel up to that this morning.

She stood when she saw him, and got in the passenger side when he reached over and unlocked the door. "Hi," she said.

"Hi."

They were shy with each other, the intimacy they'd shared on the phone, in the nighttime privacy of their own rooms, making them self-conscious in the rational light of day. Dion was embarrassed as he thought of the way he'd played with himself while talking to her, but he also found himself becoming aroused again.

Would they do it tonight?

He didn't know, but the possibility both scared and excited him.

Penelope reached into her purse, pulled out a newspaper article she'd clipped. "The fair's on Elm, outside of town. You know where that is?"

He shook his head.

"Go down to the next street and turn left. I'll tell you where to go."

"Okay."

They were silent after that, neither sure of what to say or how to act. Dion wanted to turn on the radio, but he was aware that that would only draw attention to the silence, and he kept both hands on the wheel.

He cleared his throat. "What kind of fair is this? A Lion's fair?"

"No. It's, like, a festival, a psychic festival. They have fortune tellers and tarot readers, stuff like that."

Psychic? That was a spooky coincidence.

"Turn left here," Penelope said.

He did so, glancing to the right at a grove of trees as he turned. The grove looked familiar to him, and as he looked he experienced a momentary flashback to one of last night's dreams.

Women in the forest, naked, smeared with blood, howling wildly, screaming, begging for him—

"What are you doing?" Penelope demanded.

The car was half off the road and bumping over the shoulder toward the embankment. Dion swerved quickly, too quickly, and Penelope was thrown against the door as the car reentered the lane.

"What was that about?"

"Sorry," he said sheepishly. "Daydreaming."

He felt a soft hand on his arm, and he realized that this was the first time she had touched him without his initiating the contact. "Are you okay?" she asked.

He nodded. "I'm fine."

But he was not fine. His dreams had escaped their sleep-bound confines and had entered the waking world, intruding upon reality, almost getting them into an accident, and that scared the hell out of him. What was happening? He wondered briefly if it could be something like an acid flashback. Maybe, back in the old days when he was a baby, his mom had put LSD in his milk or something, and now he was finally experiencing the side effects.

No, even at her worst, his mom would not have done something like that.

He didn't really think it was anything along those lines, though, did he? He wasn't afraid that it was drugs he'd been given as an infant or ultraviolet rays streaming through the hole in the ozone layer or even mental illness. No. He didn't know what he thought it was. But he knew that it was much scarier than any of those possibilities.

"Are you sure?" she said.

"Yeah." He looked over at Penelope and smiled, and he hoped the smile looked more real than it felt.

The Fourth Annual Wine Country New Age Music and Art Fair was scheduled to open at eleven, but when they arrived a little after ten-thirty, there were already quite a few people milling about, browsing amongst the booths, watching latecomers set up shop on the sawdust. The two of them got out of the car and, holding hands, walked across the small wooden footbridge to the fair entrance. The weekend event had been scheduled originally to be held in the park downtown, according to Penelope's article, but an inability to meet city permit registration deadlines had forced the fair organizers to move to an empty meadow near the foothills.

The change of venue did not seem to have affected attendance at all. A number of people had arrived before them, and cars were continuing to pull into the makeshift parking lot. A sign above the entry booth said that admission was a dollar for children, two dollars for adults, and that picnic baskets and water jugs were welcome. Dion pulled out his wallet, taking out a five-dollar bill and handing it to the cashier. "Did you go last year?" he asked Penelope.

She shook her head, smiling. "With who? I had no one to go with. Besides, I'd never even heard of this thing until this week."

"Really up on current events, huh?"

She hit his shoulder, and that spontaneous expression of camaraderie made him feel closer to her than he ever had before. He put an arm around her waist, drew her to him.

Taking their tickets, they walked through the gate, getting their hands stamped by a ponytailed man in case they wanted to leave the fair and come back later in the day.

Dion looked around at the posters filled with pagan symbols, the booth closest to them that was stocked with witchcraft paraphernalia.

"Are you a Christian?" Penelope asked.

He turned to face her. "Why? Are you?"

"I suppose so. I mean, I don't go to church, but I believe in God."

He nodded. "Yeah," he said. "Me too."

She smiled teasingly at him. "Scared you, didn't I? When you heard that word 'Christian,' you thought I wanted to know if you were born again."

"No," he lied.

"Be honest."

He laughed. "All right. Yeah. For a second. I thought maybe you'd been keeping this secret from me, waiting to tell me until you felt you could trust me, and you suddenly decided to spring it on me now."

"Because I was offended by all this heathenism?"

He grinned. "Something like that."

She laughed. 'That's great." They walked toward the witchcraft booth. "Oh, and I forgot to tell you—I'm a lesbian."

"I've heard that one before."

The woman in the witchcraft booth beamed at them, having obviously overheard them. "We're all lesbians in my coven," she said. "In fact, witchcraft is a celebration of our womanness."

Dion felt a tug on his arm as Penelope pulled him away from the booth.

"We have literature if you're interested," the woman said.

Penelope shook her head as they walked away. "No, thanks."

They stopped by another booth featuring exotic Third World musical instruments. Dion played with a rain stick, while Penelope used a mallet to hit what looked like a log marimba.

The two of them wandered through the fair, hand in hand.

Penelope looked toward a windowless trailer on which was painted the words: AFTERLIFE PROGRESSION.

She turned toward Dion. "Do you believe in heaven?" she asked.

He shrugged. "I guess."

"Have you ever wondered what it's like? I mean, most people think of heaven as this wonderful place where you're reunited with your loved ones for eternity, but I always wondered, which loved ones? If a woman's husband dies and she marries again, is she reunited with both husbands up there? Is there polygamy in heaven? What about first boyfriends or lovers?"

Dion laughed. "I never thought about it that way."

"And what about pets? A lot of people think that they'll meet up again with their dog or cat in heaven. But which dog or cat? Does God make you choose and only allow you to have your favorite, or are you surrounded by all the pets you had throughout your life?"

"That's weird."

"Well, how do you see heaven?"

"I don't know. I've never given it much thought, really."

"I always thought that you'd have this huge entourage. You'd be surrounded by parents and brothers and sisters and friends and lovers and husbands and wives and dogs and cats and hamsters and goldfish and anything you ever loved."

"Sounds crowded."

"That's not all. It's heaven for them too. So each of those people would have their own entourage. All of your parents' friends and lovers and pets and their friends and lovers and pets and on and on and on."

"Sounds like hell."

She nodded thoughtfully. "It does, doesn't it?"

"Well, what do you think hell's like?"

"I don't know. Do you have any ideas?"

"Oh, a hot place where I'm bent over a gym bench and

Mr. Holbrook is shoving razor blades up my ass for eternity."

She hit him, laughing. "You're bad!"

"Must be the Kevin influence."

From off to their right, Dion heard the high-pitched sound of feedback from a P.A. system. He looked in that direction and saw a group of musicians dressed in strange costumes atop a small raised platform. A crowd of about thirty was standing in front of the stage.

The musicians began playing.

"That's a weird instrument," Penelope said. "What do you think it—?"

Dion stiffened. His hand, gripping her arm, tightened.

"Hey!" she said. "What do you think you're doing?"

And then he was dancing, laughing, running down the hill naked, the women in pursuit. He could smell their ripeness, their hot arousal, mixed with the earthy odor of goat. He knew the women were going to tear him apart, rip up his flesh and drink his hot blood, but that was what he wanted, that was what he craved, and he felt wonderfully ecstatic as he ran from them, wanting to prolong this feeling, wanting to savor every moment of the chase before he felt the glorious pain of their nails and teeth as they killed him again.

He opened his eyes and he was looking up at the sky, a ring of people above him. He realized that he was lying on the ground. He could feel weeds and rocks pressing into his back through the material of his shirt.

"Dion?"

He saw Penelope, staring down at him, worried. She bent down next to him, took his hand in hers. "Are you all right?"

"What . . . ?" he began. He cleared his throat. "What happened?"

"I don't know. All of a sudden you just collapsed. Like you fainted or something."

"Should I call an ambulance?" one man asked.

"No," Dion said, sitting up. "It's okay."

"Maybe you should have a doctor look at you," Penelope suggested.

"I'm fine." He stood, and though he felt a little dizzy,

he tried not to let it show. He looked at the faces of the gathered crowd and forced himself to smile "That's it. Show's over. Leave money in the hat."

A few people chuckled, and the crowd began to disperse.

Dion felt a hand on his shoulder. "You sure you're okay?" It was the man who'd asked about the ambulance.

"I'm fine," he said. "I just tripped on a rock. Knocked the wind out of me."

The man nodded and moved off.

"You didn't trip," Penelope said.

No, he hadn't. But he didn't know what had happened. He did know that he did not want to be taken to a doctor, although he was not sure if it was because he was afraid the doctor might find something or because he already knew that there was nothing to find.

Maybe he had a brain tumor. Or some type of cancer. Maybe he'd had a mild stroke or a heart attack or something.

No. He didn't know how he knew it, but he knew it. This wasn't a medical thing. This was triggered by the sound of the pipes. And it was related somehow to his dreams and to . . .

His head hurt, and he closed his eyes against the pain.

"I think we'd better go," Penelope told him. "I'll drive."

He nodded and let her lead him out through the front gates of the fair and across the field to the car.

"I really think you should go to the doctor," she said. "What if this is something serious—"

"It's not."

"First, you swerve off the road, then—"

"It's an acid flashback," he said.

"What?" She stopped walking, letting go of his hand. Her face was white, shocked.

"A friend of my mom's put it in my milk when I was a baby," he lied. "I get these every so often."

"My God."

He took her hand again, and they continued walking toward the car. He made up a story about how his mom had found out, how the man had been arrested and jailed. He

wanted to tell her the truth, wanted to tell her that he
didn't know what was happening, but something kept him
from it. Although the truth was far more innocuous than
the lies he was spinning, it seemed more intimate somehow, and a part of him was not ready to share that intimacy.

They ended up going to a movie, a matinee that took
the rest of his ten dollars. Afterward, Penelope treated
him to dinner. McDonald's. When they finished eating,
they walked around a few of the stores not yet closed.

It was still early in the evening when he pulled to a
stop just before the entrance to the winery and turned off
the engine, killing the lights. The inside of the car was
dark with the sudden absence of dashboard illumination,
but he could clearly see Penelope's face, lit by the low
glow of the sodium lamp above the winery gate. She
looked gorgeous in the dim light, her skin smoothly pale,
her lips full and red. The darkness gave her already alluring eyes a deepness beyond that which they normally possessed. He reached over and took her hand. Her skin was
soft, warm.

"How do you feel about me?" she asked. There was a
slight trembling in her voice.

He knew what she wanted to hear but was not sure he
could say it. He had said it before, over the phone, but in
person it was harder. Besides, he had never loved anyone
before, and he did not know if he loved Penelope now. He
liked her, was obviously infatuated with her, but he was
not sure that his feelings went any deeper than that. "How
do you feel about me?" he asked.

She looked into his eyes. "I love you."

"I—I love you too," he replied, and it was true.

They kissed. His left hand was around her back, and his
right cupped her breast, squeezing it gently. His penis was
hard, and when his tongue slid between her lips and
found her own soft tongue, he felt as though he was going
to explode. His hand on her breast began to cramp from
the awkward position, and he let it fall to a more natural
position in her lap. She did not try to push him away, and
he moved his hand between her parted legs and started
massaging her crotch through the jeans.

She reached for him and her fingers lightly traced the outline of his erection.

Peripherally, through the windshield, he thought he saw movement outside. He looked up as he kissed her and saw the security camera stationed on the top of the winery gatepost swivel toward the car, but he didn't want to interrupt the rhythm they'd found and didn't want to upset her, and he pushed Penelope down on the seat as he started to unbuckle her pants.

THIRTY-TWO

April drove quickly in order to beat Dion home. She went over in her mind what Margaret and the others had told her.

It explained a lot, she thought.

It explained everything.

THIRTY-THREE

The moon was full and hung high over the hills, white now after bleaching upward from yellow. The Vintage 1870 shops were closing, and Tim South and Ann Melbury walked hand in hand across the gravel parking lot to the car, following a few other late stragglers. The air was warm but tinged with a cool autumn breeze. Tim, for one, welcomed the changing of the seasons. He was tired of sweating—his old Dart didn't have air conditioning and seemed to retain heat even with the windows open—and he was equally tired of spending the first half of each date in broad daylight. It was bad enough that his parents made him come home by eleven, but the fact that it didn't get dark until eight or eight-thirty put a further crimp in his style. He was glad the days were getting shorter. And he could not wait until Daylight Saving Time disappeared.

They reached the car, and he gallantly opened the passenger door, letting Ann in before stepping around to the driver's side.

She ran a hand through her short, spiky hair as he climbed into his seat. "So what do you want to do now?" she asked.

Tim shrugged. "I don't know."

He knew what they were going to do next. They both knew. But they always went through this hypocritical little routine anyway, pretending it was a spontaneous decision on both their parts, as though each of them hadn't thought about it all day, hadn't washed the most intimate portions of their bodies in preparatory showers, hadn't made sure they were wearing clean underwear and socks without holes.

"We could stop by Dairy Queen," Ann suggested. "They're still open."

"We could," Tim agreed. He paused. "Or we could just drive around."

She smiled. "On South Street?"

He nodded, grinning. "We could."

"Okay."

He started the car and pulled out of the parking lot onto the street. South might not be an officially recognized lover's lane, but it was *their* lover's lane, bordering as it did several of the wineries and the wooded foothills, safely away from casual traffic.

As always, they pulled onto the dirt shoulder and parked in a dark area between two large trees. Tim got out of the car and took a blanket from the backseat. Several times they had done it in the car, when it had been raining or too cold outside, but it had always been an awkward experience. The backseat was cramped and uncomfortable, and half of the front seat was taken up by the steering wheel, making movement extremely difficult, so they preferred, whenever possible, to do it outside.

That was one thing he would miss when winter arrived.

A pickup roared by, brights on, and they heard the laughter only seconds before a water balloon hit the hood of the Dart.

"Asshole!" Tim yelled.

He was answered only by a retreating honk of the truck's horn.

"Let's go into the woods," Ann suggested. "Away from the road."

"What if someone vandalizes my car?"

"They won't."

"They already did." He pointed toward the wet hood.

"You want to go home?"

"Of course not."

"Well, come on, then." She took his hand, leading him through the grass and toward the trees. "I'm not about to stay here and wait for those morons to come back and hit *us* next time."

"But—"

"No buts."

He shook his head. "You drive a hard bargain, Miss Melbury."

"You better believe it."

They walked around a copse of bushes, away from the road. "How about here?" Tim asked.

"Ground's too rough. Remember that time when my back got all cut up?"

He nodded, grimaced. They continued walking.

They reached a small clearing and he was about to suggest that they spread the blanket here when he heard a sound of rustling leaves and cracking twigs from somewhere up ahead. He stopped, grabbed her arm, put a finger to his lips. "Shhhhh."

She listened, heard it. "Do you think it's an animal?" she whispered.

"I don't know." He began walking slowly forward.

"I don't think we should—"

They both saw it at once. Movement through the trees, flashes of skin, bluish white in the moonlight.

"Come on," Tim said, creeping closer. Through the leaves he saw rounded breasts, a triangle of pubic hair. A naked woman. Dancing.

Ann shook her head, holding back. "Let's get out of here."

"Let's just see what it is." He grabbed her hand. Her palm was wet, sweaty.

"I think it's some kind of orgy."

"You think so?" Tim grinned. "Come on, let's check it out."

"No," she said, and her voice was serious. "I'm scared."

"There's nothing to be scared of."

"Nothing to be scared of? Someone's dancing naked under the full moon and you say there's nothing to be scared of? We don't know who it is. It might be a witch or satanist or something. Let's just get out of here. We'll go somewhere else."

"No," Tim said stubbornly. "I want to see." He started moving away from her, toward the dancing woman. He heard low, throaty laughter, thought he heard a sexy moan.

Maybe it *was* an orgy.

He crept forward. The ground here was littered with empty wine bottles, many of them broken, and it was almost impossible to walk quietly. He heard Ann following behind him, the ground crunching beneath her feet. He wanted to tell her to be quiet, but he was afraid of making noise himself.

Afraid?

Yes. He was afraid. He was aroused, excited, titillated, but Ann was right. There was something spooky about the whole thing, something scary. Naked women did not just dance in empty fields under the full moon for no reason at all.

He could see the woman more clearly now. And another woman. They were older, in their thirties or forties, but they were still pretty damn sexy, and they were laughing and dancing in joyous abandon. Were they lesbians? He couldn't tell. But he thought that Ann was probably right. They probably were part of some cult, performing some type of pagan ritual.

He crouched down behind a bush on the edge of the field. Ann moved behind him, pressing against his back. "Let's go," she hissed in his ear.

He shook his head, watching the women. They were laughing, obviously enjoying themselves, and his erection grew as he stared at their bouncing breasts, at the thatches of down between their legs.

The dancing sped up, became more frenzied, more frenetic. Tim was not sure when the movements crossed the border from free form into fanatic; he knew only that suddenly the women were no longer dancing, no longer celebrating. There was a wildness to their steps, danger in their motions. They seemed mad, almost maniacal, and he was frightened. His erection was gone, and he wished that they were safely back in the car and on their way home.

Now there was laughter behind them as well as in front of them, and it no longer seemed happy or joyous. He turned his head, saw a nude woman dancing in the small clearing where he'd wanted to spread the blanket.

"Let's get out of here," Ann whispered.

He shook his head. Intentionally or unintentionally, these women, whoever they were, had surrounded them. It was now impossible for them to return to the car without being seen.

But why was he so afraid of being seen?

He didn't know. But he was afraid, very afraid, and he wished he'd listened to Ann in the first place and left when they'd first heard the sounds.

He was grabbed from behind.

He tried to scream, but a hand was clamped over his mouth, a filthy hand smelling of wine and woman. He tried to lash out, tried to kick, tried to hit, but whoever was holding him was stronger than he was and held him tightly. He turned his head as far as he could to the left and saw a naked woman carrying Ann into the field. Two more carried him, following.

He couldn't see for a moment, could see only the ground and dirty legs from the angle at which he was carried. Then he was thrown onto the ground. A small branch stabbed his side. He screamed with pain and heard the noise. They were no longer holding his mouth shut. He screamed as loud as he could, "Help!" at first, then just pure sound. Ann was screaming too, and the women still holding his arms and legs turned him so he faced her.

The women were ripping her clothes off, laughing, drinking from a bottle of red wine, the thick liquid spilling down their chins, down their chests, looking like blood.

What the fuck was happening?

He was filled with not only fear but panic—and with the certainty that both he and Ann were not going to get out of this, that they were going to die.

The first woman, the dancer they'd first seen, finished off the wine. She was on top of Ann, facing backward, bottle in hand. "No!" Ann screamed, real terror in her voice. "No—!"

Her screams were cut off as the woman sat on top of her face and began shoving the thin end of the wine bottle viciously between her legs, in and out, in and out, thrust-

ng with all of the strength in her arm, until the glass was
paque with blood.

"Ann!" Tim cried, but the other women were upon him
ow, ripping his clothes, pulling his hair. He went down.
A finger found his eyeball, pressed in, and, with a stream
f hot juices, pulled out. Teeth began ripping skin, rend-
ng flesh. Fingers were shoved into his anus, pulling,
tretching, ripping. His screams were not even coherent,
ot even words. The air was filled with the smell of salt
nd sex and heavy wine.

And they tore him apart.

THIRTY-FOUR

It was long past her usual bedtime, but Penelope couldn't sleep. She had always been sensitive to moods, oversensitive perhaps, and the mood when she'd arrived home had been tense. Her mothers seldom argued, and never in front of her, but they did have disagreements, and their differences came out in subtle ways, small changes in familiar rituals, purposeful transgressions of established etiquette. They no doubt thought that they were hiding their problems from her, sparing her, but this clandestine conflict had made her that much more sensitive to small shifts of emotion.

The current fight was big.

Ordinarily there were one or two mothers involved in a dispute, and the others covered for them as best they could, acting as arbitrators, preserving the facade in front of Penelope. But tonight they had all been unusually silent, unusually solemn when she arrived home. All except Mother Margeaux, who, for some strange reason, was not there. Mother Felice asked Penelope a few perfunctory questions when she walked into the living room, but it was clear that even she was not interested in the answers, and the other mothers sat in obviously expectant silence, waiting for her to leave so they could resume their conversation.

She did leave, going to the bathroom and taking a hot shower, and when she'd gone into the kitchen afterward to get a drink of water, she'd heard her mothers talking in the living room. Their voices were low, cautious, almost conspiratorial, as if they were afraid of being overheard, and the clandestine tone of the conversation caused Penelope to tread softly and to halt in the hallway outside the door, listening.

"She's our daughter," she heard Mother Felice say.

"That doesn't matter anymore." Mother Margaret.

She moved away from the doorway, not wanting to hear any more, her heart pounding, the blood racing through her veins. She hurried up the stairs to her bedroom, closed the door and locked it.

She had not been able to fall asleep since.

Now she reached next to her, felt for her watch on the nightstand, held its vaguely luminescent face next to her eyes.

One o'clock.

She put the watch down, stared up into the blackness. More than anything, she wanted to sneak down the hall to Mother Felice's room, to crawl into her favorite mother's bed the way she used to, to find out what was wrong, what was happening, what they'd been talking about—

That doesn't matter anymore

—but that was not possible. Even though she knew her mother supported her, even though she'd heard her mother defend her, she could not be entirely certain that her mother's sympathies were completely on her side. Mother Felice loved her, yes, but she was one of them too, and perhaps those loyalties were stronger.

One of them.

When had it become that? When had it turned into *us* versus *them*?

She wasn't sure. But it was probably something that had been building for a while. She'd noticed, many times before, that although her feelings for Mother Felice had remained constant, she seemed to like her other mothers less and less as she grew older. She had never been sure if that was because she was changing or because they had changed. They had all seemed equally nice to her as a child, she had loved them all, but as she'd grown she'd begun to see the differences between them. And the difference between what they were like and what she had thought they were like. Mother Margeaux's strength and focus began to seem bossy to her, her once admirable iron will autocratic and dictatorial. Mother Janine's free-spiritedness seemed for a while flighty and irresponsible, then self-destructive, then just plain crazy. Mother Margaret's dispassionate intellectualism became cold, Mother Sheila's single-minded study of the science of the grape annoying and nerdily fanatic.

Maybe it was nothing. Maybe this was something all children went through. Teenage rebellion and all that crap.

Maybe.

But she didn't think so.

The one thing which had not changed was that they all had equal power over her. If there were divisions of labor within the business, a hierarchical order with Mother Margeaux at the top, there was no such structure in their family life. At least not in regard to her. They were all her mothers, and if there were ever conflicting orders or requests or restrictions, it was up to her to resolve them. She had learned early on that it was impossible to pit one mother against another. They always took one another's side.

Which was why she could not ask Mother Felice.

It was Dion's influence too, she thought. She had become much more assertive since she'd met him, more willing to stand up for herself and to openly disagree with or disobey her mothers. She saw her life now as he would see it, looked at it as an outsider would, and although she had always done that to a certain extent, it seemed as though now she was able to see, to know, to understand how truly strange her lifestyle was.

She didn't fit into her own life.

That was the truth of it. She had been raised this way, but it hadn't taken. She often felt like an outsider amongst her peers, but now she felt just as much an outsider around her mothers.

What would things be like if her father had lived?

She wondered about that more and more often lately. How would her life be different? How would she be different?

She wished she remembered her father, but she'd been too young when he died and everything she knew of him had come from her mothers. Even his appearance would have been a mystery had it not been for the photograph.

If he had only lived a little longer . . .

She could remember nearly everything, almost all the way back to her birth, and if her father had lived a few months longer, she would probably have retained a memory of him as well. She clearly remembered lying in the crib, in the nursery when she was only a few months old, although, to be fair, her memory was probably not as accurate as she believed it to be, comprised as it probably was of not only real events but events imagined during childhood, the visualization of extrapolations from her mothers' stories, a recollection of things she had thought about rather than seen. But the images, all of them, were so vivid, so real, that they *seemed* like things that had happened, not things that she had imagined later or heard about secondhand.

Only many of the things she remembered did not correspond to what her mothers told her.

That scared her.

In one clearly remembered dream image or flash of recollection, she saw Mother Janine, laughing, naked, covered with catsup, dancing in the moonlight in front of the nursery window. But that couldn't be right, could it? That couldn't have happened.

Maybe it could have.

That's what frightened her.

She thought of those dreams of her father. Had that happened too? She could see in her mind a particularly vivid image that had recurred in several nightmares: her father, naked, screaming, held down by the rest of her mothers while Mother Margeaux licked the blood from a gaping wound in his chest.

She sat up in bed. Her mouth was dry. She reached next to her, felt around on the top of the nightstand for her glass of water, but she'd forgotten to bring it into the bedroom with her.

She kicked off the blanket and got out of bed. She could get a drink of water from the bathroom—the cup she used when she brushed her teeth was in there—but she did not like drinking bathroom water. She'd rinse her mouth out with it, but she would not swallow it. She knew that the sink water came from the same pipe as the water in the kitchen, but somehow the fact that it was in the same room as the toilet tainted it for her.

She'd go down to the kitchen.

Penelope opened her bedroom door as quietly as she could and stepped into the hall. The house was dark, and she noticed for the first time that it was completely silent. In the morning, in the afternoon, in the evening, someone was always doing something, and there was activity, movement, sound, noise. But now her mothers were all asleep, all of the lights were off, and the dark silence seemed eerily oppressive.

She didn't want to wake her mothers, so she didn't turn on any lights but felt her way along the wall to the staircase. From somewhere below, from one of the shadeless windows in the kitchen perhaps, came a diffuse blue illumination that served to make the surrounding blackness darker. There were chills on her arms, and she almost turned around and went back into her bedroom. There was something spooky about the house tonight, and though she'd lived in it all her life, though she'd gone up and down these stairs thousands of times, it felt different to her now.

She forced herself to start down the stairs. She was just being a baby, afraid of the dark. There was nothing here that wasn't here in the daytime. And their security system made the house probably the safest structure west of the Pentagon. No one could be hiding in here. No one could have broken in.

She was not afraid of someone breaking in.

No, she had to admit, she wasn't. She was trying to look at the situation logically, but her uneasiness was anything but logical. There was no sound basis for it, no reason why it should be there.

But it was.

She reached the bottom step and hurried to her right, through the doorway into the kitchen. Here, finally, she turned on a light. The small one above the stove. As she'd hoped, illumination drove away the fear. The objects around her were recognizable now—counter, sink, refrigerator, stove—and that air of threatening unreality which had existed only seconds before was effectively dispelled.

Nothing fought off monsters like light.

She opened the dishwasher, took out a glass, and turned on the faucet.

A figure passed in front of the window above the sink.

She jumped, almost dropped the glass, catching it only at the last second. Her first thought was: ghost. The figure had been pale, a blur of movement undistinguishable as a specific form.

Then she heard the familiar sound of the alarm being deactivated as a password was keyed into the panel outside the door, and in the dim circle of light on the other side of the window she saw Mother Margeaux.

What was she doing out this late? Where had she been?

The door opened, and Penelope stood there, glass in hand, as Mother Margeaux walked into the kitchen. She saw Penelope but said nothing, moving quickly and silently past her as though she wasn't there.

Penelope said nothing either, simply watched her mother's pale form fade into the darkness of the hall, her chill returning, wondering why her mother's blouse was torn.

Wondering why it was stained with blood.

THIRTY-FIVE

Horton stared at the empty wine bottle on the table before him. He'd been staring at it now for nearly twenty minutes, trying to figure out why it was empty.

He could not remember drinking the wine.

He knew he had done so. He was drunk and acutely conscious of the fact. But he could not for the life of him recall the specifics of the event: how long it had taken to finish off the bottle, where he had gotten the wine in the first place, when he had started drinking.

Blackout.

That's what scared him. He'd known enough alkies in his time to be familiar with the symptoms, and though he had been hitting the sauce a little heavier than usual lately, it did not seem to him that he was having any difficulty controlling his drinking.

That was the problem—it never seemed that way to the person involved.

There was something else, though, something beneath the surface fear of alcohol abuse that troubled him as he stared at the bottle, and it had to do with the wine itself.

Daneam.

Lezzie label wine. He'd heard of it, perhaps even seen a bottle here and there, but it had never been available, to his knowledge, to the general public.

And he could've sworn that he picked up this bottle at Liquor Shack.

But he couldn't remember for sure.

He rubbed his eyes, massaging them until they hurt. The effect that the wine seemed to have on him was different than that of any alcohol he'd ever drunk before. Instead of feeling lonely and alone, cut off from everything except himself and his sorrows, he felt . . . connected. To who or what he didn't know, but the feeling of *communing* with others through the wine, through his intoxication, was there, and it was creepy.

He also felt . . . well, sexually excited. That was not something that usually happened either. To others, maybe, but not to him. He'd always found alcohol to be anything but an aphrodisiac. A de-sexualizer, if anything. Yet he was sitting here now with an erection, aroused after remembering the one time he and Laura had tried something kinky. She'd wanted him to cuff her to the bedposts and rape her, roughly, and he'd been happy to oblige, but when it came down to it, when she was manacled and spread-eagled before him, he'd been too inhibited and hadn't been able to maintain an erection.

Now, though, thinking back on the incident, he had no problem keeping up his erection. It pressed painfully against his slacks, and he thought that if Laura was here right now, he'd throw her on the fucking floor and shove it up her pussy until she screamed.

He picked up the bottle. It felt comfortable in his hands, familiar, and he supposed that he'd held it as he drank the wine, though he could not remember doing so.

Blackout.

What the hell was happening here?

The phone rang.

He sprang to his feet, instantly sober, already striding out of the kitchen toward the telephone in the living room. The phone never rang unless it was someone from the station calling him in, and some cop's instinct, some perpetually responsible part of his brain automatically kicked into gear, immediately negating the effects of the alcohol.

He caught the phone halfway through the second ring. "Horton."

"Lieutenant? This is Officer Deets. I'm on-site and patched through the station. We, uh, have what appears to be a double homicide here—"

"Cut the police talk. What happened?"

"Two teenagers. They were torn apart."

Horton's mouth was dry. "Where?"

"On South Street."

"I'm on my way."

Searchlights, flashlight beams, and the blue-red strobes of patrol cars lit the lonely section of road between the entrance to the Daneam vineyards and the old Mitchell ranch. Horton stood inside the roadblock next to the meat truck and lit up. The inhaled smoke felt good in his lungs. Warm. He exhaled, looked toward the Dodge Dart, where McComber and another uniform were dusting for prints. Someone had spotted the car a half hour ago and called in. Both sets of parents had already phoned the station hours earlier, worried about their kids, and when the plates of the abandoned vehicle matched the kids' plates, Deets and McComber had been sent out.

They'd found the bodies in less than five minutes.

Or what was left of them.

Horton took a deep drag on his cigarette, trying not to think of that assembled pile of flesh and bone they'd bagged and packed in the meat truck. An adult was bad enough, but teenagers, kids . . . He looked up at the stars, wondering for the zillionth time how, if there was a God, He could allow shit like this to happen.

He hated this fucking job.

They'd finally gotten a break, though. And, amazingly, old dickhead Deets was the one who'd found it.

A weapon. With prints.

Bloody prints.

He tossed his cigarette onto the asphalt past the roadblock and walked back over to the black-and-white. The weapon was still on the hood where he'd left it, bagged, tagged, and ready for the lab: a Daneam wine bottle.

He picked up the bag, thought of the bottle still sitting back on his kitchen table, and shivered.

"Lieutenant!"

Horton jumped at the sound of the voice, nearly dropped the bag. He feigned calmness, looked back toward the evidence officer. "Yeah," he said.

"You through with that?"

Horton looked down at the bag in his hand and nodded slowly. "Yeah," he said. "I'm through with it. It's all yours."

THIRTY-SIX

April awoke feeling hungover and horny.

She rolled over and squinted at the clock on the dresser but could not tell if it was eight-thirty or nine-thirty. Reaching down, she felt around on the floor next to the bed until her fingers found the wine bottle. It was not quite empty, there were still a few drops left, and she held the open neck of the bottle above her mouth and let the drops fall onto her lips and tongue.

God, it tasted good.

Her left hand slid under the sheet, between her legs. Lazily, she began rubbing herself. She was already wet, and there was a tingling within her vagina that she recognized as the need to be filled.

She'd give anything to have a hard cock inside her right now.

From the front of the house, from the kitchen, she heard the sound of the sink running, heard the rattle of silverware on pots and pans. She stopped fingering herself and let the bottle fall to the floor again. She took a deep breath, closed her eyes for a moment, then sat up, leaning against the headboard. She thought about last night, about what Margaret and Margeaux and the others had told her.

Dion?

It didn't seem possible.

She didn't *want* it to be possible.

That was the truth. That was the reason she'd gotten so drunk last night. She'd told herself even as she downed the first bottle that she was tired of being good, that she simply wanted to cut loose after being straitjacketed for so long, but the fact was that she was drinking not to feel good but to forget, trying to numb her brain and block out what they'd told her about her son.

Because she knew it was true.

That was the bottom line. She knew it was true. She'd always known, perhaps, on some subliminal level. She'd been surprised, but she hadn't been shocked or disbelieving when the others had sat her down and explained it all to her, and she'd believed it instantly. All of it.

"Mom?" Dion knocked on the door of her bedroom.

She didn't answer.

"Mom? It's almost ten. Are you getting up?"

Ten? She squinted at the clock. It hadn't said nine-thirty. It had said nine-fifty.

"Mom?"

She felt again that tingling, that maddening need between her legs, and she kicked off the covers and stood naked facing the door, not saying anything, half hoping that Dion would open the door and walk in and see her, but when he called "Mom?" again and started to turn the knob, she quickly said, "I'm up! Don't come in! I'm not dressed!"

"Okay." She heard him move away, down the hall, and she felt ashamed that she would even consider exposing herself to her son. What could possibly make her act this way? What was the matter with her?

But she knew exactly why she had acted that way, she knew exactly what was the matter with her, and as she stood there, staring at the closed door, her fingers slid down her body, through her pubic hair, and into the soft, spongy moisture between her legs.

It was hard picking up a guy on a Sunday morning.

Not impossible. But hard.

She'd left Dion at home, with a list of chores and things to do, and she'd gone cruising. She hadn't done that for a while, and it felt good. Pickings had been mighty slim at the first two taverns she'd hit: barflies, winos, old men. But the third time had been the charm, and at the Happy Hour, she'd found a handsome, athletic young man gone only slightly to seed, an obviously once hot stud now beginning to fray around the edges but still substantially intact.

She sat next to him, drank with him, talked to him, touched him, and when he offered to drive her back to his place, she'd readily agreed.

Now he was naked and whimpering on the bed, the sheets covered with sperm and blood and urine, and she looked down at him, feeling sore and satisfied, and gently ran a finger through his hair. He flinched at her touch, and she felt a warm satisfaction at the response.

She'd been about to get dressed and return home, but she was suddenly in the mood for more, and she glanced at the clock. Three-fifteen. She still had time. Dion wasn't expecting her home until six.

She knelt before him, reached between his legs, grabbed his bloody, swollen penis.

"No," he cried. "No more."

She slapped his face, smiled. "Yes," she said.

She took him in her mouth, tasted the saltiness of the sperm and the blood and the urine.

She began to suck.

On the way home she stopped at Taco Bell and picked up some tacos for their dinner.

She was home in time to see *60 Minutes*.

THIRTY-SEVEN

On Monday afternoon, Dion was suspended for fighting.

He had never been in a fight before in his life. He'd been threatened by bullies a couple of times in grammar school and junior high, but he'd always managed to avoid getting beat up: running away or not showing up at the prearranged meeting place or somehow using his brains to escape the brawn.

But this time he was the one who started the fight.

Afterward, he wasn't even sure exactly what had happened or how it had escalated so fast. One minute he was sitting on top of a lunch table with Kevin and Paul and Rick, and the next minute he and Paul were rolling on the cement ground, clutch punching. Paul had made some joke about Penelope being a lesbian, and he had defended her, responding in kind. Insults had flown back and forth. And then they were fighting.

He could not remember having made a conscious decision to try to physically hurt Paul, but all of a sudden he was lunging at the other boy, fists flying, and by the time Kevin and Rick pulled them apart, he had already drawn blood.

A crowd had gathered, and though he heard the cheers only peripherally, was aware of the crowd only as background to the fight itself, he knew that the crowd was on his side, rooting for him, and with each punch he landed, he heard the exclamations of approval, sensed the satisfaction of the watchers.

And then they were pulled apart.

The gathered students were staring at him silently, almost worshipfully, and he was trembling, pumped with adrenaline, as Mr. Barton, the counselor, led him to the

office. He was vaguely aware of the fact that he had in-
flicted much more damage on Paul than Paul had on him.
He would not have thought that possible even a few days
before, but it did not surprise him now, and he was
pleased with himself as Mr. Barton closed the office door,
sat him down in the chair opposite the desk, and told him
that he was to be suspended from school for three days.

Dion nodded numbly.

The counselor smiled at him. "I'm only doing this because I have to, you know. If it were up to me, I would've
let you kill him."

Dion blinked. "What?"

Mr. Barton opened his bottom drawer and pulled out a
bottle of wine, uncorking it. "You know how it is. We all
have to play these little games."

Dion realized belatedly that the counselor was drunk.
Mr. Barton took a swig of wine, and Dion recognized the
sweet, heady fragrance from his dinner at Penelope's. It
smelled good, and he wanted some, but when the counselor offered him a drink, he shook his head.

"Come on," Mr. Barton said.

He could practically taste it in his mouth, and he felt a
familiar stirring between his legs, but he forced himself to
say, "No."

The counselor took another long drink from the bottle.
"I understand," he said. "Saving it for later." He waved a
hand toward the door. "You're free," he said, winking.
"You're suspended. Get out of here."

Dion stood, left. It was not until he was off school
property and walking home that he began to think back
on what had happened and to wonder what had come over
him and made him behave so completely out of character.

Beating someone up? Hurting someone?

Liking it?

And that weird encounter with the counselor . . .

There were things going on here that he sensed were
related, interconnected, but that he just could not seem to
piece together. He was frustrated. It was like working on
a math problem that he almost understood but could not
quite get a handle on.

It had something to do with his dreams, though. And Penelope's mothers. And his mom. And wine.

By the time he arrived home, he was again trembling. This time it was not adrenaline, though.

It was fear.

Penelope stopped by after school. He hadn't seen her that morning in class, hadn't seen her at lunch, and he'd assumed that she'd been sick and stayed home, but when he'd tried to call her earlier in the afternoon, after he'd first arrived home, he'd gotten an answering machine and had hung up without leaving a message.

Now she and Vella walked into the house, Vella nervously, Penelope looking around with curiosity. She had never been inside before, and Dion wished he'd had time to clean up a bit. Breakfast dishes were still piled in the sink, visible through the kitchen doorway, and the living room floor was littered with Coke cans and the newspapers he'd been trying to read all afternoon. Not a good first impression.

She smiled at him. "So this is what you call home."

He reddened. "It's usually cleaner," he said, apologizing. "If you'd called and told me you were coming, I could've at least straightened up a bit."

Penelope laughed. "I wanted to catch you in your natural habitat."

Vella looked uncomfortably toward the window. "We heard what happened," she said. "We heard you got suspended."

His face felt hot, flushed. He wanted to explain but he didn't know how, wanted to apologize, but he didn't know what for. Instead he stood there stupidly, nodding, looking at Vella, not wanting to meet Penelope's eyes.

"No one likes Paul much anyway," Vella said. "You're a big hero." But he could tell from her tone of voice that she didn't think he was a hero.

"It just happened," he said. He looked over at Penelope. "He called you a lez."

She blushed.

"Hey," he said, changing the subject. "You guys want something to drink? Coke? 7-Up? Dr Pepper?"

Vella shook her head. "No. We've gotta go. I'm supposed to just drive straight to school and straight back. I'm going to be late already. My mom'll go ballistic if I'm any later."

"I thought you might want to come over," Penelope said quickly. "Vella could drop us off and I could drive you home."

"But we have to hurry," Vella said.

Dion nodded, grinned at Penelope. "Let me write my mom a note."

Ten minutes later, Vella was dropping them off in front of the winery gates. They said good-bye, Penelope thanked her friend, and then Vella drove off and Penelope opened the black security box with her key and punched in the access code. She frowned as she did so, and Dion lightly touched her shoulder, not making the gesture too intimate, aware of the security camera trained on them from the top of the fence. "Something wrong?" he asked.

Penelope started to shake her head, then nodded.

The gate swung open, and they stepped onto the driveway.

"What is it?" Dion asked.

She turned to face him. "My mothers."

He was not surprised by her words, found, in fact, that he'd been expecting them. His heart was pounding. "What about them?"

She shook her head. "That's just it. I don't know. Not exactly." They began walking slowly up the drive. She told him what had happened Saturday night after she'd gotten home, described the way in which Mother Margeaux had sneaked into the house after midnight, her blouse torn and covered with blood. "I love my mothers," she said. "But I don't know them." She took a deep breath. "I'm—I'm afraid of them."

"Do you think—"

"I think they might've killed my father."

They stopped walking, stared at each other. From the vineyard, carried on the slight breeze, came the low, musical hum of a conversation in Spanish. Somewhere near the buildings ahead, a car engine started.

"I have no proof," she continued quickly. "Nothing to

go on, really. It's just a feeling, but . . ." She trailed off. Her voice when she spoke was lower, and she glanced to the left and right as if making sure that no one was listening in. "I pretended I was sick yesterday. I stayed in my room. The reason I wanted you to come over today was not because . . . you know. It's because I was scared to come home alone." She took a deep breath, and there were tears in her eyes. "I don't know what to do."

"You should've called me."

"I couldn't."

"Is that why you weren't at school today?"

"I came after lunch. I—I spent the morning in the library."

Dion licked his lips. "What can I do?"

"I don't know."

He reached for her, hugged her, held her, and she began crying. He could feel her shaking, sobbing against his shirt, and though he wanted to be sympathetic and understanding, he could not help becoming aroused, and a powerful erection pressed outward against his jeans. She had to notice, but she didn't seem to mind, and he held her tighter, closer.

He thought of the man his mom had brought home, the man who'd been murdered, and the parallels were just too close for comfort. He thought of telling Penelope, but didn't want to worry her any further. He himself had dealt with the situation by ignoring it, not thinking about it, but Penelope was reacting in exactly the opposite way, and he tried to imagine what it must be like for her, living with people she suspected were murderers. He looked over her shoulder at the Greek-styled buildings at the top of the drive and shivered.

Too much was happening, there was too much going on. He didn't know what to do, didn't know what to say, didn't know how to react. This wasn't a simple situation where there was a problem and a solution, where there was someone he could talk to, someone he could turn to who would set things right. He couldn't just go to the police and say that he was having weird dreams and there seemed to be something creepy about Napa and, oh, by the way, Penelope thinks her mothers are murderers. He

couldn't talk to his mom because . . . well, because he had
the feeling that she might be involved somehow. He could
probably tell Kevin, but Kevin wasn't in any better position to do something about it than he was.

Do something about what?

That was the main problem. That was the most frustrating aspect of this whole business. Nothing had happened.
Nothing concrete, at least. There were hints and feelings
and hunches, but there was no one specific thing he could
point to that would convince a rational outsider that his
fears were justified.

Penelope was afraid too, though.

That counted for something.

She pulled away from him, dried her eyes, tried to
smile. "Sorry," she said. "I think I got mascara on your
shirt."

"Don't worry about it."

They were silent for a moment.

"So what do you want to do?" Dion asked.

"I want to look in the lab. I want to walk into the
woods. I want you to go with me."

"What do you think you'll find?"

"Nothing probably. But I want to know why I've been
kept away from them all these years. I thought about it
yesterday, and I feel like I'm some type of Skinner experiment, like I've been conditioned and trained to act and
feel certain ways. I mean, I've never even been curious
about the lab. I've just accepted that I can't go in there.
I've been curious about the woods, but I'm afraid of
them, and I feel like those are the responses I've been
conditioned to have." She looked into his eyes. "I want to
break my conditioning."

He nodded slowly. "What if we do find something?"

"I don't know. We'll figure that out when we come to
it."

Mother Felice was in the kitchen, baking bread, and
Mother Sheila was out in the vineyard somewhere, but
the rest of them had all gone into San Francisco for a
meeting with their distributor.

"Perfect," Penelope said to Dion over glasses of grape juice.

"What?" her mother asked.

"Nothing."

They had some fresh bread with the juice, then went upstairs for a moment, ostensibly to Penelope's room. She stationed Dion on guard at the top of the stairs and quickly ducked into Mother Sheila's bedroom, emerging a moment later, holding a key which she quickly pocketed.

They walked downstairs and outside, walking clockwise around the house from the front, coming at the main winery building from the side not visible from the kitchen window. Inside it was dark, only the security lights on, and Penelope did not turn on the rest of the lights as they went in. They walked past the pressing room in the dim halflight, and stopped in front of what looked like a small closet door. "Wait here," Penelope said, opening the door and walking in.

"What is it?"

"Security. I'm going to turn off the cameras." There was a click, a hum, and a beep, and Penelope walked back out, closing the door behind her. "Come on."

He didn't remember exactly where the lab was. He thought it was somewhere far ahead, at the opposite end of the building, and he was surprised when Penelope stopped at the next door down.

She looked at him, tried to smile. "This is it," she said. She was scared. He could hear it in her voice, and he put a reassuring hand on her arm as she inserted the key in the lock.

She glanced around, double-checking, making sure that no one had followed them, that the security cameras were not on, then quickly pulled open the door and walked inside.

He followed.

He was not sure what he had expected, but it certainly wasn't this. Sensors had turned on overhead lights the second they had walked through the door, and they stood with their backs to the entrance looking at—

Nothing.

It was a lab in name only. There were no machines, no

beakers or test tubes, no tables. There was no furniture at all. The walls were empty, the floor was spotless. There was only a circular hole surrounded by a low stone wall in what appeared to be the exact center of the room.

Dion wanted to leave. If before everything had been too vague, too nebulous, things were fast becoming far too concrete. The fact that Penelope's mothers had for years been spending time in here, telling her that they were working in a lab on stains of grape and varieties of wine when in reality there had been nothing in here but this well, scared the hell out of him. The seeming irrationality of it, the fact that he could make no sense of the situation, was what frightened him the most, and he was suddenly afraid for Penelope. He wondered if his mom would let her move in with them, if he could—

Penelope squeezed his hand, moved forward.

"No!" Dion said.

"What?"

"Don't go near it."

She smiled, but there was no humor in it. "You think a monster's going to pop up and grab me?"

That wasn't exactly what he thought, but it was close.

"I have to know," she said softly.

He held her hand tightly, and the two of them walked forward into the center of the room. They looked down into the well, expecting to see a black, bottomless pit, or an empty shaft with bones on the bottom. But instead they saw, a foot or so below the stone rim, their own reflections staring back at them from the deep, glassy burgundy surface of wine.

"What is this?" Penelope asked.

"I don't know," he said, but on some level, he thought, he did know. For the fear he'd felt before, the worry, was gone, replaced by calm. The feeling that things he didn't understand were spinning out of control was not there anymore. This room, this well, this wine, all of it felt reassuring to him, comfortable, as though he was now ensconced in familiar surroundings. He breathed deeply. The smell of the wine reminded him of the counselor's office, of Mr. Barton drinking from the bottle in his desk, and he thought back to the fight with Paul. On one level he was horrified by what had happened, disgusted with himself, but a deeper part of him approved, and as he replayed the fight in his mind, as he thought of the small changes that would have resulted in Paul's death, he smiled.

"What are you smiling at?" Penelope demanded.

He opened his eyes, looked at her, blinked. What *had* he been smiling at? The thought of killing Paul? He shook his head. "Nothing."

The two of them looked down at the well of wine.

"What now?" Dion asked.

"The woods," Penelope said.

"Are you sure?"

She nodded. "I knew I'd have to go there ever since I caught Mother Margeaux sneaking into the kitchen the other night. I tried to pretend otherwise, tried not to think about it, tried to tell myself that—that there was an explanation for it, but I knew there wasn't."

"Maybe—"

"No maybes."

He nodded. "Let's go, then. Let's see what's out there."

THIRTY-EIGHT

Horton stood against the wall as the computer checked the prints against those in its files, watching as the split screens flashed by, the left half containing the print off the bottle, the right showing the prints against which it was being compared. The process was automated but not instantaneous, and he knew that it was going to take a long time to go through all of the prints stored in the machine's memory. In addition to complete sets of fingerprints for all perps arrested in the county during the last ten years, the computer stored the prints of children fingerprinted at birth, individuals who'd undergone voluntary printing, and unidentified prints from other crime scenes. The computer also had the capability of accessing the print files of other departments across the state who were online.

The search had already been underway for nearly twenty-four hours, and according to Filbert, the technician monitoring the machine, it could take twice that long before all fingerprints were compared.

Hell, Horton thought, with his luck the print would probably end up being of someone not even on file.

He took a sip of his coffee, was about to walk back to his office when suddenly the screen stopped moving, the image locking in place. A red light flashed on and off, a small beep sounding. "Lieutenant?" Filbert said, turning around.

Horton moved forward, looked over Filbert's shoulder as the technician pressed a series of keys. The identification of the print owner was superimposed over the bottom portion of the screen.

Margeaux Daneam.

His mouth was suddenly dry, and he finished off his coffee. He hadn't suspected this, hadn't expected it, but somehow it did not completely surprise him. He stared at the name and the winery address beneath it. A ripple of cold passed through him.

"Print it," he told Filbert.

The technician pressed a key, and a copy of the screen began printing on the Laserjet adjacent to the terminal.

Daneam.

He rubbed the goose bumps on his arms. It was not the fact that a prominent local businesswoman had been implicated in the brutal rape and murder of two teenagers that spooked him. I was everything else. The peripherals. The rise in DUI's, D&D's, the other murders, his own drinking and everyone else's.

The fact that it was all related.

That was it exactly. He'd been a cop for a long time, had been involved with crimes big and small, but the crimes had always been self-contained. A crime was committed by a criminal or criminals, the case was solved, the perps put away, end of story. But this was different. The drug problem, he supposed, would be the closest analogy to this, but though drugs were related to myriad crimes, the crimes were all separate. Related, perhaps, to a root cause, but individual. They weren't . . . like this.

This was spooky.

He thought of Hammond and his wacky theories.

Maybe the detective hadn't been so far off base after all.

Filbert tore off the printed sheet and handed it to Horton.

"Print off a couple more of those," Horton said. "And give 'em to the chief."

Filbert nodded.

"And thanks." Horton opened the lab door and walked into the hallway.

The station was in chaos.

He stood there, stunned, as men ran past him in both directions down the corridor. Those policemen who were not already armed and in riot gear were in the process of becoming so. Several men were shouting at once, and something unintelligible was being broadcast over the P.A.

"What is it?" Horton demanded, grabbing a rookie by the arm.

"A riot over on State Street, sir."

"What happened?"

"No one knows. A group of fifteen or twenty people from one of the bars suddenly turned violent and started attacking people who were outside marching in the Halloween parade. Five are reported dead."

"Dead?"

"Yes, sir."

"Jesus shit."

"There might be an officer down."

Horton let go of the rookie's arm. "Go!" he said.

The officer hurried away, and Horton strode through the activity to Goodridge's office. He had a hunch about this, a weird feeling in his gut. He didn't think that the Daneams had started the riot because they knew the police had a fingerprint and had identified it and were about to come after old Margeaux. Not exactly. But he had no doubt that they were involved. He'd stake his career on it. He had never trusted those lezzies. He didn't know if they were putting something into their wine or were practicing witchcraft, but they were somehow behind all of this violence, and he was damn sure going to put a stop to it.

He walked into the chief's office, showed him the printout, told him about the match, and said that he needed a warrant and some men.

"I can't spare anyone," Goodridge said. "Why don't you hold off until tomorrow. Margeaux Daneam's not going anywhere."

Horton stared at him, stunned. "What?"

The chief looked at him coolly. "You heard me. It'll wait."

"We found her bloody fingerprint on the bottle that was used to penetrate and rupture Ann Melbury, and I'm not supposed to arrest her?"

Goodridge opened his bottom desk drawer, drew out a Daneam wine bottle. "Relax, Horton. You take things much too seriously. Have a drink. Loosen up a little."

Horton stared at the chief, cold washing over him. He turned without speaking and walked out of the office.

"Horton!" Goodridge called after him.

He ignored the chief's cry and continued walking. He spotted Deets in front of the supply room, waiting to be issued riot gear, and he grabbed the young cop. "You're coming with me," he said.

"But I'm supposed to—"

"We matched the print from the bottle. We've got our murderer. I want you in on the collar."

Deets was suddenly at attention. "Yes, sir. Thank you, sir."

Horton frowned. "How many times have I told you about that 'sir' shit?"

"I'm sorry, Lieutenant. I just got—"

"Get a black-and-white," Horton said. "Bring it around front. I'll meet you there."

"Yes, si— Okay!" He sprinted down the corridor, against the traffic.

Horton reached into his pocket, pulled out a cigarette, lit it. So they wouldn't have a warrant. No big deal. Phillips would get him one after the fact and back date it. What the chief would do . . . That was another story.

He took a long drag on his cigarette, inhaled deeply, then pushed his way past a line of uniforms toward the front door.

They pulled up in front of the winery, parking in one of the visitor spaces. He had expected someone to meet them, since they'd had to announce themselves and somebody within one of the buildings had had to open the gate for them, but the place appeared to be deserted.

He didn't like that.

He was nervous enough already, but Deets seemed not to notice anything amiss. The young officer got out of the car, straightened his belt, then started toward the front door of the main building, stopping only when he realized that Horton was not following.

"Lieutenant?" he called.

Horton lumbered around the back of the vehicle, caught up to Deets. His cop sense was working overtime. He had never before been as flat-out spooked as he was right now, and he wanted to get this over with as quickly as possible.

He didn't want to be here after dark.

It was pathetic but it was true. His uneasiness had nothing to do with Margeaux Daneam or even the unnatural gruesomeness of the murders she was going to be charged with. It was something more instinctual, more primal, and he did not want to be here when night fell.

Cop's instinct or drunk's paranoia?

He didn't know. But whatever it was, it wasn't shared by Deets. The rookie was striding purposefully toward the main building: a Greek-looking structure facing the parking lot and the drive. Horton followed his footsteps.

"Here!"

The woman's voice came from somewhere off to their left, and Horton turned to see where it was coming from. He thought he saw movement in the late-afternoon shadows that shaded the area between the main building and the structure immediately adjacent to it, but he was not sure.

"Ms. Daneam?" he called.

There was a chorus of wild female laughter, the high, manic sound of several women cackling at the tops of their lungs, and a cold shiver of fear passed through him. Again, he saw movement in the shadows.

"Ms. Daneam? We're from the—"

The door to the adjacent building opened, and for a second, against the interior light, he saw a group of naked women shoving their way inside. Then the door closed, and the wild laughter was silenced.

What the hell was going on here? He looked over at Deets. The rookie was standing in place, mouth open, an expression of dumb surprise on his face.

"Come on," Horton said, unholstering his gun, his confidence returning with the feel of the heavy revolver in his hand. "Let's go." He started jogging toward the door, gratified to hear Deets' boot steps behind him.

The two of them reached the door simultaneously, automatically positioning themselves on either side. Horton reached over and knocked loudly. "Ms. Daneam?" he called.

There was no response from inside, not even laughter, and Horton looked at Deets and said, "On three." He nodded at the rookie. "One. Two. Three."

Deets turned the doorknob and Horton swung out, pushing open the door.

Nothing.

Before them was an empty lighted hallway. There was no sight of anyone, no sound, and they looked at each other and proceeded forward slowly, guns drawn, trying doors as they passed them, though all appeared to be locked.

"They could be behind any one of these," Deets said.

Horton nodded.

"They were . . . they were naked," the rookie said.

Horton nodded again.

"Why were they naked?"

"I don't know."

"I don't like this."

That makes two of us, Horton thought, but he said nothing, tried another door. From somewhere ahead, down the hall, he heard a scream, and he looked at Deets and the two of them started running toward the sound.

The hallway turned, forking to the right, and ahead, on the left, one of the doors was open. Horton stopped, hugging the wall next to the open doorway. "Police!" he yelled. "Step out with your hands on your head!" There was no response, and he moved in front of the doorway in classic firing position.

There was no one in the room.

He quickly walked inside, and the smell hit him almost immediately. It was overwhelming, a powerfully noxious mixture of old wine and older blood, stale sex and violence. He retched, instinctively doubling over, puking on the floor in the corner next to the door.

"Jesus," Deets said behind him, gagging.

Horton wiped his mouth, straightened up. The room was windowless, furnitureless, and in its center was a gigantic empty wine vat, built into the floor and sunken like a hot tub. He walked forward. As he reached the edge of the vat, he could see that it was not empty after all. Glued to the bottom with dried blood were assorted bones and the carcasses of rotting animals.

"Holy shit," Deets said.

Horton started for the door. "Come on. Let's get out to the car and call for backup. I don't like the setup here."

"There is no backup. They're all at the riot."

"They're not *all* at the riot."

Deets followed him out the door. "What's going on here?"

"I don't know," Horton admitted. He looked down the hall the way they'd come.

And saw the women.

They were crouched near the turn of the hallway. They were dirty and disheveled, some holding spears, others wine bottles, covered with what looked like mud and blood. He stood, unmoving. He was scared. But he was also aroused, and as frightening as the women looked, as threatening as their appearance was, he found himself looking between their bent legs, trying to see their shadowed crotches. This was not the right reaction, he told himself. This was not the way he was supposed to feel. But there was something sensuous in their stances, something provocative in their complete lack of modesty and the pride they seemed to take in their filth.

He smelled alcohol, wine, and he breathed deeply, inhaling the fragrance. He imagined what it would be like to throw himself into that gaggle of women, to feel them strip him and take advantage of him, kissing him, licking him, stroking him, sitting on his lap, sitting on his face. They were all sisters too, weren't they? That would make it even better.

They screamed as one and rushed him.

He was slow to react, nearly stunned into immobility. He staggered backward, pointing his gun at the women but not ordering them to halt, the way he should have.

Deets' reactions were quicker. He moved in front of Horton, both hands on his firearm. "Stop right there!" he demanded.

They took him down.

It happened fast, too fast, and Horton wasn't even sure

what exactly occurred. He knew only that they were instantly upon the other officer, screaming, laughing, stab-
bing with spears, clawing with nails, biting with teeth.
How they had reached him so quickly, why he hadn't
fired upon them, how they disarmed him, which one was
the first to reach him, he didn't know.

Horton fired a shot over the heads of the women, not
wanting to fire into their midst for fear of hitting Deets.
The report was thunderous, and he saw a puff of plaster
explode outward from the far wall, but the women did not
even seem to notice. They continued to claw crazily at the
man buried beneath them, and Horton saw blood flying:
drops at first, then splashes.

He realized that he could not hear Deets screaming at
all. He could only hear the women.

He knew instinctively that Deets was dead, and part of
him wanted to stand there and shoot, empty his gun in the
women, kill as many of them as he could. But he was
more afraid than he had ever been in his life, and his gut
told him that if he didn't haul ass now, he probably
wouldn't make it out alive.

He ran.

He wished the women had come from the opposite direction so he could've run out the way they'd come in. He
had no choice now but to run deeper into the building,
hoping that he'd reach the other end and find an open
exit.

They were coming. He could hear them, above his
breathing and the slapping of his shoes on the concrete,
laughing wildly and jabbering in some foreign tongue. He
wanted to try some of the doors lining the corridor, see if
they were locked, but he didn't have time, and he kept
running, following the hallway as it turned and turned
again.

Ahead, the corridor ended at a door. He prayed that it
was not locked, that it led outside, but then he saw that he
didn't have to pray. There was a window in the metal, and
through the window he saw the deep purplish orange of
twilight.

He'd made it.

He reached the door, turned the handle, and it opened.

He stopped and looked behind him, pointing his revolver. He had no qualms about shooting the women. That wasn't the problem. The problem was that he did not have enough bullets for all of them.

But there weren't that many. He saw only three women running after him. Hadn't there been more?

Yes.

They grabbed him from behind. They'd split up, some chasing after him, the others sneaking around the outside of the building to trap him, and he'd been so fucking stupid that he hadn't thought ahead, he'd walked right into it.

He deserved to be caught, he thought.

But as the first fingernails sliced into his flesh, as the broken wine bottle cut open his throat, he thought: no, he didn't.

THIRTY-NINE

They stood next to the fence, looking into the woods.

The woods.

Even the word seemed ominous, and Dion suddenly wished that they had not come out here alone, that they had brought Kevin and Vella with them. Or, better still, that they had waited until morning.

For it was night now. The sun had set quickly, brightening an already extant moon, and the woods were dark, the trees silhouettes and shadows, the hills black background. Behind them, on the other side of the high hills walling in the opposite edge of the valley, the world was yellow and orange, a prolonged sunset fading slowly into the Pacific. But here there was only gloom and the pale bluish light of the moon.

He was afraid of the woods, and it had nothing to do with Penelope or her mothers or anything that he had seen or heard or imagined. It was an instinctive reaction to the sight before him, a physical sensation in response to something within the trees that seemed to be calling to him on some subliminal level.

Something within the trees.

He did think there was something within the trees, although he was not sure where, why, or how he had come up with that idea. And it *was* calling to him. He was afraid of it, but at the same time he felt attracted to it, pulled toward it.

God, he wished he could have a drink right now.

"Dion?"

He looked toward Penelope. She was pale, and he knew it wasn't only the light of the moon that made her appear that way. "Yeah?" he said.

He expected her to say something serious and profound, something that would articulate and explain the complex conflicting emotions he was feeling—that they were both feeling—but when she spoke, her words were disappointingly, disconcertingly mundane: "We should have brought flashlights."

He found himself nodding. "Yeah," he said. "We should've."

They crawled under the fence without speaking—he holding up the barbed wire so she could sneak beneath it—and he grabbed her hand as they started to walk into the woods. Penelope's hand was warm to his touch, her palm sweaty, and he liked that. Her fear excited him somehow, and he felt a stirring in his crotch.

He tried not to think about his feelings, tried not to acknowledge them, but they were as frightening to him as the woods around them. He should tell Penelope, talk to her, let her know that something was wrong not just with this place but with him, but he said nothing, held her hand, continued walking.

The world was silent. Car noises, city noises, did not reach here, did not penetrate, and the woods generated no sounds of their own: no crickets, no birds, no animals. There was only their own breathing, the snap-crackle-pop of their tennis shoes on twigs and gravel. There was something familiar about this lack of sound, Dion thought, something he couldn't quite place.

Penelope's hand stiffened in his. She stopped walking, and he turned to look at her. The woods were dark, the ceiling of trees effectively blocking out the overbright moon. Here and there, individual shafts of moonlight illuminated small sections of ground, but Penelope was in shadow, her pale face barely visible in the murk. "What?" he asked.

"Maybe we should go back."

"I thought you wanted to—"

"I'm afraid."

He pulled her close, put his arms around her. He knew that she could feel his erection, and he pressed forward, pushing it against her. "There's nothing out here," he said. He didn't believe it and didn't know why he had said it, but he repeated it again. "There's nothing here but us."

"I'm afraid," she said again.

He wished they'd brought some wine with them. A flagon of that stuff in the vat. A few swallows of that and she wouldn't be afraid anymore. Hell, a few swallows of that and she'd be out of her panties and on her fucking hands and knees, begging for it—

He pushed away from her, took a deep breath. "Maybe we *should* go back," he said.

"You feel it too."

He nodded, then realized that she couldn't see his face. "Yeah," he admitted.

She reached for him, took his hand again. "Let's—" she began, then sucked in her breath, squeezed his hand. "Look," she said.

"What?"

"Over there." She pulled him to the left, and he saw for the first time what looked like a clearing between the trunks of the trees. A meadow. He didn't want to go to that meadow, wanted instead to turn back, return the way they'd come, but he allowed himself to be pulled along, and they passed between the trees, reached the edge of the clearing, and stopped.

"Oh, my God," Penelope said. She was breathing heavily, in hiccuping spurts. "Oh, my God."

Dion felt suddenly cold.

The clearing was littered with shattered wine bottles, moonlight sparkling on the tiny pieces of broken glass. Here and there, busted kegs emerged from the sea of smashed bottles like dark whales. Scattered amongst the glass were pieces of bone. The pieces were small—carpels, tarsels, metatarsels—but there were enough of them distributed just at their feet to let them know that this had been the sight of some major carnage, that the skeletal remains of dozens, perhaps hundreds, of people could be found here.

But it was not the bones which had chilled Dion so.

It was the blood.

Beneath the glass, beneath the bones, the grass and the dirt below the grass were stained a dark blackish red, the residual sediment of a wave or river of blood which seemed to have once flowed through the clearing. Even the trunks of the trees were darker than they should have been, and the small shrubs and wild bushes which grew around the perimeter of the meadow had a distinctly reddish brown tint, as though blood had seeped into their systems through the roots and had usurped the space of chlorophyll in the leaves.

Dion took a hesitant step forward. The soles of his tennis shoes stuck for a second to the ground, pulling out blades of grass as they moved upward, sounding and feeling stickily like the adhesion of wet paint.

"Don't," Penelope breathed, pulling him back.

But he had to move forward, he had to see. He was horrified by the sight before him, he had never seen anything like it . . . but something about it seemed familiar. It was not the bottles, not the bones, not the blood. It was the clearing itself, and this layer of detritus that had been overlaid on top of it had successfully hidden what was really there, effectively blocking what he should have recognized.

But why should he have recognized it? He had never been here before.

He walked into the meadow, Penelope at his side, still holding his hand. It was larger than it had first appeared, and that brought home to him the enormity of what must have occurred here. They tread gingerly over the littered ground, carefully avoiding the bones.

Some of these might be Penelope's father's, he thought.

He said nothing.

The silence grew heavier, the already oppressive atmosphere even more oppressive. Before them, at the opposite end of the meadow, against the trees that fronted the hillside, was a low mound. Bones and skulls, many with bits of dried flesh still clinging to them, were arranged in ancient runic form on the section of cleared ground. From the center of the space rose a stone square about the size of a bed, and atop the square were arranged crude and ancient instruments of death. Grappling hooks hung from thick chains attached to the branches above. In the trees beyond there loomed a dark carved figure, a stone idol of some sort, and as they drew closer, Dion saw that it was the likeness of a god, festooned with what looked like the results of recent kills: scalps, ears, fingers, penises.

The god had Dion's face.

Penelope's fingernails dug into his palm. "Oh, shit."

Dion backed up. "No," he whispered, shaking his head.

"We have to call the police," Penelope said, pulling him back. "This isn't something we can handle."

Dion nodded dumbly.

From somewhere, from the woods, from the hill, there were screams and cries, laughter and singing, coming closer, low but getting louder. He looked at Penelope, she looked at him, and though both of them knew that they had to get out of the clearing, neither of them knew where to go. The approaching noise was coming from an indeterminate direction, and they did not know if they would be moving away from the arriving people or toward them.

There was a chaotic feel to the noise, an impression of anarchic abandonment that Dion found at once frightening and reassuring. These people, these people who were laughing and crying and screaming, they might try to kill him, but he understood them, he knew where they were coming from, whoever they were.

Whoever they were?

He knew who they were.

They both knew who they were.

Penelope's mothers.

Sure enough, a group of figures burst through the trees at the far end of the clearing, from almost exactly the same spot at which they themselves had entered the meadow. Women. Naked women. Penelope's mothers. They carried between them two unmoving policemen. They were drunk and moving jerkily, several of them carrying what looked like spears, but they were obviously heading this way, and despite the apparent randomness of their movements, they were moving at a good pace, clearly making a beeline for the altar.

"We have to get out of here," Penelope said.

Dion nodded. He wasn't sure if they had been spotted yet, but unless they quickly found some cover, they soon would be. He took Penelope's hand, pulled her toward the trees to the right of the carved idol.

And they were seen.

A cry went up, the high-pitched wail of five women screaming in unison, and Dion turned to see, over his shoulder, Penelope's mothers dashing madly toward them, still screaming identically at the same pitch, grinning hugely and carrying the unmoving policemen with them.

"Run!" Penelope screamed.

He tried. They both tried. But her mothers were moving fast, and the screams were disorienting, and the trees here were thicker, the underbrush heavier, and . . .

And part of him wanted to be caught.

That was at the root of it. He was scared out of his wits, more terrified than he had ever been in his life, and he genuinely wanted to escape. But he held tightly to Penelope's hand, started running first one way, then another, and he realized that he not so subconsciously wanted her mothers to catch up to them. He wanted to know what would happen after that. He was frightened, but at the same time he felt strong, strangely energized, and he knew that whatever happened, no matter how freaky it got, he could handle it.

He *wanted* to handle it.

Her mothers caught up to them a few yards into the trees. Strong hands grabbed his arms, long nails digging into his skin, and he was yanked harshly around to face a leering, drunken Mother Margeaux.

He was not as prepared as he'd thought he was, nowhere near as strong and brave as he'd led himself to believe, and he screamed as the women dragged him back out of the trees toward the square altar on top of the mound. He heard Penelope screaming off to his left, but he could not turn his eyes to see her, and whether she was screaming in pain or fear—or both—he could not tell.

A flagon was shoved between his lips and cool wine forced out. Most of it dribbled down his chin, but some of it ran down his throat, and it felt good, strangely calming.

The he was lifted into the air and slammed down onto the concrete slab. The breath was knocked out of him, and pain flared in his back and his head, but then more wine was being forced down his throat and the pain disappeared. His strength returned in one odd, cold shiver, and he sat up, or was allowed to sit up, and he saw that Mother Margaret and Mother Sheila were the ones holding his arms. Mother Sheila or Mother Felice? He could not remember which was which.

At the foot of the mound below him, he saw the other mothers laughing hysterically as Mother Margeaux shoved a pine cone–tipped spear into the now exposed belly of the older policeman. Blood pooled outward, not spurting but overflowing from the rent skin, cascading onto the grass.

Penelope was not being held but had been thrown on the grass to the left of her mothers and was attempting to sit up. She saw her mothers whooping and cackling as the younger policeman was stripped and gutted, Mother Margeaux ripping into the entrails with her fingers after the spears had opened the flesh.

"What are you doing?" Penelope screamed. "What's happening?"

What was happening? Dion wondered. But though he wanted to scream too, though he wanted to cry, he didn't.

Instead, for no reason whatsoever, as he watched the mothers laughing and gleefully playing in the blood, he started to smile.

FORTY

He is here.

The knowledge burst upon Dennis McComber fully formed. The officer rolled down the window of his patrol car and dumped out the coffee he'd been drinking. He reached for the bottle of wine on the seat next to him, popped the half-stopped cork, and allowed himself a long, luscious drink.

He is here.

He thought of the chief's daughter and wondered if that little minx was going to be there as well. She probably would. Hell, of course she would. She'd known about it even before he had.

He thought of the way her head had been bobbing up and down in her boyfriend's lap. Had she taken him all the way into her mouth? Had she deep-throated him? McComber was pretty sure that she had. Even if she hadn't, what the fuck difference did it make? She'd deep-throat *him*. She'd suck him all the way down to the root. He'd make her. He'd fuck that little slut's face so hard she'd be coughing up sperm for a month.

He is here.

Yes, He was here, and it was time to meet Him. It was time to get shitfaced and fuck his brains out for the glory of his new god.

Amen.

McComber took another swig from the bottle and started the car.

Someone unplugged the jukebox, and Frank Douglas was all set to scream at the little pissant, whoever he was, and kick him out on his troublemaking ear, when he saw that everyone in the bar had stopped dancing, stopped moving, stopped talking, and were all staring at him.

"He is here," someone said, whispered, and the voice was like a shout in the silent bar.

Frank felt suddenly cold.

He glanced toward the door, saw that Ted the bouncer was standing with two of the patrons, a half-finished bottle of Daneam red dangling from his hand.

What the hell was going on?

He is here.

He knew what was going on. Well, he didn't know, not exactly, but he knew that the past few weeks had been building up to this, and he was not surprised that it was occurring now. He looked over the counter at the assembled patrons, jostling one another to the left and the right, shuffling unthinkingly into a line as they continued to stare unblinkingly at him.

He reached under the bar for his shotgun, felt comfort in its familiar heft as he removed it from its perch. He did not look down at the gun, did not look away from the crowd, unwilling to give them any edge. Most of these bastards were loaded, crocked, three sheets to the fucking wind. They might be all tanked up and full of courage right now, but when it came down to it, when he started blasting, they'd scatter and run like scared jackrabbits.

When he started blasting?

He glanced over at Ted, saw the gleeful belligerence in the bouncer's face.

Yes. When.

For it was going to happen. He had been in fights before, been in more bar brawls than he cared to remember, and there was always a point past which the violence was inevitable. No matter what was said or done, no matter how much talking went on, it was going to happen.

They'd passed that point when the jukebox was unplugged.

The shotgun was loaded, in preparation for an emergency, and in one smooth motion—a motion he had practiced in front of the mirror and in back of the bar until he could do it the way he'd seen it done in a movie—he swung the weapon up, barrel pointing straight into the center of the crowd.

"Back off!" he ordered. "Back off and get the fuck out of here! Bar's closed!"

A red-haired woman laughed. Frank noticed with shock that her skirt was off—she was wearing only a blouse and panties. As his gaze moved from one person to another, he saw that many of the men and women had clothing that was ripped or missing.

"He is here!" someone yelled.

"Wine!" a woman cried. "We need more wine!"

"The bar's closed!" Frank repeated, shifting the shotgun.

The red-haired woman laughed again.

And Frank blew her face off.

He didn't mean to. Or at least he didn't think he meant to. It happened so fast. She was laughing at him and he was pointing the gun at her and his gaze went from her black panties to the look of black hatred on her slutty face and he hated that look and he wanted her to shut up and before he could even think about it he was pulling the trigger and when he could see again she was down and her face had been blown off.

And the others rushed him.

He had no time to reload, no time to do anything. Ted was in front, and he leaped the bar and yanked the shotgun from his hand, and then others were hopping over the counter. He saw breasts and fists, pubic hair and penises. He went down, punched and poked, scratched and kicked, and he heard bottles being smashed, chairs being thrown. There was laughing and whooping, the smell of newly opened alcohol. Wine spilled onto his face.

Above him, Ted grasped the shotgun like a golf club and lifted it over his shoulder, crying, "Fore!"

Frank did not even have time to scream before the butt of the shotgun smashed in the side of his head.

Pastor Robens cowered in his office, his back to the locked door, listening to what was going on in his church but afraid to confront it and put a stop to it, afraid even

to look at the blasphemies that were being performed
under his roof.

Under *His* roof.

That was the most horrifying thing of all, the utter lack
of respect for God Almighty and His Son Jesus Christ.

They had been there already when he'd returned from
his nightly visit to the AIDS hospice. They'd broken into
the church, had smashed one of the side windows to get
in, and they were dancing in the aisles, ten or fifteen of
them, teenagers and young adults, some sort of horrible
rap music blasting from a boombox that had been set up
on the dais. There were wine bottles on the carpet, wine
bottles in the hands of the dancers, and he'd stormed into
the church filled with rage and righteous indignation,
screaming at them to leave immediately. He'd charged to
the front of the church, turned off the boombox, whirled
to face the revelers—

And he'd seen the statue.

The statue of Christ, *his* statue of Christ, the one he had
received from the Reverend Morris in Atlanta. It was lying on its side on the front pew, and it had been desecrated, a garish clown's smile painted on the face with
lipstick, an enormous clay phallus appended to the crotch.

Standing on the pew next to the statue was a young
woman with blond-and-black streaked hair. She was wearing a black see-through bra and a short black skirt, but the
skirt was hiked up, and she had on no underwear. She was
fingering herself, her hips swiveling in a slow, sensual motion.

There was a topless girl in the midst of the now mo-
tionless dancers, a boy with an erection emerging from
his open zipper. Two young men, fully clothed, were lying on the floor underneath the broken window, embrac-
ing.

The lecture he'd intended to deliver died on his lips. He
saw now that there was something hard and corrupt and
vaguely threatening in the faces of these drunken teens, a
knowing belligerence he had not noticed at first.

His anger faded as he faced the trespassers, replaced by
a growing fear.

No one spoke.

Smirking, the young woman on the pew moved to the left, straddled the desecrated statue.

She spread open the lips of her vulva and peed.

There were giggles and chuckles that echoed in the silent church, titters that turned into guffaws. The young people were all still staring at him, but in their faces was not the shame at being caught that he'd expected to see, not the guilty acknowledgment of their wrongdoing that he would have thought they'd exhibit, but condescension and a smug, intimidating contempt.

A ponytailed boy swaggered up to the dais, held a bottle out. "Hey, dude, have some."

Pastor Robens wanted to smack the bottle out of the boy's hand, wanted to grab him by the collar and shake some sense into him, but he stood meekly aside as the boy took a swig of the wine and turned on the boombox.

The other youngsters started dancing again, passing around their bottles, whooping and hollering. The two young men on the floor were now partially undressed. Against the back wall a girl screamed as a boy began beating her breasts with his fists.

Pastor Robens hurried into his office, shut the door, locked it.

He heard a chorus of laughter from the partyers on the other side.

The ironic thing was that he did want a drink. He had never wanted a drink more in his life. He was trembling, his heart pounding with fear. He had never encountered anything like this before. He had counseled troubled teens, had even worked for a while in a gang-counseling center in downtown San Francisco. But nothing he had ever experienced had prepared him for this. Emotionally troubled youth and violent fledgling criminals, those he could deal with. Those kids had specific recognizable problems. But that group out there . . .

Something smashed against the door of this office, and he leaned against it, closing his eyes, offering a quick prayer to God that they wouldn't get in.

There was something wrong with them, something deep and fundamental that went beyond the surface problems caused by family or society or even mental instability, something that he sensed but could not see, something that he only partially understood.

Evil.

Yes, that was it exactly. Evil. These kids were evil. Evil not for what they were doing, not for what they were saying, but for what they *were*.

He had intended to come in here and call the police, but as he pressed his back against the door, as he heard the revelry going on in his chapel, he realized that he was afraid to do so.

There was a furious knocking on the door behind him, a powerful pounding he could feel in his bones.

"I got a big prick for you, preacher!"

He bit his lip, said nothing.

He had been in here now for over two hours. He'd heard screams of pain, cries of pleasure, drunken laughter. There'd been things knocked over, items smashed, windows broken. And through it all, the music, that horribly repetitive rap music, blaring from the front of the church, covering the softer sounds, obscuring the louder ones, making everything chaotic and unintelligible and even more frightening.

And then, all of a sudden . . . he heard them leave. The music stopped, the laughter faded, the cries died down, and they were walking, running, staggering, crawling outside. He heard the big doors open, heard the slurred conversations retreating. He wanted to peek through the curtains, through the window, to make sure that what he was hearing was actually occurring, to make sure that they were really leaving, but he was afraid to check, afraid even to move, and it was over an hour later when he finally got up the courage to open his office door and peek into his chapel to see the damage.

FORTY-ONE

"What do you think you're doing?"

Penelope stood in the center of the meadow, screaming at her mothers as they bent over Dion, smearing him with blood and fat from the gutted bodies of the policemen. Her mothers were obviously very drunk, but the intoxication seemed to flow in waves: they were crazy, frenzied and chaotically wild, one moment; sober, organized, and intensely serious the next. It seemed almost as though they were possessed.

Possessed.

Could that be what was going on here?

Penelope didn't think so. Whatever unnaturalness was at the root of all this, it was nothing new, nothing alien, nothing from the outside.

It came from her mothers.

"Leave him alone!" she screamed.

Mother Janine looked over at her, laughed manically. "He's got a nice dick here! Get it while it's hot!"

Mother Felice slapped her face.

The others laughed. Mother Janine laughed too, but she reached out and grabbed a handful of the wine-stained tunic that Mother Felice was still wearing and ripped it off.

Mother Sheila picked up a handful of blood and fat and threw it at Mother Felice.

"Stop it!" Penelope screamed. She looked from one mother to another. She was scared and confused, and she wanted more than anything else to run, to escape, to get as far away from here as quickly as possible. But where would she run to? Where would she go? The police? That's where she should go, she knew. Two policemen were dead and eviscerated, killed by her mothers. And God knew how many other people they'd murdered.

Her father.

But she could not bring herself to turn traitor, to turn her mothers in. She wanted to stop them, maybe even wanted to kill them, but at the same time she wanted to protect them from anyone else who might try to intervene.

Whatever happened, it had to stay within the family.

Which meant that if someone was going to do something, it would have to be her.

Her mothers were still playing in the blood, and all of her instincts were telling her to get out of here, to flee the meadow, to get back to lights, streets, buildings, cars, civilization, to save herself. Everything she'd ever learned, thought, or believed was telling her to get help. But she realized that she could not do that. Not to her mothers.

Besides, she couldn't leave Dion.

Dion.

He was screaming, fighting, struggling against the drunken women holding him down and smearing him with blood. As Mother Felice broke away from the others and started toward her across the meadow, she could see Mother Janine stroking his penis, massaging it with blood.

He was hard.

Penelope felt sickened. She walked toward Mother Felice. The two of them stopped less than a foot from each other. Her mother smiled, and there was both sadness and triumph in the look. "So now you know," her mother said.

"Know what?"

"What we are. What you are."

She was even more confused than before. And more frightened. What *she* was?

She suddenly realized that she was not as shocked by all of this as she should have been, not as disgusted as she would have expected to be. It was horrifying, yes, and obviously disgusting, but her reactions were intellectual, not emotional, a recognition of the response the scene would have provoked in other people, not the response that was actually evoked within her. She was reacting to this the way she thought she should react, not the way she really felt.

The fear was definitely there, but it was not a physical fear, not a fear of what might happen to her. It was more a fear of recognition, a realization that these were her mothers and that she was their daughter, that she was one of them.

Anger. That was her overriding emotion. Anger at what they were doing to Dion, at what they were putting him through. It was a focused anger, though, a localized anger, and she wondered if she would have reacted this way if it had been someone else. Did she even give a damn about the dead policemen?

No.

It was only because it was Dion.

She smelled the wine, smelled the blood, and the mingled scent appealed to her.

She looked at her mother. "What are we?"

"Maenads," her mother said.

Maenads. She knew the word. The madwomen who had worshiped Dionysus in Greek mythology. Women crazed with wine and sexual ecstasy, responsible for brutally killing Pentheus and ripping Orpheus limb from limb in a wild orgy of blood. Representatives of chaos in the otherwise orderly world of the Greek gods. The dark side of ancient religion.

But maenads weren't real. They were mythological figures. Fictional characters.

Weren't they?

"We have always existed," Mother Felice said gently, wrapping an arm around her shoulder. Penelope was acutely aware of the fact that her mother was naked, of the fact that the blood on her smelled sweet and fresh and good. "But people have forgotten us. They have forgotten the old gods."

"No one's forgotten anything," Penelope said. "They—"

"They call it mythology."

Penelope said nothing.

"These are not fairy stories or fantasies. This is not the way primitive people attempted to explain things they did not understand." Her mother touched a finger to the blood between her breasts, lifted it to her mouth. "This is truth."

Behind her mother, Dion screamed, a piercing cry that somehow metamorphosed into loud, sustained laughter.

"What are you doing to him?" Penelope demanded.

"Restoring Him." Her mother's voice was low, worshipful, filled with awe. "Calling Him back."

Penelope felt cold. "He?"

"Dionysus."

Again, she was not surprised. She should have been. The idea that her mothers were rubbing blood all over her boyfriend in order to turn him into a Greek god was not something she could have come up with in a million years. But the events here had taken on a life of their own, and things were flowing together, coalescing, in a way that seemed inevitable, almost natural, and she could only stand by and watch as they unfolded.

"We worshiped Him in the old days," her mother said. "There were no prophets or ministers then, but we served that function. We praised Him. And He rewarded us." Again, she touched a finger to the blood, brought it to her mouth. "He gave us wine and sex and violence. He participated in our kills, in our celebrations, and everyone was happy.

"The gods were our contemporaries in those days. It was not like Judaism or Christianity or any of these modern faiths. Our religion wasn't made up of stories from the distant past. It was a living religion, and we coexisted with our gods. They took an interest in our lives. They came down from Olympus to be with us, to comingle with us." Her voice faded, and behind her, Penelope heard Dion laughing.

"Then why did your gods disappear?"

"People stopped believing."

"So?"

Mother Felice smiled gently at Penelope. "Remember when you were little and we took you to San Francisco to see *Peter Pan*? Remember that part where Tinker Bell was dying and the audience was supposed to shout that they believed in her? You were shouting for all you were worth. You wanted so badly to save her life."

Penelope nodded. "I remember."

"Well, gods are like Tinker Bell. They don't need food for nourishment. They need belief. It's what feeds them, what gives them power. Without it, they . . . they fade away."

It was so strange, Penelope thought. So insane. This rational conversation about the irrational, references to her childhood and popular culture used in an attempt to explain ancient evil.

Ancient evil.

Was that what this was? It was a cliched phrase, a staple of bad horror novels and worse horror films, conjuring up images of vengeful Indian demons and cursed land. But it applied. The events her mother was talking about had taken place centuries ago. The religion to which her mothers subscribed predated Christianity by a thousand years.

"The gods faded away, but we did not. Our survival, unlike theirs, did not depend on belief. We were flesh and blood. But we were also more than human. He had bestowed upon us a gift of divinity, and we continued our rituals, or celebrations, knowing that He would return to us eventually.

" 'The gods will be borne of men,' " she recited. " 'As they went so shall they come. To take again their rightful place on mighty Olympus.' "

"And what's that supposed to mean?"

Mother Felice leaned forward until her face was next to Penelope's. "What do you think happened to the old gods, the true gods? Do you think they just died? Do you think they flew off into outer space? No. They were weakened by nonbelief but not killed. And Zeus, in His infinite wisdom, decreed that they should take shelter in the flesh of men." She smiled, and there was blood on her teeth. Her left breast pressed against Penelope's arm. 'They hid within us. In our genes. In our chromosomes. In our cells. The other gods took refuge in Dionysus. And Dionysus took refuge in us. And we believed and continued to believe and they did not die. Instead, they were passed down from generation to generation, waiting to be born again."

"But Dion—"

"His mother is a maenad too. She is one of us."

Penelope shook her head.

Mother Felice grabbed her hand, pulled her toward the altar. Dion was standing now atop the raised rectangle, flanked by Mother Sheila and Mother Janine. He was coated with blood from head to toe, looking like a red statue, only the whites of his eyes and his teeth standing out against the darkness. His erection was huge and quivering and looked bigger than she remembered.

It looked good.

Even coated with blood, it looked good.

Especially coated with blood.

No! She pushed that thought from her mind.

Mother Margeaux passed a flagon to Mother Janine, who poured wine into Dion's mouth. He spat it out, but she poured it again, and this time he swallowed.

"Dion!" Penelope yelled.

He did not seem to hear her, did not even acknowledge her.

"Ours is the easiest god to resurrect," Mother Felice explained. "Dionysus was half man already, the only half-human god, and He will bring back the other gods of Olympus."

"How come he's in Dion? I though he was in you."

"He's in all of us."

"At the same time?"

"He's in you."

"No."

"He's in our genes." She squeezed Penelope's hand. "We don't just call each other 'sister,' your other mothers and I. We *are* sisters. We all had the same father, although our mothers were different. That is the way it has always been. For generations it was believed that He could only be reborn if the son of a maenad mated with a human woman. It was thought He was in the sperm.

"Until Mother Margeaux. She was the one who discovered that He was in the sperm *and* the egg. He could not be brought back by the son of a maenad mating with a normal woman. He could be reborn only through a maenad born of that son mating with a normal man."

Penelope was lost. Too much was happening too fast, and her mother's crazy explanation sounded suspiciously like a convoluted math problem. What was she saying? That she and Dion were related?

Incest

No. They couldn't be. She could handle anything but that. Monsters and old gods. Blood sacrifices and inter-generational breeding plans. All of it was acceptable.

But she could not be related to Dion.

"How old do you think I am?" Mother Felice asked.

Penelope shook her head.

"I was born in 1920." She smiled. "We all were. Daughters of Harris, son of Elsmere."

"But you can't all be my mother."

"No," Mother Felice admitted. "I'm your real mother. I carried you. I gave birth to you."

"I knew it—"

"But you have the genes of all of us. You're a maenad too. You might look human, you might act human, but you're not."

"I am!"

Mother Felice smiled slyly. "You like blood, don't you? You like the smell of it, the way it makes you feel. You like wine. When we gave you that taste, you wanted more . . ."

It was true and she knew it was true, but she shook her head anyway.

They had reached the altar, and the smell of the blood and the wine was intoxicating. At her feet, in front of the eviscerated bodies of the policemen, she saw the bones.

Mother Sheila saw the direction of her gaze. She laughed drunkenly. "Old parties," she said. "Old celebrations."

The fear was returning. "Who were they?"

Mother Felice shrugged. "Strangers. Drifters, mostly. There used to be a lot more coming through than there are today. Lonely, dirty, hungry young men looking for work or a handout or both. We tried not to celebrate with locals."

"But it wasn't always under our control," Mother

Janine chimed in. She smiled. "When the spirit gets a hold of you . . ."

"They're not all people," Mother Felice said. "There weren't always people in the celebrations. Sometimes there were dogs or cats. Or wild animals."

"Wild animals are the best," Mother Janine said. "They put up a good fight."

Penelope shrugged off Mother Felice's hand. She wanted to punch her right now, punch her hard in the gut and shove her to the ground. Even though she was her favorite mother, Penelope hated her at this moment. She hated all of them. But fighting would not work. That was not the way to go. She might have the element of surprise on her side, might actually be able to knock her mother down, but she was still no match for Mother Janine. And all of her other mothers would be on her in a second.

No, she had to play this cool, try to find some other way out of this.

She caught Dion's eye. She saw fear there, and horror, but also . . . what? Complicity? That made no sense. Dion wasn't the reincarnation of a god. She didn't believe her mothers' story—

But she did.

Yes, she realized, she did. She believed it. She bought it all.

And the fresh blood on Dion's erection did look pretty damn enticing.

She turned forcefully away, was grabbed by Mother Sheila. "We need you."

"You're one of us," Mother Felice said. "We want you to join us."

She shook her head. "I can't."

"Run!" Dion yelled.

Mother Janine looked up from Dion's feet. "We want you to fuck him."

Penelope's refusal died in her throat. What? What was this? What were they asking? She glanced from one mother to another, saw no sign that any of them thought this even the slightest bit unusual, saw only support and encouragement.

"We can bring Him back," Mother Felice said. "But

only you can bring back the others. He must mate with you."

"Your union will bring forth gods," Mother Margeaux announced.

"Fuck him!" Mother Sheila ordered.

Penelope started crying, unable to stop herself. "No."

Mother Janine grinned. "Look how big his cock is. Don't you want to feel it inside you?

She did, and they knew she did, and that was the worst part of it all. She was what they were, and they knew it.

Maenads.

"No!" she shouted.

"No!" Dion echoed. But when she looked at him, she saw a lust in his face that mirrored her own.

She turned toward her real mother, Mother Felice. "You can't force me to do what you want."

"No, it's your decision," Mother Felice admitted, and there was a softness in her voice, an understanding that wasn't there in the words or tones of the rest of her mothers. "You don't have to go through with it if you don't want to. There are others waiting for the return of Zeus and Artemis and Aphrodite and the others, but we don't care if they come back or not. We have our god. So it's up to you. Whatever you want to do, we'll stand by you."

Penelope looked over at Mother Margeaux for confirmation. Mother Margeaux nodded.

"You'll want to when you see Him," Mother Margaret promised.

"We'll all want to," Mother Sheila said, and the others laughed.

There was an edge to the laughter that Penelope did not like, that frightened her. She was one of them, yet she was not one of them, and she did not know what was going to happen, how things were going to turn out.

She did not know what *she* was going to do, and that's what frightened her most of all. Intellectually, she still thought that the best thing was to run and get help, go to the police. Her mothers would let her go. They would not kill her, would probably not even try to stop her.

But she could not do it. She could not renounce her family, no matter what they had done. And she could not leave Dion here with them alone. Besides, chances were that even if she did try to get help, she wouldn't be back in time to save him. She wouldn't be back before he changed.

Before he changed.

It was going to happen. She didn't just believe it, she knew it.

They were chanting now, repeating what sounded like the words of a ritual in a language she could not understand. Bottles of wine had appeared from somewhere to supplement the flagons and were being passed indiscriminately from one mother to another. Mother Margaret stumbled over the eviscerated body of one of the policemen, fell to her knees, stood up laughing. Dion, still being held, twisted in the arms of Mother Janine and Mother Margaret as if he were in pain.

Mother Felice took a swig from one of the bottles and handed it to Penelope. The wine smelled good, but Penelope threw the bottle behind her, into the meadow, where it landed on the grass, its contents spilling onto the ground.

"Hey," her mother said. "What'd you do that for?" Her speech was becoming slurred, and she looked at Penelope with a hostility that made Penelope realize that maybe she wasn't as safe from her mothers as she'd originally thought.

She backed up, away from the altar, and glanced quickly around the meadow to determine which way she should run if it came down to that.

It was then that she noticed the others.

FORTY-TWO

Dion still wasn't sure what was going on.

He was on top of the altar. He knew that. And he was naked. And Penelope's mothers were holding his arms and legs and ... doing stuff to him. He tried to call out to Penelope, but his head was forced back and one mother held his mouth open with strong, sinewy fingers while another poured wine down his throat. He felt the hands of the others anointing his body with the blood. He gulped down the sweet, intoxicating liquid, swallowing it so he could breathe. Fingers grasped his penis, stroked it, and against his will he felt himself growing, becoming hard. From somewhere he heard the sound of Penelope yelling.

His head was let go, and he opened his eyes, looked down. His erection was huge, quivering, and covered with blood.

He wished he could shove it in Penelope's mouth and down her throat to gag her and stop all that infernal racket.

No, he didn't.

Yes, he did.

He turned his head around and looked into the trees at the carved god with his face.

What the hell was happening?

More wine was poured into his mouth. That was one thing that was happening: they were trying to get him drunk. He tried to spit out the wine, but it only dribbled down his chin.

God, it tasted good.

They were chanting, the mothers, singing, but he couldn't make out what they were saying. The words were all Greek to him. He giggled. Greek to him. Oh,

God, he was already getting drunk. He'd never be able to get out of here if he didn't concentrate on keeping his wits about him and trying to stay sober—

His mouth was jerked open again, more wine poured down his throat. He gagged, tried to swallow, almost choked, but the warm liquid went down smoothly and he was filled with a pleasant lightness.

He understood some of the words the mothers were saying now. Not all of them, but some of them. They were foreign, but he'd heard them before somewhere. In dreams, perhaps.

He realized that they were praying.

To him.

This wasn't right. This shouldn't be happening. He struggled against the mothers' hold, but they were stronger than he was, their fingers and wrists like iron.

They gave him more wine.

He looked out across the meadow. Others were gathering, appearing at the periphery of the field, emerging from between the bushes and the trees. They were pale, slack-jawed, and nearly all appeared to be drunk. They were walking like remote-controlled zombies, men and women, some with flashlights, some with knives, some with dead cats or dogs, some only with bottles of liquor.

They saw him, waved to him, called to him.

He was communicating with these people, he realized, acting like some sort of homing beacon. He saw in his mind's eye all of the intoxicated men and women of the valley suddenly cocking their heads to hear an invisible sound, like pod people in a monster movie, suddenly dropping what they were doing to come here, to this meadow, to him.

The mothers let go of him, but he couldn't move. He was like a statue, frozen in place. They'd done something to him, put some sort of spell on him, trapped him here in his body. Mother Janine was still rubbing blood on his toes, but he couldn't feel it. He wanted to kick her, to lash out and smash her face in with his foot, but he was unable to move. Tears of rage and frustration slid down his immobile face.

He tried to scream, but no sound would come out.

He saw his own mother off to the left. She was naked and obviously wasted, rubbing sensuously against Penelope's Mother Margaret. He wanted to call out to her, to run to her, but he could do neither, and he watched as she stared at him, glassy-eyed, then turned away.

From somewhere deep within him came a rumbling, a low, vibrating seismic sound that echoed in his brain and rose to a roar. he was not sure if it was only within him or could be heard outside as well, but it was the loudest thing he had ever heard, and it overpowered his senses and pushed everything else aside.

The sound became words. His words and yet not his words. His thoughts and yet not his thoughts. An announcement of triumph and an admission of defeat:

I AM HERE

FORTY-THREE

April could feel the desire building, the need increasing. She was not drunk, but she soon would be, and already she could smell the blood. It hung thick in the air, redolent as the wine, and she was starting to get antsy, anxious, wanting only for events to accelerate so she could satisfy her lust.

Margaret gave her a long kiss on the mouth, pressing her body against April's, and April felt the delicious softness of touching nipples, the wiry scratchiness of rubbed pubic hair. She could sense Margaret's blood pulsing just below her skin, and she wanted to rip that skin open and let the blood wash over her.

Margaret pulled away, smiling. "Almost time."

April looked toward the altar, toward where the other women were smearing the fat of the policemen on the body of her son, and her excitement faded. Dion was struggling against the hard hands that held him, grunting with exertion and pain.

She felt queasy and a little sick. Part of her, the deep part that had always guided her actions but of which she had only recently been made aware, longed for the conclusion of the ritual, craved the freedom that the transformation would bring. But another part of her, an equally strong part, the part that had borne and raised and cared for her son, wanted only for Dion to escape.

Dion.

Her son.

She knew now that she had become pregnant, had deliberately tried to get pregnant, so that this could occur. She had had a child specifically to bring about His return, and on some level she had always known that. But she had also loved her son, loved him as a mother, any mother, would. She had wanted him to grow up and go to college, fall in love and marry, be successful. The normal things.

Dion stiffened, froze.

"No!" she cried. Tears were rolling down her cheeks, and she angrily wiped them away.

Wine always made her so sentimental.

The meadow was becoming crowded. People were arriving by the carload, by the vanload, running, staggering, crawling across the grass toward the altar. She too heard the voice within her son—*His* voice—calling out to her, and she understood why everyone was here, but she could not help wishing that she and Dion were alone, that she could help him through this, explain to him what was happening.

She looked over at him, saw the pain in his eyes, looked away.

She took another long drink of wine from the bottle, felt a hand on her buttocks. She turned, saw Margaret.

"It is time," Margaret said. "He is here."

FORTY-FOUR

She saw him change.

It was the most horrifying thing she had ever witnessed, and Penelope wanted to run, wanted to turn and flee, but she was rooted to the spot, unable even to look away, wishing with all her might that it would stop, reverse, knowing that it would not.

And he started to grow.

It began with his penis, his erection expanding immediately to more than twice its natural length, the rest of his body a step behind that accelerated pace, his arms, legs, torso, and head only belatedly catching up to the first conspicuous spurt of growth. The skin didn't rip as he grew. It should have. She had touched his skin, had felt it, had rubbed it, and it was normal, average, everyday human skin. But now it was stretching impossibly, like rubber, expanding with the elongating bones, the developing muscles.

There was no sound accompanying the change. Dion's mouth was open in a scream, but his voice was silent and the only noise in the meadow was the chanting of her mothers and the drunken babbling and overloud footfalls of the arriving inebriates.

It was a terrifying thing to see, and Penelope felt the down on her arms bristle as she watched his head flop unnaturally back and forth on his strangely extended neck, watched his metamorphosing hands twitch as spurts of growth shot through them, watched his legs buckle and dance as biologically created rhythms contorted them.

It was frightening, but the most frightening thing of all was the change in his face. It was not his features exactly, though they grew and broadened in such a way that the elements of his appearance, while remaining recognizably his, distorted the original to such an extent that he looked like a different person entirely. No, it was his expression, the way that his screaming mouth straightened into a lustful grin, the way his panicked gaze grew blank, then shifted suddenly into slyness. It was power and a knowledge of that power that settled over him, settled into him. Dion, if he was still extant within that form, was squashed down, and she watched in fear and heart-wrenching agony as he shrunk and shriveled and disappeared, lost within the ever expanding body.

He was now seven feet tall.

Now eight.

Now ten.

There was a ripple in the air, a solid wave of intensified humidity that passed over her and through her, a visibly shimmering undulation that for a second distorted not only the space directly before her, but the ground, the trees, the moon, the stars.

And he spoke: *"I AM HERE."*

The words rumbled through the woods, echoed across the hillsides, low and clear and loud enough to be heard even in the center of town. Around her, the gathered people dropped to their knees, weeping and laughing, screaming and praying. Her mothers had taken up spears and were dancing around the altar, around Dion, chanting madly.

Dion?

No, he wasn't Dion anymore.

With one quick, frighteningly well-coordinated lunge, he leapt from the altar and grabbed Mother Margeaux around the waist. He spun her around, then took her bottle, downed it in a single swallow, and tossed both her and the bottle aside. Mother Janine knelt before him, buttocks up, baring herself in orgiastic ecstasy, and he impaled her with his enormous erection. The look of expectant lust on her face turned to pain as he entered her, and she screamed in agony, trying to get away, but he grabbed a handful of her hair, jerked her head back, and thrust.

Penelope felt sickened.

Things were turning ugly, getting out of control. A dog bounded across the meadow, and three women she did not recognize pounced on it, tearing at its face and fur with their fingernails. To her left, a boy from her math class hit an old lady in the face, then kicked her in the stomach as she slumped to the ground before him.

Everywhere were bottles of wine.

Daneam wine.

Where had they gotten it? she wondered. Where had it come from?

It was time to get the hell out of here. Family or no family, mothers or no mothers, she did not belong here. Dion had metamorphosed into a monster, her mothers were drunk and completely crazy, and the only thing she could do was run, escape, try to save herself before something happened to her.

Mother Janine's screech was ear-splitting as Dion—

Dionysus

—pulled out, still spurting. In two amazingly long strides he reached another woman, a younger woman, and picked her up and ripped off her top and laughingly kissed her oversize breasts.

Suddenly Penelope was grabbed from behind. She felt the tip of a stiff erection press against her buttocks and whirled to see Dr. Jones, her old pediatrician, standing there with his pants around his ankles, a look of drunken lust in his eyes. She punched him hard in the stomach and ran, trying to get through the rapidly growing crowd. Many of the men were pulling down their pants, she saw, many of the women taking off their skirts. Still more were ripping off one another's clothes: snapping bras, tearing panties, yanking briefs.

She had to get out of here. She had to get back to the house.

She pushed through a group of teenagers, skirted a crowd of biker-looking men. From behind her, she heard Dion yell. It was a bellow of lust and triumph, but buried within it was a sound of hurt, confused frustration. She heard the pain in that cry, and it wrenched at her insides, caused her vision to be blurred by tears, but she kept running, hitting the line of trees and continuing on. Vaguely, filtered through leaves and branches off to her right, she saw a line of cars on the road, their headlights visible through the foliage and distance.

In less than a minute, she was at the fence. In front of her, the winery was lit up, seemingly every light in every building turned on. There were people in the drive, in the parking lot, on the roof of the warehouse. She heard amplified music, saw small figures dancing.

There was the sound of semi-automatic rifle fire, and several lights in the main building winked off. Screams were followed by silence.

She could not go back to the house.

It was a long walk back to town, but there were probably cars with keys in them on the road. There were probably cars that were still idling. People did not seem to be behaving too rationally tonight.

That was the understatement of the year.

She started jogging through the vineyard, toward the street, keeping an eye out for anyone lurking in the rows or running toward her. There were clouds in the sky, jet against the lighter purple darkness, but the moon was uncovered and its bluish light shone down unimpeded.

What had happened? Had her mothers been secretly recruiting people all these years, luring Baptists and Methodists and Catholics and Presbyterians away from Christianity and into their Dionysus worship? It didn't seem possible, yet there was no other explanation for this . . . pilgrimage. Why else would hundreds of drunken people descend upon the winery anticipating the return of a long-dead Greek god?

Her head hurt. It was too confusing. Everything she had ever thought or been taught seemed to have been invalidated, proven wrong. Ordinary people—doctors, housewives, clerks, construction workers—had suddenly discarded their mainstream American way of life, abandoning their lifestyle as though it had been merely a mask they had been wearing, and were now drunkenly worshiping a diety that she had studied as a literary creation. Her mothers, who had raised her, whom she had lived with every day of her life, had turned out to be maenads who had mated with a human man in order to give birth to her so she could have sex with a resurrected mythological god.

It would be laughable if it wasn't so damn horrible.

She reached the fence bordering the road and followed it toward the gates. Ahead, she saw revelers staggering through the entrance and up the drive to the winery, winding their way between the abandoned cars. Several couples were furiously copulating on the ground to either side of the drive. She knew she could not get through without being seen, but the men and women near the gates were so far gone that they probably wouldn't care.

She reached the edge of the gate, stepped over a couple on the ground, and quietly slid around the side of the fence.

"I gutted the bitch with my fishing knife," one man was saying, his voice too loud. "Slit her from tongue to twat."

"What'd you do with her tits?" a woman asked excitedly.

Penelope hurried onto the road, moving between the parked and idling cars. The odor of wine was strong in her nostrils, and her body responded to it, her mouth drying out, begging for refreshment, but she forced herself to keep moving. She was still visible from the gate, and she figured she'd go down another hundred yards or so, then find a vehicle to escape in.

Escape to where?

She didn't know. She hadn't thought it out yet. The police station first, then . . .

She'd figure that out when she came to it.

"PENELOPE!"

Dion.

Dionysus.

"PENELOPE!"

It was a cry and a demand. She could hear it from the road, and it scared her but it spoke to her. It made her want to turn around and run into the woods and throw off her clothes and spread herself before Him.

It made her want to get into a car and keep driving until she reached another state.

A bolt of light shot upward from the trees, a pearly, opalescent beam in which glints of rainbow color could be discerned. She stared at it, feeling the strength in her legs give way. She had not realized until now the scope of the situation she was dealing with. Yes, she had seen Dion's metamorphosis. Yes, she knew what her mothers were and what he had become. Yes, she had seen the growing numbers of followers. But the extent of it all had not been brought home to her.

The light, though, the powerful, unwavering beam that extended upward to the heavens and seemed to illuminate the constellations, made her realize on a gut level how powerful Dionysus was. He was not just a monster. She had not witnessed merely a Jekyll-and-Hyde transformation. She had been witness to the rebirth of a god. A real god.

How could she hope to combat or run away from that?

"PENELOPE!"

There were figures now in the opalescent beam, swirling shades that resembled wraiths or B-movie ghosts. They flowed upward from the source of the light, coalescing in the sky high above the hills, rearranging positions until they formed a figure.

Her.

She sucked in her breath. The image was unmistakable. It was white, the same rainbow-flecked white as the rest of the light, but it was clearly visible, a three-dimensional portrait of her that was so perfect in its details that it looked like a photograph.

But it was not a photograph.

It had come from him.

He wanted her.

"PENELOPE!"

She made her way into the center of the road and started to run. Around her, a few stragglers were rooted in place, staring up at her form as it shimmered in the sky.

He wanted them to catch her and bring her back to him.

To her left, on the other side of the road, she heard the loud sound of a mufflerless engine. Blue smoke was billowing from the tailpipe of a riderless Ford pickup.

She dashed across the center stripe to the truck and

pulled open the door, hopping in. The vehicle had an automatic transmission, thank God, and she put it into Reverse and backed up. The truck smacked into the bumper of the small car behind it, but she didn't stop to assess the damage. She threw the pickup into Drive and took off, tires squealing as she swerved into the center of the road. She passed the winery gates, but did not look. She kept her eyes straight ahead.

And drove.

There were fires burning throughout Napa. She could see them, both the smoke and the flames, but she heard no sirens, saw no fire trucks. She turned on the radio. On the rock station, a DJ was praying to Dionysus, a drunken ramble that sounded like a plea for forgiveness. On the country station, Garth Brooks' "The American Honky Tonk Bar Association" was playing, while a group of people in the studio whooped it up in the background. The all-news station was silent.

She turned off the radio.

The streets of the city seemed curiously abandoned. There were few other cars on the road, and not many people on the sidewalks. She saw what looked like a dead body in front of the gas pumps at a Texaco station, saw a lone looter in the windowless Radio Shack, but that was about it. Where was everyone? There were a couple of hundred, maybe a thousand people back at the winery and in the woods, but that was a small fraction of the city's population. What had happened to everyone else?

She turned onto Soscol, the street that led to the civic center and the police department.

And slammed on the brakes.

The street was filled with celebrants. Police cars and fire trucks blocked off large segments of several blocks, and between them wall-to-wall people danced and drank as though it was Mardi Gras. Many of them were wearing masks or makeshift togas. Many of them were naked. She saw sparklers and fireworks fountains, champagne bottles and beer cans. Here and there fights had broken out, and partially uniformed policemen were happily beating people into submission with night sticks.

Broken Daneam bottles littered the roadway, and as Penelope started to back out, off the street, she heard the sound of glass smashing as the pickup rolled over one. Before she had even finished swinging around the corner, the left rear tire of the truck was flat, the vehicle listing badly, the steering wheel suddenly intractable in her hands.

She got out of the pickup and hurried down Third Street, away from Soscol. It was obvious that she wasn't going to get any help from the police. Two of their own were dead in the woods, eviscerated, and they were partying.

Where would she go now?

She didn't know. She had still not had time to figure out an alternate plan, and her mind was a blank. The best thing to do, probably, was to find another car and drive down to San Francisco, tell the police there, let them figure out what had to be done.

But would they be able to handle it?

Would the National Guard even be able to handle it?

She thought of that beam of light shooting upward into the heavens and shivered.

Vella.

Yes, Vella. Why hadn't she thought of that earlier? If she could get to Vella's house, she could use her friend's phone and call for help. Then they could use Vella's car to escape.

But what if Vella's parents had been converted?

What if *Vella* had been converted?

She'd cross that bridge when she came to it.

Her friend's house was only a couple of blocks from school, and school was only a mile or so away. If she could—

She saw him at the far end of the street.

He was in front of the Mobil station, towering above the hordes of drunken revelers accompanying him. He moved strangely. Not jerkily, like a figure in a stop-motion animation movie, but unnaturally. More fluidly perhaps than ordinary movement, but oddly, eerily. He glanced first one way, then another, his head swiveling in a way she had never seen before, and she quickly ducked into the doorway of the donut shop next to her. She tried the knob, but the door was locked, and she closed her eyes and hoped that he and his followers would not come this way, would not come down the street.

He bellowed what she would have guessed from the tone of his voice was an order.

But it was not an order.

It was her name.

He was looking for her.

"PENELOPE!"

She pressed harder against the door, as if that would make her more invisible.

She had never been scared by Godzilla or Rodan or any of those oversize Japanese monsters. They were so large as to be comical, their threat so grossly magnified that it was entirely impersonal. She had always found quieter, more intimate horror more frightening. She could identify with unseen whispers in a haunted house. She could not identify with a resurrected nuclear-radiated dinosaur that stomped on houses.

But this was like one of those outrageously exaggerated Japanese things, a ridiculous, parodic manhunt. And she was utterly terrified.

"PENELOPE!"

His voice echoed off the walls of the buildings, caused windows to shake in their frames.

Could he sense her? He obviously wasn't omniscient, but perhaps he could feel her presence. Perhaps he had the power to locate where she was. How else could he have gotten so close to her so fast?

"PENELOPE!"

He was moving away.

He did *not* know where she was! He could not pinpoint her location using some godlike power. He was flying blind, guessing, trying to anticipate where she'd go, what she'd do.

He might know that she'd go to Vella's house, might try to meet her there, but she didn't think so. She was pretty sure he didn't know where it was, and she could not see the great god Dionysus stopping by a phone booth to look up an address in the white pages.

She grinned at the image, imagining all of his drunken disciples waiting around while he looked up an address. The smile grew broader and gave her confidence. Where there was humor there was hope, and she took a tentative peek around the side of the doorway, saw only the tail end of his contingent lurching and staggering around the corner of Jefferson.

She moved out of the doorway and hurried across the street, intending to take Vernon to Sandalwood, and Sandalwood to Vella's.

Her mouth was even drier than it had been earlier. God, she was thirsty. She quietly cleared her throat. A glass of chilled wine sounded good.

A bottle sounded even better.

She had to get a grip. She couldn't let herself be influenced by any of this shit that her mothers had brought about. She had to keep a clear head, maintain her reason amidst this chaos. It was the only way of getting out.

She sprinted down Vernon. To her right, adjacent to the sidewalk in a small neighborhood park barely bigger than a yard, was a picnic table and a drinking fountain, and she ran over to the fountain and took a long drink of cool water. It bubbled up from the faucet, flowed smoothly down her throat, soothing, and she drank until she could feel her stomach sloshing. Water had never been so welcome or tasted so good, and she felt instantly stronger, revitalized. She straightened up and started running again. She had to take it slower since her stomach was full, but that was just as well. She didn't want to tire herself out unnecessarily. She might need her strength later.

Once again the street seemed deserted. She was jogging through a residential neighborhood now, and the houses around her were dark, the only illumination offered by the moon and the evenly spaced streetlights. There were no cars, no other pedestrians.

Again she wondered: where had everyone gone?

Three blocks later, she stopped jogging, slowed to a walk, then finally stopped to catch her breath. She glanced uneasily around. The emptiness of the street suddenly seemed much more threatening. Running, she had not had time to notice the pockets of shadow around trees and bushes, the unsettling blackness of the windows that looked onto the street. But now she was no longer passing by, traveling through the neighborhood. She was *in* the neighborhood, and it gave her a creepy feeling.

She was still breathing loudly, tired from running, but she forced herself to start walking again. Underneath her exaggerated breath and the overloud slaps of her sneakers on the concrete, she thought she heard other sounds, cracking, snapping sounds that could have been boot steps, could have been twigs snapping. She quickened her pace. She could see in front of her and there was nothing there, but she was afraid to look behind her, afraid she would see someone or something creeping through the shadows toward her.

Once again she broke into a jog. Her heart might burst from the exertion, but she'd rather take a chance on that than on being attacked.

She heard no more sounds, felt no hands on her shoulders, saw no one leap at her from the darkness, and two streets later, she reached Sandalwood.

Here there were people. Students mostly. Kids from school. Several of them appeared to be drag-racing at the far end of the street, but the competition was haphazard, disorderly, with no apparent rules, and she saw Wade Neth's red Mustang sideswipe a white Corvette and careen onto a house's lawn while a blue '57 Chevy crashed into a parked Jeep. The onlookers lining the street cheered wildly. Bottles were thrown onto the asphalt, smashing into irregular shards. Someone set off a string of firecrackers.

Directly in front of her, four drunken members of the school's football team were having a pissing contest—with Mrs. Plume, the band teacher, as the target.

Mrs. Plume didn't seem to mind.

Penelope turned away in disgust, looking down the street in the opposite direction. There were people here, but fewer, and the school a block away appeared to be deserted.

Vella's street was only a few blocks down.

She started walking quickly.

There was a scream behind her, a sudden ear-splitting

screech that made her jump. She whirled around to see a topless girl attack a young man with an ax in the middle of the street. The wedged blade lodged in his chest, and then he began screaming as the blood spurted and she pulled the weapon out and swung again. In an instant everyone was screaming, members of the crowd, dozens of them, converging as one on the combatants. Penelope saw other weapons, saw splashing blood.

She ran, away from the melee, toward the school. There were a few people here, on the sidewalk, on the street, on the lawns of the houses, but not many. Again, most of them were kids from her school. She recognized some, but they did not seem to recognize her and for that she was grateful. She sped past them, hoping to make it to Vella's without incident.

"Penelope!"

She stopped cold at the sound of the voice, glancing quickly around. It was a human voice—it was not *his* voice—but the fact that someone was calling her name at all jolted her.

"Penelope!"

She recognized the voice now. Kevin Harte. But where was he?

There. Across the street, in the shadow of a tree, kicking an old woman who was lying on the sidewalk, clawing at his ankles. He looked over at Penelope. "Over here! Help!"

She paused only for a moment, then ran across the street to where he struggled to free himself from the woman's clutches.

"Grab something!" he said. "Hit her!"

The woman looked like a zombie. She was naked save for torn, dirty panties, and she was drooling, cackling crazily as her nails dug into Kevin's legs. Penelope looked around for a branch or a stick or a broom, something she could use as a weapon, but there was nothing in the street, on the sidewalk, or on the lawn of the adjacent house. She wasn't sure she'd be able to hit the woman anyway, but at least she could provide Kevin with a weapon he could use.

"Kick her!" Kevin yelled.

But at that moment he broke free from her grip and kicked her hard in the chest. Her cackle turned into a wheeze, and he grabbed Penelope's hand and pulled her with him down the sidewalk.

"What the fuck's going on?" he said. "The whole damn world seems to have snapped."

"It's a long story," she told him.

He turned toward her, though his pace did not slow. "You know what's going on?"

"I'm part of it."

He stopped, his hand tightening on her wrist. "Wait a minute. You're—"

"It's a long story. I'll tell you later. Let's just get to Vella's so we can call for help."

"There's no one to call. The pigs are all out partying. I tried them."

"I know. I meant call for someone outside. The National Guard or something. The San Francisco police. I don't know."

"Where does Vella live?"

"On Ash." Penelope gestured down the street. "A few blocks past school."

Kevin's face paled. "Don't go there."

Chills surfed down Penelope's arms at the fear in his voice. "Why? What is it?"

"Don't go there. I've been there."

"What is it?"

"You don't want to know."

He was right. She didn't want to know. She had seen too much already, had heard too much, had experienced too much. Her limit had been reached. She wanted only to run away and escape, to have troops come in here and clean all this up, and to return in the daytime when it was all over.

"Do you think Vella is ..." She could not finish the sentence.

"If she was at her house, she's dead." He looked up and down the street. The area from which she'd come was becoming even more crowded. Others were joining the fray, the fight spreading. In the yellowish glow of the street-lights the silhouettes of unmoving bodies could be seen on the asphalt. "School," he said. "It was abandoned when I went by earlier. We can go there."

"And do what?"

"Hide. Find a classroom, lock ourselves inside, and wait for morning."

"I don't know . . ."

Kevin smiled thinly. "Dion won't care. He knows he can trust me."

Penelope blinked. He didn't know about Dion. Tears seeped out from between her eyelids and down her cheeks, and she wiped them angrily away, willing herself not to cry. She had not had the luxury of experiencing her feelings, and as far as she was concerned, that luxury was still not yet available to her. She would have time to wallow in her misery later. Right now she had to act. She had to keep herself alive.

And away from Dion and her mothers.

Kevin saw her wipe away the tears. Their eyes met, and he looked away, embarrassed. "I'm sorry," he said. "Dion's dead?"

"No."

"He's all right, then?"

"Not that either."

"He's one of them?"

She shook her head. "It's a long story. Let's find a room. I'll tell you there. We'll have a lot of time to kill."

Kevin nodded. "I was thinking Sherwood's history class. It's on the second floor, facing the street. We'll be able to see anyone coming."

Penelope nodded tiredly. "Fine with me."

They hurried, side by side, down the rest of the block, checking first to make sure no one was around before dashing across the faculty parking lot to the classroom building.

The front doors were locked.

"Come on," Kevin said. "Around the side. We'll break a window and crawl in. Too much exposure here."

Kevin took off one of his boots and used it to break and clear out the window glass of one of the science rooms. He crawled in first, then grabbed her arms and helped her in. They waited a minute, listening, ready to jump back out and escape if necessary, but there were no alarms, no voices, no sounds within the building at all.

They exited the science room, walked down the hallway and upstairs to the history classroom. It was unlocked, and they had no trouble getting in, but there seemed to be no lock on the door at all. Kevin wanted to try another room, maybe the teachers' staff room, someplace that would have a lockable door, but Penelope liked the idea of being able to see the street, and they pushed the teacher's desk against the door, then sat on two of the students' desks and stared out the window.

There were fires and searchlights, mobs of people that passed in front of the street, going first one way and then the other. In the still air, sounds were amplified, distorted. Everything sounded close. Gunshots. Car crashes. Laughter. Music. Screams.

A lot of screams.

Kevin fell asleep a few hours later, after she had told him of Dion and her mothers. It was a wild story, but the questions he'd asked made it sound as though he believed it.

Why wouldn't he after everything he'd seen?

She couldn't sleep, though. She stayed awake, staring out at the city above the rooftops and the trees. The gunshots stopped, as did the crashes. The laughter died. The music faded.

Only the screams remained.

And they continued throughout the night.

PART II

ONE

In the morning, she could almost believe that none of it had happened, that it was a normal world, that she and Kevin had merely stayed late in the classroom to study and had fallen asleep, or even that they were rebellious teenagers in love who had snuck into the building for a romantic rendezvous and had spent the night together.

Anything was easier to believe than the truth.

Getting up quietly, Penelope walked across the cold tile to the window and peeked through the closed slats of the blinds. The street outside looked the same as it always did. There were a few cars parked next to the curb, and the houses across the way were early morning still. The weather was gloomy and cold, the air touched with a tinge of fog.

Only there was no traffic on the street. Not a single car drove past, not a single pedestrian walked by.

In the center of the parking lot she saw empty, broken wine bottles.

Dion, she thought.

She felt a sickening twinge of nausea as she recalled Mother Janine bending over in front of Dion, baring her sex to him. What had happened to her mother after that? Had she been ruptured by his enormous organ? Had she died from hemmorhaging or internal bleeding?

Penelope hoped so.

No, she didn't.

Maybe she did.

She took a deep breath. She wasn't sure. The truth was, she didn't really know what she felt. Her thoughts and emotions were still in a state of shock. She peered through the blinds, at the hillside above their winery on the opposite side of the city. She thought of the orgy in the meadow last night, and though the remembrance horrified and frightened her, it was at the same time . . . enticing.

She moved away from the window. The pull was strong. There was no denying that. It was only strength and willpower that had kept her from succumbing, that had allowed her to overcome the base desires of her blood.

Blood.

That was the most frightening thing about it all. The fact that she wanted to be part of it, that she knew she *should* be part of it.

But how long could her mind hold out against her body and her emotions?

She moved away from the window. There was a telephone mounted on the wall to the side of the blackboard. She hadn't noticed it last night, but she saw it now, and she walked across the room and picked it up.

No dial tone.

The phone was dead, but that didn't really mean anything. The line just went to the switchboard in the office. If she could get to a phone on one of the outside lines, she might be able to call for help.

She walked over to the door, started pulling on the edge of the teacher's desk to move it away. There was a loud screech as one of the desk legs scraped across the floor.

Kevin awoke with a start, practically leaping to his feet from the position on the floor in which he'd fallen asleep. He was instantly awake and on the alert, glancing quickly from the door to the windows and back again, before finally letting his gaze settle on Penelope. "What are you doing?" he demanded.

"I was going to look for a phone, see if we could call for help."

"You were going to sneak out on your own?"

She looked away, embarrassed. "I didn't want to wake you up."

"Shit." He shook his head. "I guess you can't trust anyone."

"And just what the hell is that supposed to mean?"

"It means I thought we were in this together. It means that since we seem to be the only two normal people left in the whole fucking valley, I thought we were going to stick with each other and not sneak around behind each other's backs."

She looked at him apologetically. "Sorry."

He was silent for a moment. "So where were you going to call from?"

"A phone in the office. Or the pay phone by the gym if that didn't work."

"Who were you going to call?"

"I don't know," she admitted. "The police in Vallejo, maybe. Or Oakland. Or San Francisco."

He nodded. "Sounds like a plan. But I'm coming with you."

"Okay."

Together they moved aside the desk and chairs they'd used to block the door. Kevin put his ear to the door for a moment, listening to make sure no one was out there, before opening it.

The hallway was deserted. And dark. It was morning, but no windows opened onto the hallway, and, save for theirs, the doors to all of the classrooms were closed. The lights were off.

Penelope had never seen the school like this, and somehow it seemed creepier than it had last night. Buildings were supposed to be dark at nighttime, but this daytime gloom was unnerving.

They walked slowly down the hallway toward the stairs, not speaking, treading softly. There were no sounds other than their own, but instead of reassuring her, the silence made her feel uneasy, on edge. Someone could be lying in wait for them right now, hearing their every move, listening to their progress, preparing to leap out from behind one of these closed doors . . .

They made it safely to the stairway, started quietly down.

It was not as dark downstairs. A row of thin windows high above the lockers let in a dusty version of daylight. There was no noise, no indication that anyone else was present, but Penelope still felt tense. They should have

brought weapons, she thought. They were stupid. If someone attacked them, they had nothing with which to fight
back.

They walked toward the office. It was weird being in
here like this. Usually, the corridor was crammed with
students rushing to and from classes, sorting through their
lockers, talking and laughing with one another. But
empty, the hallway seemed not only sad and lonely but,
under the circumstances, ominous.

The office door was locked, but the door to the staff
lounge next to it was open, and Kevin walked in, Penelope following. There was a phone on a battered table in
front of an old sofa, and they hurried over to it. Kevin
picked it up, put it to his ear. His expression said everything.

It was dead.

He jiggled the dial tone button, then dropped the receiver disgustedly into the cradle.

"Shit," he said.

Were all the phones in the city dead, or only the ones
in the school? Penelope didn't know, but she did know
that she had to go outside and find out for herself. If telephone service had been cut off, then they'd have to try to
find someone to help them, or get a car themselves and
drive out of the valley.

Kevin had obviously been thinking along the same
lines. "The phones are down," he said. "But maybe it's
only the school. I'll go out and see if I can find a phone
that works."

"No, you won't."

He blinked. "What?"

"You can't go out there. They'll kill you. I'll go."

He glared at her. "The fuck you will."

"The fuck I won't."

"Oh, you're going to go traipsing around the city to
save us? What do you expect me to do? Sit in here all
day?"

"Yes."

"Shit!" He kicked the table, and it flew onto its side
with a loud crash. He hurried to pick it up, instantly realizing his mistake, hoping no one had heard the sound.

"Look," she said, "just calm down. You're going to have to lay low for a while. I'll go out there and try to find a phone or someone who can help us—"

"You won't go out there and do anything."

"They won't hurt me."

"Who?"

"My mothers."

"What about Dion?"

"I'll deal with him if I see him."

"You'll be easier to spot in the daytime."

"They want me to join them. They won't harm me. You're nobody. They don't care what happens to you. They'd toss you to the wolves in a second."

Kevin was silent for a moment. He nodded. "You're right," he said. "I may be an asshole, but I'm not a moron." He looked toward the blurred glass window at the far end of the staff lounge. "So where are you going to go? You can't go to the police station. We already know the cops won't help."

"Fire stations, churches . . . I don't know. I'll find somebody. If not, I'll steal a car."

Kevin nodded excitedly. "Yeah. A car. That's what we need to do. Get a car and get the hell out of here." He thought for a moment. "You need a weapon, though. Something you can use if you get attacked."

"If I get attacked, there probably won't be a whole lot I can—"

"You're not going out alone without something."

She heard the seriousness in his voice, understood the sense of what he was saying, and nodded. "We'll both get weapons."

"That's the idea."

She followed him down the hallway. If this had been a movie, she thought, he would have taken her hand. It would have been the first hint that romance would eventually bloom between them. But they had not touched, had not come anywhere close to touching, and for that she was grateful. All those fictional depictions of two people thrown together by circumstance in the midst of a great disaster and finding accelerated love had always seemed like a load of bull to her, and she was glad to discover that she had been right.

So why was she thinking about it?

Inside the custodial office, they found everything they needed and more: hammers, screwdrivers, shovels, rakes, litter spears, hedge clippers, scissors. Penelope chose a long Phillip's screwdriver and a pair of scissors, both of which she tucked into the waistband of her pants.

"Be careful how you bend," Kevin said, grinning.

"Thanks."

Kevin grabbed several screwdrivers, a hammer, clippers, and a litter spear.

"If Rambo was a gardener . . ." Penelope said.

Kevin laughed.

That was a good sign, she thought. They could still laugh about the situation. They could still joke. That gave her confidence. The fact that they were able to retain their sense of humor despite the situation made it all seem a little less ominous. Humor somehow erected a barrier between themselves and the horrors and served to keep everything else at bay.

"Do you have a watch?" Kevin asked.

Penelope shook her head.

"Here, take mine." He unfastened the band at his wrist and handed his watch to her. "Since we don't have walkie-talkies or anything and can't keep in contact with each other, we need to set up a specific time for you to meet me back here. If you're not back by that time, I'll know something's wrong and I'll come after you."

Penelope nodded as she fastened the watch to her wrist.

"What time is it now?"

She looked. "Seven-twenty. I'll be back by nine."

"Okay."

They walked back down the hall, toward the front entrance.

When they reached the front door, they stopped, looked at each other.

"Be careful," Kevin said.

"I will."

Penelope took a deep breath, opened the door, and peered out. The air was cold, punctuated with a slight chill breeze. From north of town, from the direction of the wineries, she could hear the faint sounds of screaming, cheering. This far away, it sounded almost benign, like people having a party.

She looked to the left and then to the right, making sure there was no one around. The coast was clear, and without looking back at Kevin, she ran across the parking lot to the street. She heard the door shut behind her.

She reached the sidewalk. Now she could see some of the damage that had not been visible from the classroom. Up the street, a pickup was overturned and still burning, two bodies discarded on the asphalt next to it like limp rag dolls. Beyond that she saw movement. A small group of obviously armed, obviously intoxicated people prowling the neighborhood. Half of them were naked. They moved on, heading down another street, but another group crossed an intersection farther up, and she knew she'd probably run into others. She glanced around. Under a tree on the easement was an unbroken wine bottle, still a third full, and she quickly ran over and dumped the contents on her head and shoulders, rubbing the wine into her hair and skin so she would smell as though she was drunk, as though she was one of them. She opened her blouse, exposing a breast.

She was ready.

But where would she go? Not the winery, certainly, and not to the police station.

The fire station. That's what she'd said to Kevin, and that's where she would go. Even if the firemen had been overpowered or converted, there would still be communications equipment there. Last night's destruction hadn't been purposeful, planned. It had been random and wanton, the ignorant rampage of inebriated . . . what? Dionysian revelers?

Yes.

She shook her head, trying to clear it.

Maenads.

Why had she never heard that word before? Her mothers were maenads. Hell, she was a maenad. You'd think they would have told her a little about it, hinted around . . . something.

Maybe they had.

She remembered the stories they'd told her as a child, the fairy tales of chaos and bloodlust and rethroned kings. She recalled one favorite story involving a young princess who had to drink a magic elixir to become strong enough to kill a pack of wolves who had captured her father.

Maybe they'd been trying to prepare her.

She stared down at the empty bottle on the grass. The wine on her skin smelled good, and a part of her wished she'd saved a few swallows to drink.

No!

Blood.

She had to be strong, had to keep from being sucked in. She looked back toward the building, toward the classroom. The blinds were closed and she couldn't tell if Kevin was watching her, if he was even back up there yet, but she surreptitiously waved to him anyway.

She hoped he could see her breast.

This was going to be harder than she thought.

She began walking down the sidewalk, away from the burning truck, working on her stagger, prepared to appear drunk if she ran across anyone. She wasn't sure where the closest fire station was, but she thought it was a few blocks over, toward the downtown area, and she figured she'd head in that direction.

The street was littered with debris. Torn scraps of clothing, newspaper pages, pieces of packages, smashed bottles, and crumpled cans were strewn about the road. On the lawn of one of the houses, a nude man was lying atop the bloody body of an old lady. Penelope wasn't sure if either or both of them were alive, so she hurried past, walking on the strip of grass next to the street rather than the sidewalk to avoid making noise, her hand on the screwdriver in her waistband, ready to pull it out and use it if either of them moved.

She continued down the street. The overpowering dread she'd felt last night was gone, replaced by a more subtle tension. The light of day had removed her fear of being jumped and ambushed in the shadows, but she was still uneasy, and it still felt to her as if something was waiting to happen. The street was calm, nearly empty, only traces remaining of last night's debauchery, but it was as if the city was holding its breath—and waiting to exhale.

This felt to her like the calm before a storm.

Or the eye of a hurricane.

She turned the corner, started walking toward the downtown area.

Where was Dion?

Dionysus.

That was the big question. Had he gone back to the winery, to the meadow? Was he crashed out somewhere in the city? Or was he still on the prowl, looking for her?

She shivered. The screams from the north had not stopped, had continued all along as a constant sub-noise that she'd already started to filter out, and she thought that he was probably there, at the winery. Or at one of the other wineries.

She smiled wryly. Maybe he was taking the tourist's tour of the wine country.

She looked to the right and to the left as she crossed a small street and saw, a block down, a stoplight. Hanging from the light was a red FIRE XING sign.

A fire station. She was in luck.

She hurried down the street, her right hand clamped against the screwdriver as she ran. She'd try the phone first. If that didn't work, she'd try to figure out how to work whatever other communication equipment they had.

She slowed as she neared the station. She was not alone. There were other people here as well.

Children.

She stopped on the sidewalk in front of the station. The big doors were open, and ten or twelve kids, all of them preteens, sat or stood atop the fire truck, smoking hand-rolled cigarettes, drinking from bottles. A kid of seven or eight lay passed out on the driveway in front of the truck. On the small lawn in front of the closed office, young boys and girls were loading and unloading guns.

She was not sure what was stronger, her rage or her fear. What the hell was wrong with these kids' parents? How could they allow this? Even if they had been converted to Dionysus worship, how could they abandon all responsibility for their children?

This was more than merely conversion to a different religion, she knew. This was more than simple mass hysteria. This was something totally different, totally new, a sea change, a complete shift in the fabric of previously accepted reality. The Judeo-Christian assumptions upon which lives and society had been based were no longer true.

A young girl wearing a visible diaper under her ripped pink dress pointed a handgun at Penelope and grinned as she pulled the trigger. The hammer clicked on an empty cylinder. The other kids burst out laughing.

Maybe they'd killed their parents.

Penelope turned away hurrying back the way she'd come. Fuck trying to call for help. Fuck trying to contact the outside world. She wasn't going to sit here like a dummy and wait to be rescued. She'd find a goddamn car, go back for Kevin, and the two of them would get the hell out of the valley and not look back until it was all over.

There were cars in many of the driveways she'd passed on the way over, and though she didn't think any of them had keys in the ignition, keys were probably in the houses.

It hadn't looked like any of the owners were home.

She looked behind her. She wasn't being followed. None of the kids were coming after her. She scanned the driveways in front of her, saw a van at the next house over, saw a Lexus two houses up from that. Glancing across the street, she saw a Toyota of some kind in the driveway directly across from her.

The door to the house was wide open.

She hesitated. If the door was open, something was wrong. Maybe the owners of the house were all dead in there. Maybe they were alive—and waiting.

Fuck it. Something was wrong at the house? Something was wrong all over the goddamn city. She started across the street. She'd rush in, grab the keys, rush out. If someone was inside, she'd run if she could, or, if not, she'd fight.

She pulled the screwdriver from her waistband, adjusted the scissors so she could grab them more easily should the screwdriver be knocked from her hand.

She slowed as she reached the driveway, peering into the open doorway before her, looking for any sign of movement within the dim interior of the house.

Her grip on the screwdriver tightened as she passed the front of the car.

She saw no movement inside the house, heard no sound, and she took a deep breath and forced herself to walk through the doorway.

The house was empty. There were no dead bodies, no attackers lying in wait. She walked from the entryway to the living room to the kitchen, where a ring of keys was lying atop the counter next to the stove. She grabbed the keys, hurried outside.

The first key she tried fit the car door.

She smiled to herself. This must be my lucky day, she thought.

Five minutes later, she drove into the school parking lot. Pulling into the principal's spot in front of the main building, she was about to honk on the horn when Kevin hurried out the front door. She looked around to make sure there was no one nearby, then pressed the button that automatically flipped open the Toyota's locks.

Kevin pulled open the passenger door, jumped in, and slammed the door shut behind him.

"Well?" he said.

She locked the car doors again, put the Toyota into gear.

"What's the plan?"

"We leave," she said. "We get the hell out of here."

TWO

April awoke on the grass, a rock pressing painfully against her left breast, her mouth tasting of blood. She hurt all over, and it took her fogged mind a moment to remember where she was.

Dion.

She sat up quickly. Too quickly. Agony flared behind her forehead, almost causing her to fall back down. She closed her eyes against the pain, waiting until it subsided to a dull throb, then slowly reopened her eyes.

She was still in the meadow, as were hundreds of other people, but Dion and the other maenads were gone. She remembered them leaving rather early in the proceedings, and vaguely recalled wanting to go with them, but she could not seem to recollect where they had gone or why she had stayed here.

Next to her on the ground was the half-eaten remains of a goat. She stared down at the animal's bloody chest cavity, at the snaking entrails, the deflated sac-like organs, and felt a warm tingling between her legs. She bent down, picked up a quivery piece of liver, bit into it.

Wine.

She needed to wash it down with wine.

Glancing around, April saw a partially filled bottle clutched tightly to the chest of a sleeping woman. She walked over to the woman, lay down next to her, kissed her on the lips, and gently removed the bottle from between her oversize breasts. She finished off the wine, then carefully replaced the bottle.

She sat up, stood up. The headache was almost entirely gone now, and she looked more carefully around the meadow. Her gaze alighted on the altar at the opposite end. Immediately, a sharp stab of guilt shot through her. She remembered the way her son had screamed as the other maenads had anointed him. She should've come to his rescue. How could she have allowed them to do that?

How could she not?

Her intellect and her instincts were at odds on this one. Well, maybe not her intellect. Her upbringing. No, not that either, really.

Her sexual desires and her maternal instinct.

That was more like it.

She wondered where Dion had gone.

Dionysus.

It was still hard for her to think of her son as her god. She smiled wryly. Had it been this hard for Mary?

Someone groaned nearby, then started yelling: "My leg! What happened to my leg!"

April turned toward the voice. An obviously hungover man was sitting up on the grass, staring at the bloody, half-eaten remains of his right leg. She smiled at him, then walked over, pushed him down, and sat on his face. Immediately, his tongue snaked inside her.

She stared at the red remains of the leg as she squirmed on top of the man's head. For the first time in her life she felt totally free, totally unfettered.

Happy.

She just wished that it hadn't come at the expense of her son.

THREE

It was again as it should be.

Times had changed, the world had moved on, but he was here, the females were here, the wine was here, the celebrants were here.

Woman and grape.

These things were eternal.

Dionysus strode across the hillside, the dry grass rustling pleasantly beneath his bare feet. His maenads were singing to him. He could hear them even from this far away, their song a paean to his lust, his power, his generosity, his greatness. They had welcomed him back last night, hosting a celebration that had not stopped until dawn.

It was again as it should be.

But he was not the same as he had been. He had another past now, another history, another life, and it was his as well . . . only it wasn't. He shook his head. It was all so confusing, and he didn't really want to think about it. He wanted to drink again and celebrate his return, wanted to kill some men and rape some women.

But the exhilaration and anticipation he should have felt in contemplating the sating of his desires seemed to be tempered. He felt uncomfortable, ill at ease, not himself, as if his new physical limitations were affecting his thoughts. He was joined with this other, trapped inside this too small form, mired in this overly literal body like an animal trapped in tar. He had never had the freedom of Apollo or Artemis or Hestia, had never been as ephemeral as the others, had always been tied to the flesh, and he had liked that. It was what had set him apart from the others, his ability to enjoy earthly pleasures, and he would not have given it up for anything.

This, however, was different.

He was not himself.

He was himself and this other.

He stopped walking, inhaled deeply. The scent of grape was on the breeze. It permeated the air, the redolent fragrance providing a promise of intoxication, and it made him feel calmer, more relaxed. He strode to the edge of the hill, looking down and surveying his dominion. He could see the burnings at either end of the valley, the crashed cars on the roads, the bands of revelers prowling the city in search of more fun. Sounds came to him as well, below the singing of his maenads: breaking glass, laughter, cries of joy, cries of terror, cries of pain.

It was a wonderful morning to be alive, the beginning of a beautiful day. There was no reason for him to be brooding on the inconveniences of resurrection.

To his right was a log, and on a sudden whim he strode backward, away from the edge, got a running start, and leaped atop the log. The momentum carried him forward, and then he was surfing down the hillside, laughing with glee as he leaned to the left to steer away from a tree, bumped over a series of half-buried rocks, and then crashed to a halt at the bottom of the hill.

He tumbled head over heels, then stood, brushed the dirt off his body, and willed shut the cuts that he'd gotten from the fall. He was standing before a connected corral and horse stable that backed against the side of the hill, and the sight of the worn wooden fences triggered a memory within him, a memory that despite his best efforts remained naggingly below the surface of his conscious mind.

There was something missing in this new world. He had not been aware of it before, had not had time to be aware of it, but the corral and the stable had—

A pair of horses wandered into the fenced corral from behind the low building.

Centaurs.

He smiled. Yes, that was it. That's what he hadn't been able to remember. Centaurs. He walked forward. He

missed those randy creatures. They were a bother sometimes, but they knew how to enjoy themselves, and they
were always up for a celebration. Besides, they'd like it
here. The cool weather, the plentiful wine. This was their
kind of place.

He looked back up the hill.

He would like centaurs in his new dominion.

He strode into the corral, then walked around the side
of the stable. A small herd of horses was shying against
the opposite fence, and he spotted an acceptable filly and
called the horse to him, making her back up against his
sex.

"Pretty girl," he said, grabbing her haunches. "Pretty
girl."

The horse bucked and kicked, trying to get away, but
he held tight.

She whinnied in pain as he mounted her.

FOUR

Kevin said nothing as they drove down the empty streets, on the lookout for one of the roving bands. Here and there he saw people packing station wagons in garages and carports, surreptitiously trying to leave. He even saw one man mowing his lawn as though nothing out of the ordinary had occurred. Could it be that some people were totally unaware of the events of the night before? It didn't seem possible.

There was no sign of the revelers. Nor any sign of their victims. There were broken bottles on the road, torn pieces of clothing, overturned cars and bicycles, occasional dead cats and dogs, but there were very few human bodies on either the streets or the sidewalks.

He supposed he should be grateful for small favors.

Kevin glanced over at Penelope, who stared grimly ahead as she drove. He would have suggested that they stop and get together with some of these other people who were leaving, but he knew that she would not go for it. Penelope had seen something when she'd gone looking for the car, something she didn't want to talk about, something that had profoundly affected her, and he knew that she was not in the mood to approach strangers right now, no matter how safe they might be.

He thought about what he had seen last night on Ash Street, and he shivered.

He knew exactly how she felt.

They pulled onto Third Street. Downtown was a shambles, the destruction more random and wanton than anything he had ever seen in any post-apocalyptic movie, the rubble more awkwardly strewn about and nowhere near as aesthetically pleasing as the precisely arranged disor-

der found in films. The old building that had housed
Phil's Photo had burned to the ground, and the blaze had
spread to the vacant lot next door before apparently burning itself out. Clothes, electrical equipment, and food
from the other nearby shops littered the roadway, making
it nearly impossible to drive. Penelope slowed to a crawl,
carefully maneuvering around the sharper, bulkier objects, trying to drive only on the garments and foodstuffs.

Ahead, Kevin could see that the McDonald's had been
razed. And sitting atop the still lit golden arches were two
police lights.

Nipples.

The fast-food joint's trademark had been turned into a
pair of monstrous breasts.

Kevin stared at the upcoming sign. The purposeful vandalism that it represented scared him far more than the
chaotic destruction around it, and he realized that until
this moment he had not entirely believed Penelope's
story. He'd bought the specifics of it—he'd seen enough
horrors last night to know that what she had described
had no doubt happened—but he had not been able to
completely buy the idea that Dion had been turned into a
mythological god.

The nippled arches somehow brought that truth home
to him. He did not know why. The vandalism was certainly no worse than other things he'd seen. He supposed
it was the juxtaposition of such a solidly rational symbol,
such a perfect example of normal American life, with this
lewd sexuality, this drunken crudeness, that made him realize exactly how far things had gone.

And made him realize that Penelope was obviously telling the truth.

He wondered where Dion was now.

He wondered what his friend looked like.

The emotional impact had not yet hit him, and he supposed it was because everything was happening so fast,
because he had been simply reacting to everything that
was going on and had not had the luxury of reflection. He
would miss Dion, he knew. Although they'd known each
other only since the beginning of the school year, Dion
was his best friend. It was going to be a hard loss to take.

He was already assuming that there would be a loss.
That Dion would have to be killed.

The street cleared a little past the McDonald's, and Penelope speeded up. Kevin stared out the window, saw an old lady on her hands and knees licking up what appeared to be a puddle of wine on the sidewalk. It was inevitable, wasn't it? These things always ended that way. If good was to win and triumph and all that good shit, there was no other possible ending to the situation.

He was surprised that he didn't feel sadder at the thought, more affected, but in his mind Dion was already dead, replaced by this . . . god, and so the leap wasn't that great.

It was amazing how fast the mind could adjust.

They turned onto Monticello, heading toward the highway, and Kevin sat up straighter in his seat. They would be passing his neighborhood, his house. He glanced over at Penelope. Should he ask her to stop?

He had to.

He cleared his throat, spoke. "My house," he said. "It's down Oak."

Penelope turned toward him. Her mouth was still a thin, grim line, but there was confusion in her eyes, and what looked like sympathetic understanding beneath the rage and hurt.

"Do you want to . . . stop?" Her voice was quiet, tentative.

"I have to check," he said. "I have to know."

Penelope nodded. She slowed as they reached the corner of Oak Avenue. "Which way?" she asked. "Left or right?"

"Right."

She maneuvered the car onto the street, and he pointed toward the third house on the left. His heart was pounding as she parked the car next to the curb. The lawn was littered with empty wine bottles. A pair of ripped and bloody panties hung from the branch of a bush.

The entire street was silent, and that seemed ominous.

Their driveway was empty, the car gone, but the front door was open, the screen door ripped and hanging off its hinges, and as Kevin looked through the dark doorway into the dim interior of the house, his stomach did flip-flops. He felt as if he were about to throw up.

He turned toward Penelope. "Wait here."

"No. I'm coming with—"

"Wait here," he ordered. "Keep the doors locked and the engine running. If I'm not back in five minutes, or you hear or see anything strange, take off. Don't wait for me."

Her mouth tightened as though she was about to argue, but then she looked into his eyes and nodded slowly. Her expression softened. "Okay," she agreed. "I'll wait here."

Kevin opened the car door and got out, hearing the locks click behind him. He was nervous, anxious, scared, and he wanted to run inside the house yelling, "Mom! Dad!" but he walked forward slowly, cautiously, going up the driveway one step at a time. The living room window was broken, he saw as he approached the house, and as he walked up the porch steps he prepared himself for the worst.

Inside, the house was dark. And silent. The dead air smelled of something sickly, sweetly rotten, something he did not want to think about. The living room had been ransacked, lamps and tables broken, chairs and couch overturned, but there were no bodies. His parents weren't here. He passed carefully through the living room, stepped slowly around the corner into the dining room.

Nothing.

He continued on into the kitchen. The refrigerator was open, its contents spilled onto the tile floor, lettuce rotting in milk and runny yogurt, salsa blanketing hot dogs and leftover spaghetti. He clenched his fists tightly to keep his hands from trembling. Until this point he had been more worried than frightened, but now the balance had started to shift. He hoped his parents were alive and unharmed, but if they were, he knew he didn't want to meet up with them.

He walked out of the kitchen into the hall

and almost tripped over a teenage girl's head.

His scream was so raw and uncontrolled, expelled with such force, that his throat hurt. But he could not stop

screaming, and he continued to scream as first his mother
and then his father staggered out of their bedroom. Both
were naked, both were drunk, and both were smeared
with dried blood.

Both grinned at him lasciviously.

He ran out of the house, bumping against furniture,
stumbling over debris. He leaped the porch steps and
sprinted across the yard. Penelope was already revving
the engine, and she unlocked the doors as he approached.
He yanked open the passenger door, jumped into the car,
and they took off, speeding down the street. He turned to
look through the rear window as they fled, but he could
not see if his parents had come out of the house after him.

He faced forward, heart pumping, arms shaking.

Penelope's expression was hard. "What happened?"

He took a deep breath. "My parents."

"Alive or dead?"

"Alive."

Penelope nodded. He did not have to say more.

They turned left on the next street, then left again until
they hit Monticello.

"Even if we get help, even if we get the police or National Guard or whoever out here, what are they going to
do?" Kevin asked. "How are they supposed to put a stop
to this?"

Penelope shook her head. "I don't know."

"Maybe there's nothing they can do. Maybe they—"

"We're high school kids! Shit. How are we supposed to
know how to solve this? That's their job. They'll know
how to do it. They'll figure out something."

Kevin's voice caught in his throat. "I don't . . . I just
don't want anything to happen to my parents."

"I know," Penelope said softly.

"Yeah, they're drunk and crazy and everything. But I
don't want the cops shooting them."

"I know how you feel."

Of course she did. She was in exactly the same position. Her mother—her *mothers*—had not only been
caught up in all this, they were the cause of it. They were
the ringleaders. If anyone was going to be shot and killed,
it would be them.

Penelope had to be feeling even worse than he did.

"I'm sorry," he said.

She tried to smile. "You have nothing to be sorry for."

Monticello hit the highway, and Penelope continued south. The highway was in better shape than the streets had been, the piles of debris fewer and farther between, and she took the car up to sixty.

There was no one else on the highway, no vehicles traveling in either direction, and Kevin found that unsettling. The valley seemed to have emptied of people during the night, leaving only the victims and their victimizers, with he and Penelope caught in between.

The highway curved around the side of a small hill—

—and Penelope slammed on the brakes. The car skidded, fishtailing, before finally coming to a lane-straddling halt. The highway before them was blocked, littered with stacked cars, demolished trucks and burning bodies.

Kevin, still bracing himself against the dashboard, stared through the windshield in dumb horror. The bodies had obviously been torn apart in last night's craziness and had later been separated according to part: arm, leg, head, torso. Five individual bonfires were burning, and around them danced linked circles of nude revelers, all of whom had identically blank stares on their enraptured faces.

Someone tapped on Penelope's window, and she screamed.

He jumped at the sound of her cry, looked immediately over. An old woman, face smeared with patterned blood that had been applied like war paint, laughed loonily. She breathed deeply, inhaling the thick, foul-smelling smoke. "Nose hit!" she said. "Contact high!"

"Back up," Kevin said softly. "Get us out of here before the rest of them see us."

Penelope nodded, threw the car into Reverse. As they sped backward, away from the woman, she began screeching, pointing, and several of the naked celebrants broke away from the nearest circle—the leg bonfire—and began chasing after the car.

Kevin's heart was pounding with fear, and he watched the men and women run after them, breasts and erections bouncing as legs pumped unnaturally fast. The blank expressions on their faces had been replaced by intimidating looks of grim determination, and he was suddenly certain that the revelers would catch them. They'd be yanked out of the car and torn apart, their body segments burned in the appropriate bonfire as drunken partyers danced.

Then Penelope slammed on the brakes, spun the car around, and they were off, speeding back down the highway the way they'd come, their pursuers fading into specks behind him.

Kevin coughed. The smoke from the bodies had seeped into the car, and it was nauseating. He pinched his nostrils shut, trying to breathe only through his mouth, but he could taste the horrid smoke in his throat, and he started to gag.

Penelope reached over, turned on the air conditioner. "It's pretty bad," she said.

But she wasn't having a hard time breathing, he noticed. The smoke didn't seem to have affected her at all.

He breathed in the cold, filtered air, and his nausea passed.

The car slowed as they reached the intersection at which they'd gotten on the highway. "What now?" Penelope asked.

"I don't know," he said. "We could try going north, but I bet both ends of the valley are blocked off."

"Then we're trapped here. We can't get out."

"How about one of the back roads?" Kevin suggested. "What about sneaking through Wooden Valley and circling back to Vallejo? Or taking Carneros into Sonoma?"

"We could try it," she said. "But I don't think we should hold our breath."

"If not, what then?"

She shrugged. "Hike out? I don't know. We'll figure something out when we get to that point."

They were both right. The highway was blocked by another pileup of vehicles just above Calistoga, and both the road to Sonoma and the various westbound side roads they attempted to navigate had been turned into heavily guarded obstacle courses.

"These people may be wasted," Kevin said after they'd

narrowly avoided an ambush on the road to Lake Berryessa, "but they're organized."

"It's Dion," Penelope said. "He doesn't want me to leave."

The hairs prickled on the back of Kevin's neck.

They were both silent after that, driving back down to the highway, on the watch for attackers and pursuers. What was Dion like now? Kevin wondered. Would he recognize their previous relationships with him? Would he let them go if he caught them because of that past association? Or was all that forgotten history? Was Dion gone completely, entirely overtaken by . . . Dionysus?

God, that sounded stupid.

A demon he could understand. The spirit of an old murderer even. But a mythical god? It seemed so ludicrous.

It wasn't, though. He knew that.

They reached the highway again, and Penelope pulled to the side of the road. She turned off the ignition, slumped forward.

She started crying.

"Hey," Kevin said. "Don't cry."

She began sobbing harder. He sat there uncertainly, unsure of what to do, then scooted toward her on the seat and awkwardly put a hand on her shoulder. "It's okay," he said.

Penelope sat up, nodding, and wiped her eyes. "I'm sorry. It's just . . . It's so frustrating. We keep trying all these roads and they're all blocked. We're in a cage here. We can't get out."

He moved back away from her. "You want me to drive for a while?"

She breathed deeply, nodded. "Yeah."

"Okay." He checked behind the car, in front, to the sides, making sure there was no one around, then got out of the passenger door and ran around the vehicle to the driver's side, while Penelope slid across the seat.

"There's one more road we haven't tried," he said, getting behind the wheel and locking the door.

"Think it'll do any good?" she asked.

"No, but I'm obsessive-compulsive, and I have to finish the search."

She laughed, wiping the last of the tears from her eyes. He turned on the ignition, put the car into gear, and took off.

The road, a winding, hilly route that led through Deer Park to Angwin, was cut off almost at the source by a group of over fifty who were holding some sort of bastardized, impromptu rodeo, taking turns riding what appeared to be milk cows and using broken wine bottles to goad the animals into moving.

"We could try plowing through them," Kevin suggested.

Penelope started to respond, but the words were choked off in her throat. The color drained from her face.

He thought at first that she was having a heart attack or an epileptic fit. Then he heard the noise. A voice. A voice as low and loud as the rumble of thunder. He could not make out the words, only the sounds, and he followed Penelope's gaze to the top of the hill to their left. Coming down the hillside, striding purposefully, was a giant man as tall as a billboard. He was naked, his hairy skin stained with blood and wine, and he carried under his arm the limp, dead body of a goat. The unnatural glee in his expression nearly obscured the fact that the basic structure of his face was familiar.

"It's Dion," Penelope whispered. "Dionysus."

"Fuck," Kevin breathed. "Holy mother of shit."

A wave of people topped the hill behind Dionysus, following him down. Many of them fell, tumbling down the steep side, but no allowances were made for the clumsy, and the wave continued on, trampling those who fell before it.

Kevin was already backing up, moving quickly but not too quickly, not wanting to draw attention to their vehicle. They might be able to escape ordinary runners, but there was no way they'd be able to escape Dionysus.

He'd catch up to them before they hit the highway.

Kevin's mouth was dry, his hands not shaking only because they were gripping the steering wheel. He had been frightened before. He could not have imagined being more frightened than he had been last night on Ash

Street. But nothing had prepared him for this. Intellectually, he'd known what to expect. Penelope had described the metamorphosis to him, and he had understood how frightening it had been, had known what Dion had become, but there was no way to convey in words the sheer horrifying alienness of it all. The creature hurrying down the side of the hill was not like a person, not like a horror movie monster, not like anything he had ever seen or read about or dreamed or imagined. There was a palpable power within the form, a force that could be sensed so clearly it could almost be seen, and the presence of that power skewed all other sensory perceptions in a way that left Kevin feeling not only terrified but disoriented.

Dionysus reached the bottom of the hill, held the goat aloft, and broke off its head, tossing it to his followers while he drank in the spray that shot from the neck. He screamed, a cry of joy that rumbled through the hills like an earthquake, and Kevin forgot all about not drawing attention to the car and floored the gas pedal, sending the vehicle hurling backward.

He swung into a dirt pull-out, shifted the car into Drive, and made a sliding U-turn toward the highway.

"Is he coming?" Kevin asked.

Penelope shook her head.

"Jesus." Kevin glanced in the rearview mirror, saw nothing, only trees. "Jesus," he repeated.

Penelope was quiet. He swerved south onto the highway, back toward Napa. The obstacles in the road were familiar by this time, and he sped around them, easily avoiding the crashed cars and the debris. "We're going to be out of gas pretty soon. I don't know how we're going to get some more. I don't even know if any of the pumps still work."

Penelope said nothing.

"I didn't realize he'd be so scary." Kevin's voice was softer than he'd intended, and more frightened. "I don't know what we're going to be able to do against . . . that."

"Nothing," Penelope said dully.

"I think what we have to do now is start thinking about tonight. We haven't seen a lot of people yet, but I don't think they've gone anywhere. I bet they're just sleeping.

And they'll probably come out at night. We need to find a place to hole up, get some weapons. There's a gun store over on Lincoln. We'll try there."

The gun store, Napa Rifles, was occupied. Even from the street he could see shadowed forms moving about behind the barred windows. A line of armed, overweight men, wearing sheets that had been fashioned into makeshift togas, were seated on the curb in front of the building.

"Forget it," Kevin said, catching Penelope's glance as they sped by the store. "We'll just have to make do with what we can."

Penelope leaned forward. "You want to go back to the school?"

He shook his head. "Too easy to be trapped. I think we should go to . . ." He thought for a moment. "To the tourist cabins over on Coombsville. Napa Hideaway?"

"That slummy motel?"

"A cabin would be easily defensible. We'll scrounge what we can, hit Big 5 Sporting Goods, raid some houses if we have to." He pointed at the clock on the dashboard. "If this thing's right, it's already after noon. We'll need to find some food and supplies and be settled in before dark."

He was aware that his voice sounded calm and assured, but that word—*dark*—conjured up images from the previous night and made him tremble inside. He wasn't sure he'd be strong enough to handle another night like the last one.

"You're right," Penelope said, and in her voice was all the strength he lacked. "Let's find what we need and stake out a camp for the night."

Her confidence gave him confidence, and he nodded. "Let's switch. You drive. I'll go out and find what we need. You wait."

"I don't need to sit in the car. I can help you find things."

"I don't—"

"—know if you'll live if I don't go with you? I don't either."

Kevin laughed. "All right."

* * *

They were safely ensconced within Cabin 12 of the Napa Hideaway by four-thirty. They hadn't been able to find any guns, but Kevin had picked up baseball bats from the supply cage at the Little League diamond, and they'd grabbed butcher knives and cleavers from a kitchen store. The floor of the cabin was lined with Drano and aerosol cans and lighters that they'd stolen from a 7-Eleven. The hammers and screwdrivers they'd scrounged from the janitor's office of the school were still in the car.

Penelope sat on the king-size bed, watching Kevin finish nailing boards over the windows. She'd already helped him install two extra dead bolts on the door.

The phones were out, but the electricity still worked, as did the water. The bacchantes were neither organized nor logical enough to try to shut down the utilities, and even television reception was unaffected.

She stood up and walked across the room to change the channel on the TV, switching slowly through the stations, stopping when the familiar anchor team from San Francisco's CBS news came on.

She watched the entire broadcast. She expected to hear an update on the situation, to learn that the governor was flying in troops, that law enforcement agencies were banding together to converge on the valley, but the situation in Napa was not mentioned at all.

How was that possible?

Her spirits sank as she stared at the television. She and Kevin had been planning to alert outside authorities, but she hadn't thought they'd be the only ones to do so. She'd assumed that others had escaped to tell what was going on here. And people from the outside must have been trying to contact people in the valley. Relatives, friends, business associates. What about all the people trying to order wine? What about all of the tourists trying to drive into Napa? Hadn't any of those people complained?

Apparently not.

Maybe they'd been killed.

She tried not to think of that.

Maybe the entire state had been taken over by bacchantes.

That wasn't physically possible.

Not yet.

Kevin sat down on the bed next to her. "Nothing, huh?"

She shook her head.

"Maybe there'll be something on the late news."

"Maybe," she said doubtfully.

Kevin looked toward the window. She followed his gaze and saw the deepening hues of twilight peeking in between the boards. He stood, turned on the room light, closed the venetian blinds.

"It's going to be a long night," he said, walking back to the bed.

Penelope nodded. "If we live through it."

He sat down next to her, and the two of them remained there silently, watching the TV.

FIVE

Officer Dennis McComber finished raping the corpse of the chief's daughter and pulled out, rolling off her. He wiped the sweat from his forehead and reached for the bottle next to him, finishing it off. He was sore and spent and buzzing, and that was exactly how he wanted to feel right now.

God damn, he felt good.

Freedom.

That's what this new god had brought. Freedom.

It was what he'd been craving all these years, although he hadn't really known it. As a policeman he was supposed to enforce the law, make sure people followed the rules, but he had never really been interested in that. He had joined the force so that he would be above those laws, so that he would not have to follow those rules. Speeding? He could do it. But if other people attempted it, he would give them a ticket. Ass kicking? He could do it, but if other people did it, he would arrest them.

It had not been real freedom, though, only a taste, a sample, a whetting of his appetite.

This was freedom.

McComber reached over and touched the chief's daughter's cold breast, squeezing the nipple.

He had been afraid before the god had arrived, filled with a nearly debilitating dread that had only been relieved by wine. But His arrival had been anything but dreadful. Indeed, it had been the most glorious event in McComber's life, and the liberation he had felt as the reverberations of the god's rebirth had spread throughout the valley had been stronger, purer, and more real than anything he had ever experienced.

He had been born again himself at that moment.

McComber grabbed the chief's daughter by the arm and rolled her over. He looked toward Goodridge. "You want her next?"

The chief shook his head drunkenly, then fell facedown on the desk.

McComber laughed, his laughter doubling as he saw blood from the chief's broken nose pool onto the papers spread atop the desk. He threw the bottle against the wall, was gratified to hear it shatter. He nodded toward one of the rookies lined up by the window.

"Next," he said.

SIX

They awoke in the morning to the sound of gunfire.

Penelope jerked up, disoriented to find herself dressed and sleeping in a strange bed. Then the past forty-eight hours returned in a rush, and she looked around the dim room until her eyes found Kevin crouched in front of the boarded window, peering through the slats of the venetian blinds.

She tiptoed over to where he sat crouched, ducking down next to him. "What is it?" she whispered.

He shook his head, put a finger to his lips.

She looked at him, on his knees, tightly holding his baseball bat, doing his best to defend them though he was obviously frightened. A tingling feeling passed through her. She should reward him, maybe. Give him a blow job while he waited there.

No!

She inhaled, exhaled. What the hell was she thinking about?

Blood.

Raising herself to the level of the window, Penelope spread apart two of the slats, peeked through the blinds, between the boards. Outside, in the middle of the street, a migrant farmworker had been surrounded by a group of gun-toting women dressed in motley rags. They were passing around a bottle, taking turns shooting at his feet to make him dance. Or shooting at what was left of his feet. For he was attempting to cavort now on what looked like bloody stumps as the women called out the names of various dance steps, laughing.

"Lay low!" Kevin whispered, grabbing Penelope's

shoulder and pulling her down. "Don't touch those blinds! They'll see the movement!"

She nodded, followed his lead, peering at an angle through the slats without touching them. The women on the street were shooting again, dancing and whooping as the farmworker fell screaming to his knees. Their intoxication seemed to come as much from the violence as the alcohol, and the scary thing was that Penelope knew exactly how they felt.

She sat on the floor, facing away from the window, listening but not looking.

She had awakened in the middle of the night with a craving for wine, the smell of fresh blood in her nostrils. She had gotten a drink of water instead and had forced herself to fall back asleep. The blood, she thought now, had come from the bathroom. The woman who'd stayed here before them had probably been menstruating at the time.

How could she smell that, though?

Her senses were becoming heightened.

That was a frightening thought, and she pushed it away.

What were her mothers doing now? she wondered.

Or her mother and her aunts.

That was one thing good that had come out of all of this. She had finally confirmed what she'd known all along—that Mother Felice was her biological mother, her real mother. Despite everything else that had happened, that knowledge made her feel good. The last time she'd seen her mother, she had been naked and covered with blood, but Penelope still had the feeling that after this was all over and done with—

after the rest of her mothers were dead

—the two of them would be together, and it would be different, better, than before. They would be a real family, a regular family, a normal family, and whatever difficulties they might have, whatever problems they might come up against, would be normal problems.

Outside the cabin, there was a shot, a scream, and wild laughter.

Penelope turned toward Kevin. "They killed him," he whispered. "They shot him in the head."

She closed her eyes, feeling sick, seeing in her mind the farmworker's bloody, stumpy feet as he tried to dance on the asphalt.

"They're leaving." Kevin remained at the window for a moment, then slumped down, exhaling deeply. "Fuck."

"What could we have done if they'd come after us?" Penelope asked, still whispering.

Kevin shook his head. "Pray."

A half hour later, they were clean and combed and had finished their breakfast, such as it was. Kevin was still keeping watch on the window, but the women had not come back and the street outside remained empty save for the corpse of the farmworker.

Penelope forced herself to smile. "So what are we going to do today? Have a picnic? Hit the mall?"

"We should try to get out of here," he suggested. "Out of the valley."

"We tried," she said. "We failed."

"Well, we can't just sit here and wait and . . . and hope that someone comes to rescue us."

"We could find someone to help us."

Kevin snorted. "Yeah. Right." He was silent for a moment, thinking, then a look of hope passed over his features. He turned toward Penelope. "Mr. Holbrook. He knows about things like this. We could find him, see if there's any way he can help us. His address is probably in the phone book."

Penelope blinked dumbly.

"He knows a lot about Greek mythology," Kevin continued. "Maybe he can figure out something that can get us out of this."

She shook her head. "I don't want to see him. I don't like him. He's creepy."

"Creepy or not, we don't have much choice. And he can't be any creepier than the other shit we've seen."

"If he's still here," she pointed out. "Or if he isn't one of them. Or dead."

Kevin was obviously excited. "We'll wait a little while longer, make sure no one else is out there, then we'll haul out to the car and get out of here." He started opening the dresser drawers, looking for a phone book. "Start packing our stuff. We need to be ready to roll."

Penelope thought of arguing, then nodded, saying nothing. She walked into the bathroom, where she began filling up empty sports bottles with tap water. She stopped after the second bottle, looked at herself in the mirror above the sink.

Holbrook.

Logically, it sounded good, but the thought of going out to look for the teacher gave her an uneasy feeling in the pit of her stomach. She wished she could be as optimistic about this as Kevin was, but the idea didn't sit well with her. She told herself that she was being stupid and paranoid, but she knew that she wasn't, and the worry showed on her face.

The face staring back at her looked scared.

She glanced away from the mirror, picked up another bottle, filled it up.

Outside, there was a different feeling in the air, a different emotional atmosphere. Both of them felt it. It was subtle, indefinable, but there, a tangible presence, not merely her own altered perception. She felt nervous, anxious, as though there was a wildness within her struggling to break out—or, more accurately, a wildness without her that was struggling to break in. There were still no people on the street, but the sense that there were no rules of behavior, no boundaries, that everything was acceptable, anything goes, was alive and well and struggling for supremacy with the ordinary values inside both of them. She could see it in Kevin's face, could feel it in herself.

In the sky above, an airplane, a jumbo jet, flew from east to west, toward the ocean. It was strange to realize that everything that was happening down here was merely a two-second blip on the ground to the people in the airplane. If they blinked, they'd miss the valley. While she and Kevin were desperately trying to escape the hellhole that Napa had become, those people would be served free drinks from the stewardess as they settled in to watch their in-flight movie in air-conditioned comfort.

But how long before all this spread? How long before it affected Sonoma? Vallejo? San Francisco?

She didn't want to think about it.

They loaded their supplies in the trunk of the car, then got in, Kevin driving.

He looked down at the page he'd torn out of the phone book. "Palmer," he said. "That means we'll have to go through downtown." He glanced over at Penelope. "Don't worry. We'll make it."

Penelope looked out the windshield of the car at the bloody body of the footless farmworker. "I hope so," she said.

He started the ignition, put the car into gear, and pulled onto the street. "I just hope he's there and alive and not one of them."

SEVEN

Holbrook's house was a nondescript crackerbox on a street of small, identical subdivision houses.

Kevin was not sure what he had expected, but it had not been this. Hell, Holbrook's house was even shittier than his own. He thought of Holbrook lecturing at the front of the class, giving grades, meting out punishment, and it was hard to reconcile that figure of authority and respect with a man who lived in this small, slightly run-down home.

He parked the car by the curb in front of the house and got out, leaving the engine on. He grabbed one of his screwdrivers from the storage space on the side of the door. "Same deal," he told Penelope. "Be ready to take off. I'll go up and check things out, and if something's wrong, I'll speed back, hop in, and we'll haul ass."

Penelope smiled. "You don't want me to take off without you this time, huh?"

"Fuck no!" He grinned. "I must've been crazy."

"There's a lot of that going around."

They both laughed.

"Okay," Kevin said. "I'm—"

"What are you doing out there in the street? Get inside!"

Kevin looked up, startled by the sound of the voice. Over the roof of the car, he saw Holbrook standing in the open doorway of his house, holding a shotgun.

"Get your asses in here!" the teacher roared.

Penelope looked toward Kevin, panicked.

"Now! Before they see you!"

She opened the door of the car and got out, hurrying across the lawn toward Holbrook. Kevin sped around the

front of the car and passed her, clutching his screwdriver
. . . just in case. Holbrook's fear and concern indicated
that he was probably all right, but they couldn't afford to
take any chances.

The teacher raised the shotgun to his shoulder, and
Kevin's heart lurched in his chest—it was a trap! the bas-
tard was going to blow them away!—but he stopped in
front of the stoop, screwdriver outstretched. "Are you
drunk?" he demanded.

Holbrook lowered the shotgun, smiled grimly. "Well, I
guess that answers that question. I think we're all okay
here." He moved to the side, holding the door open. "Get
inside. Quickly."

Penelope moved up the stoop and past him, into the
house. Kevin started to follow, then realized that the car's
engine was still running. He turned, sprinting back out to
the street.

"Hey!" Holbrook yelled.

"The car!" Kevin yelled back. He reached the vehicle,
opened the door, threw himself across the seat, and
switched off the ignition, turning and pulling out the key.
Closing the car door behind him, he hurried back to
where Holbrook stood frowning.

The teacher grabbed his arm as he started to walk into
the house. "What were you doing? You could've been
killed."

Kevin yanked his arm out of the man's grasp. "There's
no one on your street. And that running engine was a red
flag to every psycho out there. Besides, I don't want anyone stealing my car." He looked into Holbrook's eyes.
"I'm going to need it."

"Get inside."

Penelope was standing just inside the living room,
looking uncertainly around. Holbrook closed the door,
locked it, started throwing a series of dead bolts. Kevin
wished that Penelope had grabbed a weapon before leaving the car.

Holbrook put down his shotgun, resting it against the
wall next to the door. He turned toward Penelope. "The
Daneam women brought back Dionysus, didn't they?"

Kevin stared at him, shocked, "How—" he began.

"They're meanads."

"I know that," Kevin said. "But how did *you* know that?"

Holbrook ignored him. "Did you help them?" he asked Penelope.

She shook her head.

"Do you know how they did it?"

She looked away, looked toward Kevin, didn't answer.

"Come on, then," Holbrook said. "I have something to show you." He walked past them, through the living room into a short hallway. He opened what looked like a closet door next to the bathroom to reveal a narrow staircase leading down. "Down here."

Kevin followed the teacher, Penelope behind him. He caught her eye as he turned around, saw her trepidation. He felt more than a little apprehensive about going in here himself, but he continued down the stairs, following Holbrook.

The narrow stairwell opened into a room that was easily half as big as the entire house above.

"Jesus," Kevin said. He looked around. The entire basement was filled with ancient artifacts and poster-sized photos of friezes. Graphs and charts had been tacked up next to photographs of Greek ruins and historical sights, and everywhere were piles of books and papers. Against the far wall was what looked like a Greek shrine, or a high school drama department's conception of a Greek shrine. It was rough and amateurish, its pillars made of grey pâpíer maché, and appeared to be only half finished.

Holbrook walked over to a desk on which a battered computer terminal was flanked by two giant stacks of notebooks. He picked up the top notebook, fished a pen out from under the papers that covered the rest of the desk, and turned toward Penelope, opening the notebook to a blank page. "It's Dion, isn't it? Dion Semele?"

She nodded.

"Tell me how it happened. Tell me everything you know. Start from the beginning."

She did.

Kevin had heard it before, but the story was just as horrifying and unbelievable the second time. Holbrook listened silently, intently, scribbling furiously in his notebook.

"Fascinating." The teacher continued to write after Penelope had finished talking. "So the gods hid inside genes and chromosomes. In DNA." He shook his head, smiled to himself. "This could be the origin of Jung's conception of the universal archetype, the collective unconscious. Perhaps this is where the concept that God is to be found within us got started—"

"Write a paper later," Kevin said. "Jesus, there are people dying out there. We don't have time to sit around playing little mind games."

"These 'little mind games' are what's going to save your ass." Holbrook turned back toward Penelope. "You don't know what they were chanting when they were anointing Dion with the blood?"

She shook her head. "Not really."

"That's too bad. If you did, we might be able to reverse the process. As it is . . ." He trailed off.

"Can he be killed?" Kevin asked.

Penelope looked from Holbrook to Kevin. "Killed?" she said, her voice rising.

Kevin could not meet her eyes. "Can he?"

The teacher nodded slowly. "I think so. But I don't know for sure. I suppose we should be thankful that the first god to come back is a god of flesh. It increases our odds greatly. Dionysus is also a cyclical god. Like the other agricultural gods which sprang up in his wake, his life parallels the cycle of nature, in his case, the grape, the vine. He lives and blooms, withers and dies, is reborn again next season."

"Then he should be dying pretty soon," Kevin said. "The season's over for this year, I think." He glanced toward Penelope for confirmation, but she would not look at him.

"Perhaps not." Holbrook walked to the other side of the basement and from between two piles of books produced a McDonald's cup in which a twig was half immersed in water. He brought the cup over, pointed at a sprout of green on the side of the otherwise brown twig. "Look at that," he said. "What do you see?"

Kevin shrugged. "A bud."

"Yes. A grape vine. Blooming. In the late fall. Do you know what that means?"

Kevin shook his head.

"The cycles have changed, to coincide with Dionysus' rebirth." He put the cup down on the desk. "I don't know how far this phenomenon extends, whether it's only here in the valley, whether it's everywhere, but the vine is supposed to be dying now, to be reborn in spring." He stopped, staring into space for a moment, then began writing in his notebook again. "I never thought of that before. Dionysus and Siva."

"What?"

"Siva, or Shiva, the Hindu god of destruction and regeneration. Siva has many parallels with Dionysus. Maybe they're the same god, different name."

"Who gives a shit?" Kevin said. "Jesus. We came to you for some help."

Penelope cleared her throat. When she spoke, her voice was quieter than it had been before. "How will he die?" she asked.

Holbrook looked at her. "He'll be torn apart."

"Oh, God."

"Maybe we can speed up the season somehow," Kevin suggested. "Once he's dead, maybe the rest of them'll—"

"What are you talking about?" Penelope demanded. "That's Dion! Your friend!"

"It's not Dion," Kevin said. "Dion's dead."

"No, he's not. He's in there. Trying to get out."

Kevin shook his head, resigned. "It doesn't really matter anyway, does it? Even if we kill him, he'll only be reborn again next season."

"*Then* he'll be dead. Dionysus might be reborn, but Dion won't. If we kill him now, we'll be killing Dion."

Holbrook closed his notebook. "You're right. You're both right. It's possible that Dionysus can't be permanently killed. But the form he has taken can be. And if he was driven into dormancy for thousands of years, he can be driven so again."

"How?" Kevin asked.

"I don't know yet. But for all these centuries Dionysus has been like a seed waiting for the right soil. And that soil was Dion. If we can destroy this incarnation, it might be centuries before another compatible host can be found again."

Kevin took a deep breath. He realized that his hands were shaking, and he slipped them into the front pockets of his jeans to steady them. "What about God? Our God? What's He doing? Why doesn't He do something about this? Have we been worshiping the wrong god all this time? Was He something we just made up?"

Mr. Holbrook shook his head. "God's real. At least, *I* think He's real. But I also think that we can't and shouldn't count on Him for help. He doesn't intervene in wars, He doesn't stop natural disasters, He doesn't halt the spread of disease. These are all problems we must deal with ourselves. And I think this is the same way. You know, we refer to Dionysus and the other Old World dieties as 'gods,' and perhaps to us they are. But I don't think they're gods in the true sense of the word. I don't think they're omnipotent. The myths, in fact, tell us that they're not. I think they're beings or creatures with powers greater than our own, but I do not think that their power can be measured against that of a true god, against . . . well, *God.*"

"So they're, like, demons. Monsters."

"Yes."

For the first time since entering the basement, they were all silent. Kevin watched Holbrook as he put his notebook back on the desk. Penelope was right, he thought. There was something creepy about Holbrook, something secretive and unsettling. And though he didn't doubt that the teacher was on their side in all of this, that he was one of them and not one of *them,* he didn't feel comfortable being down here alone with the man. He wished there was another adult around. Or at least another male. Penelope was fine, but, sexist as it was, he'd feel a hell of a lot better if there was another guy here with them.

She'd probably kick him in the nuts if she knew he thought that.

He smiled to himself, then glanced over at Penelope. She did not smile back at him, but she did not turn away this time, and the look that passed between them told him that she was not angry with him, that everything was okay.

Once again he found himself glancing around the basement. His gaze alighted on a large urn, a carved marble vessel on which nymphs and satyrs frolicked between Doric columns. He turned toward Holbrook, about to ask about the photos, the artifacts, the shrine, this whole strange Grecophile basement, but Penelope beat him to it.

"So what," she asked, gesturing around the room, "is all this?"

Holbrook looked up. "All what?"

"All this . . . Greek mythological stuff."

Mr. Holbrook smiled proudly. "I knew this day was coming. I was preparing."

Kevin snorted. "Boy, you're a regular Sherlock Holmes, aren't you?"

Penelope ignored him, faced the teacher. "You knew this was coming? What made you think so?"

"Dion's last name. Semele. That's why I asked you about *your* name and your mothers and your wine. Semele was a Theban princess, the daughter of Cadmus, who was consumed by fire when she beheld Zeus in all his glory. Dionysus is the son of Zeus and Semele."

Penelope stared at him incredulously. "And that was what made you think this might happen? Dion's last name?"

"Your last name. 'Daneam.' It's 'maenad' spelled backward."

Penelope was silent. She obviously had not noticed that.

"So?" Kevin said.

"This didn't come out of nowhere. They've been preparing for this for centuries." He paused. "As have we."

Kevin's uneasiness increased, and he moved next to Penelope. "We?"

The teacher stood straighter. "The Ovidians." He looked at them proudly. "Mankind's protectors against the gods."

Kevin looked at Penelope, but her eyes remained fixed on Holbrook.

"Our order was originally formed to prevent gods from meddling in the affairs of men. In ancient Greece, during the time of the gods, they were always raping our women, playing with us, using us to combat the boredom of immortality. We attempted to put a stop to that."

"Godbusters," Kevin said.

"If you like."

"Ovidians," Penelope said. "After Ovid?"

"Yes."

"I thought he was the one who wrote down the myths and, you know, saved them for posterity."

"He was a Latin chronicler of the gods, but he thought it was all nonsense. We'd been around a few hundred years by that time, but we didn't really have a name for ourselves. It was Ovid's disparagement of the gods, his insistence that these were fictional tales, not factual recountings of actual events, that further weakened people's already waning belief. We named ourselves after him. He wasn't one of us, but he furthered our cause."

Kevin looked at the teacher. "You guys wanted to get rid of all of the gods? There weren't any of them you liked?"

Holbrook leaned forward. "They're evil. All of them." He gestured around the basement, at the pictures on the walls. "People think that the ancients lived an idyllic life in a golden age, that they were enlightened, intelligent men who lived happily amidst their temples and oracles. But do you know what horrors the gods perpetrated on men? We were slaves. They were masters. And they enjoyed that. They thrived on it. Our order grew out of the resistance to them."

"So you're the ones who killed them off?"

Holbrook shook his head. "I wish I could say we were, but no. We tried to foster disbelief, and it was disbelief that eventually weakened them to the point that they were forced to go into hiding and protect themselves before they faded away entirely. Ovid was a big help with that. But no, it was probably the emergence of Christianity, more than anything else, that caused people to stop believing in the old gods."

"But your group kept on?" Penelope said.

"We knew they'd be back. We didn't know how, didn't know where, didn't know when, but as long as the maenads and the other believers survived, we knew the gods weren't dead."

"So was, like, your dad an Ovidian?" Kevin asked. "And his dad? All the way back?"

"No. I mean, yes, my dad was, but his dad wasn't. Being an Ovidian is not a hereditary thing. You're not born into it. Usually we recruit." Holbrook sat down on the swivel chair in front of his computer terminal. "We keep in touch through an online network." He reached around to the back of the machine, turned it on.

"But the phone lines are down . . ."

"Yes. We can't communicate now. But I'm sure they know what's happening. Right now I'm trying to access the Ovidian database. I knew this would happen, so last week I downloaded everything I thought I'd need."

Holbrook's smug, I-knew-this-was-going-to-happen attitude was really starting to irritate the shit out of him, and Kevin nudged Penelope. She did not turn to look at him, but nodded as though she understood why he had elbowed her.

"The other gods," Holbrook said to Penelope. "You did not say how the other gods will be revived. Or how long it would take."

Penelope cleared her throat. "My mothers said that the other gods . . ." She trailed off, redness rushing to her face. "They said the other gods are in Dion too. And that if I had sex with him, I could give birth to them."

"Dionysus is supposed to father the others?" Holbrook smiled. "We may have gotten a break here."

"Why?" Kevin asked.

"He was always something of an outcast on Olympus. The other gods loved order and symmetry. Dionysus loved chaos. He might not be so willing to bring the others back." He typed something on his keyboard. "Dion's mother is a maenad too, right?"

Penelope nodded.

"Same parents as your mothers?"

"Same father. Different mothers."

He raised his eyebrows. "Father. That's new. You wouldn't happen to know this name, would you?"

"My mother told me, but I . . . I can't remember."

"Think."

"She said . . ." Penelope thought for a moment. "Harris," she said finally. "Harris. Son of Elsmere. Whatever that means."

"Harris," Holbrook repeated, typing. "Elsmere." He pushed a series of keys, then leaned back to wait. There was a moment of clicking and humming before a full page of text appeared on the screen. "Harris Naxos," he read, scanning the display. "He was found murdered in his town house in New York, torn apart, along with the bodies of four women who'd been drowned in his basement. The women had been chained up and had all recently given birth, although none of the infants were found. Harris' mother, Elsmere, was a known maenad. Emigrated from Greece. We knew about her, apparently, but since she'd given birth to a son, not a daughter, we concentrated our efforts at that time on keeping track of the maenad Ariadne and her children in Athens." Holbrook looked up from the screen. "If we'd known all this then, we could have killed Harris. And the babies too."

Kevin was chilled. He glanced at Penelope. Her face was pale. "You would have killed the babies?"

"Maenads, as we have always advocated, need to be eradicated. Only then will the threat of the gods' return be ended. We haven't always been able to manage it, of course, but when we can . . ." His attention returned to the screen. "We got Ariadne. And her children when they grew up."

"What about me?" Penelope demanded angrily. "Do I need to be 'eradicated' too?" She grabbed the back of his chair, swung it around until he was facing her.

He shook his head. "Of course not. You're more us than them. And as long as you don't procreate—"

She backed away from him.

"No, no. I'm not saying that we would automatically have to kill your child—"

"Shut up," Kevin told him. "Just shut your fucking mouth." He put an arm around Penelope, drew her close to him. Her body was stiff, her muscles tense, but she allowed herself to be maneuvered.

They were silent for a while, Holbrook reading the information on his computer screen, Kevin holding Penelope.

"So what about your buddies?" Kevin asked. "Are they flying in to help us?"

"No."

"No? I thought you said—"

"They don't know anything's wrong. I didn't have time to warn them before communications were cut off. They may figure it out on their own, but it might take a while." He paused. "It might be too late then."

"Are there any Ovidians in Napa?" Kevin asked. "You guys are spread out all over the world, but is there anybody here in the valley besides you?"

"Of course. This is one of the locations we've been monitoring."

"Then what are we doing here? Get off your lazy ass and find them."

"They're dead."

"How do you know?"

"We were supposed to meet here if anything happened. It's been two days. No one's showed."

"They might've—"

"They're dead."

The flat certainty of the statement cut off Kevin in mid-sentence, hanging heavily in the air between them.

"So what's your plan?" Kevin asked finally. "What are we going to do now? How are we going to get out of this?"

"We'll have to think of something."

"You'll have to *think* of something?" Penelope said, her voice rising.

Kevin glared at him. "You mean to tell me that your little group's been around for centuries and your sole purpose is to put a stop to this—and you never came up with a plan?"

"We have ideas—"

"Ideas? Shit! You should have plan A, B, C, D, all the way to fucking Z! You've certainly had enough time to think about it. Did you think that just knowing it was going to happen was enough? You'd just wing it from there?"

Holbrook was not on the defensive. "Actually, we had planned to prevent the resurrection from occurring."

"Well, you totally failed at that. Did you think that asking Penelope for a bottle of wine was an attempt to stop it?"

"You're right. I should've killed her mothers years ago, when I first found out."

Penelope sucked in her breath.

"I should have killed Dion the first day of class."

Penelope whirled around, strode out of the basement, stomped up the stairs. Kevin hurried after her, only a second or two behind.

Downstairs, at his desk, Holbrook laughed.

The two of them stopped in the living room, unsure of where to go or what to do.

"I always knew Holbrook was an asshole," Kevin said. "But I never knew he was so . . ."

"Weird?" Penelope said.

"Crazy."

She nodded. "You don't think about what teachers are like in their real lives, what they do at home, on the weekends, with their families."

Kevin gestured back toward the basement. "Now we know."

Penelope shivered. "I think we should leave. I think we'd be better off on our own."

Kevin nodded toward the shotgun, still leaning against the wall next to the door. "He's better armed than we are."

"That won't mean shit."

"Then what do you suggest we do?"

"I don't know."

"He knows more than we do," Kevin said. "Maybe he can figure something out."

Penelope snorted. "Yeah."

"The basement's a good hiding place."

She shook her head. "You don't understand . . ."

"What don't I understand?" Kevin said.

She sighed. "It doesn't matter."

"I think we should stay here. At least for now. Until we figure out a plan. It's better than being out there on the streets."

Penelope sat down heavily on the couch. "Whatever," she said.

The earth rumbled beneath their feet, a low, sustained vibration that was more than a sonic boom but less than an earthquake. Downstairs, Holbrook cried out as something crashed.

"What was that?" Kevin asked, frightened.

"Power." Penelope's mouth was set in a thin, grim line. "The power of the gods."

EIGHT

He dreamed of Penelope.

They were in school, the two of them, in a classroom, though the teacher and the other students were vague, misty figures and he could not see them. He saw only Penelope. She was talking to him about a movie she'd seen on television the night before, and he was listening happily, glad merely to be there with her, to be able to enjoy these simple everyday pleasures with her.

Dionysus awoke, tears streaming down his face.

What was wrong with him?

Hangover.

That had to be it, although he had never gotten hangovers in the old days. That physiological inconvenience had been reserved for humans. He had been immune.

Not anymore, apparently.

He wiped his eyes. One of his maenads—

one of Penelope's mothers

—was sleeping between his legs, her hands wrapped around his organ. He thought of pissing on her, but he knew that she'd like that, so he pulled up his leg and kicked her hard in the midsection. She went flying across the grass, landing on an old couple entwined with a goat. He was gratified to hear screams, to hear the crack of old bones.

He stood, strode over the strewn bodies on the grass, and jumped into the river. The cold water felt good, refreshing, and he washed off the grape stains, washed off the blood. He bent down, dunked his head, let the water clean the tears from his eyes, then stretched to his full height, shaking out his hair.

He looked down at his body. He was smaller than he

should be, closer to a human than a god. Before, he had been bigger. But this new skin was tight, confining. Even his brain felt small. He ran a hand through his hair, looked up into the overcast sky. His thoughts too were confined. He seemed unable to think clearly.

And he was not himself.

That was the most difficult adjustment to make. He knew things that he should not have known, felt things he should not have felt, thought things he should not have thought. He knew this new language, knew this new culture. He had memories of this existence. He had been reborn, but the rebirth had not happened the way he'd thought it would. He closed his eyes. The others would not have this problem. They would be reborn pure, as themselves. He was the only one who would have to suffer this dual existence.

And it was not fair.

It had always been thus. He was forever the outcast, Zeus' whipping boy, forced to endure humiliation after humiliation merely because of the fact that he was half human.

And the fact that he preferred wine to ambrosia.

Those self-important elitists never could understand sensual pleasures, the wonders of the flesh. Or perhaps they could, on a purely intellectual level. But they could never *feel* it.

He could.

And they were jealous of that.

And they took it out on him.

He walked out of the river, back onto the bank. He was supposed to mate with Penelope, who would bring forth from her golden womb the remaining gods. He desperately wanted to mate with her—a combination, he knew, of his own sexual desires and Zeus' subliminal prodding—but he was not at all sure that he wanted to share this world with the others. This was his world now, his alone, and he liked it that way. There was no reason he should share. He was as powerful as the other gods and more versatile in a lot of respects. He could assume their duties. He could take over Poseidon's role as ruler of the seas. That was a part-time job to begin with. And Ares? Who couldn't wage war? A moron could handle that.

What about an underworld? That was a much bigger responsibility. Could he maintain that?

There was only one way to find out.

He looked around, finally focusing his attention on the land across the river. Drawing upon the power within him, he loosed a withering blast of heat and fire at the location. The land scorched, burned, and was changed. In place of the trees and bushes, lawns and houses, there was charred earth and burnt air. The perfect environment for the dead.

But how to effect the dead's transition?

He glanced about him. To his left, on a slab of concrete, was the mutilated body of a young man, someone's used plaything. Grinning, Dionysus walked over and picked up the man's corpse, raising it to the level of his face. He held the body and concentrated.

The man's glazed eyes blinked, his mouth worked silently. His stiffened limbs moved slowly, with effort, the jelled blood in his joints flowing slowly across the cold skin.

Yes.

He could maintain an underworld too.

He threw the corpse across the river. It bounced against a burnt tree, cracking a branch, then stood awkwardly. The dead man remained unmoving for a moment, then shambled dumbly into the smoke away from the water.

Fuck the others. Fuck Zeus. Fuck Hera. Fuck Athena. Fuck Apollo. Fuck all of them! This was his world now. He did not need them.

He would not bring them back.

NINE

The clocks had stopped. All of them. Penelope thought at first that it was merely electric clocks that were not working, but battery-powered watches, wind-up alarm clocks, every timepiece in the house was now functionally dead.

Power had gone out sometime last night, although the water was still on. Thank God. She didn't relish the idea of not bathing, of not having a toilet that flushed.

But power? Water? Those were minor inconveniences.

The clocks worried her.

She might have imagined it, but last night had seemed unusually long, much longer than it should have, and she could not help wondering if Dion—

Dionysus

—had somehow affected time, had somehow altered the normal laws of physics. She thought of the bolt of power she'd seen shooting into the sky from the meadow that first night, and she had no trouble believing that he could do it.

Maybe he was planning to shorten the days, lengthen the nights. Maybe everything here in the valley would happen in the rest of the world's split second.

There was a sharp knock at the front door.

She glanced quickly toward Kevin, who was lying on the floor, reading a mythology textbook. He scrambled to his feet, looking as panicked as she felt.

Holbrook came rushing out of the kitchen, motioning for them to lay low. He grabbed his shotgun. "Stay down!" he ordered.

There was another series of knocks.

Penelope hit the floor, crawling next to Kevin as she

watched Holbrook first peek through the closed living room curtains, then hurry over and open the front door.

"Jack!" the teacher said. He ushered in another man, a short-haired, stern-faced, well-built, middle-aged man wearing the tattered remnants of a dark blue suit. The two of them gave each other what looked like some sort of secret handshake, a ritualized greeting that involved twisting thumbs and touching elbows.

Another Ovidian.

Penelope rose to her knees, then stood, as did Kevin.

Holbrook led the man into the living room. "Jack, these are two of my students: Penelope Daneam and Kevin Something-or-other."

"Harte," Kevin said.

"Daneam?" Jack's eyebrows went up.

"Their daughter."

"And you are?" Kevin said.

"Jack Hammond. Napa P.D."

A cop! Penelope smiled, filled with relief and a buoyed sense of hope. "Thank God you're here."

"Are you a maenad?" Jack asked her.

The relief died as quickly as it had flared. There was a flat coldness in the cop's eyes, a studied detachment in the way he looked at her that made her extremely uneasy.

"She's one of us," Holbrook said. "I think we can use her to get him."

Use her.

She moved closer to Kevin. She didn't like the way this conversation was going.

"So where are the rest of you?" Kevin asked. "Is this it?"

Jack nodded, and the coldness in his face fled, replaced by a weariness that looked closer to exhaustion. She suddenly noticed that there were bruises on his skin, dull splashes of dried blood on his torn suit.

"I couldn't get here right away," he said. "So I holed up in the H.Q."

"Were any of the others there?" Holbrook asked.

"They were all there. They'd been slaughtered. Mike was naked and drenched with wine—it looked like he'd been trying to pass—but he'd been killed just like the rest of them." He took a deep breath. "Their heads had been switched."

"Bastards," Holbrook breathed.

"They were still outside, and I only had one round in my revolver, so I stayed there, hid. This was the first day I thought it was safe to come out."

Penelope was extremely uncomfortable. She wasn't sure if Jack—or Holbrook *and* Jack—blamed her in any way for what had happened, but she felt guilty nevertheless, as though she was a spy in the enemy camp.

She wasn't a spy, though. She was on their side.

She was a traitor.

"Did you save your toga?" Holbrook asked.

Jack shook his head. "Nothing."

"That's okay. I have an extra one for you. Come on."

The two of them walked down the hallway to the basement door, started down.

Penelope looked at Kevin, standing next to her. He shook his head. "Somehow, I don't think that, in this instance, two heads are better than one."

"Maybe we should get out of here," she suggested.

"And go where? Did you see the way that guy was beat up? And he's a cop!" He shook his head. "It's dangerous out there."

"Holbrook said they could 'use' me."

"I didn't like that either," Kevin admitted.

"What do you think they plan to do?"

"From everything I can tell, they don't have any plans at all."

"What are we going to do?"

Kevin shook his head. "I don't know," he said. "I don't know."

Jack didn't turn out to be all that bad.

He was a cop, of course, a conservative, hard-nosed kind of guy, but that cold steeliness she'd sensed in their first meeting seemed to have been the result of stress and hunger and lack of sleep. Rested, fed, and relaxed, he seemed nicer than Holbrook and infinitely more human, and she and Kevin found that they were able to get along with him quite easily.

She glanced over at Jack, curled up on the couch, sleeping. Kevin was sitting on the floor, leaning against the opposite wall, reading one of Holbrook's texts. The teacher, as always, was down in his basement.

They were all starting to get a little stir crazy, starting to act a little funny, and Penelope wondered, not for the first time, if it might not have been better if they'd stayed outside, roamed around in the car, and not holed themselves up in here. She thought of all of those shut-ins who received their impressions of the world solely through television. They watched the newscasts, watched the news magazines, watched the based-on-a-true-story made-for-television movies, they saw shootings and rapes and robberies, an they were convinced that the world outside their doors was filled with danger, that violent death lurked around every corner. Paranoia fed upon itself, and she wondered if they weren't doing the same thing here, blockading themselves in Holbrook's house as they talked and worried about and demonized the frightening outside world.

But it was hard to demonize a world that had real demons in it.

Or gods.

What was Dionysus exactly? God? Monster? It was more comforting to think of him as some sort of monster or demon. She could imagine going up against that.

It was harder to think about fighting a god.

Kevin put down his book, stood, stretched. He glanced over at Jack sleeping on the couch, then silently motioned for Penelope to follow him into the kitchen.

She looked again at the stopped clock above the dead television, then walked out of the living room. Kevin was already peeking through the curtains that covered the window above the sink. "Anyone out there?" she asked.

He shook his head.

There had been earlier. A gang of wasted teenagers, dressed only in the bloody skins of domestic animals, had chased a herd of naked old men down the street using pistols and bullwhips. One old man had tripped and fallen, and they'd whipped him and trampled him, the last two kids in the pack picking the old man up by his legs and dragging him behind them as they disappeared from sight.

His head had left a bloody streak on the pavement.

Kevin turned away from the window. "I'm tired of being cooped up in here."

Penelope shrugged. "Who isn't?"

"I feel like I'm wasting my time, like I should be doing something." He waved toward the world outside the window. "You know things aren't slowing down out there."

"No," Penelope admitted.

"We need to do something before it's too late."

"It's probably already too late." She walked over to the cupboard, got out a can of warm 7-Up, sat down at the kitchen table.

Kevin sat next to her. He was silent for a moment. "So what were they like?" he asked finally.

"Who? My mothers?"

"Yeah." He paused. "Before."

She shrugged. "All right, I guess. I don't . . ." She shook her head apologetically. "I don't really know what you mean."

"I mean, were they, like, good parents? Did they read your report cards? Did they go to Open House? Did they make sure you brushed your teeth and ate properly?"

"Yes," she said. "They were good parents." And felt an involuntary twinge of sadness at the thought.

"Were they, like, radical lesbians?"

Penelope felt heat rush to her face.

"Was it 'herstory' instead of 'history' and all that?"

"No. Besides, those words come from different roots. 'History' is not '*his* story.' It comes from the Greek 'historia,' which means 'inquiry.' 'His' isn't even Greek. It comes from 'he,' which is Old English."

He looked at her, surprised. "Where'd you learn that?"

She licked her lips nervously. "I don't know," she admitted.

They were silent for a moment. "You're a little spooky yourself sometimes," Kevin said.

Penelope nodded. "I know."

They looked at each other across the table, and for the first time Penelope felt as though she *was* in one of those movie situations. He looked as though he was about to take her hand, or reach over and hug her. And she realized that she would let him.

Jack walked through the door.

"Hey," he said.

"About time," Kevin told him.

The mood was broken. If it had been there at all. Penelope picked up her 7-Up, took a sip.

They needed to get out of this house. If they spent another day in here, all four of them would end up fucking each other in one huge daisy chain.

She closed her eyes, tried to push the thought out of her head.

"So who do you want to play you in the movie?" Jack asked, leaning against the sink.

Penelope nearly choked. "What?"

The policeman grinned. "After this is all over and done with, you know they're going to make a movie out of it. This is a great story. If we play our cards right, we can cash in on it."

Penelope laughed. "Go on *Donahue* and *Oprah* and *Geraldo*?"

"Hell, no. Let Fox make a quickie TV movie out of our adventures. It's a lot more interesting than Waco or O.J."

"TV movies never get top stars," Kevin said. "They'll just get some sitcom actors play you two, have the young stud of the moment play me."

Penelope snorted. "Right."

"They always get actors who are better-looking than the people in real life." He grinned. "Maybe they'll even find a semi-attractive girl to play you."

"Ha-ha." Penelope looked around the kitchen. "Where's the king?"

Kevin shook his head. "His playroom. Where else? He's probably building a little model of the Parthenon out of matchsticks."

"No, I'm not. But I'm impressed that you knew the word Parthenon. There's hope for you yet." Holbrook walked into the kitchen, dumping the cold contents of his coffee cup into the sink behind Jack. "As a matter of fact, I've been looking through my papers, trying to discover weaknesses of Dionysus, of the maenads. Things we could exploit."

"Find anything?"

"Nothing beyond the obvious. But if I had access to my database—"

"That's exactly what I was thinking," Jack said. "If I'd just made hard copies of all of my files, I would've been able to discover some way of taking this god down."

Kevin glared at them. "Didn't you guys ever think that if the gods returned, they might disrupt the power? They might screw up the phone lines? Hell, all you had to do was plan ahead a little. If you'd bought a generator and a CB radio, you could still be communicating."

He stopped, blinked.

"Shit." He turned toward Penelope. "I'm as stupid as they are. All we have to do is hit Kmart, Walmart, Target, whatever, and find a generator or a battery or some type of power source—"

"We're all stupid," Penelope said. "All we need to do is find a car with a cellular phone."

"Fuck!" Kevin slammed his palm against the table.

"I would not advise leaving the house," Holbrook said.

"Why?" Kevin said dryly. "You planning to banish Dionysus from the earth by reading in your basement?"

The teacher faced him. "You don't even know what you're dealing with here, you arrogant little shit."

"I do," Penelope said.

"Your family's the one who caused it all."

Penelope stood, not bothering to respond, not even looking at him. "Let's get out of here," she said. "Let's find us a car phone."

"I'll go with you," Jack said. "Just in case."

"You're only encouraging them."

"They might be on to something," the policeman said. He hurried out of the room. "I'll be back in a sec!" he called back. "I'm just going to get my gun!"

It felt good to be out again, driving.

There was evidence of new destruction—felled trees and still burning piles of furniture that had not been there when they'd driven the road yesterday—but it still felt reassuring to be outdoors rather than cooped up in Holbrook's claustrophobic home. There was something about being outside, being able to travel and see the sky, that lifted Penelope's spirits. It was completely illogical, based solely on emotional preference, but more than Holbrook's arsenal of facts and tales of secret societies, it gave her hope that they could find a way out of this, that they could triumph over Dionysus and his minions.

And then they turned onto Monticello and she saw the mall.

Whatever hope had been burgeoning within her died instantly. The mall was overrun. Huge holes had been blown in the brown brick walls of the Nordstrom's department store. The Sears building was little more than a three-walled ruin. Revelers streamed in and out of the open doorways in the center of the mall, dancing and cavorting. Many of them were naked and covered with blood. Many of them were carrying severed body parts. In the parking lot, cars were crashed or overturned, their twisted metal forms gaily decorated with flowers and multicolored streamers.

She was intimidated by the enormity of it all. There were only four of them. There were hundreds of people in the mall alone. How many were there in the entire valley? How could they hope to combat something of this magnitude?

Blood.

And how could they hope to combat something from which they were not immune? She was frightened of this force that had turned all of these ordinary citizens into amoral hedonists, and she hated what was happening, but . . . but it called to her. She saw these wild, drunken people, and a part of her wanted to join them, wanted to be one of them.

Did it tempt the others as well? She glanced surreptitiously at Kevin and Jack, but could not tell what they were thinking, what they were feeling.

They sped past the mall. On the other side of the street, the supermarket had been looted, all of the front windows smashed, food thrown into the parking lot, and even within the car, the heavy smell of bad wine, spoiled milk, and rotting vegetables was strong, nearly overpowering. Ahead, on the right, a fire was burning unchecked at the site of a Shell station, foul black smoke billowing up into the air and blending with the cloud cover.

This might be the end of the world, Penelope thought. Or the end of the world as they knew it. And it had not been brought about by nuclear war or a biological agent or a threat from outer space but by the resurgence of an ancient religion.

And it had been instigated by her mothers.

"We'll cruise over to a rich area," Kevin said. "Doctors, lawyers, those guys always have car phones."

Sure enough, they found an upscale neighborhood and, hidden in the locked garage of a mock Tudor mansion, a Lexus with a car phone. Most of the other cars on the street had been overturned and burned, but this one had escaped the revelers. Jack used the butt of his revolver to smash one of the back windows of the house, and while Kevin and Penelope waited outside, he foraged through the residence until he found car keys.

They hurried back into the garage to try the phone.

The line was jammed.

They moved the car out of the garage onto the driveway, tried again.

Still jammed.

On the next block over, they found another car with a phone. A Mercedes.

Jammed as well.

"Shit!" Kevin slammed the car door. "What the fuck are we supposed to do now?"

"It was a long shot to begin with," Penelope told him.

"So let's find a CB," Jack said.

Kevin nodded, although clearly whatever hopes he'd harbored of finding a way to communicate with the outside world were dashed. "All right," he said. "Let's go."

They traded their car in for the Mercedes, which had a double gas tank, both of which were full. A gang of small children threw rocks and bottles at the car as they drove up and down streets looking for a semi or a pickup that might have a CB radio. At one point a group of naked, obviously menstruating women, wielding homemade spears constructed of broom handles and trowels, chased them for nearly two blocks before the car finally outran them.

After a several false starts they finally found a roofing-company truck with keys still in the ignition that had a CB.

They turned on the power, turned on the radio.

Every channel was filled with the sound of drunken babbling.

"Hello!" Penelope tried. "Is anybody out there?"

"Is anybody out there?" came the mocking reply.

They sat there for a half hour, taking turns, trying each channel, hoping against hope that someone some-where—a trucker out of the valley and on the road perhaps—would hear them and answer, but the only responses they received were the jeering and increasingly obscene replies of the bacchantes.

Finally Kevin hung up the microphone and turned off the CB, discouraged. "It's getting late," he said tiredly. "Let's hit the road. We don't want to be caught out here after dark."

"You're right about that," Jack said.

Penelope nodded, starting toward the Mercedes.

How long would tonight last? she wondered. Ten hours? Twenty?

They drove back to Holbrook's in silence.

TEN

April smashed the empty wine bottle against the forehead of the man she was riding, and reached her orgasm as she knocked him into unconsciousness. His fluttering eyes closed, blood gushed from the broken skin, but his organ stayed hard, and she pressed herself all the way down on it until the last shudder of ecstasy passed through her body.

She rolled off him, onto the blood-soaked grass.

The others were going to strike tonight.

She knew of their plans, though they had not told her of them, and while she wanted to be involved, wanted to share in the fun, she did not entirely approve. It was her upbringing, she supposed. She was a maenad, she was one of them, but she had been raised apart, in a considerably stricter environment, and while her true nature had eventually won out, there was still a part of her that sat back and judged, that hated what she had become.

Maybe there was more of her mother in her than her father.

Whoever her mother had been.

Or maybe there really was something to be said for environment in that old environment versus genetics debate.

Of course, everything would have been fine if it had involved only her, if she had been on her own. She would have been having the time of her life, and she'd be jumping into all this with both feet, not looking back, not having any regrets.

But there was Dion.

He'd wanted better.

He deserved better.

She tried to tell herself that there *was* nothing better,

that being a god was the pinnacle, the apex, but she did not believe it. Maybe for her that might be true, but not for Dion.

She wondered if it had something to do with having given birth. She wondered if Felice felt the same way about Penelope. She'd have to ask.

If she ever saw her again.

She had not seen much of the other maenads the past two days. And she wasn't sure if she wanted to. She'd felt closer to them before the Resurrection, when they'd been just friends who drank together in bars. She missed that camaraderie, that feeling that she had finally found soul mates, people who understood her, who had the same needs and desires she did.

But now she felt like an outcast. Ostensibly, she was one of them. Born of the same line and all that. But she felt different from them, apart, and she knew that it was because of what they'd done with Dion.

She wished she'd never been Called. She wished they'd never left Arizona.

She had caught Dionysus sleeping yesterday, lying on the grassy ground between the trees, a huddled group of women acting as his pillow, and she had stood there for a while, watching him. In sleep he looked more like Dion. The changes were still there—the size of him, most obviously—but sleep softened his expression, blunted his intensity. His face was by no means innocent, but his features were relaxed, and she could see in the dozing god her son.

She'd left before he'd awakened.

They'd been avoiding each other ever since the Resurrection. She didn't think Dionysus observed any taboos regarding incest, but the part of him that was Dion most certainly did and was no doubt responsible for maintaining the distance between them. She, for her part, had been purposely staying away from him, although the reasons were complex. As a mother, she was disgusted and repulsed by the thought of having sex with him. But as a maenad, she . . .

She wanted him.

She closed her eyes, feeling in the back of her skull the dull throb of an oncoming headache.

"Are you going with us?"

She opened her eyes, turned her head, saw Margaret and Sheila walking up to her on the left. Both were bruised and bloody. Both were grinning.

"You want to be in on the raid?" Margaret asked.

April shook her head.

"You haven't even fucked him yet, have you?" Sheila said.

"I'm not going to."

"You're one of us!" Margaret said. "Act like it!"

"I'm his mother!"

Sheila giggled. "Not anymore."

"Fuck off," April said. "Both of you."

"You're not what we'd hoped," Margaret said.

"Nothing ever is."

The two sisters turned away without speaking, walking back through the meadow the way they'd come. April saw a slice of red on Sheila's right buttock where the skin had been peeled off.

A part of her wanted to join them tonight.

A part of her wanted to kill them.

The man next to her moaned groggily, stirred.

She lay there for a moment, then picked up the bottle, smashed it again against the man's head. He sank back into unconsciousness.

She climbed back on top of him.

ELEVEN

Night.

The four of them lay in silent darkness within the back bedroom of the house. The night outside was filled with cacaphonous noise: the full-volume blast of private stereos defiantly playing their owners' favorite music, the wailing of high school band instruments, the electrified amplification of amateur and semi-professional guitarists, the racing of engines, the shouting of celebrants, the screams of victims.

Penelope imagined pockets of people like themselves, throughout the valley, waiting for the raiding parties that would rape them and kill them and tear their bodies apart. At least the four of them knew what was happening; at least they knew what they were up against. She could not imagine what other people might think.

Jack cleared his throat. "The only good thing about all this," he said, "is that these bacchanals are very public. It's not as if they're sneaking around and we have to worry about where they are and whether they're going to creep up on us."

There was a rustling of the sheets on Kevin's mattress on the floor. "But it can't last much longer, can it? I mean, people from outside will find out. They'll send in troops or something and it'll all be over."

Holbrook snorted. "All be over? What are they going to do? Bomb Napa? Shoot Dionysus down like Godzilla? We're the minority here. Most of the people are with him. Do you know how long people like that can hold out? Look at Bosnia. The siege of Leningrad. Hell, history is riddled with stories of small groups of true believers who were able to outlast the attacks of the majority."

"What if my mothers find out we're here?" Penelope asked. "What if they discover where we're hiding? Where *I'm* hiding?"

There was a note of grim satisfaction in Holbrook's voice. "I'll blow those bitches away."

"Why wait for them to come here?" Kevin asked. "Why don't you go out and hunt them down?"

"I've been thinking that's exactly what we should do," Holbrook said.

They were silent after that, and Penelope heard first Kevin's, then Jack's, and finally Holbrook's breathing shift into the regular rhythms of sleep.

It was a long time before she herself drifted off.

She woke up thirsty. It was still dark out, still night, and the others were dead asleep around her. Her mouth was dry, her tongue stuck to the roof of her mouth, and she desperately needed a drink of water.

Carefully, quietly, she drew the covers off her and slipped out of bed, tiptoeing around Holbrook's sleeping bag and Kevin's mattress on the floor, using the wall to feel her way out of the room and into the hall. Still touching the wall, she reached the doorway of the bathroom. She was about to walk in, shut the door, and turn on the light in order to get a drink out of the sink when she heard noises from the front of the house.

Pounding.

And laughing.

People were at the door, trying to get in.

She stopped moving, held her breath. There was no sound from the bedroom, the others were still asleep. She knew she should go back, wake them up, but she thought of Holbrook shooting first, asking questions later, and she decided to take a peek herself first, just in case. Maybe these were people like them, victims.

Then why were they laughing?

Her eyes had begun to adjust to the darkness, and she walked slowly out toward the living room. She knew she was being stupid. This was what she complained about idiot characters doing in horror movies—going off to search for the monster by themselves—and though logically she knew that it was a foolish thing to do, it seemed normal, felt natural.

The laughter was calling to her, she realized, beckoning her. She should be worried about that, but she wasn't. She was scared, she was frightened, but she wasn't worried.

She walked into the living room. The laughing was louder here. She could hear the door being pounded upon by several sets of hands, and the noise chilled her. The living room was dark, and she could see only the vague outlines of furniture. Unthinkingly, almost against her conscious will, she walked across the carpeted floor to the door.

Why weren't the others waking up?

She thought of screaming to get their attention, but she didn't. She thought of picking up the shotgun next to the door, but she didn't.

She reached for the first dead bolt.

The laughter was constant, at once feminine and masculine, innocent and knowing, and it remained the same as it traveled from one voice to another. It was like a melody almost, the pounding on the door like a rhythm.

She opened the door.

She did not even have time to react.

Mother Sheila punched her hard in the stomach as Mother Janine grabbed her by the hair and shoved a hand over her mouth. She was yanked through the doorway and pulled down the front walk to where Mother Margaret waited in front of a brightly painted van.

As she was shoved headfirst into the rear of the vehicle, she heard the door to the house slam loudly shut behind her.

TWELVE

Penelope was gone.

Kevin paced the living room as Jack sat silently on the couch. Holbrook remained cross-legged on the floor, cleaning his shotgun.

Where could they have taken her?

She had been kidnapped. No doubt about that. Holbrook had started to suggest that she had gone with them on her own, that the acorn doesn't fall far from the tree, but Kevin had threatened to punch him out if he said anything more, and Holbrook had shut up.

It felt weird threatening a teacher, but any ties Holbrook had to respect and educational authority had long since been worn through, and Kevin felt neither guilty nor regretful.

Jack had stayed out of the confrontation entirely.

They were assuming that Penelope's mothers had taken her, or, if they had not done so themselves, that they were behind the people who had. It had been a surgical strike; Penelope had been kidnapped and the rest of them had remained untouched. If it had been a random attack, they all would have been taken. Or killed.

Which meant that Penelope was still alive.

He hoped.

He had no idea where they had taken her, though. That was the most frustrating thing. They could be anywhere—

"The winery," Jack said.

Kevin stopped pacing, turned toward the policeman. "What?"

"They probably took her home."

Of course. He should have thought of that himself. He stared at Jack. Had he been thinking aloud?

Or had the policeman just ... known what he was thinking?

He was being stupid. There was enough to worry about without reading meaning into coincidence. They had just been thinking the same thing at the same time, that's all. Under the circumstances and given the subject, it wasn't unlikely.

"We'll go there," he said. "We'll rescue her."

"How?" Holbrook asked.

Kevin looked down at the teacher. "What?"

"How are you going to rescue her? Walk into that crowd, pass by her mothers, grab her by the arm, and walk out with her?"

"I'll figure out something," Kevin said defensively.

"You'd better figure it out ahead of time or they'll rip you to shreds."

"Well, why don't you help then?"

Holbrook grinned. "I thought you'd never ask."

Kevin faced him. "You have a plan for once?"

Holbrook laughed. "That I do," he said. "That I do."

THIRTEEN

Penelope awoke on the grass. Her mothers were nowhere to be seen, and she sat up, stood. Her mouth tasted like wine, but, thank God, she was still fully dressed. And there was no blood on her. Whatever had happened, it couldn't have been much.

She smelled sex, though. On the air, in the breeze, on the grass.

And it smelled good.

She turned her head, looking around. She was not in the meadow, in the woods behind the winery, as she would have expected. Her mothers had taken her to the field where the fair had been, leaving her at the perimeter farthest from the road.

She yawned, feeling groggy, dumb, slow. She was not sure what had happened. She could not remember being hypnotized or drugged or knocked out, but her memory of last night seemed to have stopped at the point where her mothers shoved her into the van. She could not recall anything after that.

A leather-clad woman rode past on the back of a nude man fitted with a harness and stirrups. The woman carried in her right hand an assortment of paint brushes, and Penelope watched as she galloped over to a man whose skin had been dyed blue. She handed him the brushes, and he passed them out to a group of children who were helping to paint a monstrous stone phallus that had been embedded in the ground.

Penelope looked around the enormous field, her gaze moving from one grotesque tableau to another. He had organized them. The drunken chaos of the previous days was gone, replaced by an institutionalized insanity, a har-

nessed altered consciousness. The people she saw were
obviously intoxicated, obviously behaving crazily, but
there was an overriding rationality behind their individually irrational acts.

And there were thousands of them.

As before, the sheer scope of the situation intimidated
her. Not only had the bacchantes ransacked the fair, they
had adapted its forms to their uses. A group of drunken
clowns staggered by, supporting a nude and tattooed teenager between them. A woman dressed in gypsy garb was
passing out baby balloons—dead bodies of infants that
had been filled with helium and somehow sealed and cir-
cled with string. A couple walked by, each clutching a
string, twin distended babies floating above their heads
like bloated puffer fish. A plyboard wall that she remembered seeing at the fair painted with the bodies of Merlin
and various magicians, with holes cut above the figures'
shoulders so that tourists could stick their heads through
and have their photos taken, had been inverted and re-
painted with the forms of classical monsters. Though the
holes in the wall protruded erect penises. Girls and
women were taking turns kneeling in front of the figures
or backing up against them.

At the east end of the field, a crew of inebriated laborers were beginning to erect a mock Greek edifice from
bricks and blocks that apparently had been taken from demolished buildings downtown.

It was as if they had started to build a society around
their drunkenness, as though this was now their normal
state of being and they were adjusting to it.

But where was Dion ... Dionysus? She scanned the
crowd more carefully. To her right she saw Mrs.
Pulkinghorn, the librarian, squatting over the face of Mrs.
Jessup, the school nurse, who was lying prone on the
ground and being assaulted by a bald old man. The guy
who worked at the liquor store by the school was sitting
on a folding chair, furiously playing with himself.

There were men with women, men with men, women
with women, but no Dionysus.

And everywhere were grapes. The vines had obviously
been planted only within the last few days, but they dot-

ted the field, separated it into sectors. The amazing thing was that bunches of the fruit were already hanging from between the oversize leaves. She followed a line of grape vines that crossed the field diagonally.

Then she saw her mothers.

They were near the river at the west end of the field. Mother Margeaux, Mother Felice, and Mother Margaret were crouched down in a circle by the edge of the bank, doing something she couldn't make out from this far away. Mother Sheila was bent over the battered, unmoving body of a boy, licking the blood from his chest, while Mother Janine crouched behind her, her face buried deep between the cheeks of Mother Sheila's buttocks.

Penelope looked away, disgusted and frightened. These weren't the mothers she knew. These people were totally alien to her.

Weren't they?

She started walking through the field, taking the path of least resistance, skirting the most crowded areas. She didn't know why she'd been left alone after being kidnapped in such dramatic fashion, but she knew enough to take advantage of it, and she hurried toward the road. They'd taken her, no doubt, in order to force her to mate with Dionysus, but they'd either thought she'd stay asleep longer or else they'd been so drunk that they'd forgotten about her, and if she was lucky she'd be able to escape before they even noticed that she'd gone.

She was halfway across the field when she saw it.

The satyr.

She stopped dead in her tracks. "Jesus," she breathed.

The man—the creature—was seven or eight feet tall, with the legs of a goat, the ears of Mr. Spock, and a huge red erection. He galloped toward her across the field, grinning, and there was something so alien in his gait, something so unearthly in his appearance, that Penelope felt an involuntary shiver of fear pass through her. She was hit suddenly by a bolt of objectivity, a perspective that allowed her to see this not as it appeared to her, not as a participant, but as an outsider, all of the myriad adjustments her mind had made to the horrors stripped away, and the sight terrified her so that she was unable to run, unable to move, and she remained rooted to the spot as the monster reared to a stop in front of her.

"He wants you!" the satyr said, leering. Its voice was high and manic, and though she was aware that the sounds it was making were not English, were possibly not even human speech, she had no trouble understanding it.

She tried to determine if there were some way that she could run, get away from it—

"Either you follow me on your own, or I force you to come with me." The creature grinned, and this close she could see that its teeth were pointed. "If I have to force you, you'll get to ride on my cock." Its red erection bounced up and down.

"I'll come," she said.

"I know you will!" The satyr laughed, galloping off, and Penelope ran to keep up with it.

They passed between groups of men and women performing a variety of violent and sexually deviant acts, past huge cases of wine bottles and caskets of wine. She was out of breath long before they reached the far end of the field, but she refused to allow that horrible ... thing to touch her, and she forced herself to keep going.

She followed the satyr out of the field and into the trees.

To where Dionysus sat on his throne.

She stopped running, though her heart rate accelerated. Several trees had been felled, carved, and made into the elaborately carved woodland chair that the god used as his throne. Over a portion of the trampled ground before Dionysus was a royal red carpet made from human flesh. The surrounding trees were decorated with mounted sexual organs.

The satyr bowed to its god, then galloped away, laughing maniacally.

Dionysus stood, and Penelope felt a stirring within her. Even though she was not drunk, she wanted him. Against her will she wanted him. He stood before her, proudly, gloriously nude. His skin was wet with blood and sweat, and it glistened in a way that made him look magnificent. She wanted to drop to her knees and worship him, to prostrate herself before him and allow him to do what he wanted to her, but somehow she remained standing.

"Penelope," he whispered. It was Dion's voice and yet not Dion's voice, a whisper that was loud enough to drown out the noise behind her.

"Dion?" she asked.

He walked toward her, and she noticed for the first time that he carried some sort of wineskin in his left hand, a bladder-shaped receptacle that she hoped was made from an animal. He lifted it high, squirted wine into his mouth, then tossed the object aside.

She was trembling before he reached her. "Dion?" she said again, tentatively, hopefully.

"Dionysus." The god dropped to his knees in front of her so they'd be on the same level. His massive arms snaked around her back, and he pulled her to him. "I've been searching for you for so long. Why have you been hiding from me?"

His touch was powerful yet tender, and although her mind was horrified by what was happening, her body was aroused. He sniffed the air, glanced down at her crotch, and smiled. "Penelope," he said.

There was still something of Dion in his features, in his eyes, but it was less than it had been, and she knew that when he was drunk even that would disappear. He was hard against her, and she could feel the frightening enormity of his penis against her flesh. "You know you want it," he said. "Just let go. Lose yourself in me."

She remembered when she and Dion had made love in the backseat of the car, and she felt an acute pang of loss. She could smell the god's scent, a strong, musky odor that arose from the gigantic organ pressed against her torso, and she gagged.

"I don't want you," she said. The statement was not forceful, the way she'd intended, but meek, begging, a plea. A tear rolled down her cheek. He wiped the tear away with a long grape-stained finger, and she saw a flicker of compassion in his eyes. It was there for only a second, a brief flame that flared and was quickly extinguished, but it was enough to tell her that Dion was still alive in there somewhere, struggling to break free.

"You want me!" he bellowed, and the deafening rage of the demand made her jump. The arms wrapped around her did not give, and she realized that he could crush her with ease.

She was crying now, sobbing, the tears streaming down her face, but she nodded. "Yes," she said. "I want you."

"You want me to fill you up!"

"Yes. I want you to fill me up."

He was breathing heavily, and for a moment he said nothing. She expected him to rip her clothes off, to impale her on his oversize erection, but she was not prepared for what came next.

He let go of her, stood. "No, you don't," he said quietly. His voice sounded almost human. "You don't want me at all."

He turned away, started back toward his throne. "Go," he said. "Leave. I do not want to see you again."

Her mind was filled with conflicting emotions, but she knew enough to act now and sort her feelings out later, and she started running, heading not back toward the field but to her left, through the trees, where she knew the road was.

Behind her, Dionysus cried out, an anguished sound of wrenching emotional pain, and in front of her there was a flash of bluish-white light, blindingly visible even in the daytime. She didn't know if the blast was aimed at her, but she zigzagged anyway and kept running.

She tripped as she reached the street, her foot catching on an exposed section of rebar protruding from the gravel by the side of the road, but she was quick enough to catch her fall, putting her arms out in front of her and landing on the palms of her hands. Around her, the air shimmered, bristled. A row of ants on the asphalt in front of her suddenly shot up to the size of small dogs. In a matter of seconds, by the time she had jumped to her feet, the ants had twisted, contorted, grown screaming into men.

She ran. She did not look back to see if she was being pursued, she did not stop to analyze which way she should be going, she simply ran. Sweat was dripping down her face, mingling with her tears, stinging her eyes;

her lungs felt as though she'd been breathing fire, and her mouth was so dry she felt like throwing up.

But she kept going.

She did not stop until she reached an Avis Rent-a-Car office six blocks away. She was about ready to drop—she could not move another step—and she fell to the ground, gasping for air. Only then did she turn to see if they were coming after her.

The way behind her was clear. She was not being chased.

Dion had let her go.

FOURTEEN

It was nearly noon by the time Penelope arrived back at Holbrook's, and the teacher and Kevin were in the driveway, loading the trunk of Holbrook's car with boxes from the garage.

Both stared at her in shock as she drove up the driveway and parked behind Holbrook's Subaru. She got out of the car, grinning wryly. "Hey, guys, how's it going?"

"Where were you?" Kevin said, putting his box on the ground and running over. "What happened? We were just coming over to rescue you."

"Coming over where?"

"Your winery. Didn't your mothers kidnap you?"

"Yeah, but they took me someplace else. Dionysus has moved his base of operations."

Holbrook strode over. "You escaped?"

"Sort of. He let me go."

"Who? Dionysus?"

"Dion."

"What happened?" Kevin asked again.

She shook her head. "Let's go inside. It's a long story, and I need something to drink. Some breakfast would be nice too."

"Lunch," Kevin said.

"Lunch, then." She frowned, looking around. "Where's Jack?" she asked.

Neither Kevin nor Holbrook said anything, and Penelope's gaze moved from one to the other as a sinking feeling grew in the pit of her stomach. "Where is he?"

Holbrook looked embarrassed. "He got into my wine," he said. "We were downstairs going over the rescue plans, and he went back up to get something to drink. He found the bottles in the kitchen and ... drank them."

"What? ... Why? ..." She shook her head, confused, not yet able to assimilate the information.

"I don't know," Kevin said. "Jack sure didn't seem like a risk." He glanced toward Holbrook. "And I didn't even know about the wine."

"Where is he?"

"We locked him in the bedroom."

Penelope closed her eyes, feeling suddenly exhausted, the events of last night and this morning seeming to catch up with her all at once. Kevin moved behind her, put a hand on her shoulder.

She pulled away.

"Leave her alone," Holbrook said. "She'll get over it."

"Fuck you!" Kevin yelled. "It's your fault anyway!" He touched her back, and this time she didn't pull away.

"I'm sorry," she said. "I'm just ... It's been a tough day. I didn't mean to take it out on you. It's just ... stress."

"We were just trying to find you—"

"I know."

"—before something happened."

"I know." She reached out, hugged him, and after a brief hesitation he hugged her back. If Holbrook wasn't here, she thought, she'd fuck Kevin. That would make him feel better. She'd take off his pants—

"Well, isn't that cute?" Holbrook said.

They pulled apart. "Asshole," Kevin said.

Penelope faced the teacher. "How long has Jack been locked up?"

"A couple hours. He'd taken off all his clothes and was *using* one of the wine bottles when we found him." The teacher grinned. "He attacked us with the bottle, and it took us a while to subdue him."

"How long before he dries out?"

Holbrook shrugged. "Who knows?"

"I want to talk to him."

"You can't."

Penelope glared at him. "You think you can stop me?"

"No. I mean, you can't. He doesn't listen or he doesn't

hear. And what he says doesn't make any sense." He picked up Kevin's box, put it in the car, and slammed the trunk. "But I guess you'll have to see for yourself."

She could hear Jack screaming the second they walked into the house. She passed through the living room, went down the hall, following the sound of the policeman's voice. The door to the bedroom at the end of the hallway, the one in which they'd been sleeping, was shut, a newly installed dead bolt keeping it closed.

The knob rattled.

"Jack!" Penelope called.

"Eat me!" the policeman screamed. His voice was hoarse, raspy, and unrecognizable. There was a loud thump as he threw himself against the door. "Lick my cock! Lick my balls! Lick my ass!"

"It's me! Penelope!"

"I want virgin blood!"

"It's going to be a while," Holbrook said.

Penelope nodded. She stood there for a moment, staring at the closed door, then walked tiredly back to the living room, dropped onto the couch.

"So tell us what happened," Kevin said as he and Holbrook followed her into the room.

She started with her nighttime abduction, described waking up in the field, told them of her encounter with Dionysus and the way he'd told her to leave.

"He let you go," Holbrook mused. "You say he wasn't drunk?"

"A little maybe. He'd been drinking out of that skin, and his eyes were a little red, but no, not really."

"You think if he was completely drunk, he would've let you go?"

"No. I think . . . I think he's still split. And I think he's closer to Dion when he's had less to drink. I think that's the only reason he let me go."

"And the others left you alone? In the field?"

She nodded, puzzled. "Except for the satyr, yeah. Pretty much."

"It's obvious that they take their cue from him. We suspected as much. He's not only their leader, their god, but he's the one who calls the emotional shots. If he's happy,

hey're happy. If he's angry, they're angry. They're au-
omatons, there only to do his bidding. The maenads
night be different, but the others . . ."

From his seat on the floor, Kevin snorted. "So what do
we do? Sober him up and force him to start preaching ab-
tinence?"

Holbrook raised his eyebrows. "Not a bad idea."

"Come on. Be serious."

"I am serious."

"So how do we do that? Capture him and pump him
ull of black coffee?"

Holbrook thought for a moment. "We could capture
nd isolate him. But I think it would be better if we killed
him."

"Hey," Kevin said, "why didn't we think of that
earlier? You want me to go down there and off him now?"

Holbrook ignored him, faced Penelope. "We could all
go over there. We'd wait while you went in. If you could
ust lure him over to where we were hiding, we could kill
him."

"But he let me go."

"He's not Dion."

"Part of him is."

Holbrook looked levelly at her. "You really are your
nothers' daughter."

"And what's that supposed to mean?"

"Just because he has a big dick—"

"Just because you have no dick!"

Kevin raised his hands. "Children, children . . ."

"I can't just waltz in there and lure him out," Penelope
said. "It doesn't work that way. He's surrounded by his
followers and my mothers and satyrs and God knows
what else. Besides, he said he doesn't want to see me
again. If I went back, he probably would kill me."

"Only if he was drunk," Holbrook said.

"He came after me anyway, even though he wasn't
drunk. I mean, he didn't chase me or anything, but it was
like he changed his mind after he let me go, like he
wanted me back."

"You didn't tell us—"

"You didn't let me finish!"

The teacher took a deep breath. "So finish."

"Like I said, he told me to go, and I started running toward the road. All of a sudden there was, like, this explosion in front of me. I didn't see where it came from or how it happened, but I figured he'd changed his mind and was ... I don't know, throwing lightning bolts at me. Anyway, I started zigzagging, running left and right so I'd be a harder target to hit. Nothing else happened, but when I reached the road, I fell. There was a group of ants in front of me, on the asphalt, and he turned the ants into men, into warriors. Like the Myrmidons."

Holbrook paled. "Myrmidons? But that was Zeus ..."

She nodded. "Yes."

"This is a horse of a different color. I've been basing everything on the premise that he is Dionysus and that he suffers from that god's weaknesses, attributes, and limitations." He grew silent, thinking. "Maybe ..." he said finally, "maybe because he has all of those others within him, he has their powers too."

"Maybe," Penelope said.

"Only I don't think he knows it. At least not yet. Otherwise, he would have been stretching himself, making use of all of the powers at his disposal."

"Maybe he has only limited powers. Maybe he has a little bit from each god, but not everything."

"Perhaps," Holbrook conceded.

"Maybe I do too."

Kevin shook his head. "What?"

She turned to face him. "Maybe I have power too. I'm the one who's supposed to give birth to these gods. It's half him and half me. I've been bred for the same thing he has. Maybe I have some of that power in me as well."

"But how do we figure out how to use it?"

The two of them looked toward Holbrook.

"I don't think that's something we should count on," the teacher said. "You haven't exhibited any unusual abilities yet—"

"I can smell things I didn't used to be able to smell," she said. "My sense of smell seems to have doubled in power. Or tripled."

"Hardly a godlike power," Holbrook said dryly. "Besides, your mothers apparently performed some sort of ritual with Dion. They didn't with you."

She looked down, nodded. "That's true."

"And, to be honest with you, I wouldn't know how to bring about your transformation. Assuming you wanted a transformation. Our knowledge is geared more toward protecting humans from gods, not helping people turn into gods."

"And you're doing a fine job," Kevin said.

Holbrook glared at him. "You're still alive, aren't you?"

"Yeah. And at least I'm not like Jack. Oh, I forgot. He's an Ovidian too, isn't he?"

The teacher's voice was uncharacteristically quiet. "I made a mistake there."

"So what is your plan?" Penelope asked. "How were you planning to rescue me?"

"It was a catch-22," Kevin said. "We'd have to kill Dionysus to get the others to stop partying, and we'd have to kill the others in order to get to Dionysus."

"So what were you going to do?"

"Kill your mothers," Holbrook said.

Penelope shook her head. "No."

"Yes. They're his cheerleaders. Take them out and the others will fall apart."

"But how did you plan to—?"

"We were going to burn your fucking winery."

Penelope was silent.

"They'd try to save it. Luckily for us, those bitches and all their pals are too drunk to think clearly. They're not up to using firearms. We are. We'd hide in the bushes and pick them off one by one."

Penelope tried to imagine her mothers being shot, tried to imagine bullets hitting them . . . where? In the head? In the chest? The images in her mind were all too clear. What would happen to them at the last second? What would flash through their brains? Would they think of her?

She wanted them dead, or at least a part of her did, but she did not want them *killed*. And she particularly did not want them killed by her mythology teacher.

And she wanted Mother Felice spared.

"You can't kill them," she said.

"They might not be human, but they can be killed."

"I don't mean you *can't* kill them. I mean, I won't let you kill them."

"Then we either join them or die."

"Even if we join them, we might die," Kevin pointed out. "They have no problems with killing their own."

"Maenads do not follow patterns or use reason or act logically. They are completely instinctual, living ids. They—"

"They're my mothers. They won't kill me."

"But they'll kill us."

"Maybe Kevin's idea would work. Maybe we could sober everyone up."

Holbrook looked at her disdainfully. "And how do you propose we do that?"

"We cut off their supply of wine."

Kevin snorted. "In Napa? Be serious."

"Daneam wine. It's the only wine that matters." She looked at Holbrook. "Right?"

The teacher nodded reluctantly.

"You guys were going to set fire to the winery anyway. I say we go ahead with it. They can't have been thinking logically enough to set aside a separate supply."

"She has a point," Holbrook admitted.

Kevin stood. "Then what are we waiting for? Let's do it."

"Not so fast," Holbrook said.

"What do you mean 'not so fast'? We were just going to go over there and do exactly the same thing."

"But we were going to take out her mothers."

"This is even better. It's simpler. We set the place on fire, and we don't even have to kill anybody."

"It's after noon. Maybe we should wait until tomorrow."

"There's another thing you should probably know," Penelope said quietly. "Everything's speeded up. A lot more than we thought. There were vines, new vines that they'd planted, and the grapes looked almost ready to harvest."

"It's only been a few days!" Kevin said.

"Harvest," Holbrook said. "That was the time of a major festival."

"And they'd be able to make more wine," Kevin added.

"I can get in there," Penelope said. "I can light the fuse or whatever it is I have to do. They . . . trust me. They seem to think I'm one of them. They leave me alone."

"All of them?"

"I don't know about all of them, but . . ." She breathed deeply. "I'm a maenad. They can sense it."

"Didn't you say you thought your mothers drugged you or something when they kidnapped you? They obviously knew you weren't one of them."

"I could take a few sips. Pretend to be drunk. It might fool them."

"I don't know," Holbrook said.

"We have no alternative."

"The grapes grew in two days?"

Penelope looked at the teacher, nodded.

"Then we'd better do it." Holbrook started toward the front door. "Let's finish loading the car."

"Get some food," Kevin said to Penelope as he moved to follow the teacher outside. "Get something to drink."

She smiled wryly. "Got any wine?"

"Not funny," he said, walking out the door.

She hurried into the kitchen. In the suddenly quiet house she could hear Jack screaming in the bedroom. His screams had been there throughout, a muted background babble, but with the other two outside, the noise seemed somehow louder. Penelope could hear Holbrook and Kevin in the garage, talking as they carried boxes to the car, but she was in the house and they weren't and right now the policeman's crazed ranting sounded a lot closer than it should.

And a lot creepier.

She quickly opened the refrigerator, grabbed a can of Coke and a carton of malted milk balls. Sugar. Quick energy.

She had time to notice that Holbrook's refrigerator was filled primarily with sweets and junk food, but then she closed the refrigerator door and hurried outside to get away from the policeman's incessant cries.

"So what's in the boxes?" she asked, walking over to the car.

"Gasoline," Kevin said. "And rags."

"And old newspaper," Holbrook added. "Things that'll burn."

She'd been expecting something less slapdash, something more professional, and she was disappointed. "I thought you'd have explosives and stuff."

"I'm a teacher, not a terrorist." Holbrook slammed the trunk of the car. "Come on, get in."

Penelope looked back at the house. "Should I ... you know, lock it? Jack—"

"Just get in. I want to do this quick."

Kevin opened the passenger door. "Before you lose your nerve?"

"Something like that," Holbrook said. "Get in. Let's go."

The winery was a slaughterhouse.

Even after all Penelope had seen, she was shocked by the extent of the butchery.

They had driven straight to the winery. A few of the streets had been blocked, forcing them to detour, but the blockages had been old. There was no new damage, no new fires, and Napa looked like a ghost town, like a bombed-out city after a war, its inhabitants dead or fled. They'd encountered no problems on the road.

That worried Penelope. They'd seen very few people on the streets in the daytime since Dionysus' rebirth, but the city had always seemed alive in some twisted, perverted way, the playground of destructive children who were napping and had not yet come out to play.

But the feeling now was one of abandonment, and she could not help wondering if they had moved on, up the valley, or out of the valley, or if they were simply massing around their god, in preparation perhaps for their harvest festival. She thought the latter more likely, and she hoped and prayed that Dionysus stayed on the site of the fair and did not return to the winery. They needed all the breaks they could get.

Dionysus.

She was thinking of him now as Dionysus. Dion was

still in there somewhere, but after her encounter with the god, she could no longer think of Dionysus as merely Dion in an altered form. This was a separate entity, a being that had usurped Dion's place and incorporated him within itself.

The road to the winery was strewn with garbage and debris, but it was not until they reached the gates of the winery that they started seeing bodies. At first Penelope did not pay close attention to the immobile forms lining the sides of the drive. She's seen so many bodies the past few days that she was becoming inured to the sight. But even in her peripheral vision the colors jumped out at her: red, green, blue, purple. Something was different here, something was wrong. She looked more carefully at the bodies out the window of the car, and she saw that some of them had been . . . altered. There was a man with the body of a frog, a woman with the arms of a lobster, a child with an elephant's trunk and tusks. Many of the bodies were bloody, but an equal number of them weren't, and these lay curled in fetal positions or positioned in odd angles. She could not help thinking that these people had died in the midst of metamorphosis, that they had died *because* of what they were becoming.

There was something about dying that way that disturbed her more than murder, and she looked away from the bodies, kept her eyes on the road ahead.

In contrast to that first night, there were not hordes of believers milling about the winery entrance, drinking and partying in the driveway. Save for an occasional staggerer, the narrow road was devoid of life.

Ahead, she could see the buildings of the winery, and she wiped her sweaty palms of her jeans. Holbrook's plan was frighteningly simple-minded. She was to distract whomever she had to, however she had to, so that he and Kevin could shove their boxes of combustibles in the main winery building and light it on fire. Holbrook was hoping that the blaze would spread quickly enough that the wine, the alcohol, would ignite and engulf the winery in flames before any of the bacchantes realized what was happening. They'd then run back to the car and take off.

It was a dim-witted plan, she thought, a moronic

scheme. But she could not come up with a better alternative, and she said nothing.

She looked out the window to the left. On the grapevine stakes, fluttering above the bare branches of the plants, were nailed the scalps of women and long-haired men. On the wires strung between the stakes were tied gaily colored strips of crepe paper.

The meadow now reached the vineyard. It was six or seven times the size it had been. The altar and the stone statue of Dionysus, which had been at the periphery of the meadow, nearly in the trees, were now squarely in its center and could be seen even from here. The trees had not been chopped down, they had been . . . eradicated. It was as if they had never existed. Meadow grass grew from the edge of the vineyard all the way up to the top of the hill, unobstructed by bush or tree.

And then the revelers arrived.

It was as if floodgates had suddenly opened, triggered by the movement of their car up the drive. A wave of men and women flowed into the meadow, from over the hill, from between the trees at the far end. She'd thought there'd been a lot of people at the site of the fair, but that was nothing compared to this. Her heart began pounding at the sight so many individuals, instinctively recoiling before the intimidating size of the oncoming horde.

She'd thought that the revelers had come for them, had been sent by Dionysus or her mothers to tear them apart and protect the winery. But she realized as the human wave slowed, then stopped, that the people did not even know that the three of them were there.

They had come for the festival.

Harvest.

Even the word had resonance within her. They were going to celebrate the fruition of the crop, were going to pick and then crush the grapes. She didn't know how she knew this, but she did, and a part of her wanted to join them.

The car stopped just before the parking lot as Holbrook pulled to the side, executed a three-point turn, and parked the vehicle underneath a tree, facing the street so they'd be able to make a quick exit.

The teacher opened his door, got out. "Let's make this quick," he said.

Outside, she could hear the singing. Thousands of voices blending and harmonizing. She stood next to the car, rooted in place, staring toward the vineyards and the expanded meadow beyond as Holbrook and Kevin began unloading the trunk.

From this vantage point it looked almost like the scene of a rock concert, a massive cross-generational Woodstock. The feeling was like that too, she thought. Thousands of people singing in joyful camaraderie, their happy voices blending beautifully as they sang in union the words to an ancient Greek ode, a song that her mothers had sung to her when she was young. Lines of people, arms around one another's shoulders, swayed to the music.

Only . . .

Only directly in front of the crowd and off to the sides were small spots of red, the eviscerated bodies of recent kills, bloody carcasses of men, women, children, and pets that had been strewn haphazardly about, forgotten and ignored, as though they were merely the by-products of such a large gathering, like empty paper cups and sandwich wrappers.

On the top of the hill, several silhouetted women were tearing apart what looked to be the remains of a dead horse.

The singing stopped. As one, the crowd was silenced. It was as though they were listening to something, although there was no audible sound.

Holbrook was right, Penelope realized. The people took their cue from Dionysus. His mood determined theirs. They not only worshiped him, they were connected to him in some way, their feelings and emotions an extension of his own.

Movement began again, increasingly frenzied activity that spread outward from the center of the gigantic gathering.

People began moving into the far rows of the vineyard.

"We need some help here," Holbrook said. "Stop staring and grab a box."

He had seen it too. There was fear in his voice, and as

she moved to help, she noticed that Kevin was quiet, his face pale. She wanted to reassure them, to tell them not to worry, to tell them that they would not be torn apart if they were caught, but she knew that was not true. They would be killed.

She would not.

She was one of *them*.

They left half of the boxes in the open trunk and hurried silently up the last few yards of the drive to the parking lot. She wanted to feel nervous and anxious, wanted some of Holbrook's sense of urgency transferred to her so that she would move as quickly as she needed to, but she felt no tension, no nervousness, and she hurried only because her brain told her to do so, not because her emotions deemed it necessary.

Holbrook stopped at the edge of the parking lot, ducking next to an overhanging tree. Kevin and Penelope followed suit. Ahead, between two of the buildings, next to the warehouse, was a line of four transport trucks. The vehicles were being loaded with cases of Daneam wine, and she found herself thinking of a scene from *Invasion of the Body Snatchers* where trucks were being loaded with seed pods for distribution to other cities, other states. Was that what was happening here? Were they trying to spread the debauchery elsewhere through the wine? To San Francisco? Los Angeles? Phoenix? Denver? Chicago? New York?

Yes, she thought. It made sense.

She was just surprised that they had been logical enough to think of it and sober enough to do it.

Mother Margeaux, she thought.

"We can go around," she said to Holbrook. "There's a sidewalk around the side of the house that leads to the main building, the one where we produce the wine, and it can't be seen from the warehouse."

"The warehouse? That would be better," Holbrook said. "That's where it's all stored.'

"That's where they're loading the trucks. I don't think we can get in there without someone seeing us."

"Then I hope the fire spreads to the warehouse."

"Come on," Penelope said. She led them around the

edge of the parking lot, trying to stay behind vehicles, out of sight of the truck loaders. They passed behind the back of an overturned mini-van, and she stopped. The box she was carrying was getting heavy, and she put it down for a second.

"What are you doing?" Holbrook hissed.

"My arms are tired."

"Here," Kevin said. "Switch. Maybe mine's a little lighter."

"Are you sure this is going to be enough?" Penelope asked as they traded boxes. "It doesn't seem like this'll start much of a fire."

"That's why the warehouse would be better."

"Maybe we should burn the house instead," Kevin suggested.

The house? She had not really considered the fact that the house would be burned too, but of course it would. Truth be told, she had not thought any of this through. She supposed, in the back of her mind, she'd thought that the winery would burn and the fire trucks would show up before the blaze spread to the house.

But there were no fire trucks.

She looked at the house. Her home. All her things were still in there, in her bedroom. Her books, her records, her clothes, her photographs, all of her mementos and personal memorabilia. If the house burned, there would be nothing left. She'd have only the clothes on her back. And if her mothers were killed . . .

She had to at least save her photo albums.

"There's no wine in the house," Holbrook told Kevin. "We're here to destroy the wine supply."

Penelope put down the boxes Kevin had handed her. "I have to go in there. I have to get some of my stuff."

"No!" Holbrook ordered. He looked quickly around, lowered his voice. "No."

"Yes." She didn't want to debate it, didn't want to be bullied into changing her mind, and she ran around a BMW and toward the side door of the house.

"Penelope!" Kevin called after her.

She did not look back but kept running. The door was unlocked, and she opened it, peeking in before stepping inside.

The house was untouched.

Of course. This was the home of the maenads, the god's right-hand women. No one would dare go in here.

She could run upstairs, grab her photo albums, and be out in less than a minute.

She hurried inside, not closing the door behind her, running through Mother Margeaux's study, into the hall, up the stairs, to her bedroom.

Where Dion's mom was on her bed, having sex with another woman.

They were lying side by side. The other woman's head was buried between Dion's mother's scissored legs, but Dion's mom was merely stroking the woman's vagina, and she saw Penelope instantly.

Penelope stood in the doorway, unmoving, the fear and tension she'd been unable to muster until now blooming fully formed within her.

Obviously sensing that something was wrong, the other woman withdrew her face from between Dion's mother's legs and looked lazily toward the doorway. She saw Penelope and sat up. "It's her!" she cried excitedly, pointing. "It's—"

Dion's mother broke her neck.

It happened instantly, easily. She grabbed the woman's head and twisted it. There was a loud crack, and the woman's body went limp, falling across the bed.

Penelope stared for a moment at the dead woman before meeting the eyes of Dion's mom. "I just came to get my photo albums," she explained timidly.

Dion's mother nodded numbly. She appeared dazed, drunk, but she seemed to know what was going on. "Get out of here," she said. "Take your books and go. I won't tell them you were here."

Penelope wanted to ask why, wanted to know more, but she knew how capricious maenads were, and she quickly went over to her desk, opened the bottom drawer, and withdrew her photo albums.

Should she warn Dion's mother? Penelope wondered. Dion's mom had helped her. Should she return the favor?

She turned as she reached the doorway. "Get out of the house," she said. "Quickly."

Dion's mother nodded tiredly, not asking for or needing more information, and Penelope raced downstairs, through the house, and out the side door where she'd come in. She nearly ran into Holbrook and Kevin, struggling with both her boxes and their own as they approached the side of the house.

"Got 'em," she said, holding up her photo albums.

"We thought you might get into trouble," Kevin said. "You didn't see anyone inside?"

She shook her head. "No." She took a box from Kevin, a box from the teacher, placing her photo albums on top of them.

"We're wasting time," Holbrook said pointedly.

"This way." She led them down the walkway that curved around Mother Sheila's garden in the back of the house and to the rear of the winery buildings.

The back door of the main building was open, hanging half off its hinges, and an enormous puddle of dried blood covered the slab of concrete in front of it. She hesitated for a second before going in. The open door worried her. But she did not feel comfortable staying outside when just around the corner of the building bacchantes were loading trucks with cases from the warehouse.

Holbrook shoved his way past her into the building.

She looked toward Kevin and their gazed locked for a second. Then Kevin shifted the boxes in his hand and followed Holbrook through the doorway. Penelope went in after him.

The inside of the building was filled with bodies.

The extent of the carnage took her breath away. Despite what she'd seen the past few days, despite even the scene outside in the meadow, she had started to become inured to the bodies, had begun to view them as casualties of war, a natural effect of the current situation in the valley.

But there was nothing natural about this.

The long corridor had been carpeted with viscera, wallpapered with wet skin. What remained of the bodies after their skinning and evisceration had been hung up and strung up, attached to the ceiling with the heavy wire used to tie grapevines. They were hung low and high, positioned at regular intervals, forming makeshift dividers, creating a narrow walkway that zigzagged through the wide corridor.

The thing that truly sickened her was that she recognized some of the faces on the wall. Eyeless and toothless, they were stretched tight, widened and lengthened, distorted. Yet she saw familiar features, individual attributes in the forcibly misshapen faces. There was Tony Veltri's big nose. Here was Marty Robert's close-set eyebrows.

The stench in the corridor was horrible—rot and decay; blood, bile, and excrement—and Penelope held her breath, trying to breathe through her mouth.

Only ... it wasn't quite as horrible as it should have been. The shit was bad. And the rot. But the scent of the blood was pleasant, alluring, and below it all she could make out the sweet smell of wine, and she felt a familiar tingling between her legs.

She tried to breathe in through her mouth, out through her nose, tried not to smell the odors, tried not to think about them.

Next to her, Kevin vomited loudly, bending over and facing to the left so he wouldn't throw up on the boxes in his hands.

Holbrook was already navigating the corridor, blithely shouldering aside the bloody corpses as he walked forward. "How far to the wine?" he asked.

Turning back toward the open door and taking a deep breath, Penelope followed after him, her feet sinking into the squishy organs and tissue that covered the floor. "Second door on the right should have some vats," she said.

Behind her, still gagging, she heard Kevin literally following in her footsteps, his shoes making loud, squelching sounds.

The door must have been locked, because Holbrook had put down his boxes and was kicking it when she caught up to him. He kicked, slipped, fell into the grue on the floor, then got up and did it again. On the fifth try the door gave a little, and on the sixth it swung open.

Inside, the pressing room was clean. No bodies, no gore, no blood. Holbrook let his boxes drop to the floor. He looked around the room at the huge steel vats and various pieces of machinery. He turned toward Penelope, pointing t a red-valved pipe protruding from the closest wall. "The ower here," he asked. "Is it electricity or gas?"

"Both," Penelope said.

The teacher grinned. "Gas," he said. "This may work fter all."

Kevin straggled into the room, lurching past Holbrook, rying to get as far away from the door as possible before utting down his boxes and loudly exhaling.

"Uh-oh," Holbrook said, frowning and patting his ockets. "Did anybody bring a matchbook?"

Penelope's heart leaped in her chest.

"What—" Kevin began.

Holbrook grinned. "Just joking." He opened one of his oxes. "Hurry up. Let's get to work."

Under the teacher's supervision, they soaked the rags nd newspapers in gasoline, piling them in strategic loca- ions. Penelope showed Holbrook where the runoff valves vere, and he opened three of them to a trickle. It was be- oming hard to breathe due to the fumes, and even Kevin vas taking gulps of air from outside the doorway.

"Isn't this going to explode when you put a match to t?" Kevin asked. "How are we going to get out in time efore it blows?"

Holbrook was emptying the last drops of gasoline in a rail leading from one pile of rags to another. He tossed he can aside, walked over, and grinned. "I'm not com- letely dense." He reached into his pocket and withdrew folded envelope. He opened it. Inside was a bluish- vhite crystalline powder. "Chlorine," he said.

Kevin frowned. "Yeah?"

The teacher reached into his box, withdrew a plastic ontainer of transmission fluid. "Mix these two together, nd they'll start a fire."

"So will a match. What's the point?"

"There's a delayed reaction. It'll take a minute or so to tart. I'll put it next to some paper that hasn't been loused with gas. It'll have to burn through that first. Then t'll start the rags on fire. Then the fire will spread. By the ime this place goes up, we'll be long gone."

"I hope it works," Kevin said.

"It will."

They finished placing the newspapers, rags, and boxes around the room.

"Okay," Holbrook said. "It's time." He poured some transmission fluid into the envelope and heaved the still mostly full container at the wall. He shook up the contents of the envelope to mix them, then twisted the envelope and placed it next to a long length of rolled newspaper.

"Haul ass," he said.

They ran. Penelope nearly slipped in the corridor, slamming into one of the bodies, a sticky chest cavity hitting her in the face, but she kept going, and the three of them emerged outside seconds later.

In front of them, the house was surrounded by young girls dressed in white and holding hands.

"What's that?" Kevin asked. "What are they doing?"

"They're virgins," the teacher said.

"Vestal virgins," Penelope said.

"Or Hestial virgins. They are to be consecrated to the goddess of the hearth."

"Consecrated? What the hell does that mean? Sacrificed?"

"No. They'll merely become the goddess's servants or hand maidens. Priestesses, as it were. They will devote their lives to her. They will be killed only if they break their vows."

"Jesus," Kevin breathed.

"The virgins are probably sober," Holbrook said.

"That means—"

"We have no choice," Holbrook said. "We'll just have to make a run for it." He looked at Penelope. She nodded.

They dashed between the two buildings, running toward the parking lot. They were probably spotted, probably seen, but there were not wild screams, no hot pursuit. The virgins remained in place, holding hands, and the other bacchantes continued their revelry and their harvest festival.

They made it back to the car with no problem.

They were on the road, nearly back in town, when the building blew.

FIFTEEN

The hospital room was starting to stink.

Mel Scott looked around at the mounted heads on the wall, at the bodies of the doctor and the nurses on the floor. Flies had gotten in somehow and were everywhere, buzzing, constantly buzzing, alighting on the stinking heads and corpses, then flying annoyingly back into the air again.

Paradise wasn't supposed to be like this.

His head hurt. It had been hurting all day, like a hangover, though he had remained consistently drunk enough that he should not be suffering from a hangover. The DT's perhaps, but not a hangover.

Barbara was dead.

He had tried to fuck her back to life, had taken her first in the pussy, then up the ass, then in the mouth, but she had remained cold. He had prayed to his new god, but his god seemed to have forsaken him.

And now he was running out of wine.

The room stank and he was running out of wine.

Paradise wasn't supposed to be like this.

There were people in the church again.

Praying.

To God.

Pastor Robens peeked out through the crack in the door. They had abandoned God, all of them, had forsaken Him for that drunken diety from Greece, and now they were back.

It was too late, though.

They had abandoned God, and now God had abandoned them.

He listened to the frantic prayers, the desperate voices,

and silently closed the door, locked it. He walked back to his desk and the bottle of wine. They'd been right the first time. It was the wine god whom they should be worshiping, not the Judeo-Christian deity. *He* was merely the contractor who'd put up this building.

The new god was the landlord.

And rent was due.

Nick Nicholson felt himself die.

He took a couple of them with him, the assholes who wouldn't believe that there was no more Daneam, but there were twenty of them and only one of him, and they had taken him out in the end.

The moment of death itself was not painful, but it was not pleasurable either. It was not a release or a transformation. It was merely a continuation. Different. Neither worse nor better. They killed him, beat him to death, then carried him across the river to the underworld.

He stood, walked away.

There were other dead men here—and dead women and dead dogs and dead children—but he did not talk to them. He could not talk to them.

Something was wrong. He didn't know what it was, but he could sense it. This was not where he was supposed to be. This was not the real underworld. This was a shadow of the real thing, an amateur version of a professional show.

It would not last, though. He sensed that too. It would not hold together. This would only be temporary.

He walked into a woman who had had her arms ripped off. They smacked foreheads, hard, and he wanted to apologize to her, but he could not.

He backed up, moved to the right, kept walking.

SIXTEEN

The streets were deserted, and they made it back to Holbrook's with no problem. Kevin did not know how big the explosion had been or whether the fire had spread to the warehouse, but he knew that no fire trucks had gone rushing to the scene and he considered that a good sign.

But where would they go from here? Even if they had succeeded in destroying all bottles of Daneam wine—which he doubted—why couldn't the bacchantes just get wine from another vineyard? Hell, there were some eighty-five wineries in the valley at last count. It wouldn't be that hard.

Even if that wasn't possible, even if their access to alcohol had been completely denied, that didn't mean that they'd automatically die or disappear.

They would probably just be pissed off.

And he didn't want to be here when that happened.

Holbrook parked the car in the driveway, and Kevin turned to look at the teacher. He had never much liked Holbrook, and he liked him even less now. He'd been so smug and superior when he'd lectured them about Dionysus and the maenads, when he'd bragged about belonging to his secret society, but the only plan he'd come up with had been to burn down some buildings—and he couldn't have pulled that off without Penelope.

Besides, he wanted to get into Penelope's pants.

Holbrook looked back at him, and Kevin turned away. He didn't know how he knew that, but he did. The teacher might pretend to be asexual and all business, totally above petty concerns, but Kevin had seen the way he'd looked at Penelope back at the winery, and he knew what that look meant.

Maybe it wasn't Penelope herself. Maybe he just wanted to know what it was like to fuck a maenad.

Either way, Kevin didn't like it.

He got out of the car. "So was that the Ovarians' plan?" he said. "Burning down the winery?"

"Ovidians," Holbrook said. "And no, that was my own idea."

"So what do we do now?"

"I have an idea."

"What is it?"

"You'll see." They walked into the house, and Holbrook started down the hallway toward his basement. "I'll be back in a minute!" he called.

Kevin looked at Penelope. "You think we accomplished anything?"

"I don't know."

"There were a hell of a lot of people there. I don't see how we even made a dent."

"It's not just Dionysus—Dion—that's making them this way. It's the wine. Our wine. That's why they were shipping it out."

"What's so special about your wine?"

"I don't know," Penelope admitted.

They moved over to the couch, sat down. They did not sit down next to each other, but they did not purposely sit at opposite ends of the couch either, and Kevin was acutely aware of the fact that their hands, resting on the cushion, were almost touching.

He wanted to get into her pants too.

Yes, he had to admit it. He was attracted to Penelope, and there was probably a bit of jealousy tied up with his feelings about Holbrook.

He felt guilty about wanting her. She was Dion's girlfriend, and even though Dion had turned into a monster god, he still owed it to his friend not to steal his girlfriend.

Not that he *could* steal her. She was obviously still in love with Dion.

He looked toward Penelope, then glanced down the hallway, frowning. Something was wrong. He didn'

now what it was, but he could sense it, and he suddenly
felt uneasy.

"Jack," Penelope said, as if reading his mind.

That was it.

The policeman had stopped screaming.

He stood up. It could be coincidence. Jack could be
sleeping it off, getting over it. But Holbrook had been
downstairs a hell of a lot longer than the promised minute, and Kevin had the feeling there was something seriously amiss.

He turned toward Penelope, who was also standing.
"Where are the keys?" he asked. "The keys to our car, the
Mercedes?"

"In my pocket." She met his gaze.

"Be ready," he said.

They started toward the hallway, walking quietly, listening. There were no sounds at all, and that frightened
him. He had been planning to ask Penelope to go outside
and start the car, to be ready to take off instantly if something had happened to Holbrook—

if something else was down there

—but he was not brave enough to go into the basement
alone, and he did not object to her coming along.

They reached the door to the basement.

The lights were off downstairs.

"Holbrook!" he called.

No answer.

He looked to his left, toward the end of the hall, and
noticed for the first time that while the door to the back
bedroom appeared to be closed, it was not. There was a
crack of orangish late afternoon sunlight between the
door and the doorjamb.

Jack had escaped.

"Jack!" he called.

No answer.

"Let's get out of here," Penelope whispered.

Kevin reached around the doorframe to turn on the
basement light. The switch was already up.

"Enough proof for me," he said. "Let's bail."

Downstairs, someone moaned.

They looked at each other. "One of them's hurt or it's a trap," Kevin said. "There's only two choices here."

"What do you want to do? You call it."

He looked down into the darkness, took a deep breath. "Start the car," he said. "Be ready to roll."

She nodded. "Don't wait. If there's something wrong, get out."

He smiled at her. "I have no problem with that."

Penelope sped down the hall, and Kevin gathered his courage and started down the steps. "Holbrook!" he called. "Jack!"

The moan came again.

He hurried down the stairs, stopping at the bottom. In the darkness at the opposite end of the basement he saw trolls: short, hairy creatures clutching pine cone-tipped spears. He squinted into the dimness and saw that the figures were not trolls after all.

They were Penelope's mothers.

As one the naked woman rose from their collective crouch. They were filthy, covered with mud and blood, grime and wine. Their ratted, uncombed hair stuck out wildly in all directions, and it was this that in the darkness had given them that hairy, inhuman look.

He would have known better how to react had they not been human, had they really been monsters. But somehow this revelation was even more frightening, and he found himself unable to act, rooted in place by shock.

On the floor behind them was a pulpy red mess that had to be either Jack or Holbrook.

Or both.

The women laughed, jabbering in some foreign language.

He went through his options quickly: he could try to find a weapon, he could try to fight them, he could run.

He ran.

He took the steps three at a time and sped down the hallway with the sound of the maenads screaming in back of him. He ran outside, slamming the front door behind him, and rushed to where Penelope was waiting in the idling car. "Go!" he screamed.

They took off.

They sped down the street, Penelope accelerating so fast that he was thrown back into the seat before he could get his safety belt on. "Where to?" she asked.

He was still breathing heavily, his heart pounding, and he could not speak. He shook his head.

"Don't worry," she said. "We'll find something."

Penelope lay in the darkness, staring upward.

They were holed up in a small apartment at the north end of the city, in the last unit of a single-story complex that faced away from the street. Kevin's screwdriver had still been in the car, but everything else had been left behind at Holbrook's and they'd been unable to find any other weapons save a couple of butter knives and a pair of scissors.

"Do you think we're down to the last days?" Kevin had asked as they'd driven around, looking for an easily defensible place to spend the night. "Do you think we're going to make it?"

"Of course we'll make it," she said. But it was the phrase "last days" that stayed with her, and despite her outward optimism she was not at all sure that they would survive.

Which was why she'd considered raping him.

She hadn't done it, hadn't been able to go through with it. It would not even have been rape because he so obviously wanted her—she could see the bulge of a permanent erection in his pants—but it hadn't felt right to her. Part of her wanted to reward him for the past few days, to let him experience sex at least once in his life, in case they did not make it through all this alive, but something kept her from acting on the impulse.

Strange, she thought, how one person's perceptions of another could change so completely over such a short period of time. She'd known Kevin Harte almost her entire life. He'd been in her first-grade class. She'd never much liked him, had always considered him something of a screw-up, but she now felt closer to him than anyone else alive. She trusted him totally.

Maybe life was more like a movie than she'd thought. On the radio, they heard a reference to Napa. A news

report on an AM talk station out of San Francisco. The
reporter said that there'd been an accident involving
radioactive waste on Highway 29 and that all roads leading into the Napa Valley were closed until further notice.

Radioactive waste?

She looked over at Kevin.

He shook his head. "It's probably their standard story
when they don't know what's going on. No one wants to
come and gawk at radioactive waste. It keeps the
lookeeloos away."

"How are they going to explain what really happened?"

Kevin shrugged. "Biological agents, I suppose. They'll
say it was something carried on the wind, something hal-
lucinogenic that caused mass hysteria."

"You think that'll work? Dionysus'll shoot choppers
out of the sky with lightning bolts if they come to investigate. How are they going to explain that?"

"Don't worry," Kevin said. "They will."

They drove in silence after that, looking for a place to
spend the night, finally ending up here, at this apartment.

Now she lay alone in the bed, staring up at the darkened ceiling. She wondered what would have happened
with her and Dion if none of this had occurred. She
wasn't naive. She knew that most high school romances
did not last long past graduation. And she realized that
she and Dion had not known each other that long, did not
know each other that well. But the love they'd felt for
each other was strong and real, and she could see them
remaining together, going to college together. They were
both smart, both good academically, and there was no reason to believe that they couldn't have gone to the same
university.

The only thing that bothered her was the thought that
their mutual attraction, their feelings for each other, had
been bred into them, genetically engineered, planned. She
did not know if that made their feelings any less real, but
it tainted them, and gave her the unsettling feeling of having no control over her life, having no free will.

Dion would have understood this, though, if she had
been able to talk to him about it, and maybe the fact that
they were both aware of the situation would have enabled

them to bypass the pitfalls and maneuver around the barriers that had been placed in their path.

She found herself thinking of the way he'd looked when she'd first seen him in that cafeteria line. Awkward and nervous, but appealingly so. Attractive. She remembered how frightened she'd been when he passed out at the fair, the feeling of panic that had shot through her as he'd collapsed, and the way she'd wanted to tend to him and care for him when he'd been lying helplessly there on the ground. She thought of the way his voice had sounded, the way his skin had felt.

She began to cry.

She tried to steer her mind toward something else, but the thought of her home, the place she had been born and raised, now burned to the ground, and she cried even more.

There was movement in the darkness, and then a hand was stroking her forehead, Kevin's soft voice was whispering in her ear. "It's all right," he said. "It's okay. Don't cry."

She rolled over, reached out, and put her arms around him, hugging him, and he was there for her, hugging her back, letting her cry into his shoulder.

"It's all right," he said. "It's all right."

They remained like that for a while, until her tears had dried and then after. They were still holding each other when she fell asleep.

In her dream, she was in the meadow, on her back in front of Dionysus, legs spread in the air. He was enormous, and she felt as though she was being ripped apart as he entered her, but it felt good too, and she bucked against him, trying to force him deeper inside her.

His orgasm was a violent explosion of molten semen that burned inside her like acid.

A half-human ant creature burst forth from her stomach.

She awoke screaming.

SEVENTEEN

He needed Zeus.

He had never thought it would be difficult to rule. He had often chafed under Zeus' rules and restrictions, had often suffered as a result of Hera's caprices, and more than once he had wished that *he* was in charge of Olympus, that *he* was the one calling the shots and making the decisions.

But he didn't have a head for organization or administration. Olympus had always been a loose confederation of free individuals, but he could not seem to abide order to even that extent. He was constitutionally unable to act rationally or logically, to behave responsibly. It was simply not in him.

The strain was starting to show. He felt tired, and the headaches would not go away. He had killed anything that moved, had fucked everything that walked, had consumed enough wine to poison an army, but nothing had made him feel any better. The responsibility of ruling still hung heavily over his head.

And now his stash of wine had been destroyed.

The maenads would make more wine, but that would take a while. For now they were out of the nectar. Other wine had been brought in, and he had downed a casket of it, but it was not *his* wine and it was not the same. It did not give him the same kick, it did not possess the same power.

He needed to bring the others back.

Yes, that was at the heart of the matter. He had tried to make a go of it on his own and had failed. Zeus would probably punish him for that, Hera would probably bitch about it for eternity and forever sabotage his romantic entanglements, but it would be worth it to have them back. And the other gods as well.

But how was he to resurrect them? Penelope? Penelope didn't want him. She had wanted him Before. He had *had* her Before. But that was when he had not yet been himself. Now she hated him, was afraid of him, wanted to kill him.

He could force her. He could take her and rape her, fill her up with godsperm until she was overflowing. But he did not want to do that.

He was filled with a deep and aching sense of loss.

This wasn't what was supposed to happen. This was not the way it was supposed to work out.

He looked up into the sky. Dionysus in love? It wasn't possible. For thousands of years he had not formed an emotional attachment to any of the women he had had.

But this attachment was not his.

It was *his*.

He looked down. A woman was parading herself before him. When she saw that she had his attention, she bent over and offered herself to him.

He took her, grabbing her shoulders and forcing her onto him.

He began thrusting.

And the woman started to change.

He reveled in what he was doing, he savored every scream, every tortured nuance of her transformation, but he was at the same time horrified by his own cruelty, by his complete lack of feeling for the woman.

She was a goat by the time he was through, and he yanked her off him and split her open, letting the hot blood rain down on his hair and course over his forehead and cheeks.

But try as he might, he could not fully enjoy it. Even blood didn't make him feel any better.

EIGHTEEN

In the morning she felt ... better.

It was an odd sensation, but the bleak pessimism of the night before had fled, replaced by a cautious optimism. It was as if the tears of last night had washed away her doubts and fears.

And had brought new insight.

Penelope sat up. Kevin was still asleep, having crawled back to his own bed sometime during the night, and she crept out of bed and over to the window, where she lifted one of the blinds and peeked outside. The morning was clear, sunny, a rare occurrence, and that made her feel even better.

Throughout everything, she had tried to forget the fact that she was a maenad, had tried to deny and suppress that aspect of herself.

But, she realized now, that was exactly what might save them.

It was the maenads who, each fall, tore Dionysus apart in a frenzy of bloodlust.

She stared out at the blue sky.

She knew what she had to do.

Kevin awoke an hour or so later.

Penelope turned away from the window, watched him climb out of bed. "You know," she said, "I never used to like you."

Kevin recoiled, mock offended. *"Moi?"*

She smiled. "You seemed so ... I don't know. So tough."

"Tough?" Kevin laughed. The sound was loud, natural, and seemed depressingly out of place in these circumstances. "What, you thought I was some type of gang banger?"

"Not exactly that. You just seemed . . . I don't know."

"You think I'm tough now?"

She shook her head, grinned. "You're a pussy."

He laughed again, pulled on his shirt. "So it's back down to the two of us. What now?"

"We have to kill him."

He stared at her. "I thought you said he was still Dion, that we can't kill him, you wouldn't let us."

"It's the only way." She took a deep breath. "Dion's not coming back."

"But—"

"I think he'd want us to do this."

Kevin thought for a moment. "How could we do it? How could we even get close to him?"

"I think," she said slowly, "that I need to get drunk."

"No!"

"Maybe not drunk," she conceded. "But I think I need to have some wine. It's the only way I can tap into . . . whatever it is."

"You'll be—"

"Just like them?" She shook her head. "I don't think so. I won't drink so much that I'll be out of control. I'll just drink enough to alter my perceptions a little."

"But what will that do?"

"It'll help me be what I'm supposed to be."

"A maenad?"

"A maenad."

"And what then?"

"I'll tear him apart."

The silence hung between them. Kevin cleared his throat, started to speak, then lapsed into silence.

"I didn't ask to be born this way," Penelope said softly. "But it's what I am. I can fight it, I can ignore it. Or I can use it to our advantage." She walked over to the bed, sat down next to him. "I've been thinking long and hard about this, and it's the only way. It's our only chance. It's what's supposed to happen anyway. I'm just . . . speeding things up."

He managed a small smile. "You've been thinking 'long and hard,' huh? I bet you liked that."

She punched him lightly on the shoulder. "Come on. Let's scrounge up some breakfast. We're going to need our energy."

They'd found an unopened bottle of wine in the back of one of the kitchen cupboards. The renter of the apartment was obviously no drinker, but someone had apparently given him or her a bottle of wine as a housewarming present, and the bottle, still wrapped with a red ribbon, was waiting for them behind a sack of flour.

Penelope pulled it out, read the label. "Gallo," she said, smiling. "Not Daneam, but I suppose it'll do."

She had not partaken yet, not trusting herself, wanting to wait until the last minute, until she was ready to use it, and it was on the car seat between them as Kevin drove.

Wine.

She kept glancing at the bottle, feeling anxious, expectant, wanting to open it and drink it all in one swallow.

That worried her.

She hoped she was doing the right thing.

Their clothes were filthy and smelly from the past several days, but clothes at all were unusual here, and she'd made Kevin take off his shirt, had used the scissors to turn his jeans into cutoffs. She'd felt him through the pants as she'd cut, her fingers instinctively curling around the outline of his erection, and there was a moment when she considered taking it out and putting it in her mouth, a moment when he had obviously wanted her to do just that. But then she had finished with the pant leg and stood up.

She'd ripped her own clothes to make them even more raggedy than they already were, but she still wasn't satisfied that she looked the part. She considered saying something light and humorous, turning it into a joke, but instead turned to Kevin and said simply, "When we get there, I'm going to take my top off."

He obviously thought about saying something joking in reply, but he merely nodded, saying nothing.

The street in front of the field was blocked with wreck-

age and debris, garbage and rotting animal corpses, and
they parked close to the Avis office where she'd ended up
last time. Penelope got out of the car, took a deep breath,
then pulled off her shirt. The sun was warm on her skin,
but she felt cold and more naked, more exposed than she
ever had in her life. She looked down at her breasts, saw
that the nipples were erect, and she wanted Kevin to look,
wanted him to see her, but he kept his eyes purposely
averted, trying not to glance at her at all, looking only at
her face when he could not avoid it.

She took the bottle of wine out of the car.

They walked.

The air felt good on her body, the bottle felt good in her
hand, and she realized that she was enjoying this. She
was having fun. For the first time since Dion had ...
changed, she felt happy.

God, she hoped she wasn't going to screw this up.

They reached the edge of the field. It was, if possible,
even more crowded than before. In addition to the celebrants, there were satyrs and nymphs, centaurs and griffins, and though such a scene might have looked
delightfully pastoral in a painting or a Beethoven-scored
segment of *Fantasia*, the reality was something else. The
creatures before them were not only base and dirty, they
were threatening, frightening, scary not only for the wildness of their demeanor and the anger of their expressions
but for the unnaturalness of their existence.

A centaur stomped on one of the griffins, and with an
ear-piercing screech the eagle-headed creature rose into
the air and attacked, dive-bombing the centaur, lion's
claws tearing into its horse back.

A green-tinted nymph, watching the scene, smiled
wickedly, started rubbing herself.

Penelope grabbed Kevin's hand, pulled him forward.
"Here goes."

As she'd expected, as she'd hoped, they were not mo-
lested. No one hindered their progress, no one got in their
way. No one seemed to notice that they were here at all.
Dionysus knew, she was sure, but he sent no one after
them, made no effort to stop them.

They could have done this days ago, she thought. There

was no way the celebrants would have known that they
weren't of them. They were stupid to have run, stupid to
have hidden. Dionysus and the maenads were dangerous,
but the rest of them were sheep, mindless zombies, existing only for hedonistic pleasures. She and Kevin and Jack
and Holbrook had ascribed far too much sense of purpose
to Dionysus' followers. They had given the bacchantes
more credit than they deserved.

Ahead, a homemade sign by the side of the river, written in bright fluorescent colors, read STYX. On the far side
of the waterway, the land was barren, blackened. The
dead shambled mindlessly amidst the burned trees and
charred rubble.

Mother Janine and Mother Margaret, naked and
screaming, rushed by, pine cone-tipped spears held aloft
and dripping blood. Penelope considered calling out to
them but decided against it. She did not want to deal with
them.

Where was Dion?

That was the big question. She looked across the field
to the trees where his throne had been. Was he there?
Somehow she didn't think so, but that was as good a
place to start as any.

She had started to lead Kevin across the open land
when Mother Janine jumped in front of her. Her mother
was visibly lactating, twin dribbles of runny milk marking
her sunburned skin from nipple to navel. "Are you here to
join us?"

Penelope tried to make her voice as slurred as possible.
"Where is he?"

"You want him?"

She nodded.

Her mother pointed northeast, toward the mountains.
"He is on the new Olympus, readying the house of the
gods." Her voice dropped lower, and she grinned slyly.
"He's waiting for you."

Penelope felt cold.

"You've never had a man until you've had a god." She
snickered darkly. "I bled afterward. I'm still bleeding inside."

Penelope backed away.

Mother Margaret had come up behind her. "He got tired of waiting for you, you know." Penelope smelled the wine on her mother's hot breath. "He's going to have *us* repopulate Olympus."

They were surrounding her. Did they know? Could they tell she was faking it?

"Where's Mother Felice?" she demanded.

Mother Janine laughed drunkenly. She turned away without answering, hoisting her spear and running after a teenage boy who was dashing across the meadow.

Penelope turned around. "Where is she?"

Mother Margaret grinned. "Ask her." She pointed toward Dion's mom, who was standing silently next to her.

She looked from her mother to Dion's, a growing anxiousness within her. "Where's my mother?"

April's voice was low. "She's dead.'

"What?"

The shock must have shown on her face. Dion's mother nodded, and there was real sympathy in her expression. "He used her up. He finished her off. He was done with her."

Penelope stumbled back, feeling as though she'd just had a heart attack and been punched in the stomach at the same time. Her legs were wobbly. It seemed nearly impossible to breathe. Kevin took her arm, held her up.

"Where?" she managed to get out.

April was already walking, gesturing for them to follow. Both of her mothers had fled, and Penelope walked through the crowd, across the field, after Dion's mom, using Kevin as a crutch. She felt empty inside, hollowed out, and everything around her seemed to be happening slowly, as if on a delay, a few seconds behind what should have been.

Her mother was dead.

It was still a fact to her, had not yet been translated into an emotion, and she followed Dion's mom past a daisy chain of men and nymphs, past a crowd of feasting satyrs, into the trees.

Her mother was lying on the grass in front of the god's throne.

Penelope knelt down next to her mother. She could not

see for the wash of tears, but she took her mother's dead hand in hers, stroking the cold, soft skin. "We never got to say good-bye," she said, and the act of speaking started the sobs. "We never . . ." But she could not finish the sentence.

Kevin watched Penelope crying over the body of her mother and started crying himself. What had happened to his own parents? Were they dead too? He had not had a chance to say good-bye either. Their last contact had been at the house, when they'd come after him and he'd run away.

Was that the last time he'd ever see them?

More than anything else, it was the sight of Penelope clutching her mother's hand, sobbing, tears and snot flowing unchecked down her face, that brought home to him the personal tragedy of what had happened here. They'd been so busy running and hiding, planning fights and escapes, that the dead bodies they'd seen had just been horror show props, disgusting background, objects in their way. As frightening as those corpses were, though, they were all relatives of someone: mothers, fathers, children, uncles, cousins. Each body was a loss.

He had not seen it that way before.

He stood above Penelope, wiping his eyes. It was awkward to watch her, uncomfortable to witness such unadulterated grief, but he could not look away. She cried and he cried, and it was a while before he realized that Dion's mom was crying too.

Dion's mom.

One of *them*.

He turned on her. "What are you doing here, huh? Why are you hanging around?"

"I'm here to help you," she said.

Kevin looked at her coldly. "We're here to kill your son."

She hesitated only a second. "I'm here to help you. I'll take you to him."

Penelope didn't know how long she knelt over her mother's body—too long, she was sure—but she could not seem to pull herself away. For a brief second she considered taking her mother across the river—Styx—and into the land of the dead, but she knew that her mother was gone and nothing could bring her back—especially not that travesty of afterlife.

But she could not tear herself away. It was as if her mother was not completely dead as long as Penelope sat by her, and she held her mother and cried until she had no tears left.

Finally she stood, her back hurting, her legs cramping. She wiped the last vestiges of tears from her eyes. "Let's go," she said, and the resolve was evident in her voice. "Let's kill the motherfucker."

She met April's gaze.

"I'll take you to Olympus," April said.

They drove up the highway toward Rutherford, taking small side road detours wherever the highway was blocked.

The wineries along the way had been raided and razed, drunken celebrants perched atop casks and crates as the buildings burned behind them. Inglenook had collapsed it on itself, the old winery building now looking like a bombed crater, chunks of stone wall and strands of ivy protruding from the caved-in earth. Mondavi had been flattened into nothingness by Caterpillars and steam rollers that were still having some sort of demolition derby atop the winery's remains.

Penelope was driving. Kevin had said that he still did not completely trust Dion's mom, and although she had offered to drive them, he had insisted that Penelope take the wheel instead. His right hand had been on the screwdriver tucked in his waistband as he made this demand, but April had not argued, and the two of them had gotten into the backseat, leaving Penelope alone in the front.

"Just in case," Kevin said.

They reached Rutherford, and April told Penelope to head east on Highway 128.

"I don't want to burst your bubble," Kevin said, "but we've been here, we've tried this. The road's blocked."

"Not until the last mile."

She was right. The ambush they'd encountered before was gone, and though the road was damaged and heavily rutted, they were able to drive past Lake Hennessey and into Chiles Valley before a wall of felled trees festooned with ribbons and garlands and dead Christmas lights effectively ended the highway. Penelope braked to a stop.

"You'll have to hike it from here on in." April leaned over the front seat, pointed toward the high hill before them. "It's up there."

Penelope's gaze followed her finger. "Olympus?"

"At a lake." She tried to think of the name.

"Berryessa."

"That's it."

Kevin leaned forward, looked through the windshield. "Somehow," he said dryly, "I'd imagined mighty Mount Olympus, home of the great Greek gods, as being a wee bit taller."

"Be thankful it's not," Penelope said.

They got out of the car, slamming the doors. "I want the keys," April said.

"What for?" Kevin demanded. "So you can take off? How are we supposed to get back?"

"You won't need to get back. You'll either fail or succeed. Either way it'll be over."

Penelope looked at her. "What are you going to—?"

"I'm going to go back and kill your mothers."

Penelope nodded. She felt nothing. No anger, no hurt, no pain, no regret.

"Then I'll kill myself. And that'll be it." She looked away, turned toward the hill, was silent for a moment. "But I want you to tell Dion . . ." Her voice broke. "Tell him I'm sorry. And tell him that I would have done things differently if I'd known. I wanted him . . ." She trailed off, wiped her nose. She turned back toward Penelope, trying to smile. Her cheeks were wet with tears. "What am I talking about? He's not Dion anymore. Dion's gone."

"But if he's not," Penelope prodded gently, "what do you want me to say?"

"Just tell him . . . Hell, just tell him I love him." She took a deep breath, wiped her nose and eyes. She held out her right hand, palm up. "Can I just have the fucking keys?"

Penelope nodded, handing over the key ring.

April gestured toward the bottle Penelope held in her hand. "You going to drink that or what? I could sure use it if you're not."

"We'll split it."

They had not thought to bring a corkscrew, but Dion's mom expertly uncorked the bottle with one long-nailed finger and downed half the bottle in a single gulp before passing the bottle to Penelope. She closed her eyes, savoring the flavor. "That helps."

Penelope hefted the bottle in her hands, met Kevin's worried gaze, then tilted it to her lips, drinking. The wine was sweet and smooth, filling her instantly with a comfortable warmth.

And a growing heat.

She finished the wine in four long swallows, and she tossed the bottle against the roadblock, where it smashed against the logs. She felt good all of a sudden, energized, filled with an unfamiliar euphoria, and she wondered what it would be like to fuck Kevin and April at the same time, to sit on Kevin's—

No.

She closed her eyes, reined herself in.

"Are you all right?" Kevin asked.

She nodded, eyes still closed. Gradually she opened them. It was going to be hard, but she had to maintain control, had to keep herself from losing it.

At least until they found Dionysus.

Then she'd let herself go.

"I'm fine," she said. "I think we'd better get going."

April moved forward, grabbed Penelope's shoulders, looked into her eyes, and Penelope felt a connection. An understanding, a sharing, passed between them. "Hold on to it until you need it," April said softly. "Use it, don't let it use you."

Penelope nodded.

April smiled. "If I can do it, you can do it." And Penelope realized for the first time what an effort it had been

for Dion's mother to keep herself under control for this
long, to force her mind to override her emotions.

"Good luck," Penelope said.

It was an odd wish, hoping the woman would successfully kill her mothers, but April's response was the same:
"Good luck to you."

She was wishing them success in killing her son.

Why had it worked out this way? Penelope thought.
Why had all this happened?

"Ready?" Kevin said.

Penelope nodded.

April walked around the car to the driver's side, and the
two of them slid down the small embankment at the edge
of the road. They heard the car engine start, heard the car
drive away.

They looked at each other.

And started up the hill.

NINETEEN

The other maenads were waiting for her when she arrived back at the meadow.

April staggered toward them across the littered ground, acting drunker than she felt. *They knew.* They'd somehow discovered her plan and were waiting to kill her. She wished she'd brought some type of weapon. The power was within her, coiled and ready to be unleashed, but it was in them as well, and they outnumbered her.

Where was Margeaux? Janine and Sheila and Margaret were in front of her, standing together, but Margeaux was nowhere in sight. She glanced surreptitiously to her left, to her right. No Margeaux. Sneaking up on her probably, planning to grab her from behind.

She looked warily from Janine's face to Sheila's to Margaret's.

Margaret smiled as she approached. "You did it," she said. "You brought her to Olympus."

April blinked.

They didn't know!

"Yes," she said, keeping her voice slow, slurred, calm.

"You're the only one who could've done it," Sheila said. "She doesn't trust us anymore."

Janine grinned lasciviously, rubbed her lactating breasts. "You deserve to be rewarded." She dropped to her knees, motioned April forward.

April took a deep breath, sidled next to her, felt the other woman's soft hands caress her thighs.

It was now or never.

She looked down at Janine, ran her hands through the kneeling woman's hair.

And twisted off her head.

The others were too stunned to react, and before
Janine's spurting body had hit the ground, April was already clawing at Sheila's breasts, ripping through skin,
ripping through flesh, ripping through muscle. Margaret
attacked her from behind, but she was already turning to
meet the onslaught, and the three of them went down in
a wailing, slashing frenzy of tooth and nail.

"How could you?" a voice screamed at her. "We're
your sisters!"

"He's my son!" she cried.

She'd thought it was Margaret screaming at her, but as
she rolled away from the body on top of her, spitting
blood, she realized that Margaret was dead. It was her
own voice she'd heard. She'd been screaming at herself.

She was growing weaker by the second, and she used
all of the strength within her to sit up on her elbows.

There was a hole ripped through her abdomen.

In front of her, Sheila was coughing, still alive, but the
coughs were weak, and one of them caught in her throat
and then she was silent.

April fell back onto the grass, looking upward at the
sky.

She closed her eyes, feeling the last of her strength ebb
out of her.

"Dion," she whispered.

TWENTY

The hike was tougher than she'd expected, the distance farther, and as the midday sun shone down on them and her head started to ache, she wished she'd saved the wine until after they'd reached their destination.

An hour later, as they began following a winding foot path up a fairly steep slope, the vegetation started to change. The trees thinned out, the underbrush grew scarce, and ordinary flora was replaced by wildly colored plants with strangely designed forms: magenta cacti with round umbrella-shaped leaves; Day-Glo yellow ground-cover grown into intricate doily patterns; bright orange shrubs with arrowhead-tipped leaves.

"I guess we're on the right track," Kevin said.

Penelope nodded. She did not feel like talking. Whatever sense of humor she possessed had fled, and she thought of nothing but the grim task before them.

And Mother Felice.

More than anything, she was doing this for her mother.

Halfway up the hill, they heard screaming. Loud, short bursts of what sounded like unbearable agony. A few minutes later, they saw the source of the cries: Father Ibarra, the Catholic priest, was chained to a rock on the hillside. An oversize eagle was perched on the boulder next to him, pecking at his exposed abdomen in even intervals as the priest screamed in agony.

Kevin picked up a rock, threw it at the bird. It hit the boulder just below the eagle's talons. The bird did not flinch. Kevin glanced toward Penelope. "Should we try to help him?"

Penelope shook her head. "We can't help. It's the god's punishment. There's nothing we can do."

They ignored the screams, continued on.

Twenty minutes later, they reached the top.

They emerged from between two mutated pink palm trees. Penelope walked slowly forward, wiping the sweat from her face. This was Olympus? She had expected Greek buildings, green fields, flowers. Instead, there were bodies floating on the lake and, several yards down, a cluster of rude huts made from plywood and dead tree branches.

Dionysus was nowhere in sight.

"What do we do now?" Kevin asked. "Wait for him to show?"

"We find him," Penelope said.

They started walking along the shore of the lake toward the huts. The water was dirty, brown, polluted not only with bodies but with the wreckage of boats. The mud smelled of sewage.

Kevin gagged, plugged his nose.

The plants were no longer as brightly spectacular as they had been on the climb up. They were still strange, but the colors seemed off, the bold designs closer to mutations than miracles. It was as if the closer they came to the center of the wheel, the closer they got to the god, the more things seemed as though they were beginning to unravel.

They trudged silently through the sludge until they reached the small assemblage of makeshift structures. Here, bodies were not only floating in the water, they were buried in the mud, stiffened arms acting as posts, supporting the bottoms of plywood walls. The stagnant air seemed unusually heavy, the atmosphere forbidding.

What had happened? It had not been like this when she'd seen Dionysus before. Then the atmosphere had been festive, seductively hedonistic, the opposite of this dour oppressiveness. Was he spreading himself too thin? Was he losing his power because of some inner struggle? Was he simply too drunk and dissipated to function properly?

Or had he *intended* his new Olympus to look like this?

No, she didn't think so. She walked forward slowly. The huts were all small, six feet high at the most, the size of storage sheds. One of them had a facade that looked like a smaller version of the Parthenon—the plywood and tree branches metamorphosed into white marble—but the attempt was halfhearted, and there had been no similar effort made with the other structures.

Penelope stepped around a naked leg protruding from the mud and looked inside the open entrance of the first hut.

Mother Margeaux lay naked in the mud on the floor of the darkened shack.

Penelope stepped back, startled. But she did not look away, and she instantly moved forward again, stepping into the small structure.

Mother Margeaux lay curled in a modified fetal position, her face contorted in agony. Her body was bloated, nearly bursting, the filthy skin stretched taut over a fat face, overstuffed arms, enormous legs, grossly distended abdomen. She screamed, straightened, thrusting bloody hips into the air, then slumped back, the scream turning into manic laughter.

"Mother?" Penelope whispered.

Mother Margeaux stopped laughing. She looked up, smiled slyly, knowingly. "It's Zeus. He's growing inside me."

Penelope froze, cold washing over her. She knew instantly what had happened. She had not been willing to mate with Dionysus and give birth to the other gods—so her mother had offered herself to Dionysus instead.

But Penelope could tell by looking at her mother that it had not worked. Mother Margeaux was pregnant, but she would not give birth to a god. She was not able to.

And the pregnancy was killing her.

Her mother laughed again, wildly. She reached behind her, into the shadows, and drew out a wineskin, holding it above her face and letting the red liquid squirt into her mouth. "God, what a cock he has!"

Penelope took another step into the room. Her head was buzzing, although she didn't know if it was from the wine or the stress. A ray of sunlight streamed in as she moved out of the doorframe, and for the first time she saw why her mother's thighs were bloody.

There was a huge hole torn between her legs.

She'd been split open.

Inside the hole something white and slimy moved, squirmed.

Kevin pushed past her, screwdriver raised, but Penelope held him back. "Don't," she said.

"But she's—"

"She's dying."

"She's giving birth!"

Penelope's head was pounding. She smelled blood, tasted wine, and she wanted to fuck, wanted to kill. She imagined jumping on her mother, digging her nails into her mother's skin, biting her flesh, ripping out her heart.

She closed her eyes. No. She couldn't give in. She had to save it for Dionysus.

"I had him before you did!" Mother Margeaux cackled. "Even if you fuck him, I had him first! And I'm carrying his baby! I'm carrying his father! I'm carrying Zeus!"

Penelope held on to Kevin's arm, pulled him out of the hut. "Leave her."

"I'll kill her if you can't."

"She'll die anyway."

"She might not."

He was right, she realized. As uncaring as she wanted to be, as dispassionate as she'd been about April's promise to kill her mothers, as sick and empty as she felt about Mother Felice, she could not bear to see Mother Margeaux die. As an idea, as a concept, she could deal with it, but seeing her mother here, she felt her pain. She still retained feelings for her, and that was why she was equivocating, rationalizing, stalling.

Silently, she let go of Kevin's arm.

She stared at the ground as he walked back into the hut. A part of her thought that her mother would rip him apart. No matter how sick and hurt she was, she was a maenad. He was a high school kid. But Penelope would not go in there, would not help him. Whatever happened happened. It was out of her hands.

Then she heard her mother screaming. There was no laughter this time, only pain, and there was another lower sound, a deep, wet gurgling.

Zeus?

A moment later, a hand touched her shoulder, a bloody hand that felt warm and sticky on her skin, and she saw Kevin. His face was white, blanched. He had left his screwdriver behind.

She said nothing, he said nothing, but the two of them walked through the circle of huts, peeking inside the other structures, seeing only mud and blood and bones. The other structures were empty.

She closed her eyes, took a deep breath, tried to stop the pounding in her skull.

It hadn't worked.

That's what struck her most about it all. It hadn't worked. Dionysus had returned, but he wasn't Dionysus anymore. He was this . . . half god. He was there, in that body, but Dion was too. The old gods might have planned to be resurrected, but they had not been able to see into the future and had not foreseen what this world would be like.

Their plan had failed.

And Holbrook and his fellow keepers of the flame had turned out to be little more than glorified pen pals, not the guardians of the earth they obviously aspired to be. They might have been the first to understand what was going on, but they'd had no idea how to stop it.

Wasn't that always the way of it, though? So-called experts planned for emergencies and convinced themselves and everyone else that they were prepared for any contingency, yet when something happened, they were inevitably shoved into the background by some nobody who rose to the occasion.

Like her.

Although she wasn't exactly a nobody. She was involved. A minor player perhaps, but a player nonetheless.

And now it was up to her to finish this off.

She opened her eyes, glanced around. Where was Dionysus? He didn't seem to be here. Had he gone back down to the valley? Her eyes searched the perimeter of the lake.

Nothing.

She moved forward, past the last hut.

And there he was.

He lay passed out on the ground, nearly hidden in the trees that bordered the shoreline, his feet protruding between two bushes that were half normal and half altered, their transformation obviously halted in midstream.

She glanced over at Kevin. Could it be this easy? Could they really have gotten this lucky? After everything they'd been through, after all of the difficulties they'd faced, was the ending going to be this simple? Was Dionysus going to be handed to them on a silver platter?

It felt almost anticlimactic.

And then he stirred.

They stopped walking, stood unmoving. There was a roar, a yawn, and the big feet shifted.

The god stood. He saw them.

He stared at Penelope. She stared back.

He was starting to fall apart, and it wrenched her heart to see him. The flesh on his expanded frame was beginning to wrinkle and droop; capillaries had burst in his skin, leaving flowery tendrils behind. His face now looked like neither Dion's nor Dionysus'. It was more of an unsuccessful hybrid of the two, closer to the boy one moment, closer to the god the next.

Her reaction to him must have been obvious, because he backed a few steps into the trees, trying to hide in the shadows. "The timing's off," he said, and though his voice was loud, it was no longer as commanding as it had been. There was something puzzled and vulnerable in it. "Everything is . . . happening . . . quicker than it should."

Penelope nodded.

"I was supposed to have a year."

She cleared her throat. "I know."

"The season's over already."

He was dying too. They were right. His coming had thrown off and speeded up the seasons. But though he was the cause of it, he was not in control of it. He was a victim of it.

"I know why you're here," he told her. He glanced toward Kevin. "Both of you."

Kevin's voice was quiet, the certainty gone. "Dion?"

"Not anymore." He reached into the tree next to him,

withdrew an oversize wineskin. "Fuck, I need a drink."
He held the pouch to his face, ripped it open. Wine
gushed into his mouth, spilling down his chin and onto
his chest. He sighed heavily, satisfied, and emerged from
the trees, stepped onto the shore. He grimaced, concentrating, and there was a ripple in the air, a shimmering.
His skin smoothed, his muscles flattened, the burst blood
vessels faded.

He walked toward them. His penis was hard, and he
was stroking himself, staring at Penelope's breasts. Despite everything, she wanted him. She knew she couldn't
have him, knew she had to kill him, but she wanted to lay
down before him and have him mount her. She wanted to
be ripped open like Mother Margeaux. She wanted to be
impregnated with his seed.

He smiled as if he knew what she was thinking. "Yes,"
he said.

She shook her head weakly. "No."

He smiled at Kevin. "Both of you. I'll love both of
you."

Kevin spat. "I always had my doubts about you, Dion."

A frown passed over the god's face. And something
else. A human expression. A look that seemed defiantly
out of place on the oversize features. His lips started to
speak—a retort—but then the impulse was squashed, the
face smoothed out.

Penelope felt sick. Dion *was* still in there.

"We can break the cycle," the god said. "It's a new
world. The old rules don't apply." He smiled lustily. "You
can give birth to me, and I'll never die."

She shook her head.

"I'll fuck you—"

"It won't work."

He had reached them. He touched her, picked her up.
She did not struggle. He held her, licked her breasts with
his enormous tongue. Despite her desire, it did not feel
good, as she'd expected. It felt coarse and at the same
time slimy.

That gave her the strength to twist out of his grasp.

He was surprised, as much by the attempt as by her

strength, and she fell to the mud in front of him, quickly scrambling away.

"I'd give birth to the other gods, to Zeus and Hermes and . . . whoever. I can't give birth to you."

"Yes, you can," he said excitedly. "I can do it."

"I *won't* do it."

"You'll have to do it." His face was a frightening amalgam of rage and resolve and lust. "I'll make you do it."

Dionysus, she understood, was like a child. A spoiled, petulant child. His needs were simple, his actions obvious. There was no subtlety to his behavior. He was easily predictable.

Holbrook had been right. These creatures weren't gods. Monsters, maybe. But not gods.

But had his power waned enough for her to fight him? She didn't think so.

She wished she'd drunk the entire bottle of wine. The maenads were supposed to tear apart Dionysus. As a strong maenad against a weak god, she might have had a chance.

Could she have enlisted the help of her mothers?

Would they have done it on their own anyway?

Either way, it was too late to do anything about it. Hindsight was always 20/20, and though she'd do things differently if she'd known then what she knew now, at this point she could only move forward.

She closed her eyes, let herself go, letting rage fill her. She held nothing back, took off all of the emotional restraints she'd been carefully trying to maintain. She *was* a maenad. It was about time she started acting like one.

She leaped at his crotch.

She acted instinctively, her rational mind now at the mercy of the wildness within her. Her nails touched flesh, and she dug in, clawing crazily, feeling the invigorating heat of blood, hearing the delicious sounds of pain. She squeezed a giant testicle with both hands, and then she was thrown by an astonishing bolt of power that threw her back into one of the huts. She lay there stunned as the mud surrounding her melted and blackened into glass.

Dionysus rushed her. There was lust in his eyes, an unfathomable anger in his countenance. And then ... it was gone.

He reached her, picked her up, and his touch was surprisingly gentle. "Are you all right?" he asked. "I didn't mean to hurt you."

His voice was Dion's.

She started crying. It was too much. She didn't know what to do, she didn't know how to react, she didn't know ... anything. One moment he was letting her go, the next moment he was trying to kill her. She knew Dionysus was a divided, schizophrenic god—the result of the wine—but she hadn't realized that it would throw her so off balance.

No, it wasn't anything to do with Dionysus. It was Dion. If this had been anyone else, she wouldn't be so confused. She wouldn't feel so ... conflicted.

He kissed her gently on the top of the head. "I love you," he said.

She blinked away the tears. "I love you too," she admitted.

He turned his head. "I'm sorry!" he called to Kevin.

She looked over and saw that Kevin that been thrown into the water of the lake and was furiously paddling between two dead bodies, trying to reach the shore.

They'd gotten a break. Anger, fear, love—something had allowed Dion to maintain control of the god's form for a lot longer than ever before. She knew it could disappear at any second, so she quickly took his huge face in her hands and said, "I have to kill you."

"I know." He looked into her eyes, and she saw an echo of his old self. She recognized the way he blinked his eyes, the way his eyebrows moved. She started to cry again, and he used a finger to wipe her tears. "I was going to ask you to kill me. I won't fight."

There was so much she wanted to ask, so much she wanted to say, but there was no time. His tentative hold could slip at any second, and then they'd be dead.

"Your mother loves you too," she said.

And she tore him apart.

As promised, he did not put up a fight. She let loose, and even she was shocked by the power within her, by the extent of the wildness, by the violence of which she was capable. Like a cartoon character, like a whirlwind, she burrowed into him, through him, rending flesh, breaking bone, slashing organs. She kept moving—kicking, clawing, grabbing, digging—and she was screaming and crying at the same time, the saltiness of his blood mingling with the saltiness of her own tears, and she continued on, unable to stop, tearing apart not Dion but the thing that had stolen Dion, the thing that had taken him from her.

She collapsed, exhausted. Her vocal cords were hurt from screaming, but the tears were still streaming down her blood-soaked face. There was nothing left of Dionysus. There was no head, no hand, no foot, no finger. Nothing even remotely recognizable. There were only bits of bone and flesh, scattered over an amazingly long section of shore. And blood. A lot of blood.

Kevin stood staring at her, still in the water. There was fear on his face, fear of her, and though she wanted to reassure him that everything was okay, everything was all right, she did not.

She had killed Dion.

She had loved him.

And she had killed him.

Already she felt different. Tired. She wondered what was happening down in the valley. Were the people still drinking, still partying, still celebrating? Or with the god's influence gone, were they shaking their heads and coming to, as if awakening from a bad dream, wondering where they were and what had happened? She looked up. The trees and bushes had not changed back. The ones he had transformed were still in the shapes he had made them.

What had happened to the satyrs and the centaurs and the nymphs?

God, she felt tired. She leaned back, her head resting on soft, cooling flesh.

Kevin walked over, stood next to her. He looked down at her form, but there was nothing sexual in his gaze, only worry. She realized that she did not feel anything sexual either.

Not even when she thought of Dion.

"What's to stop him from coming back?" Kevin asked finally.

"There are no maenads left. Only me."

"But he's a cyclical god, right? He dies each year and is reborn?"

"He never brought the others back. There's no one to bring him back. He was a god of flesh, and his flesh is no more."

"That's all, then? That's it?"

She nodded tiredly. "Yeah," she said. "I guess it is."

She lay there for a while, Kevin still standing next to her. She closed her eyes for a few seconds—she thought. But when she opened them, it was dark, it was night. Kevin was still standing above her, watching her with concern.

She sat up, her head thumping.

"Are you all right?" he asked.

She nodded. "Yeah," she said, and surprisingly, she did feel better. "I guess I am." She stood, walked slowly over to the edge of the lake, where she stripped off her pants. She looked at Kevin, smiled, then jumped into the cold, refreshing water to wash off the blood.

EPILOGUE

Both the state and federal government stuck by their radioactive-waste story, sending in hundreds of troops and agents dressed in white contamination suits, quarantining the area and debriefing the residents with an elaborate series of physical tests and psychological examinations that Penelope assumed were supposed to brainwash the muddled, hungover citizens into thinking that what had happened had not happened.

She and Kevin knew better.

They were close after that, nearly inseparable. Kevin's parents survived and he went back to live with them. Since her mothers were all dead and she was too old to be adopted or become a ward of the state, she had herself declared an emancipated teenager by the court and moved into a small apartment near school. She received an allowance from her mothers' estate, although the amount of the estate and its assets were still being determined by lawyers and accountants and she would probably not inherit what was left of the winery or its proceeds for several years.

Somewhere toward the end of the school year, she and Kevin officially became a couple. He moved in with her after graduation, but that did not last the summer, and she went off alone to Berkeley in the fall. They'd shared a lot, but perhaps they'd shared too much. Seeing each other, they were constantly reminded of what had happened, and the wounds that should have healed into scars seemed to be perpetually kept open.

And Dion was always between them.

But if the experience they'd gone through had torn them apart, it also permanently linked them together. No one else had gone through what they had and that was a bond that could not be broken. Two years later, after living lives apart, after adjusting to the post-Dionysus world in their own ways, they met again. Penelope had transferred to UCLA, and Kevin called her up, asking if they could get together.

She agreed.

Two years later, they were married.

A year later, she became pregnant.

Penelope sat in the window seat of what was going to be the baby's room and stared out the glass at the children playing in the street. She'd recently gotten her mothers' money, and they both had good jobs, so the baby would not be a financial hardship. And, she supposed, she was happy. Kevin was a good husband, and she loved him.

But . . .

But sometimes she wondered what her life would have been like if Dion had lived, if she had married him and was now carrying his baby.

She loved Kevin.

But she'd trade him for Dion in a second.

Why couldn't it have been the other way around?

Downstairs, she heard the front door open, heard Kevin toss the mail onto the hall tree. "I'm home!" he announced.

"Up here!" she called.

She waited for him, smiled as he entered the room. He hurried across the carpet toward her. "How are you today?" he asked.

She shrugged. "Fine."

He sat down on the window seat next to her, untied his tie. He looked at the box of sesame-cheese crackers and the empty container of yogurt by her feet. "Cravings again?"

She laughed. "Yeah."

He put a hand on her distended stomach. "Is there anything else I can get you? Pickles and ice cream? Anchovies and orange juice?"

She started to say something, then looked away, shaking her head. "No."

"Come on."

She looked up at him. "I don't—"

"I'm serious. Anything you want."

She took a deep breath. "Anything?"

He smiled. "Anything your little body desires."

She met his gaze, jumped in. "Wine," she said softly. "I'd like wine."